DANCING WITH MYSELF

CHARLES SHEFFIELD

DANCING WITH MYSELF

This volume includes works of fiction. All the characters and events portrayed in this book are fictional, and any resemblance to real people or incidents is purely coincidental.

"Out of Copyright" first appeared in *Fantasy & Science Fiction*, 1989; "Tunicate, Tunicate" first appeared in *Asimov's*, 1989; "Counting Up" first appeared in *New Destinies*, December 1988; "A Braver Thing" first appeared in *Asimov's*, 1990; "The Grand Tour" first appeared in *Analog*, 1987; "Classical Nightmares and Quantum Paradoxes" first appeared in *New Destinies*, April 1989; "Nightmares of the Classical Mind" first appeared in *Asimov's*, 1989; "The Double Spiral Staircase" first appeared in *Analog*, 1990; "The Unlicked Bear-Whelp" first appeared in *New Destinies*, September 1990; "The Seventeen-Year Locusts" first appeared in *Asimov's*, 1982; "The Courts of Xanadu" first appeared in *Asimov's*, 1988; "C-change" first appeared in *Analog*, 1992; "Unclear Winter: A Miscellany of Disasters" first appeared in *New Destinies*, May 1988; "Godspeed" first appeared in *Analog*, 1990; and "Dancing with Myself" first appeared in *Analog*, 1989. "The Biography of the Universe" is copyright 1993 by Charles Sheffield.

A Baen Books Original

Baen Publishing Enterprises
P.O. Box 1403
Riverdale, NY 10471

ISBN: 0-671-72185-2

Cover art by Stanislaw Fernandez

First printing, September 1993

Distributed by Simon & Schuster
1230 Avenue of the Americas
New York, NY 10020

Printed in the United States of America

TABLE OF CONTENTS

INTRODUCTION

This book contains sixteen stories and science articles written over the past seven years. They range in length from short stories of barely a page ("The Seventeen-Year Locusts") to long novelettes ("The Courts of Xanadu"). They also range in mood from very silly to very somber.

I ought to stop right here. There is little point in saying more before you read, because no matter what I tell you hoping to whet your appetite, each item must stand or fall on its own. An introduction, by me or anyone else, can't change that.

But I will indulge myself to this extent: *after* each story I will say a few words about how it came to be written, and what I was trying to do. You can judge if I succeeded or failed.

I have one other comment, addressed to any reader worried about the repackaging of old material under a new title: I have published four other collections of short stories and articles, *Vectors*, *Hidden Variables*, *Erasmus Magister*, and *The McAndrew Chronicles*. However, the stories in this book have never appeared before in collected form, and there is no overlap of material among any of the five volumes.

— *Charles Sheffield*
June 1992

OUT OF COPYRIGHT

Trouble-shooting. A splendid idea, and one that I agree with totally in principle. Bang! One bullet, and trouble bites the dust. But unfortunately trouble doesn't know the rules. Trouble won't stay dead.

I looked around the table. My top trouble-shooting team was here. I was here. Unfortunately they were supposed to be headed for Jupiter and I ought to be down on Earth. In less than twenty-four hours the draft pick would begin.

That wouldn't wait, and if I didn't leave in the next thirty minutes I would never make it in time. I needed to be in two places at once. I cursed the copyright laws and the single-copy restriction, and went to work.

"You've read the new requirement," I said. "You know the parameters. Ideas, anyone?"

A dead silence. They were facing the problem in their own unique ways. Wolfgang Pauli looked half asleep, Thomas Edison was drawing little doll-figures on the table's surface, Enrico Fermi seemed to be counting on his fingers, and John von Neumann was staring impatiently at the other three. I was doing none of those things. I knew very well that wherever the solution would come from, it would not be from inside my head. My job was much more straightforward; I had to see that when we had a possible answer, it *happened*. And I had to see that we got *one* answer, not four.

The silence in the room went on and on. My brains trust was saying nothing, while I watched the digits on my watch flicker by. I had to stay and find a solution; and I had to get to the draft picks. But most of all and hardest of all, I had to remain quiet, to let my team do some thinking.

It was small consolation to know that similar meetings were being held within the offices of the other three combines.

Everyone must be finding it equally hard going. I knew the players, and I could imagine the scenes, even though all the trouble-shooting teams were different. NETSCO had a group that was intellectually the equal of ours at Romberg AG: Niels Bohr, Theodore von Karman, Norbert Wiener, and Marie Curie. MMG, the great Euro-Mexican combine of Magrit-Marcus Gesellschaft, had focused on engineering power rather than pure scientific understanding and creativity, and in addition to the Soviet rocket designer Sergey Korolev and the American Nikola Tesla, they had reached farther back (and with more risk) to the great nineteenth century English engineer, Isambard Kingdom Brunel. He had been one of the outstanding successes of the program; I wished he were working with me, but MMG had always refused to look at a trade. MMG's one bow to theory was a strange one, the Indian mathematician Srinivasa Ramanujan, but the unlikely quartet made one hell of a team.

And finally there was BP Megation, whom I thought of as confused. At any rate, I didn't understand their selection logic. They had used billions of dollars to acquire a strangely mixed team: Erwin Schrödinger, David Hilbert, Leo Szilard, and Henry Ford. They were all great talents, and all famous names in their fields, but I wondered how well they could work as a unit.

All the trouble-shooting teams were now pondering the same emergency. Our problem was created when the Pan-National Union suddenly announced a change to the Phase B demonstration program. They wanted to modify impact conditions, as their contracts with us permitted them to do. They didn't have to tell us how to do it, either, which was just as well for them since I was sure they didn't know. How do you take a billion tons of mass, already launched to reach a specific target at a certain point of time, and suddenly redirect it to a different end-point with a different arrival time?

There was no point in asking them *why* they wanted to change rendezvous conditions. It was their option. Some of our management saw the action on PNU's part as simple bloody-mindedness, but I couldn't agree. The four multi-national combines had each been given contracts to perform the biggest space engineering exercise in human history; small asteroids (only a kilometer or so across — but massing a billion tons each) had to be picked up from their natural orbits and re-directed to the Jovian system, where they were to make precise rendezvous with assigned locations of the moon Io. Each combine had to select the asteroid and the method of moving it, but deliver within a tight transfer energy budget and a tight time schedule.

For that task, the PNU would pay each group a total of eight billion dollars. That sounds like a fair amount of money, but I knew our accounting figures. To date, with the project still not finished (rendezvous would be in eight more days) Romberg AG had spent 14.5 billion. We were looking at a probable cost overrun by a factor of two. I was willing to bet that the other three groups were eating very similar losses.

Why?

Because this was only Phase B of a four-phase project. Phase A had been a system design study, that led to four Phase B awards for a demonstration project. The Phase B effort that the four combines were working on now was a proof-of-capability run for the full Europan Metamorphosis. The real money came in the future, in Phases C and D. Those would be awarded by the PNU to a single combine, and the award would be based largely on Phase B performance. The next phases called for the delivery of fifty asteroids to impact points on Europa (Phase C), followed by thermal mixing operations on the moon's surface (Phase D). The contract value of C and D would be somewhere up around eight hundred billion dollars. That was the fish that all the combines were after, and it was the reason we would all overspend lavishly on this phase.

By the end of the whole program, Europa would have a forty-kilometer deep water ocean over all its surface. And then the real fun would begin. Some contractor would begin the installation of the fusion plants, and the seeding of the sea-farms with the first prokaryotic bacterial forms.

The stakes were high; and to keep everybody on their toes, PNU did the right thing. They kept throwing in these little zingers, to mimic the thousand and one things that would go wrong in the final project phases.

While I was sitting and fidgeting, my team had gradually come to life. Fermi was pacing up and down the room —

always a good sign; and Wolfgang Pauli was jabbing impatiently at the keys of a computer console. John von Neumann hadn't moved, but since he did everything in his head anyway that didn't mean much.

I looked again at my watch. I had to go. "Ideas?" I said again.

Von Neumann made a swift chopping gesture of his hand. "We have to make a choice, Al. It can be done in four or five ways."

The others were nodding. "The problem is only one of efficiency and speed," added Fermi. "I can give you an order of magnitude estimate of the effects on the overall program within half an hour."

"Within fifteen minutes." Pauli raised the bidding.

"No need to compete this one." They were going to settle down to a real four-way fight on methods, they always did, but I didn't have the time to sit here and referee. The important point was that they said it could be done. "You don't have to rush it. Whatever you decide, it will have to wait until I get back." I stood up. "Tom?"

Edison shrugged. "How long will you be gone, Al?"

"Two days, maximum. I'll head back right after the draft picks." (That wasn't quite true; when the draft was over I had some other business to attend to that did not include the trouble-shooters; but two days should cover everything.)

"Have fun." Edison waved his hand casually. "By the time you get back, I'll have the engineering drawings for you."

One thing about working with a team like mine — they may not always be right, but they sure are always cocky.

"Make room there. Move over!" The guards were pushing ahead to create a narrow corridor through the wedged mass of people. The one in front of me was butting with his helmeted head, not even looking to see who he was shoving aside. "Move!" he shouted. "Come on now, out of the way."

We were in a hurry. Things had been frantically busy Topside before I left, so I had cut it fine on connections to begin with, then been held up half an hour at re-entry. We had broken the speed limits on the atmospheric segment and there would be PNU fines for that, but still we hadn't managed to make up all the time. Now the first draft pick was only seconds away, and I was supposed to be taking part in it.

A thin woman in a green coat clutched at my arm as we bogged down for a moment in the crush of people. Her face was gray and grimy, and she had a placard hanging round her neck. "You could wait longer for the copyright!" She had to shout to make herself heard. "It would cost you nothing — and look at the misery you would prevent. What you're doing is immoral! TEN MORE YEARS!"

Her last words were a scream as she called out this year's slogan. TEN MORE YEARS! I shook my arm free as the guard in front of me made sudden headway, and dashed along in his wake. I had nothing to say to the woman; nothing that she would listen to. If it were immoral, what did ten more years have to do with it? Ten more years; if by some miracle they were granted ten more years on the copyrights, what then? I knew the answer. They would try to talk the Pan-National Union into fifteen more years, or perhaps twenty. When you pay somebody off, it only increases their demands. I know, only too well. They are never satisfied with what they get.

Joe Delacorte and I scurried into the main chamber and shuffled sideways to our seats at the last possible moment. All the preliminary nonsense was finished, and the real business was beginning. The tension in the room was terrific. To be honest, a lot of it was being generated by the media. They were all poised to make maximum noise as they shot the selection information all over the System. If it were not for the media, I don't think the PNU would hold live draft picks at all. We'd all hook in with video links and do our business the civilized way.

The excitement now was bogus for other reasons, too. The professionals — me and a few others — would not become interested until the ten rounds were complete. Before that, the choices were just too limited. Only when they were all made, and the video teams were gone, would the four groups get together off-camera and begin the horse-trading. "My ninth round plus my fifth for your second." "Maybe, if you'll throw in ten million dollars and a tenth-round draft pick for next year . . ."

Meanwhile, BP Megation had taken the microphone. "First

selection," said their representative. "Robert Oppenheimer."

I looked at Joe, and he shrugged. No surprise. Oppenheimer was the perfect choice — a brilliant scientist, but also practical, and willing to work with other people. He had died in 1967, so his original copyright had expired within the past twelve months. I knew his family had appealed for a copyright extension and been refused. Now BP Megation had sole single-copy rights for another lifetime.

"Trade?" whispered Joe.

I shook my head. We would have to beggar ourselves for next year's draft picks to make BP give up Oppenheimer. Other combine reps had apparently made the same decision. There was the clicking of data entry as the people around me updated portable data bases. I did the same thing with a stub of pencil and a folded sheet of yellow paper, putting a check mark alongside his name. Oppenheimer was taken care of, I could forget that one. If by some miracle one of the four teams had overlooked some other top choice, I had to be ready to make an instant revision to my own selections.

"First selection, by NETSCO," said another voice. "Peter Joseph William Debye."

It was another natural choice. Debye had been a Nobel prize-winner in physics, a theoretician with an excellent grasp of applied technology. He had died in 1966. Nobel laureates in science, particularly ones with that practical streak, went fast. As soon as their copyrights expired they would be picked up in the draft the same year.

That doesn't mean it always works out well. The most famous case, of course, was Albert Einstein. When his copyright had expired in 2030, BP Megation had had first choice in the draft pick. They had their doubts, and they must have sweated blood over their decision. The rumor mill said they spent over seventy million dollars in simulations alone, before they finally decided to take him as their top choice. The same rumor mill said that the cloned form was now showing amazing ability in chess and music, but no interest at all in physics or mathematics. If that were true, BP Megation had dropped two billion dollars down a black hole; one billion straight to the PNU for acquisition of copyright, and another billion for the clone process. Theorists were always tricky, you could never tell how they would turn out.

Magrit-Marcus Gesellschaft had now made their first draft pick, and chosen another Nobel Laureate, John Cockroft. He also had died in 1967. So far, every selection was completely predictable. The three combines were picking the famous scientists and engineers who had died in 1966 and 1967, and who were now, with the expiration of family retention of copyrights, available for cloning for the first time.

The combines were being logical, but it made for a very dull draft pick. Maybe it was time to change that. I stood up to announce our own first take.

"First selection, by Romberg AG," I said. "Charles Proteus Steinmetz."

My announcement caused a stir in the media. They had presumably never heard of Steinmetz, which was a disgraceful statement of their own ignorance. Even if they hadn't spent most of the past year combing old files and records, as we had, they should have heard of him. He was one of the past century's most colorful and creative scientists, a man who had been physically handicapped (he was a hunchback) but mentally able to do the equivalent of a hundred one-hand push-ups without even breathing hard. Even I had heard of him, and you'd not find many of my colleagues who'd suggest I was interested in science.

The buzzing in the media told me they were consulting their own historical data files, digging farther back in time. Even when they had done all that, they would still not understand the first thing about the true process of clone selection. It's not just a question of knowing who died over seventy-five years ago, and will therefore be out of copyright. That's a trivial exercise, one that any year-book will solve for you. You also have to evaluate other factors. Do you know where the body is — are you absolutely *sure*? Remember, you can't clone anyone without a cell or two from the original body. You also have to be certain that it's who you think it is. All bodies seventy-five or more years old tend to look the same. And then, if the body happens to be really old — say, more than a couple of centuries — there are other peculiar problems that are still not understood at all. When NETSCO pulled its coup a few years ago by cloning Gottfried Wilhelm Leibniz, the other three combines were envious at first. Leibniz was a real universal genius, a seventeenth century super-brain who was good at everything. NETSCO had developed a better cell growth technique, and they had also succeeded in locating the body of Leibniz in its undistinguished Hanover grave.

They walked tall for almost a year at NETSCO, until the clone came out of the forcing chambers for indoctrination. He looked nothing like the old portraits of Leibniz, and he could not grasp even the simplest abstract concepts. Oops! said the media. Wrong body.

But it wasn't as simple as that. The next year, MMG duplicated the NETSCO cell-growth technology and tried for Isaac Newton. In this case there was no doubt that they had the correct body, because it had lain undisturbed since 1727 beneath a prominent plaque in London's Westminster Abbey. The results were just as disappointing as they had been for Leibniz.

Now NETSCO and MMG have become very conservative; in my opinion, far too conservative. But since then nobody has tried for a clone of anyone who died before 1850. The draft picking went on its thoughtful and generally cautious way, and was over in a couple of hours except for the delayed deals.

The same group of protesters was picketing the building when I left. I tried to walk quietly through them, but they must have seen my picture on one of the exterior screens showing the draft pick process. I was buttonholed by a man in a red jumpsuit and the same thin woman in green, still carrying her placard.

"Could we speak with you for just one moment?" The man in red was very well-spoken and polite.

I hesitated, aware that news cameras were on us. "Very briefly. I'm trying to run a proof-of-concept project, you know."

"I know. Is it going well?" He was a different type from most of the demonstrators, cool and apparently intelligent. And therefore potentially more dangerous.

"I wish I could say yes," I said. "Actually, it's going rather badly. That's why I'm keen to get back out."

"I understand. All I wanted to ask you was why you — and I don't mean *you*, personally, I mean the combines — why do you find it *necessary* to use clones? You could do your work without them, couldn't you?"

I hesitated. "Let me put it this way. We could do the work without them, in just the same way as we could stumble along somehow if we were denied the use of computer power, or nuclear power. The projects would be possible, but they would be enormously more difficult. The clones augment our available brain power, at the highest levels. So let me ask you: why *should* we do without the clones, when they are available and useful?"

"Because of the families. You have no right to subject the families to the misery and upset of seeing their loved ones cloned, without their having any rights in the matter. It's cruel, and unnecessary. Can't you see that?"

"No, I can't. Now, you listen to me for a minute." The cameras were still on me. It was a chance to say something that could never be said often enough. "The family holds copyright for seventy-five years after a person's death. So if you, personally, *remember* your grandparent, you have to be pushing eighty years old — and it's obvious from looking at you that you're under forty. So ask yourself, why are all you petitioners people who are in their thirties? It's not *you* who's feeling any misery."

"But there are the relatives—" he said.

"Oh, yes, the relatives. Are you a relative of somebody who has been cloned?"

"Not yet. But if this sort of thing goes on—"

"Listen to me for one more minute. A long time ago, there were a lot of people around who thought that it was wrong to let books with sex in them be sold to the general public. They petitioned to have the books banned. It wasn't that they claimed to be buying the books themselves, and finding them disgusting; because if they said that was the case, then people would have asked them *why* they were buying what they didn't like. Nobody was forcing anybody to buy those books. No, what the petitioners wanted was for *other* people to be stopped from buying what the *petitioners* didn't like. And you copyright-extension people are just the same. You are making a case on behalf of the relatives of the ones who are being cloned. But you never seem to ask yourself this: If cloning is so bad, why aren't the *descendants* of the clones the ones doing the complaining? They're not, you know. You never see them around here."

He shook his head. "Cloning is immoral!"

I sighed. Why bother? Not one word of what I'd said had got through to him. It didn't much matter, I'd really been speaking for the media anyway, but it was a shame to see bigotry masquerading as public-spirited behavior. I'd seen enough of that already in my life.

I started to move off towards my waiting aircar. The lady in green clutched my arm again. "I'm going to leave instructions in my will that I want to be cremated. You'll never get me!"

You have my word on that, lady. But I didn't say it. I headed for the car, feeling an increasing urge to get back to the clean and rational regions of space. There was one good argument against cloning, and only one. It increased the total number of people, and to me that number already felt far too large.

I had been gone only thirty hours, total, but when I arrived back at Headquarters I learned that in my absence five new problems had occurred. I scanned the written summary that Pauli had left behind.

First, one of the thirty-two booster engines set deep in the surface of the asteroid did not respond to telemetry requests for a status report. We had to assume it was defective, and eliminate it from the final firing pattern. Second, a big solar flare was on the way. There was nothing we could do about that, but it did mean we would have to recompute the strength of the magnetic and electric fields close to Io. They would change with the strength of the Jovian magnetosphere, and that was important because the trouble-shooting team in my absence had agreed on their preferred solution to the problem of adjusting impact point and arrival time. It called for strong coupling between the asteroid and the five-million amp flux tube of current between Io and its parent planet, Jupiter, to modify the final collision trajectory.

Third, we had lost the image data stream from one of our observing satellites, in synchronous orbit with Io. Fourth, our billion ton asteroid had been struck by a larger-than-usual micro-meteorite. This one must have massed a couple of kilograms, and it had been moving fast. It had struck off-axis from the center of mass, and the whole asteroid was now showing a tendency to rotate slowly away from our preferred orientation. Fifth, and finally, a new volcano had become very active down on the surface of Io. It was spouting sulfur up for a couple of hundred kilometers, and obscuring the view of the final impact landmark.

After I had read Pauli's terse analysis of all the problems — nobody I ever met or heard of could summarize as clearly and briefly as he did — I switched on my communications set and asked him the only question that mattered: "Can you handle them all?"

There was a delay of almost two minutes. The trouble-shooters were heading out to join the rest of our project team for their on-the-spot analyses in the Jovian system; already the light travel time was significant. If I didn't follow in the next day or two, radio signal delay would make conversation impossible. At the moment Jupiter was forty-five light-minutes from Earth.

"We can, Al," said Pauli's image at last. "Unless others come up in the next few hours, we can. From here until impact we'll be working in an environment with increasing uncertainties."

"The PNU people planned it that way. Go ahead — but send me full transcripts." I left the system switched on, and went off to the next room to study the notes I had taken of the five problem areas. As I had done with every glitch that had come up since the Phase B demonstration project began, I placed the problem into one of two basic categories: act of nature, or failure of manmade element. For the most recent five difficulties, the volcano on Io and the solar flare belonged in the left-hand column: Category One, clearly natural and unpredictable events. The absence of booster engine telemetry and the loss of satellite image data were Category Two, failures of our system. They went in the right-hand column. I hesitated for a long time over the fifth event, the impact of the meteorite; finally, and with some misgivings, I assigned it also as a Category One event.

As soon as possible I would like to follow the engineering teams out towards Jupiter for the final hours of the demonstration. However, I had two more duties to perform before I could leave.

Using a coded link to Romberg AG HQ in synchronous earth-orbit, I queried the status of all the clone tanks. No anomalies were reported. By the time we returned from the final stages of Phase B, another three finished clones would be ready to move to the indoctrination facility. I needed to be there when it happened.

Next, I had to review and approve acquisition of single use copyright for all the draft picks we had negotiated down on Earth. To give an idea of the importance of these choices, we were looking at an expenditure of twenty billion dollars for those selections over the next twelve months. It raised the unavoidable question, had we made the best choices?

At this stage of the game every combine began to have second thoughts about the wisdom of their picks. All the old failures came crowding into your mind. I already mentioned NETSCO and their problem with Einstein, but we had had our full share at Romberg AG: Gregor Mendel, the originator of the genetic ideas that stood behind all the cloning efforts, had proved useless; so had Ernest Lawrence, inventor of the cyclotron, our second pick for 1958. We had (by blind luck!) traded him along with forty million dollars for Wolfgang Pauli. Even so, we had made a bad error of judgment, and the fact that others made the same mistake was no consolation. As for Marconi, even though he looked like the old pictures of him, and was obviously highly intelligent, the clone who emerged turned out to be so indolent and casual about everything that he ruined any project he worked on. I had placed him in a cushy and undemanding position and allowed him to fiddle about with his own interests, which were mainly sports and good-looking women. (As Pauli acidly remarked, "And you say that *we're* the smart ones, doing all the work?")

It's not the evaluation of a person's past record that's difficult, because we are talking about famous people who have done a great deal, written masses of books, articles, and papers, and been thoroughly evaluated by their own contemporaries. Even with all that, a big question still remains. Will the things that made the original man or woman great still be there in the cloned form? In other words, *Just what is it that is inherited?*

That's a very hard question to answer. The theory of evolution was proposed a hundred and seventy years ago, but we're still fighting the old Nature versus Nurture battle. Is a human genius mainly decided by heredity, or by the way the person was raised? One old argument against cloning for genius was based on the importance of Nurture. It goes as follows: an individual is the product of both heredity (which is all you get in the clone) and environment. Since it is impossible to reproduce someone's environment, complete with parents, grandparents, friends, and teachers, you can't raise a clone that will be exactly like the original individual.

I'll buy that logic. We can't make ourselves an intellectually exact copy of anyone.

However, the argument was also used to prove that cloning for superior intellectual performance would be impossible. But of course, it actually proves nothing of the sort. If you take two peas from the same pod, and put one of them in deep soil next to a high wall, and the other in shallow soil out in the open, they *must* do different things if both are to thrive. The one next to the wall has to make sure it gets enough sunshine, which it can do by maximizing leaf area; the one in shallow soil has to get enough moisture, which it does through putting out more roots. The *superior* strain of peas is the one whose genetic composition allows it to adapt to whatever environment it is presented with.

People are not peas, but in one respect they are not very different from them: some have superior genetic composition to others. That's all you can ask for. If you clone someone from a century ago, the last thing you want is someone who is *identical* to the original. They would be stuck in a twentieth century mind-set. What is needed is someone who can adapt to and thrive in *today's* environment — whether that is now the human equivalent of shade, or of shallow soil. The success of the original clone-template tells us a very important thing, that we are dealing with a superior physical brain. What that brain thinks in the year 2040 *should* be different from what it would have thought in the year 1940 — otherwise the clone would be quite useless. And the criteria for "useless" change with time, too.

All these facts and a hundred others were running around

inside my head as I reviewed the list for this year. Finally I made a note to suggest that J.B.S. Haldane, whom we had looked at and rejected three years ago on the grounds of unmanageability, ought to be looked at again and acquired if possible. History shows that he had wild views on politics and society, but there was no question at all about the quality of his mind. I thought I had learned a lot about interfacing with difficult scientific personalities in the past few years.

When I was satisfied with my final list I transmitted everything to Joe Delacorte, who was still down on Earth, and headed for the transition room. A personal shipment pod ought to be waiting for me there. I hoped I would get a good one. At the very least, I'd be in it for the next eight days. Last time I went out to the Jovian system the pod internal lighting and external antenna failed after three days. Have you ever sat in the dark for seventy-two hours, a hundred million miles from the nearest human, unable to send or receive messages? I didn't know if anyone realized I was in trouble. All I could do was sit tight — and I mean tight, pods are *small* — and stare out at the stars.

This time the pod was in good working order. I was able to participate in every problem that hit the project over the next four days. There were plenty of them, all small, and all significant. One of the fuel supply ships lost a main ion drive. The supply ship was not much more than a vast bag of volatiles and a small engine, and it had almost no brain at all in its computer, not even enough to figure out an optimal use of its remaining drives. We had to chase after and corral it as though we were pursuing a great lumbering elephant. Then three members of the impact monitoring team came down with food poisoning — salmonella, which was almost certainly their own fault. You can say anything you like about throwing away spoiled food, but you can't get a sloppy crew to take much notice.

Then, for variety, we lost a sensor through sheer bad program design. In turning one of our imaging systems from star-sensing to Io-Jupiter sensing, we tracked it right across the solar disk and burned out all the photo-cells. According to the engineers, that's the sort of blunder you don't make after kindergarten — but somebody did it.

Engineering errors are easy to correct. It was much trickier when one of the final approach coordination groups, a team of two men and one woman, chose the day before the Io rendezvous to have a violent sexual argument. They were millions of kilometers away from anyone, so there was not much we could do except talk to them. We did that, hoped they wouldn't kill each other, and made plans to do without their inputs if we had to.

Finally, one day before impact, an unplanned and anomalous firing of a rocket on the asteroid's forward surface caused a significant change of velocity of the whole body.

I ought to explain that I did little or nothing to solve any of these problems. I was too slow, too ignorant, and not creative enough. While I was still struggling to comprehend what the problem parameters were, my trouble-shooters were swarming all over it. They threw proposals and counter-proposals at each other so fast that I could hardly note them, still less contribute to them. For example, in the case of the anomalous rocket firing that I mentioned, compensation for the unwanted thrust called for an elaborate balancing act of lateral and radial engines, rolling and nudging the asteroid back into its correct approach path. The team had mapped out the method in minutes, written the necessary optimization programs in less than half an hour, and implemented their solution before I understood the geometry of what was going on.

So what did I do while all this was happening? I continued to make my two columns: act of nature, or failure of manmade element. The list was growing steadily, and I was spending a lot of time looking at it.

We were coming down to the final few hours now, and all the combines were working flat out to solve their own problems. In an engineering project of this size, many thousands of things could go wrong. We were working in extreme physical conditions, hundreds of millions of kilometers away from Earth and our standard test environments. In the intense charged-particle field near Io, cables broke at loads well below their rated capacities, hard vacuum welds showed air-bleed effects, lateral jets were fired and failed to produce the predicted attitude adjustments. And on top of all this, the pressure, isolation, and bizarre surroundings were too much for some of the workers. We had human failure to add to engineering failure. The test was tougher than anyone had realized — even PNU, who were supposed to make the demonstration project just this side of impossible.

I was watching the performance of the other three combines only a little less intently that I was watching our own. At five hours from contact time, NETSCO apparently suffered a communications loss with their asteroid control system. Instead of heading for Io impact, the asteroid veered away, spiralling in towards the bulk of Jupiter itself.

BP Megation lost it at impact minus three hours, when a vast explosion on one of their asteroid forward boosters threw the kilometer-long body into a rapid tumble. Within an hour, by some miracle of improvisation, their engineering team had found a method of stabilizing the wobbling mass. But by then it was too late to return to nominal impact time and place. Their asteroid skimmed into the surface of Io an hour early, sending up a long, tear-shaped mass of ejecta from the moon's turbulent surface.

That left just two of us, MMG and Romberg AG. We both had our hands full. The Jovian system is filled with electrical, magnetic, and gravitational energies bigger than anything in the Solar System except around the Sun itself. The two remaining combines were trying to steer their asteroid in to a pinpoint landing through a great storm of interference that made every control command and every piece of incoming telemetry suspect. In the final hour, I didn't even follow the exchanges between my trouble-shooters. Oh, I could *hear* them easily enough. What I couldn't do is comprehend them, enough to know what was happening.

Pauli would toss a scrap of comment at von Neumann, and while I was trying to understand that, von Neumann would have done an assessment, keyed in for a data bank status report, gabbled a couple of questions to Fermi and an instruction to Edison, and at the same time be absorbing scribbled notes and diagrams from those two. I don't know if what they were doing was *potentially* intelligible to me or not; all I know is that they were going about fifty times too fast for me to follow. And it didn't much matter what I understood — they were getting the job done. I was still trying to divide all problems into my Category One — Category Two columns, but it got harder and harder.

In the final hour I didn't look or listen to what my own team was doing. We had one band of telemetry trained on the MMG project, and more and more that's where my attention was focused. I assumed they were having the same kind of communications trouble as we were — that crackling discharge field around Io made everything difficult. But their team was handling it. They were swinging smoothly in to impact.

And then, with only ten minutes to go, the final small adjustment was made. It should have been a tiny nudge from the radial jets; enough to fine-tune the impact position a few hundred meters, and no more. Instead, there was a joyous roar of a radial jet at full, uncontrolled thrust. The MMG asteroid did nothing unusual for a few seconds (a billion tons is a lot of inertia) then began to drift lazily sideways, away from its nominal trajectory.

The jet was still firing. And that should be impossible, because the first thing that the MMG team would do was send a POWER-OFF signal to the engine.

The time for impact came when the MMG asteroid was still a clear fifty kilometers out of position, and accelerating away. I saw the final collision, and the payload scraped along the surface of Io in a long, jagged scar that looked nothing at all like the neat, punched hole that we were supposed to achieve.

And we did achieve it, a few seconds later. Our asteroid came in exactly where and when it was supposed to, driving in exactly vertical to the surface. The plume of ejecta had hardly begun to rise from Io's red-and-yellow surface before von Neumann was pulling a bottle of bourbon from underneath the communications console.

I didn't object — I only wished I were there physically to share it, instead of being stuck in my own pod, short of rendezvous with our main ship. I looked at my final list, still somewhat incomplete. Was there a pattern to it? Ten minutes of analysis didn't show one. No one had tried anything — this time. Someday, and it might be tomorrow, somebody on another combine would have a bright idea; and then it would be a whole new ball game.

While I was still pondering my list, my control console began to buzz insistently. I switched it on expecting contact with my own trouble-shooting team. Instead, I saw the despondent face of Brunel, MMG's own team leader — the man above all others that I would have liked to work on my side.

He nodded at me when my picture appeared on his screen. He was smoking one of his powerful black cigars, stuck in the side of his mouth. The expression on his face was as impenetrable as ever. He never let his feelings show there. "I assume you saw it, did you?" he said around the cigar. "We're out of it. I just called to congratulate you — again."

"Yeah, I saw it. Tough luck. At least you came second."

"Which as you know very well is no better than coming last." He sighed and shook his head. "We still have no idea what happened. Looks like either a programing error, or a valve sticking open. We probably won't know for weeks. And I'm not sure I care."

I maintained a sympathetic silence.

"I sometimes think we should just give up, Al," he said. "I can beat those other turkeys, but I can't compete with you. That's six in a row that you've won. It's wearing me out. You've no idea how much frustration there is in that."

I had never known Brunel to reveal so much of his feelings before.

"I think I do understand your problems," I said.

And I did. I knew exactly how he felt — more than he would believe. To suffer through a whole, endless sequence of minor, niggling mishaps was heartbreaking. No single trouble was ever big enough for a trouble-shooting team to stop, isolate it, and be able to say, there's dirty work going on here. But their cumulative effect was another matter. One day it was a morass of shipments missing their correct flights, another time a couple of minus signs dropped into computer programs, or a key worker struck down for a few days by a random virus, permits misfiled, manifests mislaid, or licenses wrongly dated.

I knew all those mishaps, personally. I should, because I invented most of them. I think of it as the death of a thousand cuts. No one can endure all that and still hope to win a Phase B study.

"How would you like to work on the Europan Metamorph?" I asked. "I think you'd love it."

He looked very thoughtful, and for the first time I believe I could actually read his expression. "Leave MMG, you mean?" he said. "Maybe. I don't know what I want any more. Let me think about it. I'd like to work with you, Al — you're a genius."

Brunel was wrong about that, of course. I'm certainly not a genius. All I can do is what I've always done — handle people, take care of unpleasant details (quietly!), and make sure things get done that need doing. And of course, do what I do best: make sure that some things that need doing *don't* get done.

There *are* geniuses in the world, real geniuses. Not me, though. The man who decided to clone me, secretly — *there* I'd suggest you have a genius.

"Say, don't you remember, they called me Al . . ."

Of course, I don't remember. That song was written in the 1930's and I didn't die until 1947, but no clone remembers anything of the forefather life. The fact that we tend to be knowledgeable about our original's period is an expression of interest in those individuals, not memories from them. I know the Chicago of the Depression years intimately, as well as I know today; but it is all learned knowledge. I have no actual recollection of events. I don't *remember*.

So even if you don't remember, call me Al anyway. Everyone did.

Afterword: *Out of Copyright*

The question, "Where do you get your story ideas?" is a hardy perennial for science fiction writers. It is asked all the time, and most of us have some standard answer more plausible or at least more interesting than the honest, "Don't know."

Saucers of milk set out at night; small, still voices that whisper in our ears while we are watching baseball games; an anonymous correspondent in Akron, Ohio; dreams, stimulated by late night consumption of large quantities of Stilton cheese.

In this case I can actually offer a more specific answer. I got the idea for "Out of Copyright" at the "Anglers' Inn" on Macarthur Boulevard, a few miles north and west of Washington, D.C. I can even say when I got it: June 25, 1987. That's my birthday. The weather was really hot, and I rode my bike about five miles to reach the inn and have lunch alone there. I also, reprehensibly, drank four beers. Towards the end of the meal I was hit with the idea for the story.

I have eaten lunch there on other occasions. I have even drunk beer there. But I have never again had a story come to me while at the inn. It does not seem to be that writers' heaven, a place where you can go and automatically receive a new idea.

As to the point of the story: writers are a little different from most other people, because part of us does not expire when we do. The copyright to our written work hangs on, a faint ectoplasmic shade of our bodily selves, for half a century or more after we are gone. Then our copyrights finally die, and what we have produced during our lifetimes becomes public property.

I had the thought, suppose that copyright was granted not just for written work, but for all the rest of a person, too?

Eventually that copyright would lapse; and you would have this story.

TUNICATE, TUNICATE, WILT THOU BE MINE?

Curly locks, curly locks, wilt thou be mine?
Thou shalt not wash dishes, nor yet feed the swine.
But sit on a sofa and sew a fine seam,
And dine upon strawberries, sugar, and cream.
                                    — English Nursery rhyme

This has to be set down accurately, perfectly accurately; otherwise not one of you, whoever you are, will understand the truth — the truth about Master Tunicate, I mean, and why all the people died. I never expected to be the survivor — never *wanted* to be the survivor. But some choices you don't get to make.

If it were less noisy, maybe I could put everything onto the little tape recorder — it's here, with all Jane's blank tapes that she never used, and all the little spare batteries. But there's the roaring, and the drums, and the shaking, and the water, and tape recorders are terrible for picking up every bit of background noise. You wouldn't hear me at all.

So it will have to be Walter's notebook; and what is left out is left out.

All right.

So there we were, in the middle of Africa; and I defy you to find a more improbable quartet for an expedition. Walter, and Jane, and Wendy, and me, the terrible four. All of them such seasoned African travelers, and me a-gaping at everything I saw, and not knowing half the time if they were joking or not. Don't drink that water, Steven, they'd say. Don't eat the eggs and the bread. It was all a big joke. As Wendy used to say, the closest I had been to Africa was stories from mad Uncle George.

That's not the place to start. I can't handle that. Let's go back, back to the beginning. Let's try Washington, last December.

Winter came hard, and it came quickly. The Wednesday before Christmas it was like late fall. But on Christmas Eve, when we set off for Walter and Jane's place in Great Falls, we had eight inches of snow over an icy road. We went slithering and sliding along in the Toyota, not sure we would make it up the next hill, and every two minutes we talked of turning around and heading back home for Bethesda.

We kept going. Of course we did. Not all the animals are equal. For some friends we take ridiculous risks to keep a purely social appointment, for others Wendy or I would be on the phone making our apologies at the first sign of a snow flake.

We kept going, even though I knew we were heading for a three-hand evening with me playing dummy. They were all Africa freaks. We'd have dinner, then I would drink too much Bristol Cream, while the rest of them rattled on about Africa. Bloody Africa.

And when Walter told Wendy he had slides of his last trip, and that he had been to Zaire, did I complain? No. I even helped him set up the carousel projector — even though Zaire was just a name to me, along with Zambia and Zimbabwe, and all the other bloody zzz's like Zanzibar and Mozambique that filled up the middle of Africa. And I took the worst seat, with my back to the fire, so that after fifteen minutes I was roasted.

I'm not that obliging with everyone. Wendy could tell you that. When we went over last spring to see Sheila, one of Wendy's childhood friends, and her husband, Max, and they started to show us slides of their last summer's trip to England, I'm proud to say that I fell asleep on the floor, in the middle of their exposition. They deserved it. "This is Westminster Abbey" — a dwarfed, out of focus shot of some anonymous building, with two hideous, grinning figures in the foreground. "This is Hadrian's Wall." A low, obscure something in the misty background, and the same two people. Sheila has a figure like a sack of potatoes, and Max's parents never heard of the word "orthodontist."

Let's be fair. Walter's slides weren't all like that. He had an artist's eye, and he'd no more put himself in a picture than he'd photograph his bare bottom. And he's conscientious — was, *was* — about scale and focus. A pity. If he hadn't been, none of this would have started.

His slides were in strict logical order. He was doing a vegetation study for the World Bank, and he brought us inland from the coast, past a couple of hundred kilometers of white water rapids, to Kinshasa, where the Zaire River was broad and placid. Wendy kept up a running commentary on the soils and rock types, as a sort of counterpoint to Walter's botany. And after Jane noticed my glassy-eyed look, and explained to me that Zaire used to be called the Belgian Congo, and the river we were looking at used to be known as the Congo River, my old childhood geography lessons stirred in my brain and everything began to make sense to me as well.

Congo. Magic word. Just say it to yourself. Cong-go. It's the mightiest river in Africa. Don't you feel the primitive power of the word? Congo. Africa. Heart of darkness. Enough to make you shiver.

Perhaps I ought to explain how Wendy and I met. It may seem logical to you anyway, she a geologist and I a paleontologist. We could have run into each other while she was rock-hunting and I was digging up old bones. Logical, maybe, but quite wrong. I don't dig up old bones. I work for the Smithsonian, and I arrange exhibits, and I write learned papers on taxonomy, and I spend three hundred and sixty nights of the year in the same bed. I am what Wendy's family call a stick-at-homer, not quite to my face. They are all crazy, every one of them, and like mad Uncle George they swarm all over the world, looking for oil in the Java Sea or copper in southern Argentina. I'll say it again, they're all crazy.

But Wendy and I did meet, and not in the Gobi Desert. We met at the Kennedy Center, at a concert. My neighbor had a season ticket, and he couldn't attend, and Yo-Yo Ma was playing the Dvorák Cello Concerto, which is one of my favorites. So that accounts for my presence. And Wendy was in the next seat, on a date with a new boyfriend who looked human but turned out to be a total prick. She suspected it at the beginning, during the *Overture to Die Meistersinger*, but the extent of his prickishness didn't fully emerge until he twice tried to grope her under cover of his jacket during the *adagio* of the concerto. The second time she riposted with a pair of nail scissors, and moved as close to me as the seat permitted.

I had noticed all this, and thought that she looked gorgeous, in a white flared skirt and a deep pink blouse that was just right for her complexion and dark-brown hair. But I was somewhat preoccupied. It was late May, and I had terrible hay fever, with itchy eyes and streaming nose. I couldn't stop sniffing. And along the way I was actually trying to listen to the music. At the interval Wendy turned to me and asked if I would like to go out and have a drink with her during the intermission. I accepted, and she bought me an orange juice. She had to. I had left my wallet in the parking lot, on the front seat of my car. And it was orange juice because I was so full of antihistamines that alcohol would have put me out for the whole second half of the concert. Schubert's Ninth, another favorite.

When we got back to our seats pricko had departed, leaving Wendy without transportation. After a second half in which she still sat as close to me as the seat permitted, I drove her home to Sumner (good news: my wallet was still in the car). She lived alone in a two-bedroom house, and invited me in for an explicitly non-alcoholic and non-sexual nightcap. The house was filled with mementos from her world travels — most of them hideous. I managed the non-alcohol, but I flunked the non-sex and eventually stayed the night. I think I made a big impression. I am sure that Wendy had had more skillful lovers, but never one whose nose ran all over her during lovemaking, the way that mine did.

Lovemaking.

Forgive me, Wendy. This is relevant, I have to tell it. But we re-lived and re-told parts of that night a hundred times, when people asked how we met, and now when I write of it I cannot make it sound more than a farce. My heart can break, but the words don't show it — *won't* show it. My poor Wendy, in an unmarked grave in eastern Zaire. We had a golden evening and night, but we could never reveal that side of it to others. It had to be told as a joke; and now I cannot describe it any other way.

Do Wendy and I sound an improbable couple? Compared with Walter and Jane, we were a perfectly matched duo. Hear them arguing in public, and you'd be looking in the paper the next day for news of an axe murder. Not only that, look at the difference in their personalities. You could drop Jane down in the middle of Hell, and she'd calmly begin to make plans for the best way out. If I had to be lost in the middle of nowhere with anyone in the world (and I was) it would be Jane. Walter's a lot less organized, and Jane insists that Africa without a hat has fried his brains. But he's an original thinker, and he thrives on challenges. Between them they could tackle anything.

Anything . . . except Master Tunicate.

When he first put in an appearance I was already drowsing. Wine with dinner, then a port and four large sherries, with a wood fire at my back. I knew that Wendy was sober, and would drive us home. I didn't take much notice as Walter took us farther and farther east, heading towards the source of the river. He was well out of the territory he was supposed to cover for the World Bank, but what else was new? Now he was traveling on his own budget, for the sheer hell of it.

River life, and swamps, and native huts, and dense stands of forest. And then, without warning, something that made me sit up in my chair. Walter advanced the carousel to show a new slide. Two native women stood there, stone-faced, one on each side of a massive, lumpy sculpture. I swallowed that sculpture in one look. Too big for life. But so realistically carved that I marveled at the detail.

"Walter!" He had been ready to advance the carousel again when I stopped him. "Where in God's name did you take that picture?"

"Still awake, Steven? That's a first. Wait a minute." He switched on a table lamp to look at the notebook sitting next to the carousel. "I thought so. It was a little village called *Kintongo*, or *Kitongo*, I never saw it written down. What's the interest? We thought you were asleep."

Kintongo. Soon the whole world will know the name. But when Walter said it, the rest of us had never heard of it.

"Why the interest?" said Walter again. "I snapped the picture with a telephoto lens — mainly because the people in the village refused to be photographed. Otherwise I wouldn't have wasted the film."

"What's that thing in the middle, between the two women?" I'm sure my voice was shaky.

"That depends who you believe." Walter cleared his throat, and pushed back his floppy brown cowlick with his hand — I can see him do it now, as I sit here and write. "According to them, it's a god. According to me, it's a hollowed-out lump of wood. Not near as heavy as it looks."

"No trick photography? I mean, it really was that size."

"Certainly was. You know me, I always try to get something like a human, or a hand, or a car into the picture, to fix the scale. I had to wait a while until those two lovelies came out and stood in the right place. It's maybe seven feet tall, top to bottom. So what's all the excitement?"

"You didn't know it, but you photographed a tunicate."

Jane knows a lot of biology. She picked up on it at once. "Can't be. Steven, I'm ashamed of you. You know better — a tunicate's not a fraction of that size, ever. And you wouldn't find one in eastern Zaire."

I felt the curious frustration you get when you know fifty times as much about a subject as someone else, but don't want to take the time to explain. I was a world's *expert* on tunicates, for Christ's sake — Jane was a smart amateur.

I didn't argue. Instead I said: "Walter, can you get that slide in sharper focus?"

"I doubt it. But I can do better than that. Hold on a minute, I'm sure to have an eight-by-ten print in the other room. What the fuck's a tunicate anyway?" He left the room.

All the alcohol seemed to have burned out of me. "I know, Jane." I was almost stammering, and I felt short of breath. "I know. A tunicate, that far from the sea. And that size. A giant, fossil tunicate? Impossible, right. But if it's *not* impossible — it's a discovery. A *major* discovery."

I have to digress here. There's no way this can be told in any strict time sequence, anyway — not even in a *logical* sequence. So why try?

Life's a bummer. Don't laugh now, but I've probably spent ten thousand hours studying, reading about, and writing about tunicates, and chances are good that you've never even heard of them. But you have to understand them — well — if those dark later happenings at Kintongo are ever to make any sense to you. They make only limited sense to me.

Can we talk tunicates for a moment? Let me pursue that passion of mine one last time. It would be a waste of time to try to repeat exactly what I said that night to Walter and our wives. He'd been drinking pretty steadily, and he has a lot less body weight than me. Jane and Wendy caught on fast, but I had to repeat things three or four times before it got through to him.

We can go very quickly if you'll accept some shortcuts. Wouldn't do for the Smithsonian, but that's a million miles away.

One other thing. There will be an inquiry into all this — bound to be. There are other materials, exhibits that prove everything I'm going to say. But I couldn't bring them back with me. I'll tell you where they are hidden as we come to them.

Now, having promised to talk about tunicates I realize I can't afford to say it at all. Can't afford the space. I'm a fifth of the way through Walter's notebook and I've hardly begun.

It's all in other books, anyway — look in any decent zoology text, under "Tunicata," and you'll find pages about them. They are the most fascinating creatures in the world (or out of it?). Are they plants or animals? Terrestrial tunicates are animals, definitely; but in their adult form they usually root to the bottom of the sea like plants. Are they vertebrates or invertebrates? Somewhere in the middle, with a start of a backbone that never becomes one. And they have an outer skin, sort of an exoskeleton, made of *tunicin*; tunicin is very close to plant cellulose, the nearest the animal kingdom ever gets to producing it. They have a heart and a circulation system — but no oxygen-carrying pigment like hemoglobin in the blood. What the blood *does* have is sulphuric acid; and vanadium, lots of it. They concentrate vanadium, but we don't know how or why. Sometimes they look to me more like inorganic factories than natural animals.

I didn't mean to start. It's all in the books, and time is short, space is short, the river is calm now, and the boat is going like hell. We'll be back at Kinshasa in a few hours. But I have to add one or two things more, because they are the central factors that brought us to Zaire and to Kintongo.

Size, and habitat. Tunicates don't get much bigger than a small melon, even the biggest species. And they live in the seas and oceans, never inland. But pictured on that slide I saw the remains of a huge tunicate, seven feet tall, a thousand miles from the nearest salt water. My suggestion of a giant, fossil tunicate was a desperate one. It was all I could think of. But I know the fossil forms, and they're small.

A fake? A practical joke, played on me by Walter, with the connivance of Wendy and Jane?

That's not as silly as it sounds. Wendy was my love and my soulmate. But that couldn't make us the same age as each other. Walter, Jane and Wendy were contemporaries, in college together, and they've been conspiring for a long time. Although I was in college during those same years, I took a while getting there. I'm nine years older than the others. Cross-generation talk and little friendly surprises for old Steven are no new thing. They sound bad. But I liked them. They always had a nice outcome, and they made me feel like someone special.

This wasn't a fake. Walter produced the eight-by-ten and a lens, and we all had a close look. I explained what we were seeing.

Put your finger on that fifteen minute interval, if you want a starting point. One reason for getting together on Christmas Eve was to talk about next summer's vacation. We did it each year. Usually the other three would propose Kenya, or Madagascar, or Patagonia; I would counter with Rehoboth, or Atlantic City, or Long Beach island. Mostly we settled for a middle ground, and went to the Yucatán, or Rio, or Bermuda. Good hotels, good food.

Passion outweighs logic.

This time — Great God forgive me — I spoke first. For our vacation I suggested eastern Zaire.

Witness the advantages of technology.

The others laughed at my ideas of how we would get to Kintongo. Steamboat and native bearers, I had asked.

"United to Paris, then Air Zaire to Kinshasa," said Wendy.

"Air *Zaire*?"

"Sure. Seven-forty-seven — don't worry about it, American and British crew members. We won't eat the food, and last time I wasn't too keen on the state of the toilets, but that's a detail. We *could* fly Kinshasa to Stanleyville, or whatever they changed its name to."

"Kisangani," said Walter. "Get that right, Wendy, or they'll throw us all out of Zaire."

"Kisangani. But that's not as much fun as the water. We'll rent a diesel-powered shallow-draft boat and take it along the river as far as Boyoma Falls; then on by mini-bus to Kintongo."

"Piece of cake," said Jane. "I'll handle food supplies."

"And medical, too?" said Wendy. "I'll worry about visas and letters of introduction. Walter, will you cover transportation?"

"No problem. Just a rerun from last time. I've got all my old notes. We'll need a small trailer as well as the bus."

For a change there was no discussion of vacation choice. They were planning before I had thought through my own suggestion.

And the money for all this? Ah, there's the real magic of Wendy and Jane and Walter. Grant-masters, all three of them. They knew the pools where the grant money swims, and what baited words would let you reel it in.

Piece of cake.

Sure. In my excitement I believed it. I still believed it when we set out up-river from Kinshasa, aboard a thirty-two-foot twin-engined Messerschmitt launch that drew less than two feet of water.

I was excited but uneasy. Walter's slides were accurate, but some things they couldn't tell. They didn't capture the clouds of flies that chased us over the water — big flies, with a blue-black meaty body and a vicious bite. The slides couldn't catch the feeling of the river, either, broad and lazy and somehow infinitely old and powerful. Self-satisfied. It didn't notice us. When we have wiped ourselves out, or gone into space to meet our masters, that dark river will be there unchanged. I was afraid of it.

The flies annoyed, but they did not frighten — not then. They terrify me now. They are still here, there are scores of them in the cabin. I can stand them, but I dare not close my eyes. If I did, I would see again the three blue-black swarms, buzzing densely. And at the center, Walter, and Jane, and Wendy.

The boat was capable of eighteen knots, but we didn't try for more than a fraction of that. We pushed our way steadily upriver, with Walter at the helm and the three-man "crew" sitting on the hatch, smoking and chatting to each other. They seemed able to ignore the flies. Two of them still carried automatic rifles, holding them casually across their laps. I had started to object when we first boarded, but Walter had taken me to one side.

"This is a military dictatorship," he said quietly. "We're here because the President's office allows us visas and lets us be here. But they'll keep a close eye on us — and if they don't like what they see, we'll be out."

"But they're carrying guns. Are they loaded?"

"They're loaded. Get used to loaded weapons. And remember, don't ask the crew to do any work. One of them knows how to handle the boat, but the other two are army officers. We don't need them. They go with the territory."

I dare not close my eyes to sleep now. I could not sleep then. The moment we boarded the ship I felt a throbbing tension beginning inside my head, darkening the ship and the face of the monstrous river. It was a band of pressure, the torture that I first experienced when I was just sixteen years old. It had forced me to seven wasted years of madness and despair.

I tried to eat dinner with the others, but I had no appetite. Soon I left them and went aft to watch the African sunset, a red sun plunging rapidly into gray, lifeless water.

And then I had my first hint of conspiracy among the other three. Walter, Wendy, and Jane were sitting in the forward cabin. I could see their heads, nodding back and forth beneath the electric lamp. They were leaning forward, and now and again one of them would steal a glance aft in my direction. I knew they were talking about me but I had no idea of their words. My head ached terribly, like a jet-lag that had grown worse and worse, and after a few minutes I rested it on the aluminum aft rail and gazed mindlessly down at the turbulent wake. The picture of Master Tunicate came into my mind. I felt a little easier. In ten days we would be in Kintongo, and I would have an answer.

The screws were only a few feet beneath me, threshing loud in the darkness, and I did not hear Jane approach. She put her hand down gently and rubbed the back of my neck and then my forehead. Her touch was cool and dry.

"Are you all right, Steven? Can I bring you a drink?"

That quiet, cultured voice. Just as though we were at a party back in Georgetown. I stood up and hugged her to me in that humid darkness, running my hand along her thin back and then around to cup one little breast.

"I love you, Jane," I said. I had never before offered Jane an intimate touch, never said a word to suggest that I found her attractive.

She did not pull away from me, or turn her head to see if anyone was watching. "I love you, too," she said. "We all love you. Try to be patient, Steven, we'll be there soon. Come on. Wendy is worried."

She took my hand in hers and led me forward, past the silent crew. Their cigarettes glowed in the dark, and the light of the rising moon glimmered off their eyes and the polished barrels of the guns. Walter and Wendy were still sitting in the cabin. They made a space for me and Wendy placed a brimming glass in my hand. I tasted it slowly, wanting to believe that Jane had somehow found a supply of sherry on one of her shopping trips into Kinshasa. It was bad gin and cheap vermouth. I cannot say it was a martini. We had no ice.

Six days of travel brought us to Walter's chosen transfer point, thirty miles from the seventh and last cataract of the falls. We had stopped twice for fuel and fresh food, halts so brief that the second time the army men became angry. There was no beer on board. They wanted shore time for drinks and women. When Walter shook his head and spoke back to them sharply in French, they went sullenly to the bow. For the next hour they fired single shots at the white birds that flew or floated on the oily surface of the river. At a hit they would give out hoots of pleasure, but when I went forward to watch them they lowered their guns. After a couple of minutes of uncomfortable silence, they looked sideways at me and shuffled back to sit on their usual spot on the hatch.

I returned to the cabin.

"Good for you, Steven," said Walter. "They don't give a damn what I say to them, but they're afraid of you. What do they know that Jane and I don't know?"

What indeed? It's an accident of nature that made me six-feet four inches tall and Walter eight inches shorter. The fire was in him, not me. And yet they were right. They knew.

When we left the boat and the steaming river I thought we would also leave behind the crew. The two armed men had other ideas. They piled into the bus right behind us. Walter offered no protest. He made sure that the third crew member would stay with the boat, then put us in gear and headed east. Kintongo was three days' ride, over rough tracks. With the loaded trailer we couldn't do more than twenty miles an hour.

The air lost its leaden humidity when we were half a day's journey away from the river. We travelled in the early morning and evening, resting through the middle of the day. Walter, through some mysterious system of his own, had arranged for caches of food and gasoline at villages along the way. We spent the hottest parts of the day and the middle of the nights there. The huts were filthy and primitive, and sanitation was non-existent.

Our own hygiene was not much better. I wondered what my colleagues at the Smithsonian would think of me now. I, always so careful to shower well, to shave twice a day if we went out to dinner, to remove the grime from under my finger nails. If I had to wear a shirt for the second day, or go out in the morning with unpolished shoes, it was a major event. But it is astonishing how quickly we adapt. Now I did not comb my hair for days, or do more than run a wet cloth over my hands and face. And I was still a lot cleaner than our two unwelcome guests from the Zaire army.

We drove steadily east, into rolling country that rose infinitely slowly before us. The mini-bus was like a time machine, ticking off the years. Since leaving Kinshasa we had lost a century. *This* Africa had not changed since the 1880's. Steamboats and native bearers? Not even those. There were radios, certainly, and electric flashlights in the villages. At the sprawl of huts where we paused on our second day I saw a Sears, Roebuck label on a native's plaid shirt, and a carving knife made in Japan. But that was superficial change. I think their diet had not changed in centuries: smoked monkey or fish, fruit and cassava paste — relished, it seemed, by everyone except me. And the real villages came to life after dark, with firelight, drums, and dancing. The rhythms and movements were ageless. I felt the drumbeat driving into my head, until it fused with the pounding of blood inside my brain. I knew that syncopation before I came to Africa. It was my old torture.

I sat on one side of the fire and looked at Jane and Wendy opposite me. Heads close together, and now and then glancing my way. Whispering. About me. At last I stood up and wandered off through the village, out to the dark perimeter where animal night-noises replaced the drums within my skull.

I was able to breathe again. Tomorrow we reached Kintongo.

After a few minutes Walter came away from the fireside and joined me. He had taken off his glasses, and I knew what that meant. First, he was seeing the world as an astigmatic blur; second, he was going to be very serious.

"How are you, Steven?" No beating about the bush, no winding slowly into his subject.

"Excited. We'll be in Kintongo tomorrow."

"If the weather holds up and the paths are good." Walter was the perfect project director because he took nothing for granted. "We're an eight-hour drive from Kintongo in good conditions. Last time it took me nearly eleven; and we're in a wetter season now." He cleared his throat, and his expression became embarrassed and uncertain. "I suppose I'm going to find out the answer in a day or two, and I should have asked you this question long ago; but just what in hell do you hope to find in Kintongo? It's just a little village. Nothing to get excited about."

I did not speak.

"You see, I know why the rest of us are here," he said at last. "We're on an adventure in some of the best wild country on earth. But that's not you, Steven, and I knew it before we began. You could be back home in your study, and a lot happier than you are now. We've watched you for the last week, and seen how you've hated every minute — the mosquitoes, and the food, and the heat. I know you haven't complained, not a word. But this isn't your stamping ground. So why did you want to come?"

"To see the tunicate."

He shook his head. "To see the tunicate. I shouldn't have asked. That fucking tunicate. It's a fancy piece of carving. Steven, you're going to be angry as hell in a couple of days. I hope you won't be mad at us."

His mouth puckered up, as though he were trying to inhale with his lips pressed tightly together, and I thought he was about to speak again. But he turned and went slowly back toward the fire.

He hadn't come to see me of his own volition. Jane and Wendy had put him up to it, I was sure. But it was going to be all right. Tomorrow we would be in Kintongo and we would see the tunicate.

In the weeks and months before we left Washington I had teased information about Kintongo from Walter, little by little. He was my only source. The place was unknown to the Smithsonian, or to the map rooms in the Library of Congress.

Walter spoke of a thriving village, maybe a hundred people, in a fine natural setting: a pair of small volcanic cones each rising a few hundred feet above an alluvial plain, the cones overlapping in area and the taller one about fifty feet higher than the other. As volcanoes they were long extinct, and both craters had filled with water. The lake formed in the higher caldera was perhaps four acres in extent, and it fed the lower one, half its size, through a permanent trickling stream. The village of Kintongo sat by that stream. The water of the lakes was clean and deep, and decomposed volcanic ash provided a black soil that was easily worked, deep, and fertile.

The villagers were too intelligent to take their good fortune for granted, and they wanted no competition from new settlers. They were wary with all visitors, especially those with cameras.

Walter had planned our approach and first meeting in Kintongo with care. While we were still in Washington, he and Wendy spent a long time discussing the delicate question of gifts for the village chief. "He'll remember me, you can be sure

of that," said Walter. "Lunga's a shrewd old fellow. He'll wonder why I'm back. We need a good reason."

"Touring party?"

"Not if we want to stay a while near the village — a tour
wouldn't do that. Not enough to see."

Wendy put her hand up to her forehead and rubbed at the
roots of her hair. It was a nervous habit. She would rub until
she had made a red patch at the hairline, then go to a mirror
and frown in disgust at her reflection. "Working for the World
Bank, or AID, on a development project? Bird watchers?
Traders? I don't know."

"They don't want to hear anything about development.
Lunga would be happy if he never had another visitor from
Kinshasa. Bird-watchers is better — there's actually a wonderful breeding-forest a few hours from Kintongo, and we'll visit
it. But if we were mainly interested in that we'd naturally stay
over there. No, your last shot is the best one. Traders. There
are things we can sell in Kintongo, and my first trip helps.
Lunga will suspect that my previous visit was a look at the market."

Walter had brought an interesting selection. We had
enamel pans, razor blades and disposable razors, flashlights
and batteries, plastic plates, bowls, and spoons, a couple of
pressure cookers, three boxes of candles that would light
themselves again after you blew them out, and — Walter's
pièce de résistance — a gasoline-powered chain saw.

"This will get him," he said. "They cut a lot of timber for the
village, and they always need more. The pressure cooker will
be our main gift, but he'll really want the chain saw. Lunga will
let us stay until he's talked his way into getting it."

Walter had done an amazing job pulling all his "trade
goods" in through Customs with only a pittance of duty and a
modest amount of bribes. It was all part of the game — the
challenge that made the other three enjoy Africa. And on the
way from Kinshasa he had done a little trading, just to practice
his act for Lunga.

I was in the front seat of the bus as we ascended the slope
that would take us into Kintongo. The little trailer was
crammed with our food, tents, and supplies, and the volcanic
cone was steep-sided. We jolted along in four-wheel drive, at

about five miles an hour, and I had plenty of time for a leisurely first inspection of our destination.

It was not a clinical look. My pulse was fast, and I felt light-headed from excitement and lack of sleep.

Here is what I saw: there was a tightly drawn group of huts, approaching as close as thirty yards to the little lake. Each building was made of tall vertical poles of dry timber, with dry grass stuffed between and grass sheaves plaited above to form sloping roofs. The huts looked fairly fragile, but wind-proof and rain-proof, and that was enough. Cold would almost never be a problem. It was just as well, because everything looked tinder-dry and a fire inside any of the huts would be an insanity. The communal cooking-place sat between the village buildings and the lake. An enamel bathtub had been set up to catch the overflow of the stream where it trickled down into the lake, and two women were filling pans from it as we drove slowly up the slope and stopped at a respectful distance from the huts and the cooking area.

They were ready for us. Our arrival had obviously been long expected. The top of the higher volcanic cone must provide an excellent lookout point across twenty miles of plain, and Lunga was wary enough of visitors that he would keep that post well-staffed. It seemed as though the whole village had turned out for our arrival. Walter had been on the low side with his estimate. I did a rough count before we had exchanged our first words, and there must have been two hundred people thronged around our bus.

Lunga sat in state outside the biggest hut. He was quite recognizable from Walter's description and quick pencil sketch, a pot-bellied man whose grizzled hair didn't match his smooth face and young eyes. He waited calmly, nodding to himself in a thoughtful way when he saw Walter. He looked briefly at me, then turned his attention to Wendy and Jane. I wondered if he had seen white women in Kintongo before.

My inspection of Lunga was even more cursory; for behind him, standing against the wall of the hut and supported on a well-made wooden trestle, was the object that I had traveled six thousand miles to see. It lay on its side now, rather than upright as it had shown in the slide, but it was quite unmistakably the tunicate.

I would have liked to go over and look at it at once, but even in my urgency I realized that we had to go through the formalities. What I had underestimated was the length of time that those formalities would occupy. First there had to be formal greetings. I soon discovered that in Africa even the meeting of total strangers can be time-consuming. And we had another complicating factor, one that Jane had already predicted — though in her practical way she had also pointed out that there was nothing we could do about it.

I mean the presence of the two army men, the representatives of the far-off President in Kinshasa. Lunga's immediate reaction to that was a cold aloofness during our introductions, with a suggestion through his interpreter that we were clearly just passing through his village and would be on our way within the hour. But I suspect he knew the realities of the situation very well, and could see that we liked the army presence even less than he did. For after his formal expression of displeasure he at once provided us all with cups of beer and invited us to sit on the floor with him. Then he and Walter began their discussions, in the curious mixed-language talk you hear a lot in the middle of the continent. I could understand most of the French and English phrases and guess at some others, but sometimes I was lost completely.

But then I was also preoccupied. It was certainly not a carving, or even a paper model, as Wendy had irritatingly suggested that first evening. Six feet was a better estimate than seven, because the native women in Walter's slide must have been shorter than I expected; and the surface had a glossy, finished look that had not come across in the slide, either, almost as though it had been recently varnished or polished. The opening in the upper end — the inhalant siphon — was about ten inches across, and I could see that the whole interior had been scooped clean. The big surprise was at the other end. The usual sessile nature of a mature tunicate did not allow for any form of true flexible foot. But Master Tunicate had three distinct lower pads, each looking as though it was designed for real locomotion.

I was itching for a closer look, but a roar of laughter from Lunga brought my attention back to our little circle. The cups of beer had been steadily refilled every few minutes, and with the sun beating down on the bare black earth we were all sweating hugely. I felt terrible, but Walter seemed to be enjoying himself and he was doing famously. He had done his razzle-dazzle with plastic cups and plates and trick candles, and had presented Lunga with a pressure cooker. Now he was all set to demonstrate the chain saw.

Lunga's eyes lit up at the roar of the motor and the flying sawdust. He called for more beer, and sent a villager away to bring the biggest log he could find. The noise was horrendous. When we went back to the bus, an hour later, we were all half-deafened. But everyone was tipsy and seemed well pleased with the meeting. On the way to the bus we paused by the pool. It was obviously well-used by the natives, and it didn't look as clean as Walter had advertised.

"That's it, Steven," said Walter. "In the middle of all the other chit-chat I asked about your friend. He said that Master Tunicate"— this was the first time I heard that phrase spoken —"wasn't there one day, then there was a monster rain storm and electrical storm that night, and the next day he *was* there, in this pond. Nobody saw him come. Lunga says he knew they had found a god, but he said it in a way that made me feel maybe he didn't mean it. The other villagers believe it — but. perhaps Lunga doesn't."

Walter may have been right. But that problem has been solved. Lunga is now a part of Master Tunicate's entourage.

We went closer to stare into the depths of the pool.

"How deep is it?" I asked.

Walter shook his head, and I turned to Jane. "Think I could dive it?" One of my few athletic talents, as we had found in Bermuda. I was better in water than any of them.

She looked doubtful. "You could, but I don't think you should. I saw signs of schisto in some of the villagers. And you can tell they don't try to keep this pond clean, or have any decent sanitation."

"Schisto?" I asked.

"Schistosomiasis," said Walter. "I don't know if this is a schisto area or not, but we don't want to take the risk."

"But I'd only be going in once."

"Quite enough," said Jane severely. "I'll tell you an African riddle: Do you know the difference between true love and schistosomiasis?"

"Answer: Schisto is forever," said Wendy. "It's a disease with no cure. Steven, you're not going in that pond. We've done very well so far, Walter has managed miracles here — let's not spoil it."

"Does Lunga really believe we're traders?" said Jane.

"He thinks Steven and I are," said Walter. "I told him you and Wendy are our women. He understood that."

"And he believed you brought us with you all the way from America?" said Jane. "That sounds fishy. I bet Lunga's more suspicious of us than you realize. He knows women can be had right here."

"He said that to me." Walter's face was expressionless. "But I pointed out to him that you two are spectacular-exceptional-amazing in bed. He was very interested. He asked if he could try you both, especially the long one. I told him maybe — if the trading here goes well."

He headed for the bus before Jane or Wendy could hit him with a good reply. They hurried after him, cursing. I stayed on for another look at the lake. The water was a little green and cloudy, but I imagined I could see bottom. It ought to be easy enough to dive it, even at night.

Our meeting in Kintongo had not helped my sleeping difficulty at all. It had made it worse. Lying in our tent while Wendy peacefully slumbered beside me, I found my mind running in circles over the same issues that had surfaced on that first evening in Great Falls.

Problems.

There were physical problems with a six or seven foot tunicate that I had not mentioned to the others.

To take one specific: think about *scale*. Like the idea of a six-foot ant or housefly, the existence of a very large tunicate would introduce all kinds of physiological difficulties. For example, a tunicate eats by inhaling water through a siphon, straining it for food particles, and exhaling the water through another siphon. I could see that might work quite well for a very large tunicate — after all, blue whales are the biggest animals on earth, and they eat through a similar process of straining water for food. But unlike the whale, the tunicate has no lungs. It relies on the same water that carries in the food to carry in oxygen. And for a six-foot tunicate, that supply would be totally inadequate. So a six-foot tunicate is impossible. Very good — but there were the remains of one less than a half a mile away.

That, plus a dozen other more specialized questions of tunicate anatomy and function, assured that I would be awake well before dawn. When the sun came up I was already dressed, outside the tent, and firing up the stove.

I made plenty of noise, so by the time I had boiled water the rest of them were stirring, yawning and muttering inside the tents. They joined me outside and we had a hefty but hurried breakfast. For various reasons, all four of us wanted an early start to the day's work.

An hour after first light, Walter and I were heading on foot for Kintongo. When we left, Jane and Wendy had started to re-allocate food and supplies between the bus and trailer. The plan called for a trip to the bird breeding-grounds as soon as the two of us returned — Walter insisted that it was a not-to-be-missed sight, one of the main reasons for visiting this part of Zaire. I had not objected.

Lunga was an early riser, too. He was waiting for us when we got there, yawning and scratching, chewing on a leg of monkey *boucané* that looked disturbingly like the smoked limb of a human baby, and smoking an ancient yellow-brown meerschaum pipe. He was more than ready to begin discussions, and after the obligatory few minutes of general chit-chat he and Walter got down to serious business. It was my chance to stroll over to the tunicate and take a much closer look.

There are three orders of tunicate — Ascidiacea, Thaliacea, and Copelata — and no one can pretend to know every detail of every species. I certainly won't make that claim. But I do know the features common to all the orders, and Master Tunicate — while undoubtedly a tunicate — had anomalies that perturbed me greatly. The strangest was an extension of the tunic structure *inside* the body cavity, creating what amounted to a complicated internal skeleton as well as the usual tough outer layer. No tunicate had a skeleton. And there was a great bulge between the two siphons. That was where in a normal tunicate the wad of nerve tissue that makes up the animal's "brain" should lie. Here it was preposterously well-developed, a significant fraction of the total body mass. And those lower pads; they looked less and less as though they were designed for simple attachment to a rock, and more and more like feet.

There were so many questions. If only I could find a living specimen . . .

I went back to Walter's side, and found him alone for the moment. Lunga had stepped away to another hut.

"He'll be back quickly enough," said Walter. He grinned in a self-satisfied way. "He wants to buy that saw so bad, and I told him it wasn't available for sale because you had already promised it elsewhere. But I told him maybe if he wanted to trade *that*" — he jerked his head toward the great convex cylinder on the wooden trestle — "I'd try to talk you into a deal. I said you were fascinated with it."

"Thanks, Walter." My throat was suddenly tight with nervous anticipation. But when Lunga returned I leaned back into the shade and tried to look coolly indifferent.

Lunga was carrying an oblong piece of blue-gray metal or plastic, about three feet long. The surface was scored with a regular grid, an accurate pattern of ruled lines, and the edges of the material branched many times, to terminate in a broad sheaf of tiny wires. He jabbered away at Walter for a few minutes, while I struggled unsuccessfully to follow.

Walter shook his head firmly and turned to me. "He won't trade your friend there. Quite honestly, I think he'd be happy to see the last of Master Tunicate, but the villagers would give him trouble. They think they have a powerful magic going for them. But he says that blue gadget was with the god when it arrived in the village, and he'd be quite willing to trade that to us. He asked if you wanted to buy it, and I said not."

Walter turned for another two minutes of rapid cross-talk, then suddenly he rocked back to squat on his heels. I noticed an abrupt change in his manner when he looked across at me.

"Holy Hell," he said. "Steven, you're a magician. I don't see how you could read something significant out of a casual look at one of my slides, but I think we may have hit the jackpot here." He stared across at the lake. "Lunga just told me there's a whole 'iron house' at the bottom of that pond, with a lot of stuff in it like that piece of junk he's holding. But it's all made in one piece, and too heavy for them to bring up — they ran ropes to it. When the water was clear they could see it down there. He thinks it was the tunicate's house at first, and it lived down there until they caught it in a big net and held it up at the surface. Lunga suggests that we could attach a cable from the bus, and use that to drag the whole thing up, and if we did that, he'd trade it to us — for a *lot* of goods."

My stomach felt like a lump of lead, and my heart was racing. "Ask him if he's sure there was only one. There could be others, still living down there."

Walter spat out the question, and Lunga shook his head firmly.

"No chance of that, he says." Walter sighed. "There was only the one. But he says there have been other changes in the pond since the tunicate died. There are fish in it now, and before it didn't have any. The villagers say that the tunicate's death brought those fish. They try to catch them now, that's one reason the pond is dirty." He groaned. "Steven, do you see what they did? They caught it, the only one, and they kept it as a god — kept it on the surface until they killed it."

If my heart had raced before, now it felt as though it had stopped completely. Walter didn't know much about tunicates; he didn't understand the possible significance of his own words. But what he had said suggested that one of my own fantasies could be true.

I could not speak. Luckily, Walter for his own reasons felt just as strong a need to get away to where he could think as I did. We made rapid and disorganized farewells to Lunga, promising to consider his possible deal, and staggered back down hill to our own camp.

When we arrived back at the bus we found that we had been gone less than two hours. It felt like weeks.

I didn't want Walter to tell Jane and Wendy what we had heard, but of course there was no way of stopping him. Luckily he omitted some facts that I considered relevant — Jane might have picked up their significance.

"From god knows where," he said. He was walking up and down in the camp, shaking with tension and excitement.

"Light-years, it must have been. And landed here — crash-landed, I bet. So what did they do? The stupid black bastards caught him, and named him as a god, and kept him in a net. Until the poor bugger died."

Walter was more upset that I had ever seen him before. He doesn't have a speck of racist in him. That "black bastards" revealed more of his torment than a thousand curses.

The two women were staring at him skeptically, then glancing from time to time at me.

"Calm down, Walter," said Jane. "You're jumping to conclusions again. Steven, you were there too and you haven't said a word. Do you agree with all this?"

I shook my head. "How can I? They were talking gobbledygook. You know I can't understand more than one word in four when you talk to Lunga."

"I'm damned sure I didn't misunderstand anything," snapped Walter. "I know quite well that Steven didn't follow everything — but he saw that piece of ship that Lunga had with him."

They looked at me, and I shrugged. "I certainly saw *something*. But it could have been a lot of stuff — from a television set, or a crashed airplane, or some other mechanical gadget. Hell, I couldn't tell what it was — any more than Walter could. Electronics isn't our line."

"But what are we going to *do*?" said Walter desperately. "All right, suppose there's a chance I have it wrong. We can't risk the chance that I'm correct, and do nothing. We have to *act*."

Jane and Wendy looked at each other. I could imagine their train of thought: *first we had trouble with Steven, then as soon as he seems to be behaving normally we get a problem with Walter. Just one damn thing after another. . . .*

"Sure, we have to act," said Jane. "But we don't have to do anything right away." She took Walter by the elbow and began to tug him gently towards the bus. "Nothing will happen if we delay for a day or two, will it? Kintongo won't go away, and the machine will still be there at the bottom of the lake tomorrow, or a week from now. So I say we shouldn't rush into anything. We should get out of here, take our trip, and think it over while we're gone."

"You mean, just do *nothing*? Damn it, Jane —"

"It's your own rule, Walter — you've preached it at me often enough. When in doubt, think it out. So let's do that, while we're away looking at birds."

Walter glared at her, but he still allowed himself to be towed along. I knew he was hooked, and it was time for me to get into the conversation.

"I agree with Jane," I said. "You three carry on. But I think I'll hang around here and take a day's rest. I don't feel all that good."

"Sick?" said Wendy at once, and she moved to my side.

"Not sick." I allowed her to feel my forehead. "See? I'm tired, that's all. I haven't been sleeping well since we first got off the plane."

They all knew that. On the other hand, they wanted me along with them, or it wouldn't be the right mixture. I let them talk a little more, to the point where Wendy was ready to assure me I could get lots of sleep on the trip, then I nodded my head to the tent pitched on the other side of the trailer.

"If I stay it solves another problem," I said. "Them. Can you imagine them putting out their cigarettes and keeping quiet? One shot from those rifles, and you'd scare off every bird in Africa. Those two won't shut up just because you want them to. But if I'm here, I'll bet they stay with me. They don't want to split up, and they'd rather loaf here than crawl through the bush after you three."

"I was planning on sneaking off without them," said Walter. "I parked the bus with that in mind. We can do a clear run for half a mile down the hill, with the clutch in and the engine off."

"You can still do that if you want to," I said. "But this way they'll feel no duty to chase after you. Make sure there's plenty of food and gin here, and I guarantee they'll decide to stay and guard me." I patted Walter on the shoulder, turning him to face Jane and Wendy. "Don't argue about it, now. You three go off and enjoy yourselves. And don't worry, I'll find plenty to occupy me here — even if I don't feel like sleeping and eating the whole time."

Jane, Walter, and Wendy left within the hour. The two army men were predictably irritated when they finally yawned their way out of their tent and discovered what had happened, but they showed no interest at all in pursuit on foot.

I tried friendly conversation with them. I failed completely. We understood each other easily enough, despite my clumsy French, but I was rebuffed by averted eyes and uncomfortable body language. I gave up after a few minutes. They happily accepted my offer of two bottles of gin and took them back to the shade of the trailer.

I went to our tent and lay on my camp bed all afternoon. I had a lot to do, but I could not begin at once. My activities must wait until dusk. I was in a peculiar mental state. Jittery, but peaceful. My mind felt in a turmoil, yet at the same time I was totally contented. I was doing exactly what I wanted to do.

Darkness near the equator comes fast, a heavy curtain pulled without warning across the horizon. With the last glimmer of light I was quietly approaching the lake on the side opposite from Kintongo. It was full dark when I undressed, stacked my clothes twenty yards from the lake, and straightened to look again at the village. The earth was warm beneath my feet, holding the day's heat. Across the pool the cooking fires were burning brightly enough to hinder anyone who might look across in my direction. I walked forward and eased cautiously into the calm water.

It felt pleasantly cool and soothing on my body, and the bottom sloped away steeply. In a few steps I was chest-deep. I stood motionless, took a dozen long, deep breaths, then dove out and down. As my head went under I felt a vibration through my whole body, as though the water of the pool was in small, turbulent waves.

I switched on the flashlight. Part of my afternoon had gone to making it waterproof, wrapping it tightly in transparent plastic bags and sealing them shut. It was a powerful nine-volt lamp, meant for use reading in the tent or in the bush at night, and its focused beam cut a zone of illumination through the cloudy green water. I directed the light downwards, following the incline to the deepest part of the pond, and swam along the narrow cone.

The structure that Lunga had told us about was visible at once. It was a blue-gray octahedron, about ten meters across, lying slightly tilted on the bottom. The edges and corners were beveled and smooth, and I could see large, rectangular openings in the middle of two of the faces. I swam toward one of them, halted a few feet away, and directed the beam inside. The whole interior was a maze of lines and cables, criss-crossing in all directions. The walls were riddled with small pockets, each a few inches across and about the same depth. After a few seconds I switched off the flashlight, turned, and kicked my way back to the surface.

I took another dozen long breaths. The structure made no sense. There were no mechanical controls, no dials or screens or instruments; no furnishings, nothing recognizable as living accommodation. It did not fit with our ideas for a vehicle or a home.

I went back down. This time I went closer and put my head and upper body in through one of the openings.

That action almost killed me. The gentle vibration that I had sensed at the surface became overpowering within the hull. It took me, shook me, and elevated me. I could feel happiness running wild along my veins, and for the first time in my life I understood the reason for existence. I finally had something to protect, to live for and to cherish.

In that moment of revelation I opened my mouth wide enough to gasp out air and inhale water. I choked, dropped the flashlight, convulsed, and was lucky enough to jerk away from the aperture and drift upwards toward the surface. I came out at last into open air, where I let out an agonized cough and ejected cold water from my lungs. Then I was forced to float for a couple of minutes, recovering my breath. My heart was racing at full speed, like a fast drumbeat inside my chest.

Finally I was able to dive again. I approached the octahedron cautiously and picked up my flashlight, still switched on.

And it was then, hesitating once more near the openings in the hull, that I saw them. A dozen long-tailed darting shapes, each about two feet long, flashed away from the light beam and wriggled off to the dark shelter on the other side of the pond. I swam after them until I ran out of air, watching them retreating from the flashlight and my tiring body. Then I let myself float again to the surface, paddled slowly back to the place I had entered the pond, and dragged myself out. I lay down at poolside, hardly able to move. My brain was possessed by an intolerable knowledge.

This knowledge: Lunga had looked in the pool for another tunicate, but all he had found were fish. Naturally. Neither he nor Walter knew one key fact: the larval form of a tunicate looks nothing like the mature animal; it looks like a sort of tadpole, free-swimming and with a well-developed head and tail.

Anger boiled inside me. Kintongo had found Master Tunicate, taken him as their god, and held him on the surface until starvation, asphyxiation, or chemical imbalances had brought a slow and agonizing death. But the story was not over. Now they would hunt for and catch the children of their god, to serve with their cassava and smoked monkey.

I could not live with that thought. I lay for a long time, consumed by rage and fear. At last, I dressed myself and headed back for our camp.

Our camp lay on the slope of the volcanic cones, about six hundred yards downhill from the village of Kintongo. I walked back there slowly. And I realized the distance would be a real curse for the night's work.

Not yet, though. My main worry initially was the army men. They had stayed in the camp, interested in neither wild life nor village. They would probably be there now, and maybe in a foul mood. If they interfered it might affect my plans.

I concluded that I could not permit any hint of that. But I knew what to do. My thoughts had a strange, abstract purity to them, emerging full-blown in my brain with every detail clear.

I tiptoed the last hundred yards to camp, but it was really unnecessary. They had obviously been drinking since afternoon, and were both snoring by the trailer when I approached. One of them stirred as I reached for his gun, but he gave me no trouble.

That was progress. I could take the next, laborious step.

Even if the mini-bus had been available, I dared not risk the noise. It took nearly four hours to make three heavily laden journeys on foot up to a point just outside the perimeter of the village. Each trip I piled the cans I was carrying into a neat stack by a twisted, fire-scarred tree. On the third trip I went almost into the village itself. Everything was quiet. The eating, the drinking and the late night story-telling were finished.

I realized now that I should not have attempted the fourth trip. I had enough material already. But I wanted to make doubly sure, and after a few minutes rest I set off again to our camp. I was getting impatient, too — it was full night, and the moon was shrouded in thick fast-moving clouds. Rain would be a disaster at this stage. I hurried the final couple of hundred yards into camp, making no attempt to travel quietly, and headed again for the store of gasoline cans.

I found Walter, Jane, and Wendy, waiting for me by the mini-bus.

Naturally, they had found the bodies of the two army men. I had made no attempt to conceal them. I had assumed, you see, that I would have ample time. And that should have been true. But Wendy must have worried about me, and instead of staying through the night they had cut short their watch and headed for home.

Their faces held not accusation; just bewilderment, and the sick expression that accompanies a sudden discovery of death.

"Steven!" Wendy came running to me and put her arms around me. "Something terrible has happened to the army men. They're both dead."

I could feel her shivering against me. And I felt the spasm, as though an electric shock had been applied to her, when she jerked back from me.

I peered down at her. My head was roaring, a maelstrom of conflicting needs and urges. I should have had lots of time. If they had been away most of the night, as they said they would be, everything would have been all right. We would all be together at this moment, drinking Jane's gin and ready to head back to America. But I had been too hurried and careless.

"Steven. Your jacket. Your jacket."

Her voice was puzzled. Still no accusation, but an odd and lifeless weight. I had a sudden premonition. They would want to indulge in endless discussions. They would demand explanations, and they would want to do something about the army men. Worst of all, unless I could give them a full explanation they would try to stop me.

I turned, wanting to ignore them and head back to the village at once. But then I hesitated. They might follow me there, disturb me, prevent me from taking the necessary actions. And that was intolerable. I had to explain.

"I have to go back to the village at once," I said. "There's work to be done there. They killed him, you know. You see that, don't you? He came here to help us. And they murdered him."

"Steven." Walter came up close to me and grabbed my arms. He tilted his head up, staring at my eyes in the light of the gasoline lamp. Tears were rolling helplessly down my cheeks. "My God. Pull yourself together. There's been bad work here."

Then he stopped and took a slow step away from me. Like Wendy, he had seen the blood on my jacket.

"Stay here, all of you," I said. "I must go back to the village. You won't be needed. They murdered, and they are trying to murder again. That has to be taken care of properly. It will be only an hour's work. After that we can talk as much as you want."

But they wouldn't do it, you see. They couldn't understand what *had* to happen; so instead they came and stood around and wouldn't let me leave. And I had to leave.

"Wendy," I said. "Get out of the way, please. I told you I have work to do. It's very important. If you won't help me, than at least don't hinder me."

She clutched at my arm. "He's sick again," she said to Jane and Walter. "I told you he was getting worse. Give me a hand with him. We have to get him to bed and give him sedatives."

Her words destroyed me. *Sick again.* She had promised she would never mention my problem to anyone else, ever. I broke loose from her, broke loose from Walter, avoided Jane's quick restraining lunge, and ran away from the light of the gasoline lantern. They must not follow me to the village. I did what had to be done, and then I ran off into the brush. I felt full of energy, strong and confident. But I was still worried by the danger of rain. And the tears ran free down my cheeks.

I reached the outskirts of the village in just a few minutes. I took two cans of gasoline from the heap and carried them cautiously into the middle of Kintongo. The great outer case, the sarcophagus of Master Tunicate, still stood outside the biggest hut. I splashed gasoline all around its base. I was generous in the amount, and I tried not to rush. The funeral pyre of a god deserved some time and care. Then I worked my way slowly outward, covering the walls of every building with liquid and placing a broad ring of gasoline around each one. There were ten buildings. I made four trips, each time expecting that someone would stir inside one of them. But they slept deeply.

When all the dry vegetation was thoroughly soaked, I ran a thin trail of gas thirty yards from the village and ignited it. The flame seemed to catch and hesitate for a second, close to my feet, then it ran off as fast as my eye could follow along the line I had marked. Within ten seconds there were flames everywhere in the village. The huts were all blazing.

Most of the buildings were instant infernos, flaming too fiercely for anyone to escape from them. But two huts, close to the outskirts of the village, burned less strongly than the others. Four people ran screaming out of them, two men and a woman dragging a young child.

I had worried about such a situation. It had made me sit and hold my head in my hands for many minutes. What was the correct action to take? Then I realized that the answer was obvious. This was a deity's funeral pyre, and a god had a right to his servants. *All* his servants.

I lifted the rifle, set it to automatic, and fired. They fell into the flames.

No more people came out of the huts. After a few minutes I took my camera, came as close to the blaze as I could stand, and photographed the flames that licked around the great tunicate shell. The last mortal remains of Master Tunicate vanished as I watched. I stayed for two hours, but there was nothing more to see. Nothing at all. And at last I lay down on the hard black earth and cradled my head in my arms. For the first time since I came to Africa, I slept a deep and purifying sleep.

Dawn awoke me, dawn and heavy rain. It hissed down into the blackened ash of the village, quenching every ember. And it beat on my unprotected scalp to begin again the drumming inside my brain. I got to my feet, went to a thick-canopied tree a few yards away, and stood beneath it until the downpour was over. The rain sluiced down, hammering the soil and bouncing back two feet high in a white, seething spray. It did not last long. Within half an hour the clouds had gone, the sun was well up, the ground was steaming, and I could head back to our camp.

That was where it became unendurable. I had done what had to be done. I knew I would not like what came next, and I was weeping again. But it was far worse than I expected. You see, I had not known about the flies. The heat and the rain brought them out in their millions, more than I had ever seen before. They buzzed and swirled about my head all the way to the camp, clouds of them.

Within our camp itself there were more than you would ever believe. And I had to go into their midst. There was no choice. I couldn't leave Jane and Walter and Wendy like that, of course I couldn't. They were dearer to me than anyone else in the world, my friends and my true beloved. But they lay so thickly covered by flies that all I saw through my haze of tears were three humming, purple-black mounds, their outlines indistinct and wavering.

It sickened me to go near, and it took all my strength to dig places for the three of them. Gasoline drove the flies away temporarily. After I put Wendy in I took the wedding band from my finger and placed it on her hand. We had noted this fact long ago: my third finger is just as thick as her thumb's second joint.

Jane and Walter would lie together. It was what they wanted, and it was only right. I took off Walter's glasses, and smoothed the hair back from his brow, the way he had done so often. He looked peaceful and very young.

The army officers I did not bury. I splashed gasoline over them and lit it. Then I struck camp for a final time, climbed into the mini-bus, and headed west. I did not bother with the trailer at all.

Within seventy-two hours I was back at Boyoma Falls. The boat was where we had left it, moored close to the bank. The solitary crew member was nowhere to be found, but he appeared eventually from the bush.

He looked at me and tried to run. I caught him easily. He screamed, and fell to the ground in a fetal position, covering his eyes with his hands. I lifted him with one hand, and his teeth chattered in his head.

It took a little while to make him understand my French. But I did it. He is just a few feet from me now, steering the boat, working as hard as any man ever worked. Like me, he has not slept since we left Boyoma Falls — five days. I do not think he will sleep until we reach Kinshasa and I leave for home.

I am almost done. That is good. This writing must be finished before we reach the city, before the President's office asks what has become of the army men.

The writing will be done, but it cannot end here. I know that. Even if the Zaire authorities can be satisfied easily, there will be questions in Washington. It was an expedition conducted with government grant monies — there have to be written reports.

That is good. I will report everything. I did the right thing — the only possible thing. Yet I know that I will be punished.

I can stand that. What I cannot stand is the loss of Wendy, Jane, and Walter.

I promised proof. You will find it on the outskirts of Kintongo, near the roots of the old, fire-scarred tree. There is the roll of film that I took, encased in a sealed plastic box that should withstand many tropical seasons. There are small fragments of the ship, the one that bore him here. There are the two rifles, the two shallow graves, the wedding ring. They will give you all the proof that I have written the exact truth.

For me, that type of evidence is unnecessary. I know what I am: a servant. I am a servant of the Living God.

This is the message he gave me when I visited his home: *Protect my children.*

Master Tunicate will come again. When he does, you will all be as I am.

Afterword: *Tunicate, Tunicate, Wilt Thou Be Mine?*

This story began life in the strangest possible way. During lunch with a writer friend in Atlanta, the conversation somehow ranged from marine animals, including tunicates, to English nursery songs. At that point, with nothing in my head, I thought of the old rhyme that begins, "Curlylocks, curlylocks, wilt thou be mine." So of course I said, "Tunicate, tunicate, wilt thou be mine," and sat there feeling pleased with myself.

But I had at the time no thought of writing a story; in fact, I said to my friend, "There's a title for you. You can have it. You should write a story called that."

She didn't. But after another year or so, I did. I sold it, and I published it. And then I learned that the English nursery rhyme, "Curlylocks, curlylocks, wilt thou be mine," is not a widely known and standard American nursery rhyme. And without that context, the story title is gibberish. One reviewer, though he was writing in May, gave it the prize for worst title of the year. In this collection I therefore include what was not printed in the original publication, namely, the rest of the nursery rhyme that gives point to the title.

This story is, for me, awfully unpleasant and highly disturbing; the more so, because three of the characters who die in it are based on real people. Two are friends of mine, a husband and wife who are genuinely knowledgeable of and fascinated by Africa (they were once stranded for a week in Timbuktu, when the one Air Mali jumbo jet was preempted by the country president).

The third person was at the time my wife. Since she is now my ex-wife, I hate to think what dark subterranean notions may have been lurking within my brain while I was writing this story.

COUNTING UP

1.   THE THINGS THAT COUNT

The ancient Greeks gave a good deal of thought to the definition of Man (Woman, back in the fourth century B.C., was not considered a suitable subject for philosophy). The Greeks wanted to know what it is that makes humans different from all the animals. Early attempted definitions, e.g., the Platonist one: "Man is a featherless animal with two feet," were not well-received. Kangaroos were unknown in ancient Greece, but Diogenes offered a plucked chicken and asked if it were human (he was not serious, and this must be the original chicken joke). Even when amended to "a featherless animal with two feet without claws," the Platonist definition did not exactly sparkle. The Greeks never did come up with a good answer.

By the nineteenth century, definitions were more oriented to function than to appearance. "Man is a tool-using animal," declared Thomas Carlyle, in *Sartor Resartus*, following an idea of Ben Franklin, but neither man knew, as we know now, that some chimpanzees make tools out of sticks and rocks.

"Mankind is the only animal with language," say the linguists, but not as loudly as they once did. The extent to which Washoe, the famous chimpanzee with a symbol vocabulary of 180 words, and her primate friends are capable of working with a real language remains a matter of hot debate; and the complex sounds produced by the humpback whale may not be messages at all; but in any case, the claim to uniqueness by humans is in question.

- *Man is the only animal that laughs.*
- *Man is the only animal that cries.*

- *Man is the only animal that blushes — or needs to.*
- *Man is a thinking reed.*
- *Man is Nature's sole mistake.*

All interesting, and all suspect, especially as more and more of the things that we once thought uniquely human, including murder and rape, are found to be shared with our animal relatives.

"Man is the fire-using animal" still sounds good, but my own favorite definition is this one: "Mankind is a counting animal." If I substitute "entity" for "animal" in this sentence it becomes far less persuasive, since if computers do one thing well, they count — but only with human direction. Also, certain birds are supposed to be able to count the eggs in their nests, or at least to know when one is missing. However, it is certainly true that we know of no animal able to count to more than ten. Humans can, or at least, most humans can. (It was George Gamow, in his book, *One Two Three . . . Infinity*, who told the story of two Hungarian aristocrats who challenged each other to think of the bigger number. "Well," said one of them, "you name your number first."

"Three," said the second one, after a little hard thought.

"Right," said the other. "You win.")

Humans are "the things that count." Counting is something most of us learn early and learn well, to the point where there is something unnatural about the sequence 1, 2, 3, 5, 6, 7 . . . Counting is the subject of this article, but we will be concerned ultimately with counting as it applies to physics and the natural sciences, rather than to the role of counting and numbers in mathematics. I hope to start with things familiar to everyone, and end with novelties.

2. NUMBERS

The most familiar numbers are the integers, the whole numbers that we use whenever we start counting, 1, 2, 3. They are basic to everything else, to the point where the nineteenth century German mathematician Leopold Kronecker proclaimed: "God made the integers; all the rest is the work of man." Personally, I think Kronecker had it backwards. Humans were quite capable of creating the integers, from the need to enumerate everything from cabbages to kings. It is the other sorts of number, the ones we need to describe lengths and times and weights, that may need divine intervention to explain them. We will get to them in a moment.

First, let us ask an odd question. Can we define the biggest number that we normally need for counting? The conventional answer is, no, there is no such biggest number. We start counting at 1, but we never reach a "last number." No matter how far we go, there will always be a number bigger than the one we have just reached. However, there is another way to look at this, because when we get numbers larger than about a hundred, we don't think of them as made up of a whole lot of ones. We think of them in groups. A thousand is ten hundreds, a hundred is ten tens. We need that structure, to allow us to work with anything more than we can count conveniently on our fingers and toes.

The largest number of objects that I ever have to deal with in my everyday life, where I am not able to group them into subsets in a useful way, are the bits of a jigsaw puzzle. Even here, with a 1,000-piece puzzle, I try to impose some sort of system that will help me to put the pieces into their structured form of the actual picture. I pick out all the edge pieces and do those first, and I organize pieces according to their colors. And even with this help, I take many hours to assemble a hard puzzle of more than 500 pieces. Given a puzzle of ten thousand pieces, I'm not sure I'd ever put it together; and yet ten thousand is not a particularly big number. We work with much larger ones all the time, merely by organizing them into sets of smaller ones. Ten thousand dollars is not a massive stack of singles, it's a hundred one-hundred dollar bills.

The same principle works when we have to deal with something that's too small to be handled conveniently by straight counting. For example, the heights of people, or the size of a room, are not usually an exact number of feet or meters. So we say that a foot is a group of smaller objects, inches; and if we have to, we say that each inch is also a group of still smaller objects, tenths of inches. Since we can define as many levels of subgroups as we like, we can describe anyone's height, or the size of any room, as closely as we like, just by counting.

The Greeks had reached this conclusion by about four

hundred B.C. They believed that they had a system that would allow them to define any given number. It was a horrible intellectual shock for them to discover that there were certain numbers that cannot be described in this way. The result seemed to fly in the face of common sense — to be irrational. And the name "irrational numbers" is used to this day, to describe numbers that can't be written exactly as whole numbers, and subsets of whole numbers. Numbers that can be so written are called rational numbers.

The original example of an irrational number, discovered to be so by Pythagoras and his followers, is the square root of two. It's easy to write this number approximately, as something a little bigger than 1.4 and less than 1.5. We can even specify very easily a value that is as good as we are ever likely to need for practical calculation, 1.41421356237309. In terms of our whole numbers and subsets of whole numbers, this is just 1, plus 4 one-tenths, plus 1 one-hundredth, plus 4 one-thousandths, and so on. (I should add that the Greeks themselves did not have a decimal notation. That came much later, introduced in Europe in 1586, and useful as it is, it is not popular with everyone. Jerome K. Jerome wrote of visiting the city of Bruges, where he "had the pleasure at throwing a stone at the statue of Simon Stevin, the man who invented decimals.")

The problem comes when we ask when the sequence of numbers occurring in the square root of 2, namely, $1 + \frac{4}{10} + \frac{1}{100} + \frac{4}{1,000} + \frac{2}{10,000} \ldots$, stops.

It doesn't. The first thought might be that this is a problem created because we are using the decimal system. After all, $\frac{1}{3}$ is described very nicely by dividing a unit into threes, but when we write it as a decimal, $0.3333 \ldots$, it goes on forever.

The Greeks were able to show that this was not the cause of the problem, using a very simple and elegant proof, as follows:

Suppose that the square root of 2 can be written as a fraction in the form p/q, where p and q are whole numbers with no common divisors, i.e., there are no whole numbers other than 1 that divide both p and q. For example, 1.414 would be written as $\frac{1,414}{1,000} = \frac{707}{500}$.

Then $(p/q)^2 = 2$, so $p^2 = 2q^2$.

Now if p is an odd number, then so is p^2. But p^2 is even, so p must be even, and can be written as 2r, where r is also a whole number. Then since $4r^2 = (2r)^2 = 2q^2$, we must have $2r^2 = q^2$, and so q must be even. But before we began, we agreed that p and q would have no common divisors, and now we have decided they are both divisible by two. Thus our assumption that the square root of 2 can be written as a ratio of whole numbers must be wrong.

This is such an easy proof that the reader may feel anyone could find it, and that mathematics must therefore be simple stuff. If so, here's another problem to try your teeth on. It can also be proved by very simple arguments:

Let m and n be whole numbers with no common divisors, and n have no divisors other than itself and 1 (i.e., n is a *prime number*). Then when m^n is divided by n, it will leave the same remainder as when m is divided by n. For example, if m is 15 and n is 7, then $15^7 = 170,859,375$. Divide by 7, and we get the remainder 1 — the same remainder as when we divide 15 by 7.

If you can prove this, without assistance or looking up the proof in a book on number theory, I would like to hear from you.

The implications of the fact that not all numbers can be written as fractions were disturbing to the Greeks, and they ought to be equally disturbing to us. I mentioned Kronecker's idea of divine influence in connection with the whole numbers, but many people struggling over the years with irrational numbers would give credit for them to the devil.

Let's look at one of the other peculiar facts about irrationals. If we imagine a long ruler, marked off in inches, then in any inch there will be an infinite number of points that can be marked on the ruler as rational numbers, of the form p/q; but we have found that not all points within the inch can be marked that way. There are points corresponding to irrational numbers, sandwiched in among the rationals. Thus, if you want to label *all* the points on the line, you must include the irrational numbers. Worse than that, and most surprising, it can be shown that there are *many more* irrational numbers than there are rational ones. The rational numbers, in mathematical terminology, constitute a set of measure zero on the line — which means they account for zero percent of the line's length. Almost every number is irrational.

3. INFINITY

That last paragraph may sound odd, even crazy. We have already agreed that there is an infinite number of whole numbers, so there is certainly an infinite number of rational numbers, since the rational numbers include the whole numbers as a subset. Now we are saying that there are even more irrational numbers than rational ones — more than infinity. How can anything be more than infinity?

Until a hundred years ago, the answer to that question would have been simple: it can't. Then another German mathematician, Georg Cantor, suggested a different way of looking at things relating to infinity. (Cantor died in a lunatic asylum, and that may be more than coincidence.)

Cantor said that you don't need to enumerate things to agree that there are the same number of them. You can line them up, and if to each member of one set there corresponds exactly one member of the other, then there must be the same number in each set. Just as in musical chairs, you don't need to count the players or the chairs to see if the game will work; all you need to do is give a chair to every player, then take one chair away and start the music.

This idea of exact matching, or one-to-one correspondence as it is usually called, allows us to compare sets having an infinite number of members, but it quickly leads to curious consequences. As Galileo pointed out in the seventeenth century, the whole numbers can be matched one-for-one with the squares of the whole numbers, thus:

$$1, \quad 2, \quad 3, \quad 4, \quad 5, \quad 6, \quad 7, \quad 8, \quad 9, \quad 10, \quad 11, \quad 12\ldots$$
$$1, \quad 4, \quad 9, \quad 16, \quad 25, \quad 36, \quad 49, \quad 64, \quad 81, 100, \; 121, 144\ldots$$

According to Cantor, we must say there are as many squares as there are numbers, because they can be put into one-to-one correspondence. On the other hand, there seem to be a lot more whole numbers that are not squares than numbers that are. The squares omit 2,3,5,6,7,8,10,11,12,13,14,15, and so on. Most numbers are not squares.

In spite of this, Cantor insisted that it makes sense to say that there are the same number of whole numbers as there are of squares; an infinite number of both, true, but the same *sort* of infinity. There are similarly as many even numbers as there are whole numbers. They can be put into one-to-one correspondence, thus:

$$1, \quad 2, \quad 3, \quad 4, \quad 5, \quad 6, \quad 7\ldots$$
$$2, \quad 4, \quad 6, \quad 8, \quad 10, \quad 12, \quad 14\ldots$$

Using the same idea, we find that there are as many squares as there are whole numbers, as many cubes, even as many rational numbers. But there are more *irrational* numbers, a different order of infinity. The irrational numbers cannot be placed in one-to-one correspondence with the whole numbers, and Cantor was able to prove that fact using an elementary argument.

Cantor was able to go farther. There are higher orders of infinite number than the points on the line, in fact, there is an infinite set of orders of infinity. The whole numbers define the "least infinite" infinite set. The question of whether the number of points on a line constitute the *second* smallest infinite set, i.e., there is no third infinite set which includes the set of whole numbers and is included by the set of points on a line, was a famous unsolved problem of mathematics. In 1967, Paul Cohen showed that it is impossible to prove this conjecture (called the continuum hypothesis) using the standard axioms of set theory. This negative proof diminished mathematical interest in the question.

Infinite sets are seductive stuff, and it is tempting to pursue them farther. However, that route will not take us towards the physics we want. That road is found by looking at numbers that are finite, but very large by everyday standards.

4. BIG NUMBERS

". . . Man, proud Man! Dressed in a little brief authority, most ignorant of what he's most assured . . ."

Pure mathematics, as its name suggests, should be mathematics uncontaminated by anything so crude as an application. As G.H. Hardy, an English mathematician of the first half of this century, said in a famous toast: "Here's to pure mathematics. No damned use to anyone, and let's hope it never will be."

Bertrand Russell went even farther in stressing the lack of

utility of mathematics: "Mathematics may be defined as the subject in which we never know what we are talking about, nor whether what we are saying is true."

In spite of these lofty sentiments, mathematics that began its life as the purest form of abstract thought has an odd tendency to be just what scientists need to describe the physical world. For example, the theory of conic sections, developed by the Greeks before the birth of Christ, was the tool that Kepler needed to formulate his laws of planetary motion. The theory of matrices was ready and waiting, when it was needed in quantum mechanics (and today in hundreds of other places in applied mathematics); and Einstein found the absolute differential calculus of Ricci and Levi-Civita just the thing to describe curved space-times in general relativity.

(It doesn't always work out so conveniently. When Newton was setting up the laws of motion and of universal gravitation, he needed calculus. It didn't exist. That would have been the end of the story for almost everyone. Newton, being perhaps the greatest intellect who ever lived, went ahead and invented calculus, then applied it to his astronomical calculations.)

Conversely, the needs of the applied scientist often stimulate the development of mathematics. And by the seventeenth century, the main attention of physicists and astronomers was not with counting finite sets of objects; it was with describing things that varied continuously, like moving planets, or spinning tops, or heat flow. For such studies, counting things seemed to have little relevance.

That state of affairs continued until the third quarter of the nineteenth century. By that time continuous-variable mathematics had done a wonderful job in the development of astronomy, hydrodynamics, mechanics, and thermodynamics. The main tool was the calculus, which had been developed into a dozen different forms, such as the theory of functions of a complex variable and the calculus of variations.

Now, back before 400 B.C. the Greek Democritus had already suggested on philosophical grounds that matter must be composed of separate indivisible particles, called atoms (*atomos* in Greek means "can't be cut"). However, people had rather lost sight of that idea until 1805, when John Dalton re-introduced an atomic theory. But this time, there was experimental evidence to support the notion that matter was made up of individual atoms. Thus the behavior of such atoms, regarded as separate, countable objects, must somehow be able to explain the apparently continuous properties of the matter that we observe in everyday life. Unfortunately, the numbers involved are so huge — nearly a trillion trillion atoms in a gram of hydrogen gas — that it was difficult to visualize the properties of so large an assembly of objects.

If we have direct counting experience of numbers only up to a few dozen, any number as big as a billion is beyond intuition. It is possible that some crazy human has actually counted up to a million, but it is certain that no human has ever counted up to a billion. At one number a second (try saying 386,432,569 in *less* than a second), ten hours a day, every day of the year, a billion would take 76 years to finish.

I worry when I hear talk of "this many millions" and "that many billions" from officials who I know have trouble calculating a restaurant tip. I wonder if they really know the difference. It's an old theory that the expenditure of $100 on a new bike rack will engender more debate than $500,000,000 for a weapons system. People have a personal feel for a hundred dollars. A billion is just an abstract number.

However, when we look at the counting needed to enumerate the atoms of a bar of soap or a breath of air, we are well beyond the billion mark. We are talking a trillion trillion atoms; and when we reach numbers so large, we are all like Gamow's Hungarian aristocrats. We simply have no experience base, no intuitive feel for the properties of a system with so many pieces.

To take a simple example, suppose that we toss an unbiased coin in the air. We all believe we understand coin-tossing pretty well. Half the time it will come down heads, the other half it will come down tails. Now suppose that we toss two coins. What's the chance of getting two heads? Of two tails? Of one head and one tail?

Any gambler can give you the answer. You have a one in four chance of two heads, a one in four chance of two tails, and a one in two chance of a head and a tail. The same gambler can probably tell you the odds if you toss three or four coins, and ask him for the probability of getting some given number of heads.

Now throw a million coins in the air. We know that if they are all unbiased coins, the most likely situation will be that half of the coins will land heads, and half tails. But we have no feel for the chance of getting a particular number, say, 400,000 heads, and 600,000 tails. How does it compare with the chance of getting 500,000 heads and 500,000 tails?

The probabilities obey what is known as a binomial distribution, and can be calculated exactly. Table 1 shows how many times we will get a given number of heads, divided by the number of times we will get exactly equal numbers of heads and tails. As we expected, this ratio is always less than one, because equal heads and tails is the most likely situation.

However, the general behavior of the table as the number of coins increases is not at all intuitive. For small numbers of coins, there is a good chance of getting any number of heads we like to choose. For a million coins, however, the chance of getting anything far from equal numbers of heads and tails is totally negligible. And as the number of coins keeps on increasing, the shape of the curve keeps squeezing narrower and narrower. By the time we reach a trillion trillion coins, the curve has become a single spike. The chance of getting a quarter heads and three-quarters tails, or 51% heads and 49% tails, or even 50.00001% heads and 49.99999% tails is vanishingly small.

This result may seem to have no relevance to anything in the real world. But such probabilities are now central to our understanding of everything from refrigerators to lasers.

Table 1: Coin-Tossing Probabilities

R is the probability of throwing N heads, divided by the probability of throwing an equal number of heads and tails. Probabilities less than one in a million are not printed.

NUMBER OF COINS = 6

N	R
0	0.05
1	0.3
2	0.75
3	1

NUMBER OF COINS = 10

N	R
0	0.004
1	0.040
2	0.179
3	0.476
4	0.833
5	1

NUMBER OF COINS = 100

N	R
25	0.0000024
30	0.000291
35	0.0108
40	0.136
45	0.609
50	1

NUMBER OF COINS = 1,000

N	R
420	0.0000027
430	0.000054
440	0.000739
450	0.00672
460	0.041
470	0.165
480	0.450
490	0.819
500	1

NUMBER OF COINS = 10,000

N	R
4750	0.0000037
4800	0.000335
4850	0.011
4900	0.135
4950	0.607
5000	1

NUMBER OF COINS = 100,000

N	R
49,200	0.0000028
49,400	0.000747
49,600	0.041
49,800	0.449
50,000	1

NUMBER OF COINS = 1,000,000

N	R
497,500	0.0000037
498,000	0.000335
498,500	0.011
499,000	0.135
499,500	0.607
500,000	1

NUMBER OF COINS = 10,000,000

N	R
4,992,000	0.0000028
4,994,000	0.000747
4,996,000	0.041
4,998,000	0.449
5,000,000	1

As the number of coins tossed increases, the chance of a large inequality between heads and tails rapidly decreases.

5. COUNTING AND PHYSICS

"Man is slightly nearer to the atom than the star."
—A.S. Eddington

A small room contains about 10^{27} molecules of air.* The molecules are in ceaseless random motion, and the air pressure on the walls of the room is generated by their impact. Suppose that the walls of the room face north, south, east, and west, and that the room is perfectly sealed, so that no molecule can arrive or escape. Then at any moment, some fraction of the molecules inside the room have a component of their motion taking them generally towards the north wall, and the rest are heading generally towards the south wall (the number who happen to be heading due east or due west is negligible).

All the molecules bounce off the walls, and occasionally off each other. If the motions are, as we said, truly random, then we would be most surprised if the same number were heading for the north wall at all times. Thus the air pressure on any area of the wall ought to keep changing, fluctuating from one second to the next depending on the number of molecules striking there. If we measured the pressure, we ought to get constantly changing values.

We don't. Unless the temperature in the room changes, we always measure the same pressure on the walls.

To see how this can be so, imagine that the molecules had originally been introduced into the room one at a time. They are to have random motions, so to decide on the motion of these molecules, let's suppose a coin had been tossed. If it lands heads, the molecule will move north; tails, it moves south. Since coin-tossing is random, so are the movements of the molecules.

When we have tossed 10^{27} coins, the room will be filled with air. Now recall our earlier result on tossing a very large number

---

* It is awkward to express very large or very small numbers without using *scientific notation*. In such notation, the number written as, for example, 10^{36} stands for 1 followed by 36 zeros, i.e., a million million million million million million. The number 10^{-36} is one divided by that. I will usually employ scientific notation for any number more than one billion (10^9) or less than one-billionth (10^{-9}).

of coins. The chance that *exactly* as many coins land heads as tails is extremely small, so the chance that *exactly* equal numbers of molecules are heading north and south is effectively zero. However, as we saw from Table 1, even with as "few" as ten million coins, the chance that we will get substantially more heads than tails is also negligible. This result applies even more strongly when we have trillions of trillions of coins. The ratio of heads to tails will be so close to one that we will never measure anything other than an even split. Since air pressure is generated by the impact of randomly moving molecules on the room's walls, and since there is a negligible probability that we have substantially more than half the molecules heading for any given wall, we measure the same pressure on each wall. We will also find no change in the pressure over time.

A similar argument can be used to analyze the position of the molecules. Imagine a partition drawn across the middle of the room. Since molecules move at random, at any moment any number of the molecules may be to the right of the partition. What is to prevent a situation arising where all the molecules happen to be down at one end of the room, with a perfect vacuum at the other?

The distribution of molecules within the room can again be simulated by the tossing of a coin. Let us spin the coin, and each time it lands as heads, we will place a molecule to the right of the partition; when it lands as tails, we place the molecule to the left of the partition. After 10^{27} coin tosses, the room is full of air. However, we know from our coin-tossing probabilities that there is negligible chance of, say, 60% of the molecules being to the right, and 40% to the left, or even of 50.00001% being on the right and 49.99999% on the left. The danger of finding one end of the room suddenly airless is small enough to be totally ignored. It will never happen, not in a time span billions of times longer than the age of the universe.

These examples may seem rather trivial, since we know from our own experience that the air in one end of the room doesn't suddenly vanish, and we don't feel continuous popping in our ears from fluctuating air pressure. However, the same technique, expressed in suitable mathematical form, is much more than it may seem. In the hands of the Scotsman, James Clerk Maxwell, the German, Ludwig Boltzmann, and the

American, J. Willard Gibbs, this statistical approach had by the end of the nineteenth century become a powerful tool that allowed global properties of continuous systems (such as temperature) to be understood from the statistical properties governing the movement of their individual pieces — the atoms and molecules.

The science that governs the motion of individual particles is mechanics; the science that describes the global pressure and temperatures of continuous systems is *thermodynamics*. *Statistical mechanics* — the statistical analysis of very large assemblies of particles, each governed by the laws of mechanics — provides the bridge between individual particle behavior and whole system behavior. The central mathematical technique is one of counting, enumerating the number of possible arrangements of very large numbers of particles.

What do we lose in adopting such an approach? In the words of Maxwell, "I wish to point out that, in adopting this statistical method of considering the average number of groups of molecules selected according to their velocities, we have abandoned the strict kinetic method of tracing the exact circumstances of each individual molecule in all its encounters. It is therefore possible that we may arrive at results which, though they fairly represent the facts as long as we are supposed to deal with a gas in mass, would cease to be applicable if our faculties and instruments were so sharpened that we could detect and lay hold of each molecule and trace it, through all its course."

Atoms and molecules are tiny objects, only billionths of an inch in diameter and visible only with the aid of the most powerful electron microscopes. Can the effects of their encounters as individual particles ever be seen, as Maxwell suggests? They can, under the right circumstances, with the aid of no more than a low-power microscope. In 1828, an English botanist, Robert Brown, was observing tiny grains of pollen suspended in water. He noticed that instead of remaining in one place, or slowly rising or sinking, the pollen grains were in constant, jerky, and unpredictable motion. They were moving to the buffeting of water molecules. Pollen is at the size threshold where the probability of different numbers of molecules hitting each side is big enough to show a visible effect. A detailed analysis of "Brownian motion," as it is now called, was the subject of one of three ground-breaking papers published in 1905 by Albert Einstein. (The other two set forth the theory of relativity and explained the photoelectric effect.)

6. COUNTING AND BIOLOGY

"Man is judge of all things, a feeble earthworm, the depository of truth, a sink of uncertainty and error, the glory and shame of the universe."

— Blaise Pascal

Simple counting can be the basis of a field of science, as is the case with statistical mechanics; or it can provide the logical destruction of one, as is the case of homeopathic medicine.

In 1795, the doctrine of "like cures like" was proposed by Samuel Hahnemann as the basis for a new practice of medicine, basing his "Theory of Similia" upon earlier ideas by Paracelsus. The central notion is that if a strong dose of a particular drug produces in a healthy person symptoms like those of a certain disease, then a minute dose of the same drug will cure the disease. To assure that small dose, the procedure is as follows:

The original drug forms the "mother tincture." A fixed quantity of this, say one gram, is added to a kilogram of pure water, and thoroughly mixed. From this "first dilution," one gram is taken, and added to a kilogram of pure water to form the "second dilution." The procedure is repeated, each time taking one gram and mixing with one kilogram of water, to form third dilutions, fourth dilutions, and so on. This is often done as many as ten or twenty times, arguing that the greater the dilution, the more potent the healing effect of the final mixture.

The logic behind the process is obscure, but never mind that. Let's look at the molecular counts, something that was not possible in the first days of homeopathy.

One gram of a drug will contain no more than 6×10^{23} molecules. If that gram is diluted with one kilogram of water, the number of molecules of the drug in one gram of the result is reduced by a factor of one thousand, so one gram of the first dilution will contain at most 6×10^{20} drug molecules. The second dilution will be reduced to 6×10^{17} molecules, the third dilution to 6×10^{14}, and so on. The tenth dilution has on average 6×10^{7} molecules of drug — in other words, there is less than one chance in a million that the tenth dilution contains a single molecule of the drug we started with! The tenth or twentieth dilution is pure water. There is not a trace of the original drug in it.

Even if the like-cures-like idea were correct, how can pure water with no drug cure the disease? The simple answer is, it can't.

Presented with the counting argument for number of molecules, the practitioners of homeopathic medicine mutter vaguely about residual influences and healing fields. But no one can explain what they are, or how they fit with any other scientific ideas.

So homeopathic medicine can't work.

Or can it?

At this point, skeptical as I am, I have to point out another example of large-number counting drawn from the biological sciences, one that shows how careful we must be when we say that something is impossible.

On the evening of May 6, 1875, the French naturalist Jean Henri Fabre performed an interesting experiment. He took a young female of Europe's largest moth, the Great Peacock, and placed her in a wire cage. Then he watched in amazement as male moths of the species — and only of that species — began to appear from all over, some of them flying considerable distances to get to the female.

They could sense her presence. But how?

After more experiments, sight and sound were ruled out. Smell was all that remained. The male moths could smell some substance emitted by the female, and they could detect it in unbelievably small quantities. (The female silk moth, *Bombyx mori*, secretes a substance called *bombykol* with scent glands on her abdomen; the male silk moth will recognize and respond to a single molecule of bombykol. Moths hold the record in the Guinness Book of Records, for the organism with the most acute sense of smell.)

The moth attractant is one of a class of substances known as *pheromones*, a coined word meaning "hormone-bearing."

Pheromones are chemicals secreted and given off by animals, to convey information to or elicit particular responses from other members of the same species. One class of pheromones conveys sexual information, telling the males that a female of the species is ready, willing, and able to mate.

Before we get too excited by this, let me mention that pheromones are employed as a sexual lure mainly by insects. The same thing does occur in humans, but our noses have become so civilized and insensitive that we have trouble picking up the signal. We have to resort to other methods, more uniquely human. ("Man is the 'How'd you like to come back to my place?'-saying animal.")

Female moths, ready to mate, attract their male counterparts over incredible distances — several miles, if the male is downwind.

Now let's do some counting. A female moth emits a microgram or so of pheromones, possibly as much as ten micrograms under unusual circumstances. That's a lot of molecules, about 10^{15} of them (airborne pheromone molecules are large and heavy, 100 to 300 times as massive as a hydrogen atom, and you don't get all that many to a gram), but by the time that those molecules have diffused through the atmosphere and dispersed themselves over a large airspace, they will be spread very thin.

So thin that the chance of a male moth, three miles away, receiving even a single molecule from the source female, seems to be almost vanishingly small. For example, suppose that the aerial plume of pheromones stays within 20 feet of the ground, and spreads in three miles to a width of 1,000 feet — which is a tight, narrow-angle plume. Then we are looking at pheromone concentrations of about one part in a hundred billion. Even the incredibly sensitive odor detection apparatus of the moth needs at least one molecule to work with, and chances are high that it will not get it.

The natural conclusion might be that, *Guinness Book of Records* notwithstanding, the story of a single female moth attracting a male miles away must be no more than a story. And yet the experiments have been done many times. The males, unaware of the statistics, appear from the distance to cluster around the fertile females.

Now, in England a few months ago I was offered a very intriguing explanation of how this might be possible. If other female moths who receive pheromones from a fertile female themselves produce more pheromones, then these intermediate moths can play a crucial role by serving as *amplifiers* for the pheromonal message. Each moth that receives a molecule or two of the female pheromone emits more than that of the same substance. Like tiny repeater stations for an electronic signal, the moths pass the word on, increasing the intensity of the message in the process. The distant male moth receives the pheromonal signal, and heads upwind toward the fertile female.

This is such an attractive idea that it would be hard to forget it once you have heard it mentioned. I was sure I had never encountered it before. On the other hand my ignorance of biology is close to total, so I wanted to check references. And that is where the trouble started.

I began with the obvious sources: reference texts. There are a number on pheromones, and all of them stress the incredible sensitivity of moths to these chemical messengers. However, not one of them mentioned the idea of pheromonal amplifiers. (One of the most interesting books on the subject is *Sexual Strategy*, by Tim Halliday. On its cover is a bright red frog on top of a black frog. I found the contents, all about the tricks used by animals in locating their mates, fascinating. It was only when I saw the expression on the desk clerk's face as I checked the book out of a university library that I realized the title and front illustration might cause questions.)

With no help from books, or from a search of the General Science Index, I cast my net wider. I called Jack Cohen in England, who had been present when the pheromonal amplifier idea was mentioned. He was not sure quite where or when he had encountered the idea, but he offered two key words: *Lymantria*, the genus of moth used in the experiments; and *Rothschild*, the name of the person who had done the work.

At that point, it seemed a snap. I had names. I expected to have full references in no time. All I needed was a good entomologist, and I set out to track one down.

Craig Philips is a naturalist who lives not far from me. He is worth an article in his own right. He keeps tropical cockroaches and tarantulas in his apartment, and apparently enjoys their company.

("I've only been bitten once by a tarantula," he said, "and that was my own fault. I was wearing shorts in my apartment, and the tarantula was sitting on my bare leg. Suddenly the mynah bird" — not previously mentioned at all in our conversation — "swooped down to have a go at the tarantula. I covered it with my hand to protect it. And naturally it bit me."

A perfectly ordinary day in the life of a dedicated naturalist. "It didn't hurt," he added, "the way that a bee sting would. But after a while a kind of ulcer developed that took weeks and weeks to heal.")

Well, we had a very enjoyable conversation, but he had not heard of pheromonal amplifiers, either. Nor had another friend of mine, an amateur entomologist in Oklahoma City (my phone bills were mounting) but he had a vague recollection of hearing something odd like this about a different moth. *Cecropia*, he thought.

I checked that one in the reference texts, too. *Cecropia*, certainly. Pheromone amplifiers, no. No writer had heard of it.

Nor had any of the many entomologists that I spoke to over the next few days. Moths may not pass on pheromonal messages, but entomologists sure pass on interesting questions. I heard from Sheila Mutchler, who ran the Insect Zoo at the National Museum of Natural History; Gates Clark, an entomologist at the same organization; Mark Jacobson, who works on moths and pheromones at the U.S. Department of Agriculture; and Jerome Klun, who works in the Agricultural Research Service and who told me more intriguing things about moth mating habits than I had dreamed existed.

All very helpful, all knowledgeable, all fascinating to talk to. But no pheromonal amplifiers. Everyone agreed what an interesting concept it was — the sort of thing that *ought* to be true, in an interesting world. But no one could give me a single reference, or recall anything that had ever been written about the idea.

So where do I stand now?

I think the pheromonal amplifier idea not true. Other, statistical arguments can explain the male moth's abilities in long-range female detection. But I've become a shade more reluctant to use the word "impossible" when something seems to be ruled out on counting arguments alone.

7.   THE FUTURE OF COUNTING

"Man is the measure of all things."

—Protagoras

Counting has been important to humans since the beginning of recorded history, but I can make a case for the idea that the real Age of Counting began only in 1946. That's when the world's first electronic computer, the ENIAC, went into operation.

Computers count wonderfully well. Although no human has ever counted to a billion, today's fastest computers can do it in less than one second. And that is going to have profound effects on the way that science is performed, and on everything else in our future.

To take one minor example, consider the values in Table 1. I did not copy them from some standard reference work, but computed the necessary ratios of binomial coefficients from scratch, on a lap-top computer that is small and slow by today's standards. The number of arithmetic operations involved was no more than a few million. The program took less than half an hour to write, and maybe the same to run — I went off to have lunch, so I didn't bother to time it.

Compare that with the situation only forty years ago. I would have been forced to use quite different computational methods, or spend months on calculating that single table. For small values of N, say, less than 30, I would have computed the coefficients directly on a mechanical or an electric calculating machine. That would have been several hours of work, with a non-negligible chance of error. If the results were important, I would have had a second person repeat the whole computation as an independent check. For larger values of N, direct calculation would have taken far too long. Instead, I would have made use of an approximation known as Stirling's formula, calling for the use of logarithm tables and involving me in several more hours of tedious calculations. Again, there would be a strong possibility of human error.

This example illustrates the general principle: what could

have been done a hundred years ago only by ingenious analysis and approximation will be done in the future more and more by direct calculation — i.e., by counting.

The trend can be seen again and again, in dozens of different problem areas. The motion of the planets used to be calculated by a clever set of analytic approximations known as general perturbation theory. Many of history's greatest scientists, from Kepler to Newton to Laplace, spent years toiling over hand-calculations. Today, planetary motion (and spacecraft motion) are computed by direct numerical integration of the differential equations of motion. Instead of being treated as a continuous variable, time is chopped up into many small intervals, and the motion of the body is calculated by a computer from one time interval to the next.

This method of "finite differences" and numerical integration is used in everything from weather prediction to aircraft design to stellar evolution. The time and space variables of the continuous problem are chopped up into sufficiently large numbers of finite pieces, and the calculation consists of coupling neighboring times and places so as to calculate global behavior.

Statisticians have rather different needs. Instead of using finite difference methods to solve their problems, they often rely on repeated trials of a statistical process. A random element is introduced in each trial to mimic the variations seen in nature. Many thousands of trials are usually needed before a valid statistical inference can be drawn. Often the number of trials is not known in advance, since it is the behavior of the computed solution itself that tells you whether you can safely stop, or must keep on going to more trials. These appropriately named "Monte Carlo" methods are quite impractical without a fast computer.

That's the situation in 46 A.C. — and the Age of Computers has just begun. Whole new sciences are emerging, relying on a symbiosis of computer experiment and human analysis: nonlinear stability theory, irreversible thermodynamics, chaos theory, fractals. Even pure mathematics is being changed. The proof a few years ago of the four-color theorem ("Any plane map can be colored, with neighboring regions having different colors, using no more than four colors") was done using a computer to enumerate the thousands of possible cases.

The diversity of available computing equipment is increasing, as well as its speed. I'm writing these words on a small portable computer with limited memory and only one programing language (BASIC). On the other hand, it weighs less than four pounds and I can easily carry it with me for use on planes and trains. For heavy-duty work I wouldn't dream of using it. I have access to a Connection Machine, a large parallel-logic computer with 16,384 separate processors, able to perform about three and a half billion floating-point multiplications a second (that's 3.5 *gigaflops*, a word I like very much). That's where the real number-crunching takes place. Thirty years from now, I expect to have available a machine the size and weight of the portable, but with the computing power of the Connection Machine.

Implausible? Not if we look at the past. Today's small portables have the computer power of a large mainframe of 1958 vintage, and they are infinitely easier to use. The rate of increase of computer speed shows no signs of slowing, and arithmetic calculations are only the beginning. Computer hardware is as dumb as ever, but software gets smarter all the time. We are entering the age of expert systems, where human experience is captured in complex programs and used as a starting point for efficient computer algorithms.

The list of applications grows all the time, everything from messy algebraic manipulations to real-time flight simulators to crop forecasting to department store management. In addition to counting, today's computers can do algebra and complex logic far faster and more accurately than humans. A few years ago, a computer was used to make an algebraic check of the Delaunay theory of the motion of the moon, a vast mass of complicated formulae that took the French astronomer C. E. Delaunay over twenty years to develop. Most people find it amazing that his 1,800 pages of working, contained in two huge volumes published in 1860 and 1867, are correct except for a couple of insignificant errors. But should we be more amazed by this, or by the fact that today's computers can perform a complete check of the algebra in a few hours? Or that ten years from now, the same calculations will take minutes or maybe seconds?

Time to stop.

We have come a long way from the simple 1, 2, 3 . . . counting that we learn before we can read. How far can computers go, in performing functions that only a few decades ago were considered solely the prerogative of humans?

A long way. I don't want to get into the old argument about whether or not a computer can ever think, particularly when there is so much evidence that people can't. But let me summarize my own opinions, by suggesting that a thousand years from now there will (finally) be a new and wholly satisfactory definition of humankind:

"Man is the ideal computer I/O unit."

A BRAVER THING

The palace banquet is predictably dull, but while the formal speeches roll on with their obligatory nods to the memory of Alfred Nobel and his famous bequest, it is not considered good manners to leave or to chat with one's neighbors. I have the time and opportunity to think about yesterday; and, at last, to decide on the speech that I will give tomorrow.

A Nobel Prize in physics means different things to different people. If it is awarded late in life, it is often viewed by the recipient as the capstone on a career of accomplishment. Awarded early (Lawrence Bragg was a Nobel Laureate at twenty-five) it often defines the winner's future; an early Prize may also announce to the world at large the arrival of a new titan of science (Paul Dirac was a Nobel Laureate at thirty-one).

To read the names of the Nobel Prize winners in physics is almost to recapitulate the history of twentieth-century physics, so much so that the choice of winners often seems self-evident. No one can imagine a list without Planck, the Curies, Einstein, Bohr, Schrödinger, Dirac, Fermi, Yukawa, Bardeen, Feynman, Weinberg, or the several Wilson's (though Rutherford is, bizarrely, missing from the Physics roster, having been awarded his Nobel Prize in Chemistry).

And yet the decision-making process is far from simple. A Nobel Prize is awarded not for a lifetime's work, but explicitly for a particular achievement. It is given only to living persons, and as Alfred Nobel specified in his will, the prize goes to "the person who shall have made the most important discovery or invention within the field of physics."

It is those constraints that make the task of the Royal Swedish Academy of Sciences so difficult. Consider these questions:

• What should one do when an individual is regarded by his peers as one of the leading intellectual forces of his generation, but no single accomplishment offers the clear basis for an award? John Archibald Wheeler is not a Nobel Laureate; yet he is a "physicist's physicist," a man who has been a creative force in half a dozen different fields.

• How does one weight a candidate's *age*? In principle, not at all. It is not a variable for consideration; but in practice every committee member knows when time is running out for older candidates, while the young competition will have opportunities for many years to come.

• How soon after a theory or discovery is it appropriate to make an award? Certainly, one should wait long enough to be sure that the accomplishment is "most important," as Nobel's will stipulates; but if one waits too long, the opportunity may vanish with the candidate. Max Born was seventy-two years old when he received the Nobel Prize in 1954 — for work done almost thirty years earlier on the probabilistic interpretation of the quantum mechanical wave function. Had George Gamow lived as long as Born, surely he would have shared with Penzias and Wilson the 1978 prize, for the discovery of the cosmic background radiation. Einstein was awarded the Nobel Prize in 1921, at the age of forty-two. But it cited his work on the photoelectric effect, rather than the theory of relativity, which was still considered open to question. And if his life had been no longer than that of Henry Moseley or Heinrich Hertz, Einstein would have died unhonored by the Nobel Committee.

So much for logical choices. I conclude that the Nobel rules allow blind Atropos to play no less a part than Athene in the award process.

My musings can afford to be quite detached. I know how the voting must have gone in my own case, since although the work for which my award is now being given was published only four years ago, already it has stimulated an unprecedented flood of other papers. Scores more are appearing every week, in every language. The popular press might seem oblivious to the fundamental new view of nature implied by the theory associated with my name, but they are very aware of its monstrous practical potential. A small test unit in orbit around Neptune is already returning data, and in the tabloids I have been dubbed Giles "Starman" Turnbull. To quote *The New York Times*: "The situation is unprecedented in modern physics. Not even the madcap run from the 1986 work of Müller and Bednorz to today's room-temperature superconductors can compete with the rapid acceptance of Giles Turnbull's theories, and the stampede to apply them. The story is scarcely begun, but already we can say this, with confidence: Professor Turnbull has given us the stars."

The world desperately needs heroes. Today, it seems, I am a hero. Tomorrow? We shall see.

In a taped television interview last week, I was asked how long my ideas had been gestating before I wrote out the first version of the Turnbull Concession theory. And can you recall a moment or an event, asked the reporter, which you would pinpoint as seminal?

My answer must have been too vague to be satisfactory, since it did not appear in the final television clip. But in fact I could have provided a very precise location in spacetime, at the start of the road that led me to Stockholm, to this dinner, and to my first (and, I will guarantee, my last) meeting with Swedish royalty.

Eighteen years ago, it began. In late June, I was playing in a public park two miles from my home when I found a leather satchel sitting underneath a bench. It was nine o'clock at night, and nearly dark. I took the satchel home with me.

My father's ideas of honesty and proper behavior were and are precise to a fault. He would allow me to examine the satchel long enough to determine its owner, but not enough to explore the contents. Thus it was, sitting in the kitchen of our semi-detached council house, that I first encountered the name of Arthur Sandford Shaw, penned in careful red ink on the soft beige leather interior of the satchel. Below his name was an address on the other side of town, as far from the park as we were but in the opposite direction.

Should we telephone Arthur Sandford Shaw's house, tell him that we had his satchel, and advise him where he could collect it?

No, said my father gruffly. Tomorrow is Saturday. You cycle over in the morning and return it.

To a fifteen-year-old, even one without specific plans, a Saturday morning in June in precious. I hated my father then, for his unswerving, blinkered attitude, as I hated him for the next seventeen years. Only recently have I realized that "hate" is a word with a thousand meanings.

I rode over the next morning. Twice I had to stop and ask my way. The Shaw house was in the Garden Village part of the town, an area that I seldom visited. The weather was preposterously hot, and at my father's insistence I was wearing a jacket and tie. By the time that I dismounted in front of the yellow brick house with its steep red-tile roof and diamond glazed windows, sweat was trickling down my face and neck. I leaned my bike against a privet hedge that was studded with sweet-smelling and tiny white flowers, lifted the satchel out of my saddle-bag, and rubbed my sleeve across my forehead.

I peered through the double gates. They led to an oval driveway, enclosing a bed of well-kept annuals.

I saw pansies, love-in-a-mist, delphiniums, phlox, and snapdragons. I know their names now, but of course I did not know them *then*.

And if you ask me, do I truly remember this so clearly, I must say, of course I do; and will, until my last goodnight. I have that sort of memory. Lev Landau once said, "I am not a genius. Einstein and Bohr are geniuses. But I *am* very talented." To my mind, Landau (1962 Nobel Laureate, and the premier Soviet physicist of his generation) was certainly a genius. But I will echo him, and say that while I am not a genius, I am certainly very talented. My memory in particular has always been unusually precise and complete.

The sides of the drive curved symmetrically around to meet at a brown-and-white painted front door. I followed the edge of the gravel as far as the front step, and there I hesitated.

For my age, I was not lacking in self-confidence. I had surveyed the students in my school, and seen nothing there to produce discomfort. It was clear to me that I was mentally far superior to all of them, and the uneasy attitude of my teachers was evidence — to me, at any rate — that they agreed with my assessment.

But this place overwhelmed me. And not just with the size of the house, though that was six times as big as the one that I lived in. I had seen other big houses; far more disconcerting were the trained climbing roses and espaliered fruit trees, the weed-free lawn, the bird-feeders, and the height, texture and improbable but right color balance within the flower beds. The garden was so carefully structured that it seemed a logical extension of the building at its center. For the first time, I realized that a garden could comprise more than a hodge-podge of grass and straggly flowers.

So I hesitated. And before I could summon my resolve and lift the brass knocker, the door opened.

A woman stood there. At five-feet five, she matched my height exactly. She smiled at me, eye to eye.

Did I say that the road to Stockholm began when I found the satchel? I was wrong. It began with that smile.

"Yes? Can I help you?"

The voice was one that I still thought of as "posh," high-pitched and musical, with clear vowels. The woman was smiling again, straight white teeth and a broad mouth in a high-cheekboned face framed by curly, ash-blond hair. I can see that face before me now, and I know intellectually that she was thirty-five years old. But on that day I could not guess her age to within fifteen years. She could have been twenty, or thirty, or fifty, and it would have made no difference. She was wearing a pale-blue blouse with full sleeves, secured at the top with a mother-of-pearl brooch and tucked into a gray wool skirt that descended to mid-calf. On her feet she wore low-heeled tan shoes, and no stockings.

I found my voice.

"I've brought this back." I held out the satchel, my defense against witchcraft.

"So I see." She took it from me. "Drat that boy, I doubt it he even knows he lost it. I'm Marion Shaw. Come in."

It was an order. I closed the door behind me and found myself following her along a hall that passed another open door on the left. As we approached, a piano started playing rapid staccato triplets, and I saw a red-haired girl crouched over the keyboard of a baby grand.

My guide paused and stuck her head in for a moment. "Not so fast, Meg. You'll never keep up that pace for the whole song." And then to me, as we walked on, "Poor old Schubert, 'Impatience' is right, it's what he'd feel if he heard that. Do you play?"

"We don't have a piano."

"Mm. I sometimes wonder why we do."

We had reached an airy room that faced the back garden of the house. My guide went in before me, peered behind the door, and clucked in annoyance.

"Arthur's gone again. Well, he can't be far. I know for a fact that he was here five minutes ago." She turned to me. "Make yourself at home, Giles. I'll find him."

Giles. I have been terribly self-conscious about my first name since I was nine years old. By the time that I was twenty I had learned how to use it to my advantage, to suggest a lineage that I never had. But at fifteen it was the bane of my life. In a class full of Tom's and Ron's and Brian's and Bill's, it did not fit. I cursed my fate, to be stuck with a "funny" name, just because one of my long-dead uncles had suffered with it.

But there was stronger witchcraft at work here. I had arrived unheralded on her doorstep.

"How do you know my name?"

That earned another smile. "From your father. He called me early this morning, to make sure someone would be home. He didn't want you to bike all this way for nothing."

She went out, and left me in the room of my dreams.

It was about twelve feet square, with an uncarpeted floor of polished hardwood. All across the far wall was a window that began at waist height, ran to the ceiling, and looked south to a vegetable garden. The window sill was a long work bench, two feet deep, and on it stood a dozen projects that I could identify. In the center was a compound microscope, with slides scattered all around. I found tiny objects on them as various as a fly's leg, a single strand of hair, and two or three iron filings. The mess on the left-hand side of the bench was a half-ground telescope lens, covered with its layer of hardened pitch and with the grinding surface sitting next to it. The right side, just as disorderly, was a partially assembled model airplane, radio-controlled and with a two cc diesel engine. Next to that stood an electronic balance, designed to weigh anything from a milligram to a couple of kilos, and on the other side was a blood-type testing kit. The only discordant note to my squeamish taste was a dead puppy, carefully dissected, laid out, and pinned organ by organ on a two-foot square of thick hardboard. But that hint of a possible future was overwhelmed by the most important thing of all: everywhere, in among the experiments and on the floor and by the two free-standing aquariums and next to the flat plastic box behind the door with its half-inch of water and its four black-backed, fawn-bellied newts, there were *books*.

Books and books and books. The other three walls of the room were shelved and loaded from floor to ceiling, and the volumes that scattered the work bench were no more than a small sample that had been taken out and not replaced. I had never seen so many hard-cover books outside a public library or the town's one and only technical bookstore.

When Marion Shaw returned with Arthur Sandford Shaw in tow I was standing in the middle of the room like Buridan's Ass, unable to decide what I wanted to look at the most. I was in no position to see my own eyes, but if I had been able to do so I have no doubt that the pupils would have been twice their normal size. I was suffering from sensory overload, first from the house and garden, then from Marion Shaw, and finally from that paradise of a study. Thus my initial impressions of someone whose life so powerfully influenced and finally directed my own are not as clear in my mind as they ought to be. I also honestly believe that I never did see Arthur clearly, if his mother were in the room.

Some things I can be sure of. Arthur Shaw made his height early, and although I eventually grew to within an inch of him, at our first meeting he towered over me by seven or eight inches. His coordination had not kept pace with his growth, and he had a gawky and awkward manner of moving that would never completely disappear. I know also that he was holding in his right hand a live frog that he had brought in from the garden, because he had to pop that in an aquarium before he could, at his mother's insistence, shake hands with me.

For the rest, his expression was surely the half-amused, half-bemused smile that seldom left his face. His hair, neatly enough cut, never looked it. Some stray spike on top always managed to elude brush and comb, and his habit of running his hands up past his temples swept his hair untidily off his forehead.

"I'm pleased to meet you," he said. "Thank you for bringing it back."

He was, I think, neither pleased nor displeased to meet me. It was nice to have his satchel back (as Marion Shaw had predicted, he did not know he had left it behind in the park), but the thought of what might have happened had he lost it, with its cargo of schoolbooks, did not disturb him as it would have disturbed me.

His mother had been following my eyes.

"Why don't you show Giles your things," she said. "I'll bet that he's interested in science, too."

It was an implied question. I nodded.

"And why don't I call your mother," she said, "and see if it's all right for you to stay to lunch?"

"My mother's dead." I wanted to stay to lunch, desperately. "And my dad will be at work 'til late."

She raised her eyebrows, but all she said was, "So that's settled, then." She held out her hand. "Let me take your jacket, you don't need that while you're indoors."

Mrs. Shaw left to organize lunch. We played, though Arthur Shaw and I would both have been outraged to hear such a verb applied to our efforts. We were engaging in serious experiments of chemistry and physics, and reviewing the notebooks in which he recorded all his earlier results. Even in our first meeting he struck me as a bit strange, but that slight negative was swamped by a dozen positive reactions. The orbit in which I had traveled all my life contained no one whose interests in any way resembled my own. It was doubly shocking to meet a person who was as interested in science as I was, and who had on the shelves of his own study more reference sources than I dreamed existed.

Lunch was an unwelcome distraction. Mrs. Shaw studied me as openly as my inspection of her was covert, Arthur sat in thoughtful silence, and the table conversation was dominated by the precocious Megan, who at twelve years old apparently loved horses and boats, hated anything to do with science, school-work, or playing the piano, and talked incessantly when I badly wanted to hear from the other two. (I know her still; my present opinion is that I was a little harsh in the assessment of eighteen years ago — but not much.) Large quantities of superior food and the beatific presence of Marion Shaw saved lunch from being a disaster, and finally Arthur and I could escape back to his room.

At five o'clock I felt obliged to leave and cycle home. I had to make dinner for my father. The jacket that was returned to me was newly stitched at the elbow where a leather patch had been working loose, and a missing black button on the cuff had been replaced. It was Marion Shaw rather than Arthur who handed me my coat and invited me to come to the house again the following week, but knowing her as I do now I feel sure that the matter was discussed with him before the offer was made. I mention as proof of my theory that as I was pulling my bike free of the privet hedge, Arthur pushed into my hand a copy of E.T. Bell's *Men Of Mathematics*. "It's pretty old," he said offhandedly. "And it doesn't give enough details. But it's a classic. I think it's terrific — and so does Mother."

I rode home through the middle of town. When I arrived there, my own house felt as alien and inhospitable to me as the far side of the moon.

It was Tristram Shandy who set out to write the story of his life, and never progressed much beyond the day of his birth.

If I am to avoid a similar problem, I must move rapidly in covering the next few years. And yet at the same time it is vital to define the relationship between the Shaw family and me, if the preposterous request that Marion Shaw would make of me thirteen years later, and my instant acquiescence to it, are to be of value in defining the road to Stockholm.

For the next twenty-seven months I enjoyed a double existence. "Enjoyed" is precisely right, since I found both lives intensely pleasurable. In one world I was Giles Turnbull, the son of a heel-man at Hendry's Shoe Factory, as well as Giles Turnbull, student extraordinary, over whom the teachers at my school nodded their heads and for whom they predicted a golden scholastic future. In that life, I moved through a thrilling but in retrospect unremarkable sequence of heterosexual relationships, with Angela, Louise, and finally with Jennie.

At the same time, I became a regular weekend visitor to the Shaw household. Roland Shaw, whom my own father described with grudging respect after two meetings as "sharp as a tack," had a peripheral effect on me, but he was a seldom-seen figure absorbed in his job, family, and garden. It was Marion and Arthur who changed me and shaped me. From him I learned concentration, tenacity, and total attack on a single scientific problem (the school in my other life rewarded facility and speed, not depth). I learned that there were many right approaches, since he and I seldom used the same attack on a problem. I also learned — surprisingly — that there might be more than one right answer. One day he casually asked me, "What's the average length of a chord in a unit circle?" When I had worked out an answer, he pointed out with glee that it was a trick question. There are at least three "right" answers, depending on the mathematical definition you use for "average."

Arthur taught me thoroughness and subtlety. From Marion Shaw I learned everything else. She introduced me to Mozart, to the Chopin waltzes and études, to the Beethoven symphonies, and to the first great Schubert song cycle, while steering me clear of Bach fugues, the Ring of the Nibelung, Beethoven's late string quartets, and *Winterreise*. "There's a place for those, later in life," she said, "and it's a wonderful place. But until you're twenty you'll get more out of *Die Schöne Müllerin* and Beethoven's Seventh." Over the dinner table, I learned why sane people might actually read Wordsworth and Milton, to whom an exposure at school had generated an instant and strong distaste. ("Boring old farts," I called them, though never to Marion Shaw.)

And although nothing could ever give me a personal appreciation for art and sculpture, I learned a more important lesson: that there were people who could tell the good from the bad, and the ugly from the beautiful, as quickly and as naturally as Arthur and I could separate a rigorous mathematical proof from a flawed one, or a beautiful theory from an ugly one.

The Shaw household also taught me, certainly with no intention to do so, how to fake it. Soon I could talk a plausible line on music, literature, or architecture, and with subtle hints from Marion I mastered that most difficult technique, when to shut up. From certain loathed guests at her dinner table I learned to turn on (and off) a high-flown, euphuistic manner of speech that most of the world confuses with brain-power. And finally, walking around the garden with Marion for the sheer pleasure of her company, I picked up as a bonus a conversational knowledge of flowers, insects, and horticulture, subjects which interested me as little as the sequence of Chinese dynasties.

It's obvious, is it not, that I was in love with her? But it was a pure, asexual love that bore no relationship to the explorations, thrills, and physical urgencies of Angela, Louise, and Jennie. And if I describe a paragon who sat somewhere between Saint and Superwoman, it is only because I saw her that way when I was sixteen years old, and I have never quite lost the illusion. I know very well, today, that Marion was a creature of her environment, as much as I was shaped by mine. She had been born to money, and she had never had to worry about it. It was inevitable that what she *thought* she was teaching me would become transformed when I took it to a house without books and servants, and to a way of life where the battle for creature comforts and self- esteem was fought daily.

I looked upon the world of Marion Shaw, and wanted it and her. Desperately. But I knew no way to possess them.

"It were all one that I should love a bright particular star, and think to wed it, he is so above me," Marion quoted to me one day, for no reason I could understand. That's how I, mute and inglorious, felt about her.

And by a curious symmetry, Megan Shaw trailed lovelorn after me, just as I trailed after her mother. One day, to my unspeakable embarrassment, Megan cornered me in the music room and told me that she loved me. She took the initiative, and tried to kiss me. At fourteen she was becoming a beauty, but I, who readily took the part of eager sexual aggressor with my girlfriends, could no more have touched her than I could have played the Chopin polonaise with which she had been struggling. I muttered, mumbled, ducked my head, and ran.

Despite such isolated moments of awkwardness, that period was still my personal Nirvana, a delight in the sun that is young once only. But even at sixteen and seventeen I sensed that, like any perfection, this one could not endure.

The end came after two years, when Arthur went off to the university. He and I were separated in age by only six months, but we went to different schools and we were, more important, on opposite sides of the Great Divide of the school year.

He had taken the Cambridge scholarship entrance exam the previous January and been accepted at Kings College, without covering himself with glory. If his failure to gain a scholarship or exhibition upset his teachers, it surprised me not at all. And when I say that I knew Arthur better than anyone, while still not knowing him, that makes sense to me if to no one else.

Success in the Cambridge scholarship entrance examinations in mathematics calls for a good deal of ingenuity and algebraic technique, but the road to success is much smoother if you also know certain tricks. Only a finite number of questions can be asked, and certain problems appear again and again. A bright student, without being in any way outstanding, can do rather well by practicing on the papers set in previous years.

And this, of course, was what Arthur absolutely refused to do. He had that rare independence of spirit, which disdained to walk the well-trod paths. He would not practice examination technique. That made the exams immeasurably harder. A result which, with the help of a clever choice of coordinate system or transformation, dropped out in half a dozen lines, would take several pages of laborious algebra by a direct approach. Genius would find that trick of technique in real time, but to do so consistently, over several days, was too much to ask of any student. Given Arthur's fondness for approaching a problem *ab ovo*, without reference to previous results, and adding to it a certain obscurity of presentation that even I, who knew him well, had found disturbing, it was a wonder that he had done as well as he had.

I had observed what happened. It took no great intellect to resolve that I would not make the same mistake. I worked with Arthur, until his departure for Cambridge in early October, on new fields of study (I had long passed the limits of my teachers at school). Then I changed my focus, and concentrated on the specifics of knowledge and technique needed to do well in the entrance examinations.

Tests of any kind always produce in me a pleasurable high of adrenalin. In early December I went off to Cambridge, buoyed by a good luck kiss (my first) from Marion Shaw, and a terse, "Do your best, lad," from my father. I stayed in Trinity College, took the exams without major trauma, saw a good deal of Arthur, and generally had a wonderful time. I already knew something of the town, from a visit to Arthur halfway through Michaelmas Term.

The results came just before Christmas. I had won a major scholarship to Trinity. I went up the following October.

And at that point, to my surprise, my course and Arthur's began to move apart. We were of course in different colleges, and of different years, and I began to make new friends. But more important, back in our home town the bond between us had seemed unique: he was the single person in my world who was interested in the arcana of physics and mathematics. Now I had been transported to an intellectual heaven, where conversations once possible only with Arthur were the daily discourse of hundreds.

I recognized those changes of setting, and I used them to explain to Marion Shaw why Arthur and I no longer saw much of each other. I also, for my own reasons, minimized to her the degree of our estrangement; for if I were never to see Arthur during college breaks, I would also not see Marion.

There were deeper reasons, though, for the divergence, facts which I could not mention to her. While the university atmosphere, with its undergraduate enthusiasms and overflowing intellectual energy, opened me and made me more gregarious, so that I formed dozens of new friendships with both men and women, college life had exactly the opposite effect on Arthur. As an adolescent he had tended to emotional coolness and intellectual solitude. At Cambridge those traits became more pronounced. He attended few lectures, worked only in his rooms or in the library, and sought no friends. He became somewhat nocturnal, and his manner was increasingly brusque and tactless.

That sounds enough to end close acquaintance;but there was a deeper reason still, one harder to put my finger on. The only thing I can say is that Arthur now made me highly *uncomfortable*. There was a look in his eyes, of obsession and secret worry, that kept me on the edge of my seat. I wondered if he had become homosexual, and was enduring the rite of passage that implied. There had been no evidence of such tendencies during the years I had known him, except that he had shown no interest in girls.

A quiet check with a couple of my gay friends disposed of that theory. Both the grapevine and their personal observations of Arthur indicated that if he was not attracted to women, neither was he interested in men. That was a vast relief. I had seen myself being asked to explain the inexplicable to Marion Shaw.

I accepted the realities: Arthur did not want to be with me, and I was uncomfortable with him. So be it. I would go on with my studies.

And in those studies our new and more distant relationship had another effect, one that ultimately proved far more important than personal likes and dislikes. For I could no longer *compare* myself with Arthur.

In our first two years of acquaintance, he had been my calibration point. As someone a little older than me, and a full year ahead in a better school, he served as my pacer. My desire was to know what Arthur knew, to be able to solve the problems that he could solve. And on the infrequent occasions when I found myself ahead of him, I was disproportionately pleased.

Now my pace-setting hare had gone. The divergence that I mentioned was intellectual as well as personal. And because Arthur had always been my standard of comparison, it took me three or four years to form a conclusion that others at the university had drawn long before.

His lack of interest in attending lectures, coupled with his insistence on doing things his own way, led to as many problems in the Tripos examinations as it had in scholarship entrance. His supervision partner found him "goofy," while their supervisor didn't seem to understand what he was talking about. Arthur was always going off, said his partner, in irrelevant *digressions*. By contrast, my old approach of focusing on what was needed to do well in exams, while making friends with both students and faculty, worked as well as ever.

In sum, my star was ascendant. I did splendidly, was secretly delighted, and publicly remained nonchalant and modest.

And yet I knew, somewhere deep inside, that Arthur was more creative than I. He generated ideas and insights that I would never have. Surely that would weigh most heavily, in the great balance of academic affairs?

Apparently not. To my surprise, it was I alone who at the end of undergraduate and graduate studies was elected to a Fellowship, and stayed on at Cambridge. Arthur would have to leave, and fend for himself. After considering a number of teaching positions at other universities both in Britain and abroad, he turned his back on academia. He accepted a position as a research physicist with ANF Gesellschaft, a European hi-tech conglomerate headquartered in Bonn.

In August he departed Cambridge to take up his new duties. I would remain, living in college and continuing my research. When we had dinner together a few days before he left he seemed withdrawn, but no more than usual. I mentioned that I was becoming more and more interested in the problem of space-time quantization, and proposed to work on it intensely. He came to life then, and said that in his opinion I was referring to the most important open question of physics. I was delighted by that reaction, and told him so. At that point his moodiness returned, and remained for the rest of the evening.

When we parted at midnight there was no formality or sense of finality in our leave-taking. And yet for several years I believed that on that evening the divergence of our worldlines became complete. Only later did I learn that from a scientific point of view they had separated, only to run parallel to each other.

And both roads led to Stockholm.

When one sets forth on an unknown intellectual trail it is easy to lose track of time, place, and people. For the next four years the sharp realities of my world were variational principles, Lie algebra, and field theory. Food and drink, concerts, vacations, friends, social events, and even lovers still had their place, but they stood on the periphery of my attention, slightly misty and out of focus.

I saw Arthur a total of five times in those four years, and each was in a dinner-party setting at his parents' house. In retrospect I can recognize an increasing remoteness in his manner, but at the time he seemed like the same old Arthur, ignoring any discussion or guest that didn't interest him. No opportunity existed for deep conversation between us; neither of us sought one. He never said a word about his work, or what he thought of life in Bonn. I never talked about what I was trying to do in Cambridge.

It was the shock of my life to be sitting at tea in the Senate House, one gloomy November afternoon, and be asked by a topologist colleague from Churchill College, "You used to hang around with Arthur Shaw, didn't you, when he was here?"

At my nod, he tapped the paper he was holding. "Did you see this, Turnbull," he said. "On page ten? He's dead."

And when I looked at him, stupefied: "You didn't know? Committed suicide. In Germany. His obituary's here."

He said more, I'm sure, and so did I. But my mind was far away as I took the newspaper from him. It was a discreet two inches of newsprint. Arthur Sandford Shaw, aged twenty-eight. Graduate of King's College, Cambridge, son of etc. Coroner's report, recent behavior seriously disturbed . . . no details.

I went back to my rooms in Trinity and telephoned the Shaw house. While it was ringing, I realized that no matter who answered I had no idea what to say. I put the phone back on its stand and paced up and down my study for the next hour, feeling more and more sick. Finally I made the call and it was picked up by Marion.

I stumbled through an expression of regret. She hardly gave me time to finish before she said, "Giles, I was going to call you tonight. I'd like to come to Cambridge. I must talk to you."

The next day I had scheduled appointments for late morning and afternoon, two with research students, one with the college director of studies on the subject of forthcoming entrance interviews, and one with a visiting professor from Columbia. I could have handled them and still met with

Marion. I canceled every one, and went to meet her at the station.

The only thing I could think of when I saw her step off the train was that she had changed hardly at all since that June morning, thirteen years ago, when we first met. It took close inspection to see that the ash-blond hair showed wisps of gray at the temples, and that a network of fine lines had appeared at the outer corner of her eyes.

Neither of us had anything to say. I put my arms around her and gave her an embarrassed hug, and she leaned her head for a moment on my shoulder. In the taxi back to college we talked the talk of strangers, about the American election results, new compact disk recordings, and the town's worsening traffic problems.

We did not go to my rooms, but set out at once to walk on the near-deserted paths of the College Backs. The gloom of the previous afternoon had intensified. It was perfect weather for *weltschmerz*, cloudy and dark, with a thin drizzle falling. We stared at the crestfallen ducks on the Cam and the near-leafless oaks, while I waited for her to begin. I sensed that she was winding herself up to say something unpleasant. I tried to prepare myself for anything.

It came with a sigh, and a murmured, "He didn't kill himself, you know. That's what the report said, but it's wrong. He was murdered."

I was not prepared for anything. The hair rose on the back of my neck.

"It sounds insane," she went on. "But I'm sure of it. You see, when Arthur was home in June, he did something that he'd never done before. He talked to me about his work. I didn't understand half of it"— she smiled, a tremulous, tentative smile; I noticed that her eyes were slightly bloodshot from weeping —"you'd probably say not even a tenth of it. But I could tell that he was terrifically excited, and at the same time terribly worried and depressed."

"But what was he doing? Wasn't he working for that German company?" I was ashamed to admit it, but in my preoccupation with my own research I had not given a moment's thought in four years to Arthur's doings, or to ANF Gesellschaft.

"He was still there. He was in his office the morning of the day that he died. And what he was doing was terribly important."

"You talked to them?"

"They talked to us. The chief man involved with Arthur's work is called Otto Braun, and he flew over two days ago specially to talk to me and Roland. He said he wanted to be sure we would hear about Arthur's death directly, rather than just being officially notified. Braun admitted that Arthur had done very important work for them."

"But if that's true, it makes no sense at all for anyone to think of killing him. They'd do all they could to keep him alive."

"Not if he'd found something they were desperate to keep secret. They're a commercial operation. Suppose that he found something hugely valuable? And suppose that he told them that it was too important for one company to own, and he was going to let everyone in on it."

It sounded to me like a form of paranoia that I would never have expected in Marion Shaw. Arthur would certainly have been obliged to sign a non-disclosure agreement with the company he worked for, and there were many legal ways to assure his silence. In any case, to a hi-tech firm Arthur and people like him were the golden goose. Companies didn't murder their most valuable employees.

We were walking slowly across the Bridge of Sighs, our footsteps echoing from the stony arch. Neither of us spoke until we had strolled all the way through the first three courts of St. Johns College, and turned right onto Trinity Street.

"I know you think I'm making all this up," said Marion at last, "just because I'm so upset. You're just humoring me. You're so logical and clear-headed, Giles, you never let yourself go overboard about anything."

There is a special hell for those who feel but cannot tell. I started to protest, half-heartedly.

"That's all right," she said. "You don't have to be polite to me. We've known each other too long. You don't think I understand anything about science, and maybe I don't. But you'll admit that I know a fair bit about people. And I can tell you one thing, Otto Braun was keeping something from us. Something important."

"How do you know?"

"I could read it in his eyes."

That was an inarguable statement; but it was not persuasive. The drizzle was slowly turning into a persistent rain, and I steered us away from Kings Parade and towards a coffee shop. As we passed through the doorway she took my arm.

"Giles, do you remember Arthur's notebooks?"

It was a rhetorical question. Anyone who knew Arthur knew his notebooks. Maintaining them was his closest approach to a religious ritual. He had started the first one when he was twelve years old. A combination of personal diary, scientific workbook, and clipping album, they recorded everything in his life that he believed to be significant.

"He still kept them when he went to Germany," Marion continued. "He even mentioned them, the last time he was home, because he wanted me to send him the same sort of book that he always used, and he had trouble getting them there. I sent him a shipment in August. I asked Otto Braun to send them back to me, with Arthur's personal things. He told me there were no notebooks. There were only the work journals that every employee of ANF was obliged to keep."

I stared at her across the little table, with its red-and-white checkered cloth. At last, Marion was offering evidence for her case. I moved the salt and pepper shakers around on the table. Arthur may have changed in the past four years, but he couldn't have changed that much. Habits were habits.

She leaned forward, and put her hands over mine. "I know. I said to Braun just what you're thinking. Arthur always kept notebooks. They had to exist, and after his death they belonged to me. I wanted them back. He wriggled and sweated, and said there was nothing. But if I want to know what Arthur left, he said, I can get someone I trust who'll understand Arthur's work, and have them go over to Bonn. Otto Braun will let them see everything there is."

She gazed at me with troubled gray eyes.

I picked up my coffee cup and took an unwanted sip. Some requests for help were simply too much. The next two weeks were going to be chaotic. I had a horrendous schedule, with three promised papers to complete, two London meetings to attend, half a dozen important seminars, and four out-of-town visitors. I had to explain to her somehow that there was no way for me to postpone any part of it.

But first I had to explain matters to someone else. I *had* been in love with Marion Shaw, I told myself, there was no use denying it. Hopelessly, and desperately, and mutely. She had been at one time my *inamorata*, my goddess, the central current of my being; but that was ten years ago. First love's impassioned blindness had long since passed away in colder light.

I opened my mouth to say that I could not help.

Except that this was still my Maid Marion, and she needed me.

The next morning I was on my way to Bonn.

Otto Braun was a tall, heavily built man in his mid-thirties, with a fleshy face, a high forehead, and swept back dark hair. He had the imposing and slightly doltish look of a Wagnerian *heldentenor* — an appearance that I soon learned was totally deceptive. Otto Braun had the brains of a dozen Siegfried's, and his command of idiomatic English was so good that his slight German accent seemed like an affectation.

"We made use of certain ancient principles in designing our research facility," he said, as we zipped along the Autobahn in his Peugeot. "Don't be misled by its appearance."

He had insisted on meeting me at Wahn Airport, and driving me (at eighty-five miles an hour) to the company's plant. I studied him, while to my relief he kept his eyes on the road ahead and the other traffic. I could not detect in him any of the shiftiness that Marion Shaw had described. What I did sense was a forced cheerfulness. Otto Braun was uneasy.

"The monasteries of northern Europe were designed to encourage deep meditation," he went on. "Small noise-proof cells, hours of solitary confinement, speech only at certain times and places. Well, deep meditation is what we're after. Of course, we've added a few modern comforts — heat, light, coffee, computers, and a decent cafeteria." He smiled. "So don't worry about your accommodation. Our guest quarters at the lab receive high ratings from visitors. You can see the place now, coming into view over on the left."

I had been instructed not to judge by appearances. Otherwise, I would have taken the research facility of ANF Gesellschaft to be the largest concrete prison blockhouse I had ever seen. Windowless, and surrounded by smooth lawns that ended in a tall fence, it stood fifty feet high and several hundred long. All it needed were guard dogs and machine-gun towers.

Otto Braun drove us through the heavy, automatically opening gates and parked by a side entrance.

"No security?" I said.

He grinned, his first sign of genuine amusement. "Try getting out without the right credentials, Herr Doktor Professor Turnbull."

We traversed a deserted entrance hall to a quiet, carpeted corridor, went up in a noiseless elevator, and walked along to an office about three meters square. It contained a computer, a terminal, a desk, two chairs, a blackboard, a filing cabinet, and a book-case.

"Notice anything unusual about this room?" he said.

I had, in the first second. "No telephone."·

"Very perceptive. The devil's device. Do you know, in eleven years of operation, no one has ever complained about its absence? Every office, including my own, is the same size and shape and has the same equipment in it. We have conference rooms for the larger meetings. This was Dr. Shaw's office and it is, in all essentials, exactly as he left it."

I stared around me with increased interest. He gestured to one of the chairs, and didn't take his eyes off me.

"Mrs. Shaw told me you were his best friend," he said. It was midway between a question and a statement.

"I knew him since we were both teenagers," I replied. And then, since that was not quite enough, "I was probably as close a friend as he had. But Arthur did not encourage close acquaintance."

He nodded. "That makes perfect sense to me. Dr. Shaw was perhaps the most talented and valuable employee we have ever had. His work on quantized Hall effect devices was unique, and made many millions of marks for the company. We rewarded him well and esteemed his work highly. Yet he was not someone who was easy to know." His eyes were dark and alert, half-hidden in that pudgy face. They focused on me with a higher intensity level. "And Mrs. Shaw. Do you know her well?"

"As well as I know anyone."

"And you have a high regard for each other?"

"She has been like a mother to me."

"Then did she confide in you her worry — that her son Arthur did not die by his own hand, and his death was in some way connected with our company?"

"Yes, she did." My opinion of Otto Braun was changing. He had something to hide, as Marion had said, but he was less and less the likely villain. "Did she tell *you* that?"

"No. I was forced to infer it, from her questions about what he was doing for us. Hmph." Braun rubbed at his jowls. "Herr Turnbull, I find myself in a most difficult situation. I want to be as honest with you as I can, just as I wanted to be honest with Mr. and Mrs. Shaw. But there were things I could not tell them. I am forced to ask again: is your concern for Mrs. Shaw sufficient that you are willing to withhold certain facts from her? Please understand, I am not suggesting any form of criminal behavior. I am concerned only to minimize sorrow."

"I can't answer that question unless I know what the facts are. But I think the world of Marion Shaw. I'll do anything I can to make the loss of her son easier for her."

"Very well." He sighed. "I will begin with something that you could find out for yourself, from official sources. Mrs. Shaw thinks there was some sort of foul play in Arthur Shaw's death. I assure you that he took his own life, and the proof of that is provided by the curious manner of his death. Do you know how he died?"

"Only that it was in his apartment."

"It was. But he chose to leave this world in a way that I have never before encountered. Dr. Shaw removed from the lab a large plastic storage bag, big enough to hold a mattress. It is equipped with a zipper along the outside, and when that zipper is closed, such a bag is quite airtight." He paused. Otto Braun was no machine. This explanation was giving him trouble. "Dr. Shaw took it to his apartment. At about six o'clock at night he turned the bag inside out and placed it on top of his bed. Then he changed to his pajamas, climbed into the bag, and zipped it from the inside. Sometime during that evening he died, of asphyxiation." He looked at me unhappily. "I am no expert in 'locked room' mysteries, Professor Turnbull, but the police made a thorough investigation. They are quite sure that no one could have closed that bag from the outside. Dr. Shaw took his own life, in a unique and perverse way."

"I see why you didn't want Mr. and Mrs. Shaw to know this. Let me assure you that they won't learn it from me." I felt nauseated. Now that I knew how Arthur had died, I would have rather remained ignorant.

He raised dark eyebrows. "But they *do* know, Professor Turnbull. Naturally, they insisted on seeing the coroner's report on the manner of his death, and I was in no position to keep such information from them. Mrs. Shaw's suspicion of me arose from a quite different incident. It came when she asked me to return Dr. Shaw's journals to her."

"And you refused."

"Not exactly. I denied their existence. Maybe that was a mistake, but I do not pretend to be infallible. If you judge after examination that the books should be released to Dr. Shaw's parents, I will permit it to happen." Otto Braun stood up and went across to the gray metal file cabinet. He patted the side of it. "These contain Arthur Shaw's complete journals. On the day of his death, he took them all and placed them in one of the red trash containers in the corridor, from which they would go to the shredder and incinerator. I should explain that at ANF we have many commercial secrets, and we are careful not to allow our competitors to benefit from our garbage. Dr. Shaw surely believed that his notebooks would be destroyed that night."

He pulled open a file drawer, and I saw the familiar spiral twelve-by-sixteen ledgers that Arthur had favored since childhood.

"As you see, they were not burned or shredded," Braun went on. "In the past we've had occasional accidents, in which valuable papers were placed by oversight into the red containers. So our cleaning staff — all trusted employees — are instructed to check with me if they see anything that looks like a mistake. An alert employee retrieved all these notebooks and brought them to my office, asking approval to destroy them."

It seemed to me that Marion Shaw had been right on at least one thing. For if after examining Arthur's ledgers, Otto Braun had *not* let them be destroyed, they must contain material of value to ANF.

I said this to him, and he shook his head. "The notebooks had to be kept, in case they were needed as evidence for the investigation of death by suicide. They were, in fact, one of the reasons why I am convinced that Dr. Shaw took his own life. Otherwise I would have burned them. Every piece of work that Dr. Shaw did relevant to ANF activities was separately recorded in our ANF work logs. His own notebooks . . ." He paused. "Beyond that, I should not go. You will draw your own conclusions."

He moved away from the cabinet, and steered me with him towards the door. "It is six o'clock, Professor, and I must attend our weekly staff meeting. With your permission, I will show you to your room and then leave you. We can meet tomorrow morning. Let me warn you. You were his friend; be prepared for a shock."

He would make no other comment as we walked to the well-furnished suite that had been prepared for me, other than to say again, as he was leaving, "It is better if you draw your own conclusions. Be ready for a disturbing evening."

The next morning I was still studying Arthur's notebooks.

It is astonishing how, even after five years, my mind reaches for that thought. When I relive my three days in Bonn I feel recollection rushing on, faster and faster, until I reach the point where Otto Braun left me alone in my room. And then memory leaps out towards the next morning, trying to clear the dark chasm of that night.

I cannot permit that luxury now.

It took about three minutes to settle my things in the guest suite at the ANF laboratory. Then I went to the cafeteria, gulped down a sandwich and two cups of tea, and hurried back to Arthur's office. The gray file cabinet held twenty-seven ledgers; many more than I expected, since Arthur normally filled only two or three a year.

In front of the ledgers was a heavy packet wrapped in white plastic. I opened that first, and almost laughed aloud at the incongruity of the contents, side-by-side with Arthur's work records. He had enjoyed experimental science, but the idea of car or bicycle repair was totally repugnant to him. This packet held an array of screwdrivers, heavy steel wire, and needle-nosed and broad-nosed pliers, all shiny and brand-new.

I replaced the gleaming tool kit and turned to the ledgers. If they were equally out of character . . .

It was tempting to begin with the records from the last few days of his life. I resisted that urge. One of the lessons that he had taught me in adolescence was an organized approach to problems, and now I could not afford to miss anything even marginally significant to his death. The ledgers were neatly numbered in red ink on the top right-hand corner of the stiff cover, twenty-two through forty-eight. It was about six-thirty in the evening when I picked up Volume Twenty-two and opened it to the first page.

That gave me my first surprise. I had expected to see only the notebooks for the four years that Arthur had been employed by ANF Gesellschaft. Instead, the date at the head of the first entry was early April, seven and a half years ago. This was a notebook from Arthur's final undergraduate year at Cambridge. Why had he brought with him such old ledgers, rather than leaving them at his parents' house?

The opening entry was unremarkable, and even familiar. At that time, as I well remembered, Arthur's obsession had been quantized theories of gravity. He was still coming to grips with the problem, and his note said nothing profound. I skimmed it and read on. Successive entries were strictly chronological. Mixed in with mathematics, physics, and science references was everything else that had caught his fancy — scraps of quoted poetry (he was in a world-weary Housman phase), newspaper clippings, comments on the weather, lecture notes, cricket scores, and philosophical questions.

It was hard to read at my usual speed. For one thing I had forgotten the near-illegible nature of Arthur's personal notes. I could follow everything, after so many years of practice, but Otto Braun must have had a terrible time. Despite his command of English, some of the terse technical notes and

equations would be unintelligible to one of his background.
Otto was an engineer. It would be astonishing if his knowledge
extended to modern theoretical physics.

And yet in some ways Otto Braun would have found the
material easier going than I did. I *could* not make myself read
fast, for the words of those old notebooks whispered in my
brain like a strange echo of false memory. Arthur and I had
been in the same place at the same time, experiencing similar
events, and many of the things that he felt worth recording had
made an equal impression on me. We had discussed many of
them. This was my own Cambridge years, my own life, seen
from a different vantage point and through a lens that imposed
a subtle distortion on shapes and colors.

And then it changed. The final divergence began.

It was in December, eight days before Christmas, that I
caught a first hint of something different and repugnant.
Immediately following a note on quantized red shifts came a
small newspaper clipping. It appeared without comment, and
it reported the arrest of a Manchester man for the torture,
murder, and dismemberment of his own twin daughters. He
had told the police that the six-year-olds had "deserved all they
got."

That was the first evidence of a dark obsession. In successive months and years, Arthur Shaw's ledgers told of his
increasing preoccupation with death; and it was never the
natural, near-friendly death of old age and a long, fulfilled life,
but always the savage deaths of small children. Death unnatural, murder most foul. The clippings spoke of starvation,
beating, mutilation, and torture. In every case Arthur had
defined the source, without providing any other comment. He
must have combed the newspapers in his search, for I, reading
those same papers in those same editions, had not noticed the
articles.

It got worse. Nine years ago it had been one clipping every
few pages. By the time he went to live in Bonn the stories of
brutal death occupied more than half the journals, and his
sources of material had become world-wide.

And yet the Arthur that I knew still existed. It was
bewildering and frightening to recognize the cool, analytical
voice of Arthur Shaw, interspersed with the bloody deeds of

human monsters. The poetry quotes and the comments on the weather and current events were still there, but now they shared space with a catalog of unspeakable acts.

Four years ago, just before he came to Bonn, another change occurred. It was as though the author of the written entries had suddenly become *aware* of the thing that was making the newspaper clippings. When Arthur discovered that the other side of him was there, he began to comment on the horror of the events that he was recording. He was shocked, revolted, and terrified by them.

And yet the clippings continued, along with the lecture notes, the concerts attended, the careful record of letters written; and there were the first hints of something else, something that made me quiver.

I read on, to midnight and beyond until the night sky paled. Now at last I am permitted the statement denied to me earlier: The next morning I was still studying Arthur's notebooks.

Otto Braun came into the office, looked at me, and nodded grimly.

"I am sorry, Professor Turnbull. It seemed to me that nothing I could say would be the same as allowing you to read for yourself." He came across to the desk. "The security officer says you were up all night. Have you eaten breakfast?"

I shook my head.

"I thought not." He looked at my hands, which were perceptibly shaking. "You must have rest."

"I can't sleep."

"You will. But first you need food. Come with me. I have arranged for us to have a private dining-room."

On the way to the guest quarters I went to the bathroom. I saw myself in the mirror there. No wonder Otto Braun was worried. I looked terrible, pale and unshaven, with purple-black rings under my eyes.

In the cafeteria Braun loaded a tray with scrambled eggs, *speckwurst*, croissants and hot coffee, and led me to a nook off the main room. He watched like a worried parent to make sure that I was eating, before he would pour coffee for himself.

"Let me begin with the most important question," he said. "Are you convinced that Arthur Shaw took his own life?"

"I feel sure of it. He could not live with what one part of him was becoming. The final entry in his journal says as much. And it explains the way he chose to die."

Enough is enough, Arthur had written. *I can't escape from myself. "To cease upon the midnight with no pain." Better to return to the womb, and never be born . . .*

"He wanted peace, and to hide away from everything," I went on. "When you know that, the black plastic bag makes more sense."

"And you agree with my decision?" Braun's chubby face was anxious. "To keep the notebooks away from his parents."

"It was what he would have wanted. They were supposed to be destroyed, and one of his final entries proves it. He said, 'I have done one braver thing.'"

His brow wrinkled, and he put down his cup. "I saw that. But I did not understand it. He did not say what he had done."

"That's because it's part of a quotation, from a poem by John Donne. 'I have done one braver thing, Than all the worthies did, And yet a braver thence doth spring, And that, to keep it hid.' He *wanted* what he had been doing to remain secret. It was enormously important to him."

"That is a great relief. I hoped that it was so, but I could not be sure. Do you agree with me, we can now destroy those notebooks?"

I paused. "Maybe that is not the best answer. It will leave questions in the mind of Marion Shaw, because she is quite sure that the books must exist. Suppose that you turn them over to my custody? If I tell Marion that I have them, and want to keep them as something of Arthur's, I'm sure she will approve. And of course I will never let her see them."

"Ah." Braun gave a gusty sigh of satisfaction. "That is a most excellent suggestion. Even now, I would feel uneasy about destroying them. I must admit, Professor Turnbull, that I had doubts as to my own wisdom when I agreed to allow you to come here and examine Dr. Shaw's writings. But everything has turned out for the best, has it not? If you are not proposing to eat those eggs . . ."

Everything for the best, thought Otto Braun, and probably in the best of all possible worlds.

We had made the decision. The rest was details. Over the next twelve hours, he and I wrote the script.

I would handle Marion and Roland Shaw. I was to confirm that Arthur's death had been suicide, while his mind was unbalanced by overwork. If they talked to Braun again about his earlier discomfort in talking to them, it was because he felt he had failed them. He had not done enough to help, he would say, when Arthur so obviously needed him. (No lie there; that's exactly how Otto felt).

And the journals? I would tell the Shaws of Arthur's final wish, that they be destroyed. Again, no lie; and I would assure them that I would honor that intent.

I went home. I did it, exactly as we had planned. The only intolerable moment came when Marion Shaw put her arms around me, and actually *thanked* me for what I had done.

Because, of course, neither she nor Otto Braun nor anyone else in the world knew what I *had* done.

When I read the journals and saw Arthur's mind fluttering towards insanity, I was horrified. But it was not only the revelation of madness that left me the next morning white-faced and quivering. It was excitement derived from the *other* content of the ledgers, material interwoven with the cool comments on personal affairs and the blood-obsessed newspaper clippings.

Otto Braun, in his relief at seeing his own problems disappear, had grabbed at my explanation of Arthur's final journal entries, without seeing that it was wholly illogical. "I have done one braver thing," quoted Arthur. But that was surely not referring to the newspaper clippings and his own squalid obsessions. He was appalled by them, and said so. What was the "brave thing" that he had done?

I knew. It was in the notebooks.

For four years, since Arthur's departure from Cambridge, I had concentrated on the single problem of a unified theory of quantized spacetime. I made everything else in my life of secondary importance, working myself harder than ever before, to the absolute limit of my powers. At the back of my mind was always Arthur's comment: this was the most important problem in modern physics.

It was the best work I had ever done. I suspect that it is easily the best work that I will ever do.

What I had not known, or even vaguely suspected, was that Arthur Shaw had begun to work on the same problem after he went to Bonn.

I found that out as I went through his work ledgers. How can I describe the feeling, when in the middle of the night in Arthur's old office I came across scribbled thoughts and conjectures that I had believed to belong in my head alone? They were mixed in hodge-podge with everything else, side-by-side with the soccer scores, the day's high temperature, and the horror stories of child molestation, mutilation, and murder. To Otto Braun or anyone else, those marginal scribbles would have been random nonsensical jottings. But I recognized that integral, and that flux quantization condition, and that invariant.

How can I describe the feeling?

I cannot. But I am not the first to suffer it. Thomas Kydd and Ben Jonson must have been filled with the same awe in the 1590's, when Shakespeare carried the English language to undreamed-of heights. *Hofkapellmeister* Salieri knew it, to his despair, when Mozart and his God-touched work came on the scene at the court of Vienna. Edmund Halley surely felt it, sitting in Newton's rooms at Trinity College in 1684, and learning that the immortal Isaac had discovered laws and invented techniques that would make the whole System of the World *calculable*; and old Legendre was overwhelmed by it, when the *Disquisitiones* came into his hands and he marveled at the supernatural mathematical powers of the young Gauss.

When half-gods go, the gods arrive. I had struggled with the problem of spacetime quantization, as I said, with every working neuron of my brain. Arthur Shaw went so far beyond me that it took all my intellect to mark his path. "It were all one that I should love a bright particular star, and think to wed it, he is so above me." But I could see what he was doing, and I recognized what I had long suspected. Arthur was something that I would never be. He was a true genius.

I am not a genius, but I am very talented. I could follow where I could not lead. From the hints, scribbled theorems, and conjectures in Arthur Shaw's notebooks I assembled the whole; not perhaps as the gorgeous tapestry of thought that

Arthur had woven in his mind, but enough to make a complete theory with profound practical implications.

That grand design was the "braver thing" that he knew he had done, an intellectual feat that placed him with the immortals.

It was also, paradoxically, the cause of his death.

Some scientific developments are "in the air" at a particular moment; if one person does not propose them, another will. But other creative acts lie so far outside the mainstream of thought that they seem destined for a single individual. If Einstein had not created the general theory of relativity, it is quite likely that it would not exist today. Arthur Shaw knew what he had wrought. His approach was totally novel, and he was convinced that without his work an adequate theory might be centuries in the future.

I did not believe that; but I might have, if I had not been stumbling purblind along the same road. The important point, however, is that Arthur *did* believe it.

What should he do? He had made a wonderful discovery. But when he looked inside himself, he saw in that interior mirror only the glassy essence of the angry ape. He had in his grasp the wondrous spell that would send humanity to the stars — but he regarded us as a bloody-handed, bloody-minded humanity, raging out of control through the universe.

His duty as he saw it was clear. He must do the braver thing, and destroy both his ideas and himself.

What did I do?

I think it is obvious.

Arthur's work had always been marred by obscurity. Or rather, to be fair to him, in his mind the important thing was that he understand an idea, not that he be required to explain it to someone of lesser ability.

It took months of effort on my part to convert Arthur's awkward notation and sketchy proofs to a form that could withstand rigorous scrutiny. At that point, the work felt like my own; the re-creation of his half-stated thoughts was often indistinguishable from painful invention.

Finally I was ready to publish. By that time Arthur's ledgers had been, true to my promise, long-since destroyed, for whatever else happened in the world, I did not want Marion Shaw to see those notebooks or suspect anything of their contents.

I published. I could have submitted the work as the posthumous papers of Arthur Sandford Shaw . . . except that someone would certainly have asked to see the original material.

I published. I could have assigned joint authorship, as Shaw and Turnbull . . . except that Arthur had never presented a line on the subject, and the historians would have probed and probed to learn what his contribution had been.

I published — as Giles Turnbull. Three papers expounded what the world now knows as the Turnbull Concession Theory. Arthur Shaw was not mentioned. It is not easy to justify that, even to myself. I clung to one thought: Arthur had wanted his ideas suppressed, but that was a consequence of his own state of mind. It was surely better to give the ideas to the world, and risk their abuse in human hands. *That*, I said to myself, was the braver thing.

I published. And because there were already eight earlier papers of mine in the literature, exploring the same problem, acceptance of the new theory was quick, and my role in it was never in doubt.

Or almost never. In the past four years, at scattered meetings around the world, I have seen in perhaps half a dozen glances the cloaked hint of a question. The world of physics holds a handful of living giants. They see each other clearly, towering above the rest of us, and when someone whom they have assessed as one of the pygmies shoots up to stand tall, not at their height but even well above them, there is at least a suspicion. . . .

There is a braver thing.

Last night I telephoned my father. He listened quietly to everything that I had to tell him, then he replied, "Of course I won't say a word about that to Marion Shaw. And neither will you." And at the end, he said what he had not said when the Nobel announcement was made: "I'm proud of you, Giles."

At the cocktail party before tonight's dinner, one of the members of the Royal Swedish Academy of Sciences was tactless enough to tell me that he and his colleagues found the speeches delivered by the Nobel laureates uniformly boring. It's always the same, he said, all they ever do is reca-pitulate the reason that the award had been made to them in the first place.

I'm sure he is right. But perhaps tomorrow I can be an exception to that rule.

This is a birthday present for Bob Porter.
—*Charles Sheffield, February 17, 1989*

Afterword: A Braver Thing

In 1988 I wrote a story called "The Double Spiral Staircase." It can be found later in this collection, and I am giving nothing away when I say that it concerns a great discovery, and an attempt at its suppression. I sent it off to Analog magazine, but I didn't feel completely happy with it. I wondered if perhaps I had told the story from the wrong character's point of view. So I sat down to re-tell it in the first person.

In the re-telling, everything changed: mood, pacing, length, style. What emerged was "A Braver Thing." To me it was at heart the same story, but I could find no one who agreed. Friends looked at the two, and shook their collective heads. The two stories, they said, had nothing to do with each other. I read "A Braver Thing" again, and disagreed. It was the same story. I liked it, too, although I decided that it was no longer science fiction. It was fiction about science. I thought it was probably unsalable.

I sent it off anyway, to Gardner Dozois at Asimov's magazine. He, showing why he is a successful editor and I am not, bought it, and it became a Hugo finalist for 1991.

Meanwhile, Stan Schmidt of Analog had written back to me. The problem was not in the point of view, as I had thought, but in the ending. I changed that at his suggestion, and he bought the story. It seemed to me that I had in some sense sold the same story to two magazines. But no one has ever complained.

One other thing ought to be said about this story. There is a big lump of autobiography here. In it, however elliptically, I approached for the first time the 1977 death of my first wife, Sarah. It was almost certainly her final illness that led me to write fiction at all, after never having considered that before as even a remote possibility. But I could not write about Sarah for another eleven years. And I could not write directly about her for three more years, until last winter the story "Georgia On My Mind" appeared on my computer almost without my knowing it.

THE GRAND TOUR

Tomas Lili had won the Stage, square if not fair, and now he was wearing the biggest, sweatiest grin you have ever seen. Tomorrow he would also wear the yellow jersey on the next-to-last Stage of the Tour.

Ernie Muldoon had come second. In one monstrous last effort of deceleration, I had almost squeaked in front of him at the docking, and hit the buffer right on the maximum allowable speed of five kilometers an hour. We had been given the same time, and now we were collapsed over our handlebars. I couldn't tell about Ernie, but I felt as though I were dying. For the last two hours I had been pedalling with a growing cramp in my left thigh, and for the final ten minutes it was as though I had been working the whole bike one-legged.

After five minutes' rest I had recovered enough to move and speak. I unbuckled my harness, cracked the seals, and climbed slowly out of my bike. As usual at the end of a Stage, my legs felt as though they had never been designed for walking. I did a couple of deep knee-bends in the half-gee field, then straightened up and staggered over to Muldoon. He had also flipped back the top of his bike and was slowly levering himself free.

"Tomas was lucky," I said. "And he cheated!"

Muldoon looked at me with eyes sunk back in his head. He was even more dehydrated than I was. "Old Persian proverb," he said. "Luck is infatuated with the efficient."

"You don't think he cheated?"

"No. And he wasn't lucky, he was smart. He bent the rules, but he can't get called on it. Therefore, he didn't cheat. He was just a bit smarter than the rest of us. Admit it, Trace, you'd have done it too if you'd thought of it."

"Maybe."

"Maybe, schmaybe. Come on. I've been cramped in this bike for too long. Let's beat the crowd to the showers."

He was right, the others were streaming in now, one every few seconds. As we left the docking area a whole bunch zoomed in together in practically a blanket finish. I saw five riders from Adidas, so close I was sure they'd been slip-streaming for a sixth member of their team. That *was* outside the rules, and they were bound to be caught. Five years ago, slipstreaming had been worth doing. Today, it was marginal. The teams did it anyway — because the man who benefited from the slipstreaming was not the one doing anything illegal. The rider who had given the momentum boost would be disqualified, but that would be some no-hoper in the team. Illogical? Sure. The Tour had a crazy set of rules in the first place, and as more and more riders became part of the big teams, the rules became harder to apply. Ernie Muldoon and I were two of the last independents racing the Grand Tour. Ernie, because he was famous before the team idea caught on; me, because I was stubborn enough to want to win on my own.

Tomas was already sitting in the cafeteria as we walked through it, surrounded by the microphones and cameras. He was enjoying himself. I felt angry for a moment, then decided that it was fair enough. We waved to the media and went on to the showers. Let Tomas have his day of glory. He was so far down in the overall ratings that there was no way he could be the outright Tour de Système winner, even if he won tomorrow's and the final Stages by big margins.

Ernie Muldoon thought that the overall Grand Tour winner was going to be old and wily Ernest Muldoon, who had already won the Tour de Système an unprecedented five times; and I thought it was going to be me, Tracy Collins, already identified in the media coverage as the Young Challenger; or maybe, as Ernest put it, the Young Pretender. Which made *him*, as I pointed out, the Old Pretender.

I had modelled my whole approach to the Tour on Ernie Muldoon, and now it was paying off. This was only my third year, but unless I were disqualified I was certain to be in the top five. My cumulative time for all the Stages actually placed me in the top three, but I hate to count them little chickens too soon.

The shower facilities were as crummy as we've grown to expect. You've got one of the premier athletic events of the Solar System, with coverage Earth-wide and Moon-wide, and still the showers at the end of each Stage are primitive. No blown air, no suction, no spin. All you get are soap, not-warm-enough water, and drying-cloths. It must be because we don't attract top video coverage. People are interested in us, but what sort of TV program can you build out of an event where each Stage runs anything up to thirty-six hours, and the competitors are just seen as little dots for most of the time? Maybe what the media need are a few deaths to spice things up, but so far the Tour has been lucky (or unlucky) that way.

Muldoon slapped me on the back as we were coming out of the shower area. "Three quarts of beer, three quarts of milk, thirty ounces of rare beef, and half a dozen potatoes from the original Owld Sod, and you'll not even notice that leg of yours. Are you with me, lad?"

"I'm with you — but not this minute. Don't you want to get a weather report first, for tomorrow?"

"A quick look, now. But I doubt if we'll see anything special. The wind forecasts for tomorrow have all been quiet. It's my bet we'll see stronger winds for the final Stage. Maybe a big flare-up."

Muldoon was casual, but he didn't really fool me. He had told me, a dozen times, that the solar wind forecast was the most important piece of a rider's knowledge — more relevant than local gravity anomalies or super-accurate trajectory calculations. We went over to the weather center and looked at the forty-eight hour forecast. It was pretty calm. Unless there were a sudden and dramatic change, all the riders could get away with minimal radiation shielding.

That wasn't always the case. Two years ago, the second half of the Tour had taken place when there was a massive solar flare. The solar wind of energetic charged particles had been up by a factor of a hundred, and every rider added another two hundred kilos of radiation shielding. If you think that doesn't make a man groan, when every ounce of shielding has to be carried around with you like a snail carrying its shell — well, then you've never ridden the Tour.

Of course, you don't *have* to carry the shielding. That's a rider's choice. Four years ago, on the eleventh Stage of the Tour, Crazy-legs Gerhart had done his own calculation of flare activity, and decided that the radiation level would drop nearly to zero a few minutes after the Stage began. When everybody else crawled away from Stage-start loaded down with extra shielding, Crazy-legs zoomed off with a minimal load. He won the Stage by over two hours, but he just about glowed in the dark. The wind level hadn't become low at all. He docked so hot with radiation that no one wanted to touch him, and he was penalized a hundred and fifty minutes for exceeding the permissible dosage per Stage by ninety-two rads. Worse than that, they dumped him in the hospital to flush him out. He missed the rest of the Tour.

Every rider had his own cookbook method for guessing the optimal shielding load, just as everyone had his own private trajectory program and his own preferred way of pacing the race. There were as many methods as there were riders in the Tour.

Muldoon and I made notes of the wind — we'd check again, last thing at night — and then went back to the cafeteria. A few of the media people were still there. Without looking as though we were avoiding them, we loaded our trays and went off to a quiet corner. We didn't want the Newsies tonight. The next-to-last Stage was coming up tomorrow morning, and it was a toughie. We had to ride nearly twenty-five thousand kilometers, dropping in from synchronous station, where we had docked today, to the big Sports Central station in six-hour orbit.

Some people complain because we call it the "Tour de Système" when the only part of the Solar System we travel is Earth-Moon space. But they've never ridden the Tour. When you have, the six-hundred-thousand kilometer course seems quite long enough. And the standards of competition get tougher every year. All the original Stage records have been broken, then broken again. In a few years' time it will be a million-kilometer Tour, and then we'll zip way out past the Moon before we start the inbound Stages.

Muldoon and I stuffed ourselves with food and drink — you can't overfeed a Tour rider, no matter what you give him —

then went off quietly to bed. Two more days, I told myself;
then I'll raise more Hell than the Devil's salvage party.

Next morning my first worry was my left thigh. It felt fine
— as it ought to, I'd spent an hour last night rubbing a foul
green embrocation into the muscles. I dressed and headed for
breakfast, wanting to beat the rush again.

"Well, Tracy, me boyo." It was Muldoon, appearing out of
nowhere and walking by my side. "An' are you still thinking ye
have the Divil's own chanst of beating me?"

He can speak English as well as I can, but when he senses
there are media people around he turns into the most dreadful
blarney-waffling stage-Irishman you could find.

"Easily." I nudged him in the ribs. "You're a tough man,
Muldoon, but your time has come. The bells will be pealing
out this time for handsome young Tracy Collins, overall winner
of the Grand Tour de Système." (So maybe I respond to the
media, too; I sounded confident, but Muldoon couldn't see my
fingers, crossed on the side away from him.)

"Not while there's breath in this breast, me boy," he said.
"An 'tis time we was over an' havin' a word here with the grand
Machiavellian Stage winner himself."

Muldoon stopped by Tomas Lili's table, where a couple of
press who must have missed the Stage winner the previous
night were sitting and interviewing. "Nice work, Tomas me
boy," Muldoon said, patting the yellow jersey. "An' where'd
you be getting the idea of doin' that what yer did?"

A couple of media people switched their recorders back on.
Tomas shrugged. "From you, Ernesto, where we all get our
ideas. You were the one who decided that it was easier — and
legal — to switch the ion drive around on the bike at midpoint, rather than fight all the angular momentum you'd
already built up in your wheels if you tried to turn the bike
through a hundred and eighty degrees. I just built from there."

"Fair enough. But your trick won't work more than once,
Tomas. We'll be ready."

Tomas grinned. He had won a Stage, and that's more than
his Arianespace sponsors had expected of him. "What trick
ever did work more than once, Ernesto? Once is enough."

The media rats at the table looked puzzled, and now one of

them turned to Ernest Muldoon. "I don't understand you. What 'trick' is this you're talking about?"

Muldoon stared at the woman, noted she was young and pretty, and gestured at her to sit down. He poured everyone a liter of orange juice. We competitors sweat away seven or eight kilos, pedalling a Stage, and we have to make sure we start out flush-full with liquids. Tomas took the opportunity to slide away while Muldoon was pouring. He'd had his juice, and some of the other competitors who were still straggling in might have a less enlightened attitude towards Tomas' innovation of the previous Stage.

"D'you understand how we change directions round in the middle of each Stage?" Muldoon asked the reporter. One reason Ernie is so popular with the Press is that he's never too busy to talk to them and explain to them. I noticed that now he had her hooked he had dropped the stage-Irish accent.

"I guess so. But I don't understand *why*. You're out in empty space, between the Stage points, and you've pedalled hard to get the wheels rotating as fast as you can. And then you shift everything around!"

"Right. An' here's the why. Suppose the rider — say, Trace here, the likely lad — hasn't reached halfway point yet, and let's for the moment ignore any fancy maneuvers at Stage turn points. So he's pedalling like a madman — the only way he knows — and the wheels are whizzing round, and he's built up a voltage of something respectable on the rotating Wimshurst disks — say, a couple of million volts. That voltage goes into accelerating the ion stream out of the back of the bike, eh? The faster he pedals, the higher the voltage, the better the exhaust velocity on the ion drive, and so the faster goes our lad Tracy. And he's *got* to get that exhaust velocity as high as he can, because he's only allowed fifty kilos of fuel per Stage, total. All right?"

"Oh, yes." The lady looked into Muldoon's slightly squinty eyes and seemed ready to swoon with admiration. He beamed at her fondly. I was never sure that Ernie Muldoon followed through with a woman while we were riding the Tour — but I'm damned sure if he *didn't* have them between Stages, he saved up credits and used them all when the Tour was over.

"All right." Muldoon ran his hand out along the table top. "Here's Trace. He's been zooming along in a straight line, faster and faster. But now he gets to the halfway point of the Stage, an' now he's got to worry about how he'll get to the finish. See, it's no good arriving at the final docking and zooming right on through — you have to *stop*, or you're disqualified. So now Trace has a different problem. He has to worry about how he's going to *decelerate* for the rest of the run, and finish at a standstill, or close to it, when the bike gets to the docking point. The old-fashioned way — that means up to seven years ago — was pretty simple. Trace here would have turned the whole bike round, so that the ion drive was pointing the other way, towards the place he wanted to get to, and he'd keep on pedalling like the dickens. And if he'd planned well, or was just dumb lucky, he'd be slowed down by the drive just the right amount when he got the final docking, so he could hit slap against the buffers at the maximum permitted speed. Sounds good?"

She nodded "Fine." I didn't know if she was talking about the explanation, or Ernie-the-Letch Muldoon's hand resting lightly across hers. "But what's wrong with that way of doing it?" she went on. "It sounds all right to me."

Someday they're going to assign reporters to the Tour de Système who are more than twenty-two years old and who have some faint idea before they begin of the event they are supposed to be covering. It will ruin Muldoon's sex-life, but it will stop me feeling like an antique myself. All the young press people ask the same damned questions, and they all nod in the same half-witted way when they get the answers.

I wanted to see how Ernest handled the next bit. Somehow he was going to have to get across to Sweet Young Thing the concept of angular momentum.

"Problem is," he said, "while the wheels are spinning fast the bike don't want to turn. Those wheels are heavy glassite discs, rubbing against each other, and they're like flywheels, and so the bike wants to stay lined up just the way it is. So in the old days, the biker would have to stop the wheels — or at least slow 'em down a whole lot — then turn the bike around, and start pedalling again to get the wheels going. All the time that was happening, there was no potential difference on them Wimshurst's, no ion drive, and no acceleration. Big waste of time, and also for the second half of the Stage you were flying ass-backwards. So I did the obvious thing. I mounted a *double* ion drive on my bike, one facing forward, one facing back — turned out that the rules don't *quite* say you can't have more than one drive. They only say you can't have more than one ion drive on your bike *in use at one time*. They don't say you can't have two, and switch 'em in the middle of the Stage. Which is what I did. And won, for about two Stages, until everybody else did the same thing."

"But what was it that Tomas Lili did? He seemed to have come up with something new."

"He installed an ion drive that had more than just the two positions, fore and aft. His can be directed in pretty much any way he wants to. So, first thing that Tomas did on the last Stage, he went off far too fast — at a crazy speed, we all thought. And naturally he got ahead of all of us. *Then* what he did was to direct his ion beam at whoever was close behind him. The ions hit whoever he was pointing at — me, or Trace, or one of the others — and just about canceled out our own drives completely. We were throwing a couple of tenths of a gram of ion propellant out the *back* of the bike at better than ten kilometers a second, but we were being hit on the front by the same amount, traveling at the same speed. Net result: no forward acceleration for us. It didn't *hurt* us, physically, 'cause we're all radiation shielded. But it slowed us. By the time we realized why we were doing so badly, he was gone. Naturally, Tomas wasn't affected, except for the tiny bit he sacrificed because his exhaust jet wasn't pointing exactly aft." Muldoon shrugged. "Neat trick. Works once — next time we'll stay so far out of his wake he'll lose more forward acceleration turning off-axis to hit us than he'll gain."

"You explain everything so clearly!" Their hands were still touching.

"Always try to help. But we've got to get ready for the Stage now. Will you be there at the finish?"

"Of course! I wouldn't miss it for anything."

Muldoon patted her hand possessively. "Then why don't we

get together after it, and we can go over the action together?
Next to last Stage, there ought to be fireworks."

"Oh, yes! Please."

As we left for the start dock, I shook my head at Muldoon.
"I don't expect any particular fireworks today. No tricky course
change, no solar flares — it should be the tamest leg of the
Tour."

He stared back at me, owl-eyed. "And did I say the action
would be on the course, boyo?"

We walked side by side to the main staging area. In twenty
minutes we would be on our way. I could feel the curious
internal tension that told me it was Tour-time again — more
than that, it was the final Stages of the Tour. Something in my
belly was winding me up like an old-fashioned watch. That was
fine. I wanted to hang there in that start space all ready to
explode to action. I touched Muldoon lightly on the shoulder —
good luck, Muldoon, it meant; *but don't beat me* — then I went
on to my station.

There was already a strange atmosphere in the preparation chamber. As the Tour progresses, that strangeness
grows and grows. I had noticed it years ago and never
understood it, until little Alberto Maimonides, who is probably the best sports writer living (my assessment) or ever (his
own assessment) sampled that changing atmosphere before
the Stages, and explained it better than I ever could. Either
one of Muldoon's tree-trunk thighs has far more muscle on it
than Maimonides' whole body, but the little man understood
the name of the game. "At the beginning of the Tour," he
said to me one day, "there are favorites, but everyone may be
said to have an equal chance of winning. As the Tour progresses, the cumulative time and penalties of each rider are
slowly established. And so two groups emerge: those with
the potential to win the whole thing, and those with no such
potential. Those two different potentials polarize the groups
more and more, building tension in one, releasing tension in
the other. Like the Wimshurst disks that you drive as you
turn the pedals, the competitors build up their own massive
potential difference. Beyond the halfway mark in the Tour, I
can tell you into which group a competitor falls — without
speaking a word to him! If a rider has a chance of winning, it

is seen in the tension in neck and shoulders, in the obsessive attention to weather data, in the faraway look in the man's eyes. I can tell you at once which group a rider is in."

"And can you—" I began.

"No." He interrupted me. "What I cannot do, Trace, to save my life, is tell you who will win. That will be, by definition, the best man."

I wanted to be that best man, more than I had ever wanted anything. I was thinking of Alberto Maimonides as I lifted open the shell of my bike and began to inspect the radiation shielding. It was all fine, a thin layer in anticipation of a quiet day without much solar wind. The final Stage was another matter — the forecasts said we would see a lot more radiation; but that was another day, and until we finished today's effort the final Stage didn't matter at all.

The fuel tank came next. The competitors were not allowed to charge the fuel tank themselves, and the officials who did it always put in an exact fifty kilograms, correct to the microgram. But it didn't stop every competitor worrying over the tank, afraid that he had been short-changed and would run out of fuel in the middle of the Stage. People occasionally used their fuel too fast, and ran out before the end of a Stage. Without ion drive fuel they were helpless. They would drift miserably around near the docking area, until someone went out and fished them in. Then they would be the butt of all the other competitors, subject to the same old jokes: "What's the matter, Tish, got thirsty and been drinking the heavy water again?" "You're four hours late, Sven, she gave your dance to somebody else." "Jacques, my lad, we all warned you about premature ejaculation."

I climbed into the shell, and checked my trajectory. It was too late to change anything now, except how hard I would pedal at each time in the Stage. It would need something exceptional to change even that. I had planned this Stage long ago, how I would pace it, how much effort I would put in at each breakpoint. I slipped my feet into the pedal stirrups, gripped the handlebars hard, looked straight ahead, and waited. I was hyperventilating, drawing in the longest, deepest breaths I could.

The starting signal came as an electronic beep in my

headset. While it was still sounding I was pedalling like mad, using low gears to get initial torques on the Wimshursts. After a few seconds I reached critical voltage, the ion drive triggered on, and I was moving. Agonizingly slowly at first — a couple of thousandths of a gee isn't much and it takes a while to build up any noticeable speed — but I was off.

All the way along the starting line, other bikers were doing exactly the same thing. There were various tricks to riding the Tour in the middle part of a Stage, but very little choice at the beginning. You rode as hard as your body would stand, and got the best speed as early as possible. Once you were moving fast you could relax a little bit, and let the bike coast. At the very end of the Stage, you made the same effort in reverse. Now you wanted to hold your speed as long as possible, to minimize your total time for the Stage. But if you had been too energetic at the beginning, or if your strength failed you at the end, you were in real trouble. Then you'd not be able to decelerate your bike enough. Either you'd shoot right through the docking area and whip out again into open space, or you'd demolish the buffers by hitting them at far more than the legal maximum. These both carried disastrous penalties.

After half an hour of frantic pedalling I was feeling pretty pleased. My leg was giving me no trouble at all — touch wood, though there was none within thirty thousand miles. I could see the main competition, and it was where I wanted it to be. Muldoon was a couple of kilometers behind, Rafael Rodriguez of the NASDA team was almost alongside him, and Tomas Lili was already far in the rear. I looked ahead, and settled down to the long grind.

This was a Stage with few tricky elements. During the Tour we started from low earth orbit, went all the way to L-4 in a series of thirty variable-length Stages, and then looped back in halfway to the Moon before we began the drive to Earth. Some Stages were geometrically complex, as much in the calculations as the legs. This one was the sort of Stage that I was thoroughly comfortable with. The only real variables today were physical condition and natural stamina. I was in the best shape I had ever been, and I was convinced that if my legs and determination held out I had everyone beat.

Twenty-six hours later I was even more convinced. We

had passed the crossover point long ago, and I had done it without any complication. I could still see Muldoon and Rodriguez in my viewfinder, but they had not closed the gap at all. If anything, I might have gained a few more seconds on them. No one else was even in sight. There was a terrible urge to ease off, but I could not do it. It was *cumulative* time that decided the Tour winner, and Muldoon and Rodriguez had both started this Stage nearly a minute ahead of me. I wanted to make up for that today, and more. The yellow jersey might be enough for Tomas Lili, but not for me. I wanted the whole pie.

I had taken my last liquid three hours ago, draining the juice bottle and then jettisoning it to save mass. Now my throat was dry and burning, and I'd have given anything for a quarter liter of water. I put those thoughts out of my head, and pedalled harder.

It turned out that I left my final sprint deceleration almost too late. Twenty-five kilometers out I realized that I was approaching the final docking area too fast. I would slam into the buffers at a speed over the legal limit. I put my head down, ignored the fact that my legs had been pumping for nearly twenty-seven hours straight, and rode until I thought my heart and lungs would burst. I didn't even see the docks or the final markers. I guess my eyes were closed. All I heard was the loud *ping* that told me of an arrival at legal speed. And then I was hanging on the handlebars, wishing some person would shoot me and put me out of my misery.

My chest was on fire, my throat was too dry to breathe, my heart was racing up close to two hundred beats a minute, and my legs were spasming with cramps. I clung to the handlebars, and waited. Finally, when I heard a second *ping* through my helmet's radio, I knew the second man was in. I looked up at the bigboard readout. It was Muldoon, following me in by one minute and seventeen seconds. He had started the day one minute and fourteen seconds ahead of me on the cumulative total. I had won the Stage — and I was now the overall Tour leader.

I groaned with pain, released my harness, and cracked open my bike. I forced a big grin onto my face for the media — more like a grimace of agony, but no one would know the difference — and managed to climb out onto the docking facility just as though I was feeling light and limber. Then I sauntered along to where Muldoon was slowly opening his bike. One cheery smile for the benefit of the cameras, and I was reaching in to lift him lightly clear of the bike.

He glared up at me. "You big ham, Trace. What was your margin?"

"One minute and seventeen seconds."

"Ah." It was more a groan of physical agony than mental as he tried to stand up on the dock. His thigh muscles, like mine, were still unknotting after over a day of continuous effort. "So you're ahead then. Three seconds ahead. And with a new Stage record. Damn it."

"Thanks. You're just a terrific loser, Muldoon."

"Right. And it takes one to know one, Trace." He did a couple of deep knee-bends. "What about the others. Where did they finish?"

"Schindell came in two minutes after you. He's about four minutes behind us, overall. Something must have happened to Rodriguez, because he's still not in."

"Leg cramps. We were riding side by side for a long time, then he dropped way behind. I'm pretty sure he had to stop pedalling."

"So he's out of the running."

We stared at each other. "So it's me an' thee," said Muldoon after a few moments. "Barring a miracle or a disaster, one of us will be *it*."

It! Overall Tour winner. I wanted that so much I could taste it.

Muldoon saw my face. "You're getting there, Trace," he said. "Muscle and heart and brains will only take you so far. You have to *want* it bad enough."

I saw *his* face, too. His eyes were bloodshot, and sunk so far back that they were little glowing sparks of blue at the end of dark tunnels. If I had reached a long way into myself to ride this Stage, how far down had Muldoon gone? Only he knew that. He *wanted it*, as much as I did.

"You're getting old, Ernie," I said. "Alberto Maimonides says that the Tour's a young man's game."

"And what does he know, that little Greek faggot!" Muldoon

respected Maimonides as much as I did, but you'd never know it if you heard them talk about each other. "He's talking through his skinny brown neck. The Tour's a *man's* game, not a *young* man's game. Go an' get your yellow jersey, Trace, and show your fine profile to the media."

"What about you? They'll want to see you as well — we're neck and neck for overall Tour position. How long since non-team riders have been one and two in Tour status?"

"Never happened before. But I've got work to do. Weather reports to look at, strategy to plan. You can handle the damned media, Trace — time you learned how. And I'll tell you what." He had been scowling at me, but now he smiled. "You look at all the pretty young reporters, and you pick out the one who'd be my favorite. An' you can give her one for me."

He stumped off along the dock. I looked after him before I went to collect the yellow jersey that I would wear for the final Stage, and pose with it for the waiting mediamen. Ernie hadn't given up yet. There was brooding and scheming inside that close-cropped head. He was like a dormant volcano now, and there was one more Stage to go. Maybe he had one more eruption left in him. But what could it possibly be?

I was still asking that question when we lined up for the beginning of the final Stage. Yellow jersey or no yellow jersey, I hadn't slept well last night. I dreamed of the swoop towards the finishing line, with its massed cameras and waiting crowds. There would be hordes of space tugs, filled with spectators, and video crews from every station on Earth or Moon. And who would they be homing in on, to carry off and interview until he could be interviewed no more?

In the middle of the night I had awakened and wandered off to where the rows of bikes were sitting under twenty-four hour guard. The rules here were very simple. I could go to my bike, and do what I liked with it; but I could not touch, or even get too close to, the bike of another competitor. The history of the rule was something I could only guess at. It made psychological sense. No competitor wanted *anybody* else touching his beloved bike. We suffered the organizers to fill our fuel tanks, because we had no choice; but we hovered over and watched every move they made, to make sure they did not damage so much as a square milli-meter of paint.

The bike shed was quiet when I got there. A couple of competitors were inside their bikes, fiddling with nozzles, or changing the position of juice bottles or viewfinders or com-puters. It was all just nerves coming to the fore. The changes they were making would not improve their time by a tenth of a second. Ernie Muldoon was inside his bike, too, also fid-dling with bits and pieces. He stopped when he saw me, and nodded.

"Can't sleep, either?"

I shrugged. "It's not easy. Plenty of time for sleep tomorrow night, when the Tour's over."

"Nobody wants to sleep when it's over. We'll all be partying, winners and losers."

"Wish it were tomorrow now."

He nodded. "I know that feeling. Good luck, Trace."

"Same to you Ernie."

I meant it. And he meant it. But as I sat at the starting line, my feet already in the pedal stirrups, I knew what that well-wishing meant. Neither of us wanted anything bad to happen to the other; all we wanted was to *win*. That was the ache inside. I looked around my bike for one last time. The radia-tion shielding was all in position. As we had surmised the day before yesterday, the weather had changed. There was a big spike of solar activity sluicing through the Inner System, and a slug of radiation was on its way. It would hit us close to the halfway point of the final Stage, then would diminish again when the Tour was over. The maximum radiation level was nowhere near as high as it had been in the Tour two years ago, but it was enough to make us all carry a hefty load of shielding. The prospect of hauling that along for twenty-six thousand kilometers was not one I was looking forward to.

The electronic beep sounded in my helmet. We were off. A hundred and six riders — we had lost thirty-four along the way to injuries and disqualification — began to pedal madly. After half a minute of frenzied, apparently unproductive activity, the line slowly moved away from the starting port. The airlock had been opened ten minutes before. We were heading out into hard vacuum, and the long solitary ride to the finish. No one was allowed to send us any information during the Stage, or to respond to anything other than an emergency call from a competitor.

The optimal trajectory for this Stage had been talked about a good deal when the competitors held their evening bull sessions. There were two paths that had similar projected energy budgets. The choice between them depended on the type of race that a competitor wanted to ride. If he were very confident that he would have a strong final sprint deceleration, then trajectory one was optimal. It was slightly better overall. But if a rider were at all suspicious of his staying power at the end, trajectory two was safer.

The two trajectories diverged early in the Stage, and roughly two-thirds of the riders opted for the second and more conservative path. I and maybe thirty others, praying that our legs and lungs would stand it, went for the tougher and faster route.

Muldoon did neither of these things. I knew the carapace of his red-and-black bike as well as I knew my own, and I was baffled to see him diverging from everyone else, on another path entirely. I had looked at that trajectory myself — we all had. And we had ruled it out. It wasn't a disastrous choice, but it offered neither the speed of the one I was on, nor the security of the path most riders had chosen.

Muldoon must know all that. So where was he going?

I had plenty of time to puzzle in the next twenty-four hours, and not much else to occupy my attention. Before we reached midpoint where I reversed my drive's direction, all the other riders in my group had diminished to dots in my viewfinder. They were out of it, far behind. I had decided that after today's Stage I would take a year to rest and relax, but I wouldn't relax now. I pushed harder than I had ever pushed. As the hours wore on I became more aware of the radiation shielding, the stone that I was perpetually pushing uphill. A *necessary* stone. Outside my bike was a sleet of deadly solar particles.

Even though the group of competitors who had ridden my trajectory were just dots in the distance behind me, I didn't feel at all relaxed. On the Tour, you *never* relax until the final Stage is ridden, the medals have been awarded, *and* the overall winner has performed the first step-out at the Grand Dance.

At the twenty-third hour I looked off with my little telescope in another direction. If anyone in the slow, conservative group had by some miracle managed to ride that trajectory faster than anyone had ever ridden it, they ought to be visible now in the region that I was scanning. I looked and saw nothing, nothing but vacuum and hard, unwinking stars.

The final docking area was at last in sight, a hundred kilometers ahead of me. I could begin to pick up little dots of ships, hovering close to the dock. And unless I was very careful, I was going to shoot right through them and past them. I had to shed velocity. That meant I had to pedal harder than ever to slow my bike to the legal docking speed.

I bent for one last effort. As I did so, I caught sight of something in my rear viewfinder.

A solitary bike. Red and black — Muldoon. But going far too fast. He was certainly going to overtake me, but he was equally certainly going to be unable to stop by the time he reached the dock. He would smash on through, and either be disqualified or given such a whopping time penalty he would drop to third or fourth place.

I felt sorry for him. He had done the almost impossible, and ridden that inefficient alternate trajectory to within a few seconds of catching me. But it was all wasted if he couldn't dock; and at the speed he was going, that would be just impossible.

Then I had to stop thinking of him, and start thinking of myself. I put my head down and drove the cranks around, gradually increasing the rate. The change in deceleration was too small for me to feel, but I knew it was there. The ions were pushing me back, easing my speed. I was vaguely aware of Muldoon's bike moving silently past mine — still going at an impossible pace.

And so was I. It was the mass of all the shielding, like a millstone around my bike. The inertia of that hundred extra kilos of shielding material wanted to keep going, dragging me and the bike with it. *I had to slow down*.

I pedalled harder. Harder. The docking area was ahead. *Harder!* I was still too fast. I directed the bike to the line instinctively, all my mind and will focused on my pumping legs.

Stage line. Docking guide. Docking. Docked!

I heard the *ping!* in my helmet that told of a docking within the legal speed limit. I felt a moment of tremendous satisfaction. *All over. I've won the Tour!* Then I rested my head on my handlebars and sat for a minute, waiting for my heart to stop smashing out of my rib cage.

Finally I lifted my head. I found I was looking at Muldoon's red and black racing bike, sitting quietly in a docking berth next to mine. He was slumped over the handlebars, not moving. He looked dead. The marker above his bike showed he had made a legal docking.

His bike looked different, but I was not sure how. I unlocked my harness, cracked the bike seals, and forced myself outside onto the dock. As usual my legs were Jell-O. I wobbled my way along to Muldoon's bike. I knocked urgently on the outside.

"Muldoon! Are you all right?" I was croaking, dry-throated. I didn't seem to have enough moisture left in my body for one spit.

I hammered again. For a few seconds there was no response at all. Then the cropped head slowly lifted, and I was staring down into a puffy pair of eyes. Muldoon didn't seem to recognize me. Finally he nodded, and reached to unlock his harness. When the bike opened, I helped him out. He was too far gone to stand.

"I'm all right, Trace," he said. "I'm all right." He sounded terrible, anything but all right.

I took another look at his bike. Now I knew why it looked different. "Muldoon, you've lost your shielding. We have to get you to a doctor."

He shook his head. "You don't need to. I didn't get an overdose. I didn't *lose* that shielding. I shed it on purpose."

"But the radiation levels —"

"Are down. You saw the forecasts for yourself, the storm was supposed to peak during the Stage and then run way down. I spent most of last night fixing the bike so I could get rid of shielding when the solar flux died away enough. That happened six hours ago."

I suddenly realized how he had managed that tremendous deceleration at the end of the race. Without an extra hundred kilos of shielding dragging him along, it was easy. I could have done the same thing.

And then I felt sick. Any one of us could have done what Muldoon had done — if we'd just been smart enough. The rules let you jettison anything you didn't want, empty juice bottles, or radiation shielding. The only requirement is that you don't interfere with any other rider. Muldoon had thrown a lot of stuff away, but by choosing a trajectory where no one else was riding, he had made sure he could not be disqualified for interference.

"You did it again," I said. "How far ahead of me were you when you docked?"

He shrugged. "Two seconds, three seconds. I'm not sure. I may not have done it, Trace. I needed three seconds. You may still have won it."

But I was looking at his face. There was a look of deep, secret joy there that not even old stoneface Muldoon could hide. He had won. And I had lost. Again.

I knew. He knew. And he knew I knew.

"It's my last time, Trace," he said quietly. "This one means more than you can imagine to me. I'll not win any more. Maimonides is quite right, the Tour's a young man's game. But you've got lots of time, years and years."

I had been wrong about the moisture in my body. There was plenty, enough for it to trickle down my cheeks. "Damn it, I don't *want* it in years and years, Ernie. I want it *now*."

"I know you do. And that's why I'm sure you'll get it *then*." He sighed. "It took me eight tries before I won, Trace. Eight tries! I thought I'd never do it. You're still only on your third Tour." Ernie Muldoon reached out his arm and draped it around my shoulders. "Come on now, lad. Win or lose, the Tour's over for this year. Give a poor old man a hand, and let's the two of us go and talk to them damned media types together."

I was going to say no, because I couldn't possibly face the cameras with tears in my eyes. But then I looked at his face, and knew I was wrong. I could face them crying. Ernie Muldoon was still my model. Anything he could do, I could do.

Afterword: *The Grand Tour*

It would be a mistake to look for deep significance here. This is a lighthearted sports story. The fact that it happens to be a bicycle story set in space is almost irrelevant.

Why biking? Well, I grew up in Hull, a town in the north of England that happens to sit in the middle of a very flat area called the plain of Holderness. The biggest "hills" to be found in Hull were the river bridges and the railway bridges. It was a very benign environment for a push-bike. Even eighty-year-olds rode, creaking their way along flat streets that during the rush hour carried cyclists seven abreast. Automobiles were regarded as interlopers, resented and almost ignored.

Naturally, the big events of my youth were the casual weekend rides to the coast, and the competitive time trials. In the latter, riders were released at one minute intervals early on Sunday morning. We raced a 25-mile fixed course on the open road, trying to beat one hour, or, for the most successful, fifty-seven minutes or even fifty-five. It was forbidden to "slipstream" by riding close behind a truck. It was also extremely dangerous, but that wasn't enough to discourage people, so observers were planted along the route to look for cheaters.

The reader will probably see Tour de Système *in this story, and think* Tour de France. *But the memory for me is of brisk mornings in East Yorkshire, looping out on roads that carried me to the first gentle slopes of the Yorkshire Wolds. And then painfully back, convinced during the final five miles home that my legs were turning to iron and my heart was about to freeze in my chest.*

CLASSICAL NIGHTMARES . . .
. . . AND QUANTUM PARADOXES

". . . the quantum mechanics paradoxes, which can truly be said to be the nightmares of the classical mind . . ."

—Ilya Prigogine

1. THE MIGHTY ATOM

The theory of special relativity tells us that we cannot accelerate an object to move faster than the speed of light. Worse than that, it tells us that as we try to accelerate a body to speeds closer and closer to light speed, we must apply more and more energy because the mass of the accelerating object increases. The same theory tells us that we can't send messages faster than light, either.

These results are unpopular in science fiction, where ways are needed to get from star to star quickly, cheaply, and easily, or at the very least to communicate over interstellar distances. This has led writers to seek a variety of loopholes. They include such things as:

• warp drives — largely undefined, though there is usually a suggestion that the drives can warp space-time in such a way that points physically far apart in real space become closely separated in the warped space;

• wormholes — there are singularities in space-time, formed by black holes; wormholes are connections between these black holes and white holes, and the intrepid traveler who enters a black hole will emerge from a white hole;

• hyperdrives — which suppose that there are other space-times, loosely connected to ours, in which either the speed of light is far bigger than in our own universe, or the distances between points are far less. You move to one of these other spacetimes to do your traveling.

The advantage of these devices is obvious: they permit interesting stories. The disadvantage of all of them is that they have no relationship to today's accepted physical theories (for instance, no one has ever fully defined a white hole, or seen any evidence that such a thing can exist). This does not mean that the devices *cannot* exist — only that they are very, very unlikely. Today's theories will be supplanted by tomorrow's, but surely not in any simple-minded way arranged for the convenience of science fiction writers. Warp drives and their relatives are varieties of wishful thinking.

A much better way to look for faster-than-light travel techniques is to seek the places where today's theories are incomplete or, better still, *inconsistent*. For if two independent theories tell us two different and incompatible things, something must be wrong, and that is fertile ground for discovery.

Where incompatible theories meet, there may be loopholes. We want a particular loophole that allows an object to move from one place to another faster than the speed of light, or permits a piece of information to be transferred faster than light. There is one obvious place to look: at the meeting place of quantum theory and relativity. In the first part of this century, the quantum theory was developed in parallel with, but almost independent of, the theories of special and general relativity. Despite sixty years of effort, the two have never been put consistently together in what John Archibald Wheeler, the physicist who among other things gave us the modern name "black hole" to the end-point collapse of massive stars, has termed "the fiery marriage of general relativity with quantum theory."

Moreover, when we explore the bases of quantum theory we are fishing in very strange waters. The techniques allow us to compute the right answers, i.e., they seem to describe the way the universe behaves, but they often run counter to the way we feel things *should* behave. That's our problem, of course, and not Nature's. As the late and much-lamented Richard Feynman, one of the sparkling intellects of the century, put it, the problem "is only a conflict between reality and your feeling of what reality 'ought to be.'"

Part of the difficulty is that, until recently, quantum

theory seemed to be confined to describing what happened in the world of the very small — atoms, and electrons, and sub- nuclear particles far too little for us to have any hope of seeing them. There was thus no direct physical experience to guide us as to their behavior, and a simple extrapolation of intuition derived from large objects was likely to prove false.

In the next sections we will look at quantum theory and ask how the world would appear if atoms were big, say as big as a basketball. Before we roar with laughter at such a silly idea, we ought to look back forty-some years. When the first atomic bomb was dropped on Hiroshima on August 6, 1945, the average citizen knew not a thing about atoms. Even the name, "atomic bomb," was evidence of public confusion. Every bomb since the invention of gunpowder was an atomic bomb, since it involved the chemical bonds between the outer electrons of atoms. The new bomb should have been called a *nuclear* bomb" — but the media could get away with the term "atomic bomb" because few people seemed to know about atoms.

When a poll was made in 1945, asking the general public among other things how big they thought atoms were, "about the size of a tennis ball" was one popular answer. And have you ever heard the word "atom" before, Mr. & Mrs. Average Citizen? Well, it was the title of a popular book, *The Mighty Atom*, by Marie Corelli (a book which had nothing to do with atoms in the scientific sense).

And how about the word "nucleus" applied to atoms? Sorry, that's new to us.

The bomb was such a sensation that a number of truly amazing rumors made the rounds: e.g., that the bomb itself was far too small to be seen with the naked eye; that Albert Einstein — the one scientist the public had heard of — had personally piloted the plane that dropped the bomb. And my own favorite, the rumor, repeated over British radio, that the container for the first atomic bomb was designed by Bing Crosby. People seemed ready to believe anything.

(Before we laugh, ask if we are smarter now. A country that *pays* farmers to grow a crop that kills three hundred and fifty thousand of us every year, or cheerfully accepts astrology in the White House, can't afford to do much mocking of anyone. I'd be interested to hear the answers if you held a poll *today* and asked people how big an atom is.)

My point is this: Most people knew nothing about atoms, and once they found out just how small atoms were, their amazement took a new direction. How is it possible, they said, for anyone to count, measure, and know the properties of objects that we can't even see?

That is a very basic and reasonable question, and in some ways the general public was smarter than the scientists. There is no reason to expect that objects too small to see or touch *should* behave in any way like the large objects of everyday experience. In fact, they don't. And therein lies quantum theory.

Before we can get to the quantum paradoxes and faster-than-light communications, we will have to say something about the theory itself: where it came from, what it means, why it's needed.

2. THE BEGINNINGS OF QUANTUM THEORY

Quantum theory has been around, in much its present form, for over sixty years. The basic rules for quantum theory calculations were discovered by Werner Heisenberg and Erwin Schrödinger in 1925. Soon afterwards, in 1926, Paul Dirac, Carl Eckart, and Schrödinger himself showed that the Heisenberg and Schrödinger formulations can be viewed as two different approaches within one general framework.

It quickly became clear that the same theory allowed the internal structure of atoms and molecules to be calculated in detail, and by 1930, quantum theory, or quantum mechanics as it was called, became *the* method for performing calculations in the small world of molecules, atoms, and nuclear particles.

There have been great improvements since that time in computational techniques, and in our understanding of such things as nuclear models, nuclear scattering processes, and sub-nuclear structure. However, the basic ideas have not changed much since the late 1920's; and the same mysteries that plagued and puzzled the workers of that time are worries now.

It is, in fact, fair to say that although we have *recipes* that allow us to compute almost anything we want to, underneath those recipes lurk deep paradoxes and open questions, and they have been there since the beginning. To quote Feynman again, "I think it is fair to say that no one understands quantum mechanics." We are like people who know very well how to drive a car, but have never looked under the hood and have no idea how the engine works.

If you ask how I have the nerve to write about a subject that I am saying no one fully understands, let me admit the validity of the criticism and point out that such considerations never yet stopped a politician or a preacher. I'm not going to let it stop me.

Harder to answer is the need for yet another discussion of quantum theory and its paradoxes, when so many high-quality detailed discussions already exist in the literature. I argue that my objective is a rather brief article, not a book, and in the final section I point out some of the excellent texts that treat in detail what here I will only mention.

While in confessional mode, I also have to say that I can't possibly describe quantum theory fully in a few thousand words. There's too much to it, and it's a truly difficult subject. If everything I say seems to be perfectly clear, chances are that either I'm missing the point, or you are.

The need for quantum theory emerged gradually, from about 1890 to 1920. Some rather specific questions as to how radiation should behave in an enclosure had arisen, questions that classical physics couldn't answer. Max Planck in 1900 showed how a rather *ad hoc* assumption that the radiation was emitted and absorbed in discrete chunks, or *quanta* (singular, *quantum*), solved the problem. He introduced a fundamental constant associated with the process, Planck's constant. This constant, denoted by h, is a tiny quantity, and its small size compared with the energies, times, and masses of the events of everyday life is the basic reason why we are not aware of quantum effects all the time.

Most people thought that the Planck result was a gimmick, something that happened to give the right answer but did not represent anything either physical or of fundamental importance.

That changed in 1905, when Einstein used the idea of the

quantum to explain another baffling result, the *photoelectric effect*. (The year 1905 was unbelievable for Einstein. He produced the explanation of the photoelectric effect, the theory of special relativity, and a paper explaining Brownian motion [see the article, "Counting Up"]. The only comparable year in scientific history was 1666, when Isaac Newton developed the calculus, the laws of motion, and the theory of universal gravitation.)

The photoelectric effect arises in connection with light hitting metal. In 1899, the Hungarian physicist Phillip Lenard had shown that when a beam of light is shone on a metallic surface, electrons begin to pop out of the metal provided that the wavelength of the light is short enough. Note that the result depends on the *wavelength* of the light, and not its brightness. If the wavelength is short enough, the *number* of emitted electrons is decided by the brightness, but if the wavelength is too long, no electrons will appear no matter how bright the light may be.

Einstein suggested that the result made sense if light were composed of particles (now called *photons*) each with a certain energy decided by the wavelength of the light. These photons, hitting atoms in the metal, would drive electrons out if the energy provided by the impact was enough to overcome the binding of the electron within the atom. Einstein published an equation relating the energy of light to its wavelength, and again Planck's constant, h, appeared.

Quanta looked a little more real, but Einstein was only twenty-six years old and still an unknown, so the world did not hang on his every word as they did in his later years. There were certain exceptions, people who recognized Einstein for what he was from the beginning. Max Born, whom we will meet again in the 1920's, wrote: "Reiche and Loria told me about Einstein's paper, and suggested that I should study it. This I did, and was immediately deeply impressed. We were all aware that a genius of the first order had emerged." Born here is typically modest. *He* certainly knew that a genius of the first order had arisen; but he was himself a genius. It takes one to know one.

It might seem that there was nothing particularly surprising in Einstein's suggestion that light was composed of particles. After all, Newton, over two hundred years earlier, had believed exactly the same thing, and it was known as the *corpuscular theory of light*. However, early in the nineteenth century, long after Newton's death, a crucial experiment had been performed that seemed to show beyond doubt that light had to be a form of wave motion. All the evidence since that time had pointed to the same conclusion.

The key experiment was a deceptively simple one performed in 1801 by an English physicist and physician, Thomas Young. (Young was also one of the men who deciphered Egyptian hieroglyphics, thus allowing ancient Egyptian writings to be understood; he can hardly be given the label of narrow scientist.)

Young took light from a point source and allowed it to pass through two parallel slits in a screen. When this light was allowed to fall on a second screen held behind the first, a pattern of dark and light, known as an *interference pattern*, was seen. Young's result is explained easily enough if light is a form of wave, but is incomprehensible if light is assumed to be made up of particles. And in the 1860's, Maxwell had gone further, showing that light as a form of wave motion appeared as a natural solution of his general theory of electromagnetism. Thus in 1905, when Einstein published his paper on the photoelectric effect, no one but Einstein was willing to concede that light could be anything but waves. And no one was willing to throw overboard the wave theory of light on the word of a twenty-six-year-old unknown, still working for the Swiss Patent Office.

While Einstein was analyzing the photoelectric effect and re-introducing the corpuscular theory of light to physics, other scientists had begun to put together a picture of an atom that was more than the old Greek idea of a simple indivisible particle of matter. Over in Canada, the New Zealand physicist Ernest Rutherford had been studying the new phenomenon of radioactivity, discovered in 1896 by Henri Becquerel. Rutherford found that radioactive material emits charged particles, and when he moved to England in 1907 he began to use those particles to explore the structure of the atom itself. Rutherford found that instead of behaving like a fairly homogeneous sphere of electrical charges, a few billionths of an inch across, the atom had to be made up of a very dense central region, the *nucleus*, surrounded by an orbiting cloud of electrons. In 1911, Rutherford proposed this new structure for the atom, and pointed out that while the atom was small — a few billionths of an inch — the nucleus was *tiny*, only about a hundred thousandth as big in radius as the whole atom. In other words, matter, everything from humans to stars, is mostly empty space and moving electric charges.

Our own Solar System is much the same sort of structure, of small isolated planets, far from each other, orbiting the central massive body of the Sun. And to many people this analogy, though no more than an analogy, proved irresistible — so irresistible that it was taken to extreme and implausible lengths. The nuclei were imagined to be *really* like suns, and the electrons like planets (despite the fact that all electrons appear to be identical, and all planets to be different). Each electron might have its own tiny life forms living on it, and its own infinitesimal people. And the same argument could be taken the other way. Perhaps, it was suggested, our own Solar System was no more than an atom in the hind leg of a super-dog, barking in a super-universe.

That was perhaps a tongue-in-cheek comment that no scientist took too seriously, but there was a problem with the Rutherford atom, much more fundamental than the breakdown of a rather far-fetched analogy. The inside of the atom, in fact, must be far stranger and more alien than any miniature Solar System. For if electrons were orbiting a nucleus, then Maxwell's general theory of electromagnetism insisted that the electrons ought to radiate energy. But if they *did* lose energy, then according to all classical rules they would quickly have to fall into the nucleus and the atom would collapse.

This didn't happen.

Why didn't it? Why was the atom a stable structure?

That question was addressed by the Danish physicist, Niels Bohr, who at the time was working with Rutherford's group in Manchester, England. He applied the "quantization" notion — that things occur in discrete pieces, rather than continuous forms — to the structure of atoms.

In the Bohr atom, which he introduced in 1913, electrons do move in orbits around the nucleus, just like a miniature solar system. But the reason they don't spiral in is because they can only lose energy in chunks — quanta — rather than continuously. Electrons are permitted orbits of certain energies, and can move between one and the other when they emit or absorb light and other radiation; but they can't occupy *intermediate* positions, because to get there they would need to emit or absorb some fraction of a quantum of energy, and by definition, fractions of quanta don't exist. The permitted energy losses in Bohr's theory were again governed by the wavelengths of the emitted radiation and by Planck's constant.

It sounded crazy, but it worked. With his simple model, applied to the hydrogen atom, Bohr was able to calculate the right emitted wavelengths (known as the *emission spectrum*) for hydrogen. No earlier theory had been able to do that. Thus, although the idea that electrons orbit the nucleus, rather than reside outside the nucleus with a certain amount of energy, was found misleading and subsequently dropped, the quantum nature of the electron energy levels within the atom remained and proved of central importance. Electrons jump from one level to another, and as they do so they give off or absorb quanta of radiation.

How long does it take an electron to move from one quantum level to another quantum level?*

Here we seem to catch our first glimpse of speeds faster than light. According to Bohr's theory (and subsequent ones), we can't speak of an electron "moving" from one state to another. If it moved, in any conventional sense of the word, then there would have to be intermediate positions that corresponded to some intermediate energy. There is no evidence of any such intermediate, fractional, energies. The electron "jumps," disappearing from one state and appearing in another without any discernible transition. It's meaningless to ask how fast it went.

---

* Termed *states* in the vocabulary of quantum theory; any possible unique situation in a system forms one state.

It may seem natural to ask if there might *really* be a whole sequence of transition states, ones that we are simply unable to observe. Quantum theory is quite insistent upon this point: if we can't *observe* it, it is not a part of physics; it belongs to the realm of metaphysics. *"Only questions about the results of experiments have a real significance and it is only such questions that theoretical physics has to consider"* —Dirac. This is in contrast to the nineteenth century view of physics, in which Nature was thought to be evolving like some great machine, with all questions about that machine permitted and potentially answerable, even if we could not give answers with present theories.

The next step came in 1923, and it was made by Louis de Broglie. He knew that Einstein had associated particles (photons) with light waves. He asked if wave properties ought to be assigned to particles, such as electrons and protons, and if so, how. He found that the Bohr "orbits" of electrons in atoms were just right for a whole number of waves to fit into the available space. He also suggested that there should be direct evidence that particles like electrons can be diffracted, just as a light wave is diffracted by an aperture or an object in its path.

His suggestion proved to be entirely correct. If waves behaved like particles, particles also behaved like waves.

The situation in 1924 can now be summarized as follows:

1. Radiation came in quanta — discrete bundles of energy.

2. Those quanta, the photons, interacted with matter as though they were particles, but everything else suggested that radiation was a form of wave.

3. The structure of the atom could be explained by assuming that the permissible positions for electrons corresponded to well-defined, discrete energy values.

4. Particles show wavelike properties, just as waves seem to be composed of particles.

5. One fundamental constant, Planck's constant, is central to all these different phenomena.

The stage was set for the development of a complete form of quantum mechanics, one that would allow all the phenomena of the subatomic world to be tackled with a single theory.

It was also set for an unprecedented confusion about the nature of physical reality, and a debate that still goes on today.

Before we go any farther, let us note a few things about the five points just made. First, the papers which presented these ideas were not difficult *technically*. They did not demand a knowledge of advanced mathematics to be comprehensible. Some of the mathematics used in these ground-breaking papers has a simple, almost homemade look to it. (This was equally true of Einstein's papers on special relativity.) However, the new ideas were very difficult *conceptually*, since they required the reader to throw away many cherished and long-held "facts" about the nature of the universe. In their place, scientists were asked to entertain notions that were not just unfamiliar — they seemed positively perverse. Energy was previously supposed to be a continuously variable quantity, with no such thing as a "smallest" piece of emitted energy — but now people were asked to think that energy came in separate units of precise denomination, like coins or postage stamps. And light was waves, electrons were particles; there should be no way they could both be both, depending on how you looked at them or (as William Bragg jokingly suggested) on which day of the week it happened to be.

The other thing to note is the power of hindsight.

It is easy for us today to sit back and pick out the half-dozen fundamental papers that paved the way for the development of quantum theory, just as it is easy to point to seminal papers by Heisenberg, Schrödinger, Born, and Dirac that created the theory. But at the time, the right path for progress was not clear at all. The crucial papers and the ideas that worked were not the only ones being produced at the time. Everyone had more or less equal access to the same experimental results, and hundreds of attempts were made to reconcile them with existing, nineteenth century physics. Many of those attempts employed the full arsenal of nineteenth century theory, and they were impressive in their complexity and in the mathematical skills that they displayed.

It called for superhuman brains to sit in the middle of all

that action and distinguish the real advances from the scores of other well-intentioned but unsuccessful attempts, or from totally alien and harebrained crank theories. A handful of physicists were able to see what was significant, and build upon it. If we think that the developments of quantum theory are hard to follow, we should reflect on how much harder it was to create.

The same strangeness of thought patterns was there in all the creators of quantum theory — the whiz kids, Heisenberg and Wolfgang Pauli and Dirac* and Pascual Jordan, all in their middle twenties; the wise advisers Bohr and Einstein and Born, men in their mid-forties; the young mathematicians Hermann Weyl and John von Neumann; and the odd man out — Schrödinger, thirty-nine when he published his famous equation in 1926, and an old man for such a fundamental new contribution to physics.

(Of that original legendary group from the mid-20's, I met only one. Paul Dirac, the most powerful theorist of the lot, taught the first course that I ever took in quantum theory. In retrospect, I think of it as a Chinese meal course. Dirac would derive his results, and they were all so clear and logical that they seemed self-evident. Then I would go away, and a couple of hours later I would try to reconstruct his logic. It was gone. What was self-evident to him was not so to me.

I also met him on several occasions socially, though that may be the wrong word. Dirac was a famously shy man. At cocktail parties in the senior common room at St. Johns College, Cambridge, the professors and the graduate students got together a couple of times a year, to drink sherry and make polite conversation. Dirac was always very affable, but he had no particular store of social chit-chat. And we were too in awe of him, and too afraid of looking like idiots, to ask anything about quantum theory, or about the people he had worked with in developing it. Talk about wasted opportunity!)

The logical next step in this article would be to go on with

---

* Einstein, writing in 1926 of Dirac, whom he came to admire greatly, said, "I have trouble with Dirac. This balancing on the dizzying path between genius and madness is awful."

the historical development of the theory. We could show how in 1925 Schrödinger employed the apparent wave-particle duality to come up with a basic equation that can be applied to almost all quantum mechanics problems; how Heisenberg, using the fact that atoms emit and absorb energy only in finite and well-determined pieces, was able to produce another set of procedures that could also be applied to almost every problem; and how Dirac, Jordan, and others were able to show that the two approaches were just different ways of representing a single construct, that construct being quantum theory in its most general form.

We will not proceed that way. Interesting as it is, it would take too long. Instead we will take advantage of hindsight. We will move at once to what writers from Dirac to Feynman have agreed is the single most important experiment — the one which is totally inexplicable without quantum theory, and the one which is the source of endless argument and discussion within quantum theory.

It is an experiment that Thomas Young would recognize at once.

3.   THE KEY EXPERIMENT

We start, as did Thomas Young, with a pair of slits in a screen. Instead of light, this time we have a source of electrons (or some other atomic particle). Electrons that go through a slit hit a sensitive film, or some other medium that records their arrival. As Louis de Broglie predicted, when we do the parallel slit experiment and look at the pattern, we see a wave-like interference effect, showing that the electron has wave properties.

The problem is, to get that pattern it is necessary to assume that *each single electron goes partly through both slits*.

This sounds like gibberish. The obvious thing to say is, it can't go through both, and it should be easy enough to see which one it did go through: you simply watch the slit, to see if the electron passes by. If you do that, you will always observe either one electron, or no electron — and when you make such an observation, the interference pattern goes away.

Quantum theory says that before you made the observation, the electron was partly heading through one slit, partly through the other. In quantum theory language, it had components of *both states*, meaning that there was a chance it would go through one, and a chance it would go through the other. Your act of observation forced it to pick one of those states. And the one it will pick cannot be known in advance — it is decided completely randomly. The probability of the electron ending in one particular state may be larger than for another state, but there is absolutely no way to know, in advance, which state will be found when we make the observation.

This "probabilistic interpretation" of what goes on in the parallel slit experiment and elsewhere in quantum theory was introduced by Born in 1926. It is usually referred to as the "Copenhagen interpretation," even though Born worked at Göttingen. (That was because Niels Bohr, of Copenhagen, included Born's idea as part of a general package of methods of quantum theory, allowing anyone to solve problems of atoms and molecules.) The Copenhagen interpretation said, in effect, that the theory can never tell you exactly where something is, before you make a measurement to *determine* where it is. Prior to the observation, the object existed only as a sort of cloud of probability, maximum in one place but extending over the whole of space. And it is the observation itself that forces the particle to make a choice (I *think* I am speaking anthropomorphically) as to where it is.*

Many people found this idea of *"quantum indeterminacy"* incomprehensible, and many who understood it, hated it — including Einstein and Schrödinger. Schrödinger said: "I don't like it, and I'm sorry I ever had anything to do with it," and "Had I known that we were not going to get rid of this damned quantum jumping, I never would have involved myself in this business."

But one man's poison may be another man's bread and butter. Science fiction writers have regarded the probabilistic

---

* This idea has been challenged recently by Roger Penrose, in his book, *The Emperor's New Mind*. See the final section.

element of quantum theory as providing not a problem, but a great deal of license. The logic runs as follows: If there is a finite probability of an electron or other subatomic particle being anywhere in the universe, then since humans are made up of subatomic particles, there must also be a finite probability that we are not here, but somewhere else. Now, if we could just make a quantum jump to one of those other places, we would have achieved travel — instantaneously.

This is a case where the term "finite probability" is true, but totally misleading. If you work out the probability of a simultaneous quantum jump (presumably you want to all go simultaneously, and to the same place — no fun arriving in a distributed condition, or half of you a day late) you get a number with so many zeros after the decimal that the universe will end long before you could write them all down. As in so many things in science, calculation kills off what seems like a good idea until you look at the numbers.

It's perhaps a good thing that this probabilistic aspect of quantum mechanics was emphasized only after people already knew that the methods gave results corresponding to experiment. Otherwise, the lack of determinacy that the theory implies might have been enough to stop any further work along those lines. As it was, Einstein always rejected the indeterminacy, arguing that somewhere behind it all there had to be a theory without random elements. (Perhaps Einstein's most quoted line is: "God does not play dice." He also said, in the same letter to Max Born, "Quantum mechanics is certainly imposing. But an inner voice tells me that it is not yet the real thing.")

Can we dispose of the idea that the electron is in a mixed-state condition before we observe it, perhaps on some logical grounds?

Suppose that atoms, protons or electrons were as big as tennis balls, or at least weighed as much, as the average citizen was apparently quite ready to believe forty years ago. We could still perform the double slit experiment, and we could watch which slit any particular electron went through. Moreover, a single photon, reflecting off a passing electron, would be enough to give us that information. It then sounds totally ridiculous that the infinitesimal disturbance produced by the impact of one photon could cause a profound change in the results of the experiment.

What does quantum theory tell us in such a case?

It provides an answer that many people find intellectually very disturbing. When we observe large objects, says the theory, the disturbance caused by the measuring process is small compared with the object being measured, and we will then obtain the result predicted by classical physics. However, when the disturbing influence (e.g., a photon) is comparable in size with the object being observed (e.g., an electron), then the classical rules go out of the window, and we must accept the world view offered by quantum theory. Quantum theory thus provides an absolute scale to the universe — a thing is small, if quantum theory must be used to calculate its behavior.

The converse notion, that quantum theory is only important in the atomic and subatomic world, is false. Quantum indeterminacy is quite capable of revealing itself at the level of everyday living. For example, superconductivity is a macroscopic phenomenon, but it arises directly from the quantum properties of matter.

However, perhaps the most famous example of the macroscopic implications of quantum indeterminacy, one which has been quoted again and again, is the case of Schrödinger's cat. This paradox was published in 1935.

Put a cat in a closed box, said Schrödinger, with a bottle of cyanide, a source of radioactivity, and a detector of radioactivity. Operate the detector for a period just long enough that there is a fifty-fifty chance that one radioactive decay will be recorded. If such a decay occurs, a mechanism crushes the cyanide bottle and the cat dies.

The question is, without looking in the box, is the cat alive or dead? Quantum indeterminacy insists that until we open the box (i.e., perform the observation) the cat is partly in the two different states of being dead and being alive. Until we look inside, we have a cat that is neither alive nor dead, but half of each.

There are refinements of the same paradox, such as the one known as Wigner's friend (Eugene Wigner, born in 1902, was an outstanding Hungarian physicist in the middle of the action in the original development of quantum theory). In this version, the cat is replaced by a human being. That human being, as an observer, looks to see if the glass is broken, and therefore automatically removes the quantum indeterminacy. But suppose that we had a cat smart enough to do the same thing, and press a button? The variations — and the resulting debates — are endless.

To get out of the problem of quantum indeterminacy, Hugh Everett and John Wheeler in the 1950's offered an alternative "many-worlds" theory. The cat is both alive and dead, they said — but in different universes. Every time an observation is made, all possible outcomes occur, but the universe splits at that point, one universe for each outcome. We see one result, because we live in only one universe.

This suggestion is of philosophical but not apparently of practical interest. It will always get just the same experimental results as those of the Copenhagen interpretation.

We will not try to decide between the Copenhagen interpretation and the Everett-Wheeler many-worlds theory, or other more recent suggestions such as John Cramer's "transactional interpretation," published in 1986. Instead, we will accept that quantum indeterminacy is real, and explore the reasons why some people feel that it could be the key to faster-than-light communication.

4.   ACTION AT A DISTANCE

With waves looking like particles and particles behaving like waves, with energy coming in lumps, with determinacy gone, what was left that the physicists of the late 1920's could rely on?

Well, there were still the conservation principles. In any process, momentum had to be conserved, and so did angular momentum. And energy had to be conserved (though since Einstein's relativity papers in 1905, mass had to be recognized as convertible to energy, and vice versa, according to a precise rule — if "God does not play dice" are Einstein's most famous words, $E = mc^2$ is certainly his most famous formula). Insisting on these general conservation laws within the new quantum theory not only imposed some order on the confusion, it also led to new physical predictions. Wolfgang Pauli predicted the existence of a new particle, the *neutrino*, in 1931, based on the conservation principles. That particle was not actually seen until 1954, but most people accepted its existence during that quarter-century wait.

Angular momentum, or spin, is a variable that quantum theory tells us can take on only a finite set of values. Like the energy levels of atoms, it is *quantized*. If an object with zero spin breaks into two equal pieces, then conservation of angular momentum tells us that the spins of those pieces must be equal and opposite. (By opposite we mean that the spins are in the opposite sense — imagine two spinning tops, that looked at from above are rotating in clockwise and counterclockwise directions.)

Now consider one of the two pieces. Quantum indeterminacy tells us that until we look at it, we don't know the sense of its spin. The two pieces may fly far apart from each other, without our knowing the sense of spin of either one of them, but we can be sure that they must continue to have opposite spins, since their total angular momentum must be zero.

Suppose that, when the two particles are far apart, we measure the spin of one of them. According to quantum indeterminacy, until that measurement is performed, the particle doesn't have a defined sense of spin — it has a mixture of two possible spins, and it is only the measurement that forces it into one particular spin.

But when that happens, the other particle, no matter how far away, must at once take on a spin of the opposite sense to the one that was just measured. Otherwise angular momentum would not be conserved. One particle has affected the other, and the influence has traveled faster than the speed of light.

A version of this experiment was proposed (as a thought experiment, not a real experiment) by Einstein, Rosen, and Podolsky, in 1935. Their objective was not faster-than-light communication. It was rather to assert that the possibility of measuring a property of one of the particles, without affecting the other, undermined the whole idea of indeterminacy in quantum theory, and therefore that quantum theory was missing some basic element.

However, another way of looking at the situation can be

adopted: suppose that we accept quantum theory. Then the second particle *is* affected by the measurement we made on the first one. We have achieved "action at a distance," something that most physicists object to on general philosophical grounds. Any theory that allows action at a distance is called a *non-local* theory. We are led to one of two alternative conclusions:

(a) There is something incomplete or wrong in quantum theory; or

(b) The universe permits non-local effects, where one action here can instantly affect events far away.

Starting in 1976 and continuing today, experiments have been performed to test which conclusion is correct. They are done by evaluating an expression known as Bell's inequality, first published in 1964, which gives different results in the two situations (a) and (b).

The experiments are difficult, but they come down firmly in favor of (b). The universe is non-local; action at a distance is part of nature; and an event here can, under the right circumstances, affect (immediately!) another one far away.

Faster-than-light communication?

Unfortunately, no. To achieve communication, some information must be *transferred* after we have made our observation on one of the two particles. Say that we created a thousand particle pairs. Half the particles fly away together on a spaceship, and their sister particles stay here. Now we test the ones that are here, and observe their spin. We now know what the spins of the other particles must be — but we can't tell our colleagues on the ship! And they don't know if we have done those measurements or not, since when *they* do measurements, they find no pattern to the spins, even if those spins were determined by what we did here. If we could somehow *affect* the spins that we measure, then the other spins, far away, would change, and we would have a message. But that's exactly what quantum indeterminacy tells us we can't do. We have no control over what we will find when we make the measurements.

Let's change the question. Quantum theory seems to give us a non-local universe, one in which two events can affect each other unconstrained by the speed of light. Once we accept the idea of action at a distance, is there anything else in the quantum world to give us hope that faster-than-light travel or communication might be possible?

There is. We remarked earlier that the quantum jumps between electron states in the Bohr atom do not take place via a succession of intermediate states. They sit in one state, and then they are, with no time of transition, instantaneously in another state. We also pointed out that quantum phenomena are not, as one might think, restricted to the world of the very small, such as atoms and electrons. Superconductivity is a purely quantum phenomenon. Might there be some sort of "quantum jumping" associated with it, which could allow events in one place to affect events in another, unconstrained by the speed of light?

Ten years ago, I think that every physicist would have said no, just as every physicist would probably have said we would not have superconductors operating at liquid nitrogen temperatures before 1990. Today, we are at the "could be" stage. If we can, by our experiments, show that *some* events — even one pair of events — far apart in space are coupled, then the universe permits action at a distance. Once we admit that, since *all* the universe was once intimately coupled (at the time of the Big Bang — see the article, "Something for Nothing") then it may be just as coupled today, albeit in unobservable ways.

In the case of superconductivity, the theory tells us that the whole superconductor constitutes a single quantum state. If it changes that state, *all* the superconductor changes. However, we can make a superconducting ring or cylinder of any size we choose. If a change of state is induced at one end of it, that state change appears immediately at the other end, and should be measurable.

With the increased availability of superconducting materials, we seem to be just one step away from a great potential breakthrough — a practical test to make one part of a superconducting device respond to another, unconstrained by the limitation of light-speed.

And if it does not? Then we are back to the drawing boards. Quantum theory is even more subtle and complex than it appears today. The soul-searching and agonizing of the world's greatest physicists for the past sixty years will go on, perhaps until a unified understanding of gravity and quantum theory is achieved.

5. THE COMING TRIUMPH

We suddenly had a new view of the world, one which was so radically different from all that came before that the older generation of scientists could never fully comprehend it. Many of them would, in fact, spend their remaining years trying to refute it.

The new theory was full of totally unfamiliar concepts; just as bad, it called for the use of mathematical techniques quite unlike any needed for earlier models of the universe. Worse yet, the mathematics contained at its heart deep paradoxes, with processes of thought that defied all logic.

Only the new, upstart generation of scientists were able to master that new mathematics, resolve those paradoxes, absorb and be comfortable with the new world-view, and finally transform it to a subject easy enough to be taught in any school. . . .

I am not referring to quantum theory.

I am talking about the theories of motion and universal gravitation developed by Isaac Newton, and presented to the world in the "Principia Mathematica" in 1687.

Newton introduced the concepts of absolute space and absolute time, alien ideas to people who had always thought in terms of the *relative* positions of objects. He suggested that one set of laws — mathematical laws — governed the whole universe. And he spoke a mathematical language that was too hard for almost all his contemporaries.

Before Newton, astronomical calculations and proofs were geometrical or algebraic. He invented the calculus, and then made it a central mathematical tool, to be learned and used if the new system of the world was to be explored and understood. That same calculus, in its notions of limiting processes, brought into existence philosophical questions and logical paradoxes that would take a century and a half to dispose of.

And it was only the later generations who would become totally comfortable with the use of the calculus. Not until half a century after Newton's death did the theory become, in the hands of Euler and Lagrange and Laplace, the easy tool, powerful and flexible, that it is today.

Scientists have been struggling with quantum theory, what it means, and what lies at its roots, for over half a century. If the earlier revolution in thought that took place in Newton's time is any guide, a century from now our descendants will look back at our difficulties, and wonder what all the fuss was about. They will see in the 1980's and 1990's the clear trail of the most significant papers, the ones that removed the paradoxes and made quantum theory so simple. They will have absorbed the quantum world-view so thoroughly and so early that they will be unable to comprehend the source of our confusions.

Hindsight is a wonderful thing.

But there's no need to envy our great-great-grandchildren. A hundred years from now, they will surely be struggling with their own surprises, their own paradoxes, their total inability to fathom some new mystery that grew, oak-like, from a small acorn of inconsistency between observation and theory that we are not even aware of today.

Or do I have it completely wrong? Will they be sitting back, with all of nature fully understood and nothing left to baffle them?

I don't know. As Pogo remarked in another context, either way it's a mighty sobering thought.

6.   SOME READING

The articles in this book are intended to be self-contained. However, occasionally I will recommend a few works that I consider well worth finding and reading. Usually these are books, and books moreover written for the non-specialist, rather than journal articles.

This has three advantages. It shortens the list of references. It directs the reader to works available in bookstores rather than only in university libraries; and it points to works with a higher level of readability than the original source material.

It also has three less desirable consequences. First, the reader is always at least one step away from primary data sources. Second, popular texts sometimes gain readability at the expense of accuracy and detail. And third, books normally lag journals by at least a year or two, thus the information that they contain is less current.

Gribbin, J. *In Search Of Schrödinger's Cat*. Bantam, 1984. Clear, readable, and complete (as much as any book *can* be complete, when the subject is quantum theory).

Gamow, G. *Thirty Years That Shook Physics*. Dover reprint of Doubleday text, 1966. With the author's own strange sketches of the people described. Here is one quotation that gives you the feel for the whole thing: "It often happens that 'absent-minded professor' stories grow up around famous scientists. In most cases these stories are not true, merely the invention of wags, but in the case of Dirac all the stories are really true, at least in the opinion of this writer. For the benefit of future historians we give some of them here."

The Born-Einstein Letters. Max Born, Editor. Walker & Company, New York, 1971. Great men, in every sense, and great letters. You see quantum theory as it was being developed.

Feynman, R.P. *The Character of Physical Law*. MIT Press, 1967. Thoughts on the nature of physics, by another of the century's greatest physicists.

Penrose, R. *The Emperor's New Mind*. Oxford University Press, 1989. This book is fascinating but controversial, since its main thesis is that the human brain is not an algorithmic device (i.e., we are not "computers made of meat"). However, it is not that thought, but an important sub-text, that concerns us here. Penrose argues that the collapse of the quantum wave function upon observation is caused not by anything as subjective as the observation itself, but by the fact that the observation creates a critical space-time curvature, at which point the assumption of linear superposition of quantum theory breaks down.

NIGHTMARES OF
THE CLASSICAL MIND

". . . the quantum mechanics paradoxes, which can truly be said to be the nightmares of the classical mind."
> —Ilya Prigogine, Nobel Prizewinner, 1977

We had come to re-animate a corpse.

GOG filled the sky ahead of us, eight kilometers long, a dark, silent figure nailed to a giant cross of metal girders.

We were silent, too. Vilfredo Germani was taking us to a rendezvous at the center of the crucifix, but until we arrived at the Glory Of God there was nothing to do but gather around the forward screen and stare at the looming figure.

"Not a glimmer there," said Celia Germani at last. "Nothing."

"What did you expect? A pilot light?" Her father did not turn to look at her. We were less than ten kilometers from GOG.

She gave me a nudge in the ribs with her elbow, and a second later her hand crept like a little mouse into mine. She scratched her nails gently against my palm.

"That's not so daft as you might think," said Malcolm McCollum. He was the fourth member of the experimental crew, and our expert on anything to do with power systems. "If GOG was set up to run off solar power, there might still be systems ticking over. In fact, I'm hoping there will be. It'll make start-up a lot easier."

Vilfredo Germani said nothing more, but he shook his head. He must have checked the status of the Glory Of God before he made his proposal, and if he thought there was no power on GOG he was probably right. But after Thomas Madison's death, the return to Earth had been so random and disorganized that anything was possible. No one had a clear idea which sections were still airtight, which power systems had been left on to drain the reserves, or even if everyone on GOG had got away safely. Was there still the possibility of a desiccated corpse or two in one of the station's convoluted corridors?

I said nothing at all about that thought. As a late addition and supernumerary to the party, I was supposed to work hard and keep my mouth shut. The original exploration group was to have been just the Germanis, father and daughter, plus McCollum and the shuttle pilots. It was only Celia's wheedling that had persuaded her father to add me to the group at the last moment.

We drew steadily closer to the main dock. The detailed plans of the Glory Of God had been a big secret, but we knew the general layout. The long arm of the cross was eight kilometers long, and the short arm five kilometers. However, the living quarters were all contained in a sphere about three hundred meters in diameter on the far side of the cross, and the Christ-figure itself was no more than a thin translucent skin stretched over a metal frame of girders. The purpose of the Glory Of God had been effect. Thomas Madison had planned the whole system with that in mind. GOG moved in sun-synchronous polar orbit, roughly eight hundred kilometers high, which meant that the cross was visible at nine-thirty every evening (prime time, if you want to be cynical) from almost everywhere on Earth. Seen from the surface, GOG was a shining emblem in the sky, bigger than the full Moon. As its designer had intended, the sight was breathtaking.

But Vilfredo Germani was a theoretical physicist, not a religious leader. He was interested in other uses of GOG, and visual effects were of no interest to him. As the Shuttle performed its final closing he became more intense and preoccupied. The funding foundations and government grant committees knew Germani as a gregarious, affable man, the most lucid and persuasive salesman for his ideas that could be imagined. They would not have recognized the twitchy, dark-faced fanatic who peered anxiously at the forward screen.

To be honest, I was no less nervous. GOG had been the home and personal vision of Thomas Madison, the Hand of

God, the People's Friend, the Living Word, the Great Healer. Thomas Madison, born Eric Kravely, poor and lecherous and angry until at thirty-two he had given up selling perfumes and found his true vocation. Contributors who gave enough (five million dollars, according to the Press, but they had that figure too low) were flown out to GOG, for a personal audience and special treatment. That included visions guaranteed to send them home reeling, their minds receptive to even bigger suggestions of support. Those special effects had never been documented. If they were still operating, our visit might be wilder than Germani realized.

We docked, and that ended my speculations. The Shuttle operated in a shirt-sleeve environment, but the inside of GOG would be, at least initially, exposed to the vacuum and temperatures of open space. The four of us climbed into our suits. In spite of all our practicing, Celia seemed to have no idea what she was doing, and I had to help her with the clasps and seals.

The attitude control system of GOG was still functioning, and it held the Christ-figure always pointing toward Earth. That displayed a clean-lined, beautiful design, the best that money could buy. However, the dock and living quarters were on the far side, hidden from Earth-view, and our final approach had told quite a different story. The back of GOG was little more than an open frame, with the habitation sphere attached to the center of the cross. We could see the crude welds on the girders, and a tangle of cables that held the whole structure in balance. Everything looked dark, and somehow dirty, as though it had hung there in space for a million years. The Shuttle ship that Thomas Madison used to bring his visitors to GOG had, by no accident, lacked observation ports.

It was typical of Vilfredo Germani that our approach to GOG was televised, and that his first act when we were inside the Glory Of God was to tape a lecture for subsequent transmission. He had his sponsors to satisfy, and although he was a superb scientist he had even better showman's instincts. Thomas Madison would have appreciated him.

However, the television program could also be considered a foolhardy act. Madison's followers had not died with him. To millions of the faithful, back on Earth, the invasion of the Glory Of God for secular purposes was simple sacrilege. It had been six years now, but the followers were still loyal and Madison had always attracted extremists. When he returned home, Germani would be a target for everything from vilification to assassination attempts.

With McCollum's help I set up the camera just inside the dock. A corridor leading to the interior of GOG stretched away dark behind Germani's suited figure, and added a suitable element of mystery. While I adjusted the camera angle, McCollum searched around for a power outlet. He tested it with an ammeter, and grunted with satisfaction.

"Still juice here. That's going to save us a whole lot of trouble." Bright fluorescents came on, and threw a harsh pattern of yellow light and black shadows across the beams and partitions of the chamber. Germani looked around him, nodded at me to start recording, and stared straight into the camera.

"The question has been with us now for more than forty years," he said easily. "Is spacetime quantized, and if so, how? We hope that in the next two weeks we will be able to provide a definite answer."

I had heard him talk before, and he knew all the tricks. If he had not happened to have the talent to be a top scientist, he would have made his living easily as a salesman. Grab them in the first second, and then you can give your spiel at leisure. Not that the average person would consider spacetime quantization much of a grabber, but Germani was now addressing his funding agencies, science writers, and fellow scientists (in roughly that order).

"Planck and Einstein and Bohr started this," he went on, "over a century ago. Planck first proposed that in certain circumstances energy must be emitted only in discrete units — quanta — rather than being continuous. Einstein extended that idea to more general circumstances, and then Bohr applied it to the electronic transitions in atoms. We can call this process *first quantization*, the quantization of energy levels and energy emission."

It was astonishing to see how his manner changed when the camera was on him. Germani modeled his public presence on his fellow-countryman, fellow physicist, and idol, Enrico Fermi. A few minutes ago he had been nervous and jumpy, now even with the confining presence of the spacesuit he was all relaxed affability. There was even a self-deprecating little smile on his face, as though to say that he knew the audience was familiar with all this, but he had to repeat it anyway.

"The next step was taken about 1930," he went on. "Heisenberg, Pauli and Dirac quantized the electromagnetic field itself — *second quantization*." As he spoke the lights in the chamber flickered and dimmed to a level much too low for the cameras. Germani swore, changed at once into an irritable physicist, and swung round to McCollum.

"What the devil's this? I thought we had electric power."

While he was speaking, the lights dropped even further. A deep, throbbing hum sounded in my ears (radio-frequency induction in my suit). A blue haze filled the airless chamber, and within it flashing letters formed: THE GLORY OF GOD, THE GLORY OF GOD, THE GLORY OF GOD.

I heard Celia's gasp. "What's happening?"

"Part of the visitors' reception routine." I was already heading along the entry corridor, followed closely by Malcolm McCollum. "The system must still be turned on, we triggered it when we docked. Now we have to find the power control center."

McCollum was moving on past me. "Which way?" he asked over his suit phone. We had come to a branch in the corridor.

"This one, for a bet." I took the upward leg and followed it for twenty meters, until I found myself at an airlock. "This is the way to the real interior. I'll go back for the others. I'll bet the welcoming system switches off as soon as there's no one in the chamber."

McCollum grunted as he moved to study the lock controls. "You may be right, Jimmy. Go do it. Maybe you'll be more useful than I thought. I'm going to have a go at this airlock. If we have a breathable atmosphere inside things will go a lot easier setting up our experiment."

As I returned to the docking area I took a closer look at the corridor walls. GOG had been deserted and empty for six years now, circling the globe like a dark monument to Madison's dreams. We were the first people to set foot on the habitat in all that time, but once the lights were on everything still shone new and gleaming. The Glory Of God.

By the time that I got there Germani had become tired of waiting and returned to the Shuttle to oversee the unloading of his experimental equipment. The crates were floating in now, seven of them. Celia was opening each one and inspecting the contents. These instruments would remain in vacuum — they were designed to do so — until they could be deployed in precise positions along GOG's unequal arms.

Everything had survived the trip up from Earth, and by the time that Germani reappeared and heard that the equipment was fine, air and full power were available in the interior. Suddenly the head of the party was beaming again, waving his hands and eager to get out of his suit.

Time to celebrate. We had finished Phase One of what Vilfredo Germani unblushingly described as "the most important physics experiment ever performed by humans."

Celia Germani is short and blond; ash blond, North Italian blond. Left uncombed — as it usually is — the hair of her head clusters to tight ringlets. She disdains the use of makeup. Her skin is naturally dark, and she loves to sunbathe naked. It is a surprise to find fair, sun-baked hair on her tanned legs, in her armpits, and in a broad, golden swath along her belly from pubes to navel.

Before I sought out Celia she was, in her own charming words, "almost a virgin" at twenty-seven. Blame that on her father. He had turned the mind of his only child so effectively to physics that until I came on the scene there had been no time for much else. Now Celia wanted to make up for lost opportunities.

Five hours after our arrival at GOG, the first stage of the occupation was complete. We had chosen living quarters not far from the main lock, set up our monitors for air and power, eaten a makeshift meal, and gone to bed. In the excitement of liftoff, ascent, and rendezvous, no one had slept for thirty-six hours.

As soon as McCollum and Germani were out of sight, Celia drifted into my room. She slipped off her clothes and wriggled into my sleeping bag. "Jimmy?"

"No."

She giggled. "Here I am."

"Don't you ever sleep?" I responded to her kiss, but my head was full of my own thoughts and worries. I did not want company.

"Jimmy, we're in freefall. Remember?"

I remembered. It had been a point of persuasion to Celia, one reason for my presence with the experimental party. Sex in zero gee. I had talked of it as an ecstatic experience, making up the details as I went along. Now Celia was calling me on it.

My body did its part, willingly if not enthusiastically. Perhaps the lack of gravity did add some extra dimension to our actions, for although my mind was calm and detached as Celia gasped and shuddered against me, I had the feeling of consciousness expanding outward, concentric waves of my awareness that swelled to encompass the whole of GOG. Something was out there, something strange.

While we lay coupled I wandered mentally through the rest of the habitat's interior, the part that we had not yet explored. We had encountered no more of Thomas Madison's planned miracles, but even without them the Glory Of God induced a feeling of uneasiness, of events poised to happen.

I wondered. What had they left behind here, the followers of Madison, when they fled to Earth?

The Church of Christ Ascendant, the heart of Madison's empire, had collapsed at the moment of his death, days before the organization was due to be hit by Earth authorities with tax evasion and criminal charges. The staff had hurried away from the Glory Of God, panic-stricken that they might be stranded five hundred miles above the Earth. Many of them had arrived on the surface just in time to be sent to jail for fraud and extortion.

The habitat had emptied with no long goodbyes, no attempt to put the place into mothballs, no time to put the power supplies on standby status. (Will the last person to leave the Glory Of God please turn out the lights.)

I had learned the details of Madison's death through the news media, just like anyone else. To his devout followers it was not the fact of his death that was intolerable; it was its ignominious nature.

Part of Madison's plan required that he return to Earth from GOG every month or two for personal contacts and minor miracles. Everywhere he went he offered gifts: printed prayers, signed photographs, little silvery reproductions of GOG. To his minor contributors, people who had given fifty dollars, there was a little plastic telescope, cost maybe a quarter, that would let you see the details on the orbiting cross quite easily. For the skeptics, or those who were wavering, he would call on the power of Faith and hold his hand in a naked flame without being burned, stop his heart for two minutes, or stare full into the sun without being blinded.

The little tricks were nothing in themselves, but they added to his image.

Image: he was all image, crafted by the most skillful and professional public relations campaign in history. GOG's messages were sent by television and radio to two hundred countries, and to every one he projected a different personality, even used a different name. He was Thomas Madison only in the United States. Was he really an American, a Chinese, a Russian, Brazilian, or European? No one could say. Subtle plastic surgery had shaped his nose just so, adjusted the spacing and shape of his eyes, modelled his cheekbones, defined his hairline. Surgery had given him the features of the world, made him a face for all nations. Few people knew the man behind the facade, but everyone agreed on one thing: compared with Thomas Madison, every previous religious leader and fund-raiser had been a fumbling amateur.

And then he had been destroyed, six years ago, by something so stupid.

Women threw themselves at Madison when he visited Earth; young and old, ugly and beautiful, rich and poor. He could have had discreet affairs with a hundred or a thousand of them. Instead he took the wife of Jack Burdon, his oldest friend and staunchest supporter. Burdon led the Church of Christ Ascendant in Australia. He would do anything for Madison, but when he caught the two of them in the act on Madison's two-hundred foot yacht he had gone temporarily crazy. According to his own confession he had shot Madison five times in the head, slit his throat, and thrown the body to the sharks and saltwater crocodiles that patrol the coast of northern Australia. He had beaten his wife so severely that she was now a grinning vegetable. Then Burdon had told everything he knew to the international police and the taxation authorities, providing the evidence that sent a couple of hundred top people in the Church to jail.

A great financial empire (fifty billion dollars, tax free, and still growing) had vanished between a woman's thighs. Audits revealed that most of the money had vanished with it, like rain on dry sand, leaving no sign of its existence.

There remained of Madison's ministry only the bewildered followers, still grieving for what they had lost, and this empty shell, the Glory Of God, sweeping dark and silent through the star-filled sky. How many people, every night, still looked up longingly and hoped for the return of the glittering cross?

Celia interrupted my thoughts, gripping me hard and whispering in my ear. "Jimmy. What's that — do you hear it?"

It was a murmur of sound, coming from all around us. The whole body of GOG was in tiny movement, creaking and flexing, a Titan stretching in his sleep.

I groped at my side until I found my watch and looked at its luminous dial. "It's nothing bad. We'll get this every fifty minutes or so."

"But what is it?"

"Thermal cycling. GOG goes in and out of Earth-shadow every orbit, cools down or heats up. Everything contracts or expands."

She snuggled against me, enfolding me with her arms and legs. "You're so smart. You could be anything you want to be. How did I live before I had you?" She moved one hand to stroke my chest, running her fingers up along my collarbone and into the hollow of my neck. "You'll never find anyone who loves you as much as I do. Never. Tell me you love me, Jimmy. Tell me you don't know how you lived before you found me."

Just a couple more days, I said to myself. Then I told Celia that I loved her. I did not tell her how I lived before I found her.

The next morning we were ready to go on with Germani's experiment. Malcolm McCollum was at GOG's main power board, checking circuits. I was with him, making my own analysis of the places where power had been available when we first arrived at the habitat.

McCollum patched in the compact fusion unit that we brought up from Earth, then paused with his big fist clamped on one of the switches. "Now this would be a real fun test. If I throw it, we light up the whole of GOG. Ninety megawatts. We only draw half that for the experiment."

I looked at my watch and shook my head. "Don't do it, Mac. We're on the night side. People down there would get the wrong idea."

"Ah." He grinned at me. "Nice thought, though — get the religious maggots a bit excited. But you're probably right, Jimmy. Stay here while I tell Germani we're all set."

I was happy to have time to myself. While McCollum was with Vilfredo Germani I confirmed what I already suspected. One power board, fully operating, was linked to a hidden part of GOG. Some region of the habitat was inaccessible to normal entry. I could trace it by following the power lines.

I did not have time to follow up at once. Germani was bursting with impatience, and Celia and I were sent outside to string the array of interferometers and magnetometers along GOG's jutting arms. The placement was critical, and tightly controlled through an array of lasers. It called for no real thought, but for concentration and steadiness. I found my hands trembling within my suit. I had slept for only a couple of hours. Once Celia had fallen asleep I had wandered the interior of GOG, studying the layout of the habitation sphere.

As we slowly installed the instruments she now reviewed the whole experiment for me. She went into details that I could not possibly have understood. After a few minutes I realized that she was doing it for her own benefit, not mine. It had dawned on me some time ago that although Vilfredo Germani was the showman and fund-raiser, the fundamental ideas came from Celia. She had devised the crucial test for "third quantization" — the test to see if space-time itself had a granular structure, rather than being continuous.

"Not really grains," Celia said now. "More like little loops in twelve-space. And the loops are so small, they can never be observed. Every probe we can devise is twenty orders of magnitude too big. The uncertainty principle guarantees that we will never do any better."

"If you can't hope to measure it, what's the point of the experiment?"

"We look for what's left over. Residual effects." She was peering at a Mössbauer calibrator, locking the position of an array of magnetometers to one part in a million billion. "The individual twists can't be observed, but there are residual effects of their interaction. Remember, things don't have to be seen directly to have physical meaning. Think of black holes. Think of quarks."

Soon after I found Celia, I had asked her what *use* the Germani theory and experiment could be. What did it matter what was going on, if it was happening at a scale a sextillion times too small to see?

Celia had chided me. "It doesn't matter *today*, but in fifty or a hundred years it will change the whole world. We're not talking a minor experiment, you know. This is a lot bigger than Michelson-Morley, it's probing the roots of reality itself. What we're doing will go into all the schoolbooks one day, like Newton's apple and Einstein's falling elevator. When experiment confirms our theory, we'll kill all the quantum dragons with one thrust."

Quantum dragons. The way Celia described them, the quantum paradoxes were real dragons, destroying physicists everywhere with their razor teeth and fiery breath. Schrödinger's cat, Wigner's friend and infinite regression, Everett and Wheeler's many worlds, Chang's cascade, Ponteira's dilemma; the dragons gnawed away at the roots of the tree of physics, and no one had been able to slay them. They all involved the same questions: what was the condition of the quantum state vector, before and after observation? How did observation change it? For most of a century, scientists had possessed a set of computational procedures that allowed them to make calculations of quantum phenomena. But it was a set of *ad hoc* methods that happened to give the right answers. Beneath them was the void, populated only by paradoxes.

If spacetime itself were quantized in a certain way, said the Germani theory, then all those paradoxes could be disposed of at once. The theory also suggested a crucial experiment, and until that was performed Vilfredo and Celia Germani had done no more than propose an interesting hypothesis. Fortunately the experiment was within reach of today's technology — just. It called for the use of a large, minimally-active structure and a microgravity environment. There was exactly one known body that fitted the requirement: GOG.

The media found a certain irony in the fact that Germani could use Thomas Madison's facilities on GOG to seek a truth that Madison himself would have hated. In his preaching, he had described science as a sinful delusion and a tool of Satan.

Germani, gifted fund-raiser that he was, could not afford to buy GOG, or even to rent its use. No one could. After Madison died his revenues had been declared taxable income, and the Church was hit for billions in unpaid taxes. It had no money left, and the top officials were lucky if they stayed out of jail. So the property had been taken over by the U.S. Government. But it was worthless — and inaccessible — to almost everyone. The habitat had a good orbit for an automated spacecraft, but a very bad one for most crewed facilities.

Vilfredo Germani had gone to the government with a clever proposal. He asked for the use of GOG and all its facilities, free, for six months. It would remain government property, and any inventions or patents that developed as a result of the experiment would belong jointly to the government and to Germani. The government would also share revenue from sale of media rights. More than that, Germani would pay all costs of the transportation and the experimental equipment. From the government point of view, it was a no-risk proposal.

From our personal point of view, though, it was far from risk-free. We would be generating a huge pulse of power, confined and applied in a novel way. Germani had made one fact very clear to me and to Malcolm McCollum: a second reason for performing the experiment out in space was because of possible unpredicted physical effects.

The experiment had been scheduled to take place when GOG was traveling over the United States. In addition to our live broadcast, television cameras in every major city would be pointed upwards, hoping to observe some visible evidence of the result — hoping also, I suspected, for unforeseen calamity and associated fireworks. Successful physics experiments make less interesting news than disasters.

Two hours before the experiment was scheduled to begin, we had evidence that GOG was still capable of producing its own surprises.

McCollum was concluding a full-scale dry run, feeding energy through the network. As the power input reached a maximum, every sound in the interior — even the ones that we were making ourselves — faded to inaudibility. In that unnatural hush, a whispering voice spoke in our ears, just loud enough to be understood, "Vengeance is mine, saith the Lord. I will repay. Vengeance is mine."

It was Thomas Madison's recorded voice, we knew that. Just as we knew that the God of Thomas Madison was the rough god of the Old Testament, a deity of revenge, blood, and savage justice. "Vengeance is mine," could have been the slogan of the Church, a *leitmotif* that ran through all the broadcasts and promotional materials. Madison had made the fate of unbelievers very clear. They would burn in hell — he described that hell in gruesome detail — for eternity, with no hope of salvation. Curiously, this seemed to be one of the Church of Christ Ascendant's main attractions. The faithful sent letters in with their contributions, proposing new torments.

Madison's enemies mocked him and denounced his miracles as expensive fakes. Just gimmicky effects. That was easy to do sitting in front of a television screen on Earth, but here on GOG, with that soft, menacing voice in your ear . . .

Well, we all shivered a little, I think, before McCollum could isolate the circuit involved, and cut it out of the power system. There was no thought of postponing the experiment. Germani had made commitments. The show must go on.

He had the action organized as tightly as a ballet, with himself at the center of attention. Celia had a minor role, and no one else would appear. I had been banished to the power control room with Vilfredo Germani's direct order to "keep an eye on things." And stay out of the way, said his tone. The experiment was in three phases, extending over a four-hour period. Germani did not want to see me in the main chamber with the recording cameras during that interval.

It suited my needs perfectly. I had decided that the best possible time for me to do what I had to do would be during the experiment. The others would be so focused on that, they wouldn't even think of me.

I went to the power control room and waited. Forty minutes before zero hour, I left that assigned position and moved down the long axis of GOG, heading for a region that was supposed to be nothing more than unused storage space. Within two hundred meters I had come to the outer bulkhead and triple hull. Beyond them should be nothing but vacuum. I knew differently. Hidden power lines, concealed within ventilation shafts, ran on and through the thick metal wall. They had to lead somewhere.

It took five minutes to find the key. Electrically activated, part of the bulkhead slid aside, producing a circular opening six feet across. I had put on my suit before I left the power room, but I did not need it. The aperture led to another set of chambers, each with a breathable atmosphere. The different parts of GOG when we had arrived had been at wildly differing temperatures, depending on the orientation of each section relative to the Sun and on thermal coupling to other parts. This set of chambers had its own triply-redundant thermostats and was precisely controlled to twenty degrees above freezing point.

The first three rooms were concentric shells of living space, each well-equipped with entertainment materials and with receiving equipment for broadcasts from Earth. They also possessed heavy wall shielding against the effects of solar flares, but they were otherwise conventional.

The fourth, and innermost . . .

I opened the door, held my breath. In the center of the room stood the blue-gray barrel of a Schindler hibernation unit. Eighteen million dollars of desperation. Badly wounded or sick patients could live in one of these almost indefinitely, intravenously fed and with body functions ticking over at just a few degrees above zero, until donor organs or improved medical techniques gave them a chance of recovery.

But you didn't have to be sick. I examined the settings and found a quintuply-redundant group of timing units, each set to trigger nine months from now. I overrode all of them, initiated immediate reawakening, and sat down on the floor in front of the unit.

Even at fastest reanimation, it would take a while. The heart activity trace had been showing one beat per minute. Now as drugs dripped in through the I/V's, the body temperature crept up, a degree every hundred and forty seconds. The pulse rate rose with it.

The minutes dragged on. I waited. In half an hour the over-head lights flickered.

I looked at my watch. The first part of Germani's experiment was in full swing, and I was seeing the effects of the power drain. Helical surges of magnetic field ran the length of GOG now, tightening on themselves. This was the most direct test of third quantization, but also the least sensi-tive. Celia didn't hold out much hope for it — the second test, two hours from now, was the one she said she would bet her money on.

Body temperature, seventy-eight degrees. The bronchospi-rometer showed that breathing was at normal levels and had near-normal gaseous composition. There ought to be stirrings of consciousness within the Schindler unit. I peered in through the narrow plastic cover on the upper rim, and could see nothing. The heartbeat was strong at forty-seven. My own pulse was up over a hundred. I closed my eyes, and told myself that three quarters of an hour was nothing compared with six years.

I had never seen a Schindler unit in operation before. When the reawakening cycle was complete, what happened? The reanimated subject was not likely to pop out like a piece of bread in a toaster, but I dared not open it from the outside in case I was too soon.

Finally there was a sigh from inside the unit, a protest at sleep disturbed. The lock on the front of the unit clicked. The door did not open, but it was now unsecured. I reached out a cold and trembling hand, pulled gently, and a moment later I was staring in on the dazed face of Thomas Madison.

"Jack?" he said uncertainly. He lifted his head a few inches from the supporting web. "Jack?"

"Jack Burdon is dead, Eric." I spoke slowly and clearly. "This is Jim."

He gasped, and his face took on the expression I had waited years to see. "Where am — what did—" He could speak, but only just.

"You're up here on the Glory Of God, Eric. Everything worked out just the way you planned."

He was doing his best to move forward, but he was still feeble. I thrust him back with one hand. He shivered and cowered away within the unit. "But Jack — what happened to Jack?"

"*Vengeance is mine*, Eric. Remember? Your favorite line. You want to know how I found out? There were rumors, they came through the grapevine even when I was in prison. Wild talk of resurrection. It made no sense, not with Thomas Madison dead. But they never found a body, did they? That made me think. And then I learned that they never found the Church's money, either. I went to see Jack when I got out, and he told me everything he knew."

He shook his head.

"He wouldn't talk, you mean?" I said. "Not loyal old Jack. Ah, but you're wrong. He just needed persuasion, some of the treatment he gave his wife. Why did you make Jack an insider, Eric, and not me? I was with you longer than he was."

He couldn't speak, but I knew the answer. Even Jack Burdon had been told only a small part of it. When you plan something so big, the fewer people involved, the better.

"Jim, I couldn't tell you. Don't you see that, I had to keep everything tight — keep it secret." His voice was coming back, his face showed a trace of color, and with that came a little more courage. "It was falling apart on us, you knew that as well as I did. We had to wrap it up, lie low and start over. But I wouldn't have forgotten you."

I leaned forward and pressed his windpipe, not hard enough to cut off breathing. "Now that, I'm prepared to believe. I know the grand design. Want me to tell it to you? I had it from Jack when he was too far gone for lying."

It was clean and simple. Thomas Madison dead and gone, vanished for seven years, until the heat was off the Church. Jack Burdon and a couple of others with enough money and resources to make sure that the Glory Of God went unvisited. Then, the whispers around the Earth. Thrilling words, of death and transfiguration. After exactly seven years (numbers are important) the Glory Of God, long dead and lifeless, blazes forth again in the night sky. Thomas Madison, resurrected on GOG, broadcasts again to all the people of Earth.

"The New Dawn," I said. "That would be the Word. And for anyone from the old order? Most of us died in prison, the way we were supposed to. Special bad treatment, bought and paid for with Church funds. But you wouldn't have forgotten the rest of us — until we were gone, and it was safe to forget us."

He didn't bother to deny it. His eyes looked from side to side, avoiding me. I noticed that his appearance was slightly different. He had been *enhanced*, features thinner, eyes wider and more gleaming to fit the image of a reborn prophet.

"I wouldn't have hurt you, Jim," he said at last. "I wouldn't. Not my own brother."

"Wouldn't hurt me? Five years in that stinking South American prison, with the filth and the lice and the bad water." I pressed harder on his throat. "I was supposed to die there. But we're tough, aren't we, the Kravely boys? You don't kill us with rat bites and with rotting garbage instead of food. We thrive on it. We lie in our rags, and we think."

He was slowly suffocating. His hands were pushing at me, but he was too weak.

"I got out of prison, Eric, and I did what I had to." I couldn't help myself, I was pressing harder on his windpipe. "I had my talk with Jack Burdon. Found out about Vilfredo Germani, then fawned and grovelled to meet him, that egocentric little Italian shit. Screwed Celia Germani until she couldn't see straight, even though she's hairy and sweaty and I've had more fun fucking the monkeys they brought in to the Sao Paulo jail. Ass-kissed and fornicated my way up here. I did it, Eric. I did it all, whatever it took. You wouldn't hurt me, you say? Then I'm not hurting you."

He was dying, jerking in the harness. I wanted to slow down, to keep him alive, to make it last. I had looked forward to this moment for a year, savoring the idea. But I couldn't hold back. When I had myself under control he lolled already lifeless in the Schindler hibernation unit.

I looked at his starting eyes and swung the unit closed. All my anger drained away as I turned to leave the chamber. And there, in the doorway, stood Celia Germani.

Her face was pasty-white and her eyes lacked focus. She was not wearing a suit, and I could see her midriff quivering. "I came to find you," she said tonelessly. "The second phase of the experiment is going to start. I wanted you to be there with me. There were signs from Phase One that this will give us just what we need, so I wanted you with me to see it."

Celia was on autopilot, babbling randomly because she did not know what else to do. But I knew exactly what to do. She had seen me kill my brother, probably heard what I said, knew who I was.

She had to go out of the airlock. I could snap my suit closed, take her there, and hold her during evacuation. Accident, someone new to space. Nothing to point to me.

I started forward.

She must have read my face, because she turned and tried to flee. Too late. I grabbed a fistful of her blond, curly hair and stopped her before she could move two feet. At that point her legs and arms went limp and I was able to drag her along with me easily.

No point in speech. I reached up with one hand to close my suit, holding her firmly in the other, and moved as fast as I could. It was more than a hundred meters to the nearest lock, back the way I had come. We seemed to take forever, but I did not expect to meet anyone. Germani and McCollum were too wrapped up in the experiment. When we had gone maybe fifty meters, a whining sound came from the walls of GOG.

Celia began to struggle in my grasp. "Phase Two," she cried, in the tones of a prayer. "Oh, Phase Two."

We were close to the maximum point of field intensity. The whine became a shriek, the shriek an insane howl; the whole structure went into rapid vibration. The oscillation continued. The outlines of walls and fixtures softened like a tuning fork at the moment of striking.

I froze and tightened my grip on Celia. After a few more seconds our surroundings steadied and firmed.

But Celia was no longer distinct to my eyes. She blurred, split, became two fuzzy images. One of them was pulling hard to free herself, the other slumped hopelessly in my arms. The images shivered, split again.

Celia was free, flying away down the corridor.

Celia was pulling hard against my grip.

Celia had bent her head to my right hand and was biting it hard.

Celia was fainting in my arms.

Celia was stabbing at my eyes with a knife from the pocket of her uniform.

Celia lay senseless where I had flung her against the corridor wall.

Celia . . .

. . . blurred and split, blurred and split, blurred and split. The chamber was filled with phantom Celia's, running, turning, struggling, attacking, biting, fainting, bleeding, weeping, screaming.

I tried to grapple with them, all of them. But now I was dividing, holding Celia with a hundred hands that became a thousand hands that became an uncountable infinity of hands. I beat at the flying shapes and felt myself spread all along the corridor. I willed my body — all my bodies — to turn and fly back the way I had come. The spectral Celia's suddenly vanished. At last I could move. There was a wrenching, sideways jerk as I encountered and passed through some central focus of the field, then I was coalescing once more to a single body.

Back I went to the innermost chamber, slamming the external lock. I sagged against it as it clanged tight. Suddenly I felt safe.

But how safe? For all I knew the rest of GOG had been destroyed completely by Phase Two of Germani's experiment. After I had felt reality crumble and fission and fragment, it was hard to know what was left.

I went to the display screens and turned them on with frozen fingers. They showed news broadcasts beamed up from Earth. At least that much of GOG was working. I flicked from channel to channel, expecting every one to have live coverage of the experiment.

There was nothing, not a single mention. Finally I discovered a news show with one small item about Vilfredo

Germani. He had just announced that he would seek government permission to perform some type of experiment on the Glory Of God space habitat. The show was mostly interested in the protests of Madison's old followers.

That had happened nine months ago. I remembered the event. Yet here I was, alive, breathing. Nine months ago neither Vilfredo nor Celia Germani knew that I existed.

A frightening realization crept into my mind. No one knew I was here. I was alone on GOG, without food or water. I could not survive for nine months, not even for one month. Even a crash rescue operation would take longer than that to reach me.

I switched off the display screens and moved to a chair.

Action, not panic. There was an answer, and it was here in the chamber with me: the Schindler hibernation unit. It could sustain me almost indefinitely, until a Shuttle could be sent from Earth.

But first I had to remove Eric's body and dispose of it. I moved across to the unit, studying it for the first time since I had re-entered the chamber. I stopped in shock. The chamber was active. A heartbeat trace showed, forty beats a minute. Body temperature, sixty-eight degrees. Light but steady breathing.

I thought I had killed Eric — surely I had killed him. But my brother had returned from the dead. *Vengeance is mine.*

I shivered. After a moment, rational thought returned. There must have been a flicker of life in him when I left, and the hibernation unit had done what it was supposed to do for a sick occupant. It had taken the steps necessary for survival.

I hesitated for no more than a moment. What I had done once, I could do again; this time, more thoroughly. Eric would have to die.

Action. I seized the door and canceled the lock, noting the warning message — PREMATURE OPENING MAY BE A LIFE-THREATENING ACT — that appeared on the display. A flurry of activity came from the unit's monitors, determined to sustain the life within in every way possible.

I ignored the messages and the sensor readings. If it came to a fight between me and the hibernation unit, I was sure I could win. I knew more roads to death than it knew to life.

I heaved the heavy door open. As I did so it occurred to me that Eric was not dead only because I had never killed him. I laughed at the logic of it. If all that the Germani experiment had done was to throw me back nine months, Eric at that time was still alive. But that could be changed.

I peered inside the unit. And then I could no longer act. I knew I could not win. Reality was not that simple.

I could not win. I *cannot* win, no matter how long I stay here, no matter what I do within this chamber. The quantum dragons, the razor claws that rend the fabric of reality, are too complex. They have won already.

Thomas Madison, the prophet that Eric and I designed together, is no more. A long time ago it had been a joke between us: would he be the incarnation of our ideas, or would I? It had been decided by the toss of a coin, the simplest chance event. Eric became Thomas Madison.

That Thomas Madison is gone now. And Eric may be dead, or perhaps in this Universe he never was. But the living, breathing face that stares peacefully from the hibernation tank is familiar to me, so familiar.

It is my own.

Afterword: *Nightmares of the Classical Mind*

This story developed directly from the article that precedes it. The quotation at the beginning of both, from the works of Ilya Prigogine, seems equally apt for either. And although the one is presented as simple fact and the other as no more than fiction, many people may find the idea of a religious leader who amasses fifty billion dollars from ignorant followers far easier to believe than the counter-intuitive strangeness of quantum theory.

I said the story rose from the article, and that is mainly true; but there was one other influence at work. A few years ago, Sprague de Camp's splendid book, The Ancient Engineers, *was reprinted by Dorset Press. Browsing through the new edition, I was impressed by the desire of the early Egyptian kings to build the biggest possible monuments to their own memory. All they had to work with was stone, earth, and human labor; yet they created the huge Pyramids, and used them to house their own tombs.*

I wondered, what could a modern leader, taking full advantage of television fund-raising methods and modern technology, do to match that? What would he build, and where would he build it to maximize its impact? What is today or tomorrow's equivalent of the Egyptian sarcophagus?

At that point I had a sudden vision of a monstrous illuminated cross, sweeping around the planet in sun-synchronous evening orbit. That at once became GOG, the Glory Of God, a vast crucified Christ figure. My own deep suspicion of the motives of all televangelists did the rest.

I find this a most unpleasant tale, told by an awful person. When it was first published in Asimov's magazine I asked that the first page contain a disclaimer, pointing out that I was not to be confused with the narrator of the story. I would just like to repeat that statement here.

THE DOUBLE SPIRAL STAIRCASE

Seventy degrees. February 1st in Washington. It had no right to be so warm and pleasant. But who was going to complain?

Not Jake Jacobsen. A Waldorf salad, a flounder shipped over fresh that morning from the fishing boats on Maine Avenue, a medium steak, a couple of drinks — well, make that three or four, enough to get a nice little buzz on but not enough to show — and then a leisurely stroll across the Mall back to Independence Avenue; that was what today's blue skies demanded. That was what they got. As he walked, skirting the banners and noisy fervor of a group of Animal Rights Activists, he thought of the old Navy traditions; of raging seas, salt pork and weevil-filled hard tack, foul water, shipwreck, starvation and scurvy. Things had improved quite a bit in two hundred years.

In fact, the only thing missing now was a cigar, a nice Havana Corona.

He vowed to remedy that, as soon as he was back in his office. Smoking was illegal in government offices, but RHIP.

He didn't wear his uniform in the daytime (no point in rubbing it in with the old staff, they still resented the change) but the guards on the front entrance saluted him anyway. As they should. They were all Navy now. He returned the salutes automatically, and walked to the elevators that would take him to the seventh and highest floor, up to his corner office that looked north toward the green expanse of the Mall.

Now *there* was one hell of a contrast. He had been five years locked up in the windowless bowels of the Pentagon, designing the master plan, choreographing industry and OMB and congressional support. And then, at last, had come the exquisitely timed *coup* — there was no other word for it —

that brought the agency under Navy's wing, and him his third star and the position of NASA Administrator.

In fact, he thought as he left the elevator, today's lunch could well be thought of as a small celebration. It was six months to the day since the Act had gone into effect, just two months since his hearings had confirmed him in this job. The war was certainly not over — the damned Air Force would never stop trying to take the lead role in space, he knew that. There were tough times ahead, but he had won the first two battles.

Admiral Jacob Jacobsen pushed open the door of his office, walked to his desk without looking around him, and sat down.

And at that point all of his lunchtime euphoria evaporated.

Someone was already there, in the Important Visitor's seat. There, despite his sternest orders that no one, not even his own wife (hell, least of all his wife) was to be permitted entrance to his office without his approval. And he would certainly never have approved the admission of the scruffy object who sat opposite him.

It had to be that witless oaf Trustrum again, the worst apology for an aide that a man ever had to endure, ignoring direct orders and letting people in using his own sadly inadequate judgment.

Jacobsen thought for a wistful moment of the Old Navy. Not everything today was an improvement. Two hundred years ago he would have had Trustrum flogged for such a gross failure to obey orders. Today, with NASA's insistence on retaining some elements of civilian function, about all he could do was to put an unfavorable and strongly worded memo into Trustrum's personnel file when what he really wanted was to have the man keelhauled and hung from the yardarm. But Trustrum's wife was the Vice President's cousin, and even a memo would probably be pulled before it got into the record. Christ. *Everyone* was somebody's cousin, or uncle, or bedmate, or best college friend. Sometimes he felt that the whole of Washington was glued together into one vast, incestuous, and inefficient snotball.

He stared at the stranger slumped in the chair opposite. The man was overdressed for the warm weather, in thick and shapeless woolen trousers and a heavy, leather-patched tweed jacket. He was also short and stooped and thin to emaciation, with an unhealthy pallor and jutting cheekbones. His remaining hair was combed forward in an unsuccessful attempt to disguise creeping alopecia, and his brown eyes bulged out like a dyspeptic frog's. And, unless Jacobsen's nose was playing tricks, the man smelled. No, he didn't smell, he *stank*. Of something worse than body odor.

Jacobsen grabbed a cigar from the humidor, lit it hurriedly, and put up a defensive smokescreen between them. He leaned far back in his seat.

"I've no idea who you are, Mister, or why you're here, but you can just answer me one question. How in the name of Nelson did you talk that jackass Trustrum into letting you into my private office? And when you've answered that, you can get the hell out of here."

The stranger didn't blink. He held up his hand and displayed a Naval Academy class ring. "I showed Trustrum your picture, Porky. Your picture and mine, next to each other — in the year book. That was all it took."

"Porky! Nobody's called me that for—" Jacobsen leaned forward, peering more closely at the other's protruding eyeballs. "Jesus Christ. The year book. Buggsie. Bug-eyes Bates? Is it really you? For God's sake, what happened? You look like hell."

The other man frowned. "Same thing as happened to you, old buddy. We got old. Take a peek in the mirror, you don't look too hot yourself. I bet your blood pressure is double your IQ. And that's not styrofoam stuffed down your suit, it's a hundred pounds of lard. But we'll not get much done if we sit here trading smart-ass insults, the way we did in the old days. Don't you have the graciousness to offer a cigar to a classmate and a might-have-been — except for what you did, Porky — fellow *matelot*? Remember that?"

Buggsie Bates leaned forward and helped himself to a cigar as he spoke. He didn't light it, but sat there smiling an inscrutable smile.

Jacobsen cleared his throat.

"Hey, Buggsie, that was a long time ago. We were all young and wild. Nobody meant you any harm. I'm damned sure I didn't."

"Mebbe. But you doped her up and knocked her up and put her in my bed. And you went on and got the three stars, while I just got the shaft." Bates waved the cigar in a circular motion in the air. "It's all right, Porky. No need to start hunting for the panic button, I'm not here to settle thirty-year-old scores from Academy days. And I'm going to give you more stars than you ever dreamed of. When they canned my ass from the Navy, that turned out to be the best thing that ever happened to me. I'd have made a terrible middy."

"You were already pretty bad." Jacobsen's curiosity was roused. "Buggsie, what happened to you? I know you left the Navy, but where did you go? You disappeared. I mean, if you're out on the street, I'll be glad to do what I can to . . . you know, you smell like — God, I don't know what. You smell like — no offense now — like you've been rolling around in a pile of ape-shit."

"Not too far from the truth. Add in bear-shit, and you're close." From the smile on Bates's face, the insult didn't worry him. Already, in less than five minutes, the two men had dropped right back into the easy relationship that had ended thirty years earlier. "Thanks for the offer of help, Porky, but I don't need it. In fact, I'm here to do *you* a favor. A big one."

Jake Jacobsen peered at Bates from beneath his most prominent feature, bushy eyebrows that together with his porker's nose and ample belly were the delight of the political cartoonists. "Yeah, sure. Buggsie, the last person who told me he'd come to do me a big favor is doing five years in Leavenworth instead. If you're working for a lobbyist, leave now. You can keep the cigar for old times' sake."

"No lobbyist, Porky. I don't really work for anyone, at least no one you'd recognize. You've moved up in the world, but so have I. After I got kicked out I did what I should have done anyway. Went to college — serious science college, not tin soldiers — and did a Ph.D., then moved west for a faculty position. Big man on campus. Full chair and tenured position now, at Simi Valley State."

"But you *smell*."

"There's a big animal experiment lab, and I spend time in it. Like they say, shit sticks." He lit his cigar, and nodded his head in satisfaction at the aroma.

Jacobsen pulled his desk calendar over to him and stabbed at it with a thick finger. "I don't have much time to chat, Buggsie." His voice was apologetic. "I have a meeting downstairs in fifteen minutes. Why did you come here?"

Bates was peering unashamedly at the calendar, reading it upside-down. "SETI. You're going to talk about the Search for Extraterrestrial Intelligence?"

"Sort of. There's been a two-day meeting on the fifth floor, all the big names. I met 'em. They're a bunch of dumb turkeys. So I'm going to drop the big one on them today, tell 'em their budget just went bye-byes."

"You're cutting them out?"

"To zero. They're not even going in below the line. It's a new ball game here, Buggsie. Since Navy took over this place, we're cutting out all the chickenshit and doing what we should have been doing in space for the past thirty-five years. Consolidating our position. Building space infrastructure and the permanent supply ports. Making a *policy*, and a real space program. You know, I'd give half my pension for a cheap space transportation system, but over the years we've pissed away billions on third world training programs and space telescopes and listening for little green men. And what do we have to show for it? You tell me. Well, all that stopped when I got the job.

"Here." Jacobsen stared at Bates with sudden suspicion. "You're not one of *them*, are you? That SETI crowd?"

"Not any more. I was interested for a while, and I guess I owe them something, because they got me interested in finding and deciphering hidden messages." Bates was rummaging around in the pocket of his tweed jacket. "That's certainly not why I'm here. I didn't know anything about your meeting, but I'm going to make it very easy for you to break the news to them. SETI just became irrelevant. Take a look at this."

He was holding a small oval cylinder of white plastic, the size of a packet of cigarettes. The curved top was featureless except for a stud that could be moved to five positions along a sliding scale, and a round dial like a tiny watch face in the center. Bates leaned forward and placed the unit on the desk in front of Jacobsen. He put his hand flat on top of it.

"Ready?" He moved the stud to the first position, then pulled his hand clear. The cylinder rose to eye level and hovered there, two feet above the top of the desk. "Position one. Stasis mode, I call it. It's set to cancel and return to position zero — off — after thirty seconds, but that's programmable. If you want it to, it will hover indefinitely long at any height."

Jake Jacobsen's eyes were bulging more than Bates's ever did.

"Or it will do this," said Bates. "Position two. Constant velocity."

He reached out to the little unit and moved the stud one notch farther along the scale. At a steady foot per second, the white plastic rose until it reached the soundproofed ceiling and remained there, pressing gently upwards. Jacobsen stared up at it, mouth gaping open.

"It's smart enough to know there's an obstacle," continued Bates, "so it just stays there without exerting any upward force. If the ceiling weren't in the way, it would keep on moving up at the same speed until cut-off time is reached. Then — depending how it's programed — it will either stay where it is, or return at once to the starting point."

As he finished speaking the smooth-sided box drifted downwards until it was sitting on the desk top. Jacobsen reached out a pudgy hand and touched the side of the cylinder tentatively, as though it might be red-hot.

"It's not some sort of trick, is it? I mean, it really did what I saw it do."

"I'm not a hypnotist or a magician, if that's what you mean. You ought to know me better than that. And it's not a trick. It does what you saw."

"Then . . ." Jacobsen picked up the flattened white cylinder and put it on the palm of his hand, gauging the weight. "Then it's . . . it's. Christ. Did you *invent* this thing?"

"Not quite. Let's say I *discovered* it. And of course, all that I have here is a demonstration model. To be really useful, the cylinder ought to be as big as this room, then it could carry people. I didn't have the facilities to do that in the university machine shop, and anyway, that's not my department. It's yours. All I wanted to do is be sure it worked."

"Is it anti-gravity?" Jacobsen peered at the red button on

top of the smooth surface. "When you pressed it to that second position, it just went straight up."

"That's right. But it's more than anti-gravity, because it can go at a constant speed in any direction I choose. And it does a lot more even than that. See the other three settings? The first one puts the cylinder into a state of constant acceleration, for as long as the timer is set. I've tested it outside, and it went up, faster and faster, for twenty seconds. If I hadn't programed it to switch off and return to its starting point, I guess it would just have kept on going forever. I've only tested the other settings in a lab environment, so there could be a surprise or two. But the fourth position seems to be a constant rate of *increase* of acceleration. You'd have to be careful with that in a passenger version. Even with only a tenth of a gravity increase per second — and it can do a lot more than that — you'd be up to six gee in one minute, enough to start flattening everyone on board. By that time you're going a mile a second. You'd make a sizable dent in anything you hit. Don't touch that setting, by the way, I have no timer in the program."

Jacobsen put the cylinder down on the desk and pulled his hand away as though the plastic had suddenly become radioactive.

"The fifth position, though." Bates casually retrieved the object. "That's the real pay dirt. The unit just seems to disappear for a moment, then appear again at some pre-set distance away. I haven't been able to use separations big enough to measure the transition speed, but I know it's very fast. Maybe instantaneous."

The other man's face had been moving through a sequence of expressions as Bates described the functions of the flattened cylinder, running from amazement and disbelief to nervousness, and finally to squint-eyed cunning. When Bates finished speaking, the admiral sat in silence for a few seconds, drumming pudgy fingers on the desk top.

"What's the power source? Some humongous generator, somewhere?"

"No. What you see is what you get. It doesn't have one. I'm not a physicist, but from what I've been reading it has to draw its energy from vacuum fluctuations. There's no practical limit."

"You say you didn't invent it?"

"I discovered it. Sort of stumbled across it."

"So where's the guy who *did* invent it. Why isn't he here?"

"There isn't any other guy." Bates raised a skinny hand. "Look, I know that what I'm going to tell you sounds off the wall, but the important thing is *this*." He hefted the cylinder. "You don't have to trust me. Fix your eyes on this whenever what I have to say sounds strange to you. The machine's *real*. You're seeing it work. Keep that in your head."

Bates turned the dial on top of the cylinder and moved the stud to its first setting. The unit rose to hover in the air just above eye-level, between the two men.

"Let's start easy," Bates continued. "While you've been here at NASA you must have had questions about flying saucers, and visitors from space."

Jacobsen snorted. "Too damned many. We get a new inquiry every day. I told my staff what to tell 'em, that there's been a dozen investigations and they all show it's a bunch of garbage. Don't do much good, though, next day there's some other nut case on the line. I hope you're not going to sit there and tell me that a little man in a flying saucer dropped in on you and gave you the gadget?"

"Not quite. But you're warm. The best explanation I've been able to come up with is that somebody from far away *did* visit Earth, just the way your saucer fanatics insist. But it happened a long time ago. I don't know quite when, but it was over twenty million years. And before you ask me anything else, let me say I have no idea what they looked like, or their main reason for coming here. Whatever it was, they decided they'd leave a gift behind when they left. You're looking at it — the secret of easy access to space. Probably of interstellar travel, too, with that fifth setting."

"Wait a minute." Jacobsen was puffing furiously on his cigar, scowling from beneath those fierce eyebrows. "First you tell me you didn't *invent* it. Now you're saying they *left* it, whoever the hell they are. But you also said *you* built it."

"I did build it. What they left were instructions as to how to do it. I could follow the directions, but I still don't know *why* it works."

"Instructions?" Jacobsen's fat cheeks were turning crimson. Overdue for a stroke, he seemed to have decided that now was the time. "*Instructions!* Written in English, I suppose. Buggsie, I've had enough of this. You never did know when to stop joshing. If you think I was born yesterday—"

"Look at the machine, Porky. See it, hanging there? Have faith. Not instructions in English, of course not. Not in any human language. The instructions came as coded digit sequences, and they had to be deciphered. Your SETI friends waiting down on the fifth floor have worried the same problem for a long time: if you did receive a signal from space that was of artificial origin, how would you figure out the message?" Bates had finally lit his cigar, and now he was staring thoughtfully at the glowing tip. "You know, I used to be quite a SETI fan myself, but when you look at it logically, sending radio signals here from space is a terrible way to communicate with anybody. If you're not listening at just the right time with an antenna pointing in the right direction, the signal has been and gone while you're looking the other way. It's worse than putting a note in a bottle, and throwing it into the ocean. Much better to do it this way, leave a message *here*, where it will be around whenever someone gets smart enough to look for it."

He glanced up at Jacobsen. "Where was I? I flew the redeye from the Coast to get here, and I'm feeling a bit muzzy. Anyway, after a while I became convinced that what I had found *was* a message, but it took me forever to decipher it. The digital signal was a string of binary numbers, tens of millions of bits long. I knew it wasn't random, but I couldn't read it. Finally I discovered that the key was to convert the long string of digital signal into a two-dimensional array, laying a thousand and twenty-four digits down as each row, and then viewing the result as a pictorial form. And then I still had to puzzle out what the pictures *meant*. You see, until I actually had a working model, I couldn't be sure what I was building. For a while, I wondered if I might be making a gadget that would blow up the whole world — a sort of self-sterilizing device, left on Earth to get rid of any species smart enough to expand off the planet." He smiled unpleasantly. "Then I decided, what the hell, I'd build it anyway. I've learned a lot about animals. *Humans* might be that sneaky and horrible, but nothing else would."

The bright red had receded from Jacobsen's face, but he was stirring restlessly in his chair. "How many people have you told about all this, Buggsie? The message, and everything else?"

"Hardly anyone. Just a couple of coworkers at the lab, and I don't think they believed me. And as soon as I finished the working model I headed straight here."

"No public talks? No papers written?"

"None. Before I had a working model there was a problem of, let's say, credibility. This sort of thing isn't my academic specialty, and electronics is only a hobby. I'd have been laughed at until I had proof. Then when I had this working, I decided it was too important for anything like the usual publication route. We're talking a major press conference."

"Sure." Jacobsen picked up the interoffice phone and said: "Trustrum? Postpone my meeting with the SETI group. I know, I know. Screw 'em. And send a security officer up here to my office. Second thoughts, better make that *two* security officers, OK?"

He turned to Bates. "Buggsie, in the last year at the Academy I had you blackballed for the Jacks-off Five Society because I said you were all brains and no common sense. I have to apologize for that. I was wrong. You did exactly the right thing coming here to me without telling anybody. Do you realize the importance of what you have there?"

"Of course I do." Bates was scowling. "Why do you think I came to NASA? This gives us the stars — as it was designed to do."

"Nuts to the stars." Jacobsen walked across to the door to make sure it was securely closed. "I get too much crap in this job about stars and black holes and galaxies. That's for those SETI fruitcakes and their buddies in their meeting on the fifth floor. What we need right now are the *planets*. And that means a low-cost system to get off Earth, for starters. Navy and I took over NASA with a mission: to make it get its act together. The name of the space game today is *easy access*. I don't give the Russians credit for much, but they have the right attitude when they say that the upper atmosphere is the shore of the universe. The first real spacefaring nation will control the solar system, the way that Spain and Portugal and England used to control the seas. And that's going to be *us*, not a bunch of Russians and Japanese and Chinese and Frenchmen." He stared at Bates. The other man was shaking his head and there was a tired smile on his face. "We can do it, Buggsie. What you're holding in your hand guarantees it."

"It gives *humanity* easy access to space. Not just America."

"Oh, sure. Others will get to go eventually — they'll ride our coattails. But you had the same history lessons as I did, back at the Academy, and you know how the world works. Control the ports, and you control everything else. Trade follows the flag. Our flag."

Bates sighed. "Porky, I hoped for better things from you. I read all those noble things you said when you were testifying at the hearings to become head of NASA. 'I conceive it as my sacred duty to build a staircase, one that will allow all of humanity to ascend to the stars.' And I was dumb enough to believe you meant what you said. I'm delivering the staircase to you, but you want to restrict its use. Well, it doesn't make any difference what you want to do, or what I want to do. This staircase can't be kept secret."

"We'll see about that." There was a buzz on the office phone, and Jacobsen levered himself out of his chair and went to open the door. Two jg's stood to attention outside. Jacobsen nodded to them.

"I want you to stand guard as long as this meeting is going on. We're at TS level in here until further notice." He closed the door and returned to his desk. "Buggsie, you've spent too long in that ivory tower. Isn't it obvious that what you've shown me makes this a national security issue, too? The future of this whole country is at stake, and if that" — he pointed at the cylinder, still hovering above the desk — "got into the wrong foreign hands, our defense systems wouldn't be worth a packet of peanuts. You started out right, coming to me. Don't blow it now. Work with Navy, and you'll be sitting right on the inside — I'll make sure you get all the clearances, and if you need money one of my contractors can write you a nice fat subcontract. But don't give me any crap about this being 'too important to keep secret.' Let me tell you, *anything* can be kept secret, if the screws are turned down tight enough. And this has to be."

Bates laid his dead cigar down on the desk ashtray. For the past two minutes he had forgotten to smoke it. "You still don't understand, Porky. I said this can't be kept secret, no matter how much you or I might want to do that. I told you I found a message. Where do you imagine I found it, written on a wall somewhere?"

Jacobsen glowered. "Damned if I know. But it was somewhere in this country, wasn't it?"

"Yes. I haven't been abroad for over ten years."

"Then let me tell you something, Buggsie old buddy. I spent years in Naval Intelligence, and I can guarantee that we'll be able to put a lid on the place — any place in the U.S. of A. — where that message came from; a cap so tight Harry Houdini couldn't get his little finger in or out of it. And we can make sure nothing appears in the press, and nothing gets published. Your space transport system will be produced in a maximum security environment that makes standard DOD Top Secret facilities look leaky as colanders. If that's not keeping a secret, I don't know what is."

"It won't work." Bates gestured at the hovering cylinder. "You say you thought I had no common sense. Use yours, Porky, if you have any left after twenty years of military BS. Suppose you were an alien, visiting Earth twenty million years ago, and you wanted to leave a message that could be read today. What would you do?"

Jacobsen puffed out his full cheeks. "Carve it somewhere permanent, on rock, or on a steel plate. No, gold or glass would be better. But twenty million years . . ."

"You're getting there." Bates had an irritating smile on his face. "Take your time. Twenty *million* — not two hundred, or two hundred thousand. No artifact on Earth is that old. Any message would be worn away by the weather in less than a million years, so anything left on the surface would be eroded or buried hundreds of feet deep. Think, Porky. *Twenty million.*"

"It's impossible. Nothing can last that long."

"Right. That's what I wanted you to conclude. Nothing we could build would be recognizable twenty million years in the future."

"Not on Earth. But maybe if you left it on the Moon, where there's no weather to wear it out . . ."

"Hey, nice try. I didn't expect that. But you'd still have to worry about meteor impact. There's a better way, right here on Earth. A way that allows messages to persist for *hundreds of millions* of years, with small danger of being lost. And it's a form of recording we almost know how to do ourselves, if we wanted to."

Jacobsen growled his annoyance. "I know you think you're so damn smart, Buggsie, you always did. It sounds impossible, but if you're going to tell me, get on with it. And while you're at it you can tell me why *you* found this, and nobody else."

"Because I smell of ape-shit and bear-shit. I told you I wasn't a physicist, but I didn't tell you what I am. I'm a biologist — a molecular biologist. And one of the hottest topics today in molecular biology is DNA sequencing. Do you know anything about it?"

"Never heard of it, and I'm not sure I want to."

"You do, if you follow Government research financing. DNA is the molecule that carries genetic information. DNA also gets duplicated, unchanged except for very rare mutations, every time a cell divides. The Department of Energy and the National Institutes of Health have been given a billion dollars each to do DNA mapping of humans."

"A *billion*?" Jacobsen was finally dealing with something he understood. "That's not chickenfeed."

"Not even by Defense Department standards."

"Sounds like another big R&D boondoggle to me. NASA is full of 'em."

"No. This one is important. You see, the DNA of an organism decides exactly what that organism *is*. If I specify your DNA, in full, I specify you. It might sound easy to do that, because although a DNA molecule is shaped like a double helix — a pair of interlocking spirals — you can think of it as one long string, open-ended or joined in a circle, of just four different chemicals called nucleotide bases. The chemicals are thymine, adenine, guanine, and cytosine—"

"In English, goofball. You're starting to gibber."

"Sorry, Porky. I forgot you're a meathead. Just think of the bases in terms of their initials, T, A, G, and C, and imagine you have a whole lot of beads, with one of those letters written on each. Now you can make a necklace using those beads, with no

restriction on which bead sits at which position on the necklace. A complete DNA sequence — it's called a *genome* — is
just the listing of the order of the beads along the spiral necklace. That's enough to describe the organism completely. The
difference between me and you and a cabbage or a mosquito
or a chicken is in the length of the DNA sequence, and the
order of the four chemicals along the sequence. The trouble is,
we're talking of billions of beads for any sort of complex organism. Genome mapping is a monstrous job."

"And a damned useless one, I'd have said. What's the good
of it?"

"All sorts of things. If we knew the DNA mapping exactly
we could tackle all sorts of hereditary diseases. That's been
known for thirty years. But techniques to map the DNA
sequence, and find the exact order of the T, A, G, and C beads
on the genetic necklace are more recent, ten years old or less.
We do it using electron microscopes and crystallography and
other chemicals called restriction enzymes. That's what I do.
I'm good at it. The Department of Energy gave me a grant of a
million dollars to look at a particular question relating to DNA
sequencing, what you might call the problem of 'junk' DNA
that doesn't seem to do anything useful.

"You see, the DNA in any cell tells that cell how to
operate, especially how to produce proteins. So you might
think that every bit of DNA would be used that way. But it
isn't. As little as ten percent of the DNA is used to control
production processes in the cell. So what's the rest of it there
for? Nobody knows. And yet the *introns*, those intervening
sequences that don't direct production of cell materials, can
make up nine-tenths of the total DNA. My grant was to examine the introns, and see if I could discover what purpose
they serve."

Bates had been sitting completely motionless in his chair.
With the explanation almost over, he seemed exhausted. Now
he stirred, picked up the cigar again, and pointed with it at the
hovering cylinder. "So here's the exciting bit. I found out,
Porky. At least, I found out part of the answer. It's right there,
hanging in front of you. *Somebody planted a message*, over and
over again, in the introns, in the DNA sequences that look at
first sight like some sort of junk. All I did was discover it and

decode it."

Jacobsen was staring at the palm of his own fleshy hand with bemusement. "Are you saying that's where your space transportation system design is? Hidden away in the damned DNA sequence, like a coded signal? It's even inside *me*?"

"It sure is. It's in your hand there, hidden in the part of the DNA sequence that's not expressed in protein production. It's repeated many times, in case a bit of the sequence in one place is destroyed by a mutation. And don't you see the beauty of the idea? If DNA does one thing superbly well, it's this: it makes copies of itself, from generation to generation, with a minuscule error rate. Maybe after a few hundred million years you'd get enough DNA mutation to make the message unreliable, but not in a mere twenty million. It's the nearest thing to an eternal form of a message that you can imagine. Our friends who came to Earth and left the design for your stellar staircase didn't have to worry about it being obliterated by weather or accident. It would be there, as long as anyone who might get smart enough to find it was there. And the other nice thing is that you can't read the message until you're ready to use it. DNA sequence analysis needs *technology*, electricity and computers and matching algorithms and scanning tunneling microscopes, before it can be performed."

"But the sequence is in every cell? A message tens of millions of digits long?"

"Every cell, in every human, in every country." Bates was picking up energy again, talking faster. "The information in DNA is tight-packed. It can define an entire human being, in a few trillionths of a gram of material. Compared with that, specifying a space-drive is nothing. But now do you see why I say it can't be kept a secret? I'm in touch with other researchers in my field, all around the world, and I know of fifty people who are moving along the same track as me. You can try as hard as you like to keep my work away from them, but it won't hold for more than a couple of years. Someone else will see the same anomalies in the sequence, and decode them independently. Then they'll have the same 'staircase to the stars' that you told Congress you wanted to provide."

Jacobsen leaned back in his seat, breathing loudly through

his nose. "Damn you, Buggsie." He growled the words. "You come in here and tell me you're going to give me something. You show it to me, and then you take it right away again. If every tinpot upstart country can get to space, it makes my job *harder*, not easier."

"That depends what you think your job is. If you believe you were put here to sit on your fat behind and make space off-limits to everyone except the U.S. Navy, then you're right. That job won't just be hard now, it'll be impossible. That's fine with me. I never came here for that. But if you see your job as I do — as you once did — as building the system that gives everyone on Earth a stake in space development and a chance to go there, then I've done it for you. Or rather, the beings who left the design have done it for you. All I did was act as the messenger."

He reached out for the hovering cylinder, switched it off, and placed it on the desk. "Think positive, Porky. We've got the planets, and maybe we've got the stars, too, and I'm giving you a couple of years start on the competition. With any luck, you'll be going into space *yourself* before then."

Jacobsen's hand had been moving irresistibly towards the white plastic unit. He paused. "Me!?"

"You. Who else?" Bates watched the changing expression on the other man's face. "Ah, now I'm getting to you, aren't I? And about time. You may have kidded yourself that you wanted to be head of NASA because it was a good career move. But I remember a different Porky Jacobsen. You were the one who used to bend our ears at the Academy, telling us how humans were meant to go to space, and how nothing would stop us. How nothing was going to stop *you*. And what you told me a few minutes ago is spot on, easy access is the key. That's what we have, now. You can go, Porky, *yourself*. You're too old for the Shuttle, but you're not too old for this. D'you hear me? You can go."

"I can." Jacobsen stared down at the cylinder, now gripped possessively in his hand. "By God, I can and I will. You know, the very idea of meeting them terrifies me — they've waited twenty million years for us. I wonder how we'll shape up. But you're right, if there's any way on Earth I can get onto that prototype ship I'll be there. Nothing will stop me."

He moved the stud on the cylinder to its second setting, and watched as it rose lazily to meet the ceiling. "But there's something even scarier, in a way, than this gadget itself. It's that *they knew*, so long ago, that we humans would be the ones to make it. They knew we'd find a way, all the way, up to intelligence. And there were no humans around at that time, were there?"

"Not a one. Just primitive apes." Bates had a dreamy smile on his face. "But don't assume that when they left that message, they knew just who'd be coming up to meet them. I said they left it *at least* twenty million years ago. How do you think I know that?"

Jacobsen shook his head. The white cylinder floated quietly down to rest on his hand.

"Because we weren't the only candidates," went on Bates. "I told you, I work with animals as well as humans. I found the same message in the DNA sequence of animals that split off the human genetic line up to twenty million years ago. We and chimps and gorillas and orangutans and gibbons separated from a common genetic line at different times, but we all have the same coded introns. Chances are the message was planted just once, maybe as a virus in a common ancestor to all of us, and that means over twenty million years ago. We were all given the message. But no one really has it until they can *read* it."

The other man looked up from his gloating over the tightly held cylinder. "You were the one who *did* read it, Buggsie. Just you. You were the only one smart enough to do it. I want to go, but it seems to me that if anyone *deserves* to go, it's you. And I'm sure I can arrange it."

"No rush. I'll take my turn — I don't have to be on that first ship."

Jacobsen shook his head. "Don't make my mistake, Buggsie. Don't leave it until you find you're too old, and too fat, and too battered, and it's too late to go."

"Oh, I don't think that will happen." Bates hesitated. "As a matter of fact, I'm pretty confident it won't."

He rummaged in his jacket pocket, and pulled out a white, spidery structure with multiple shiny connectors. "You see,

Porky, what you've got there wasn't the only thing coded into the introns. I'm not a hundred percent sure of this one, and I have to check it with the experts. But that shouldn't be hard — The National Institute on Aging is only a couple of blocks away from here, isn't it."

Afterword: *The Double Spiral Staircase*

One problem that I have with the whole idea of UFOs is the frequency of their visits. Humans have been developing on this planet for at least a couple of hundred thousand years. Surely it would be difficult for an alien, no matter how advanced, to know in advance at what point in time we and our ancestors would become smart and civilized enough for rational communication. (If we ever become so civilized. When Mahatma Gandhi was asked what he thought of Western civilization, he said that he thought it would be a good idea.)

It seems monstrously inefficient for a supposedly advanced species to drop in on us every year or two, waiting and waiting until the time is right. They must have better things to do with their time. Wouldn't our rational aliens adopt a different solution? Wouldn't they choose to come here very rarely, and then leave messages that we could read and understand only when we were smart enough to do so?

Very good. How would they know when we were smart enough?

Well, one way acceptable to me, although perhaps unpopular at the moment with many people, is to correlate smartness with the development of technology. If the message were then written on something so small that it could not be read without a microscope, that would filter out false alarms. If it were also written on a medium that is present anywhere potentially intelligent life was likely to be found, it would be unlikely to escape notice. And if it was stored in a form that could be copied unchanged over many centuries and millennia, it would not matter how long it took for developing intelligence to find it.

Here is a problem for the reader: if you don't accept DNA as the message medium, what else can you suggest that satisfies the requirements?

THE UNLICKED BEAR-WHELP

A Worm's Eye Look at Chaos Theory

"So when this world's compounded union breaks,
Time ends, and to old Chaos all things turn."

— Christopher Marlowe

1. INTRODUCTION

The Greek word "chaos" referred to the formless or disordered state before the beginning of the universe. The word has also been a part of the English language for a long time. Thus in Shakespeare's *Henry VI, Part Three*, the Duke of Gloucester (who in the next play of the series will become King Richard III, and romp about the stage in unabashed villainy) is complaining about his physical deformities. He is, he says, "like to a Chaos, or an unlick'd bear-whelp, that carries no impression like the dam." *Chaos*: something essentially random, an object or being without a defined shape.

Those lines were written about 1590. The Marlowe quotation that heads this article comes from close to the same year, and it is a wonderful (though unintentional) foreshadowing of the idea of the heat-death of the Universe, first formulated in the late nineteenth century.

Chaos is old; but *chaos theory* is a new term. Ten years ago, no popular article had ever been written containing that expression. Today it is hard to pick up a science magazine *without* finding an article on chaos theory, complete with stunning color illustrations. I must say that those articles, without exception, have failed to make the central ideas of chaos theory clear to me. That's why I went grubbing into it on my own, and why I am writing this, adding yet another (possibly unintelligible) discussion of the subject to the literature.

Part of the problem is simple newness. When someone writes about, say, quantum theory, the subject has to be presented as difficult, and subtle, and mysterious, because it *is* difficult, and subtle, and mysterious. To describe it any other way would be simply misleading. In the past sixty years, however, the mysteries have had time to become old friends of the professionals in the field. There are certainly enigmas, logical whirlpools into which you can fall and never get out, but at least the *locations* of those trouble spots are known. Writing about any well-established subject such as quantum theory is therefore in some sense easy.

In the case of chaos theory, by contrast, *everything* is new and fragmented; we face the other extreme. We are adrift on an ocean of uncertainties, guided by partial and inadequate maps, and it is too soon to know where the central mysteries of the subject reside.

Or, worse yet, to know if those mysteries are worth taking the time to explore. *Is* chaos a real "theory," something which will change the scientific world in a basic way, as that world was changed by Newtonian mechanics, quantum theory, and relativity? Or is it something essentially trivial, a subject which at the moment is benefiting from a catchy name and so enjoying a certain glamor, as in the past there have been fads for orgone theory, mesmerism, dianetics, and pyramidology?

We will defer consideration of that question until we have had a look at the bases of chaos theory, where it came from, and where it seems to lead us. Then we can come back to examine its long-term prospects.

2. HOW TO BECOME EXTREMELY FAMOUS

One excellent way to make a great scientific discovery is to take a fact that everyone knows must be the case — because "common sense demands it" — and ask what would happen if it were not true.

For example, it is obvious that the Earth is fixed. It *has* to be standing still, because it feels as though it is standing still. The Sun moves around it. Copernicus, by suggesting that the Earth revolves around the Sun, made the fundamental break with medieval thinking and set in train the whole of modern astronomy.

Similarly, it was clear to the ancients that unless you keep on pushing a moving object, it will slow down and stop. By taking the contrary view, that it takes a force (such as friction with the ground, or air resistance) to *stop* something, and otherwise it would just keep going, Galileo and Newton created modern mechanics.

Another case: to most people living before 1850, there was no question that animal and plant species are all so well-defined and different from each other that they must have been created, type by type, at some distinct time in the past. Charles Darwin and Alfred Russel Wallace, in suggesting in the 1850's a mechanism by which one form could *change* over time to another in response to natural environmental pressures, allowed a very different world view to develop. The theory of evolution and natural selection permitted species to be regarded as fluid entities, constantly changing, and all ultimately derived from the simplest of primeval life forms.

And, to take one more example, it was clear to everyone before 1900 that if you kept on accelerating an object, by applying force to it, it would move faster and faster until it was finally traveling faster than light. By taking the speed of light as an upper limit to possible speeds, and requiring that this speed be the same for all observers, Einstein was led to formulate the theory of relativity.

It may make you famous, but it is a risky business, this offering of scientific theories that ask people to abandon their long-cherished beliefs about what "just must be so." As Thomas Huxley remarked, it is the customary fate of new truths to begin as heresies.

Huxley was speaking metaphorically, but a few hundred years ago he could have been speaking literally. Copernicus did not allow his work on the movement of the Earth around the Sun to be published in full until 1543, when he was on his deathbed, nearly 30 years after he had first developed the ideas. He probably did the right thing. Fifty-seven years later Giordano Bruno was gagged and burned at the stake for proposing ideas in conflict with theology, namely, that the universe is infinite and there are many populated worlds. Thirty-three years after that, Galileo was made to appear before the Inquisition and threatened with torture because of his "heretical" ideas. His work remained on the Catholic Church's Index of prohibited books for over two hundred years.

By the nineteenth century critics could no longer have a scientist burned at the stake, even though they may have wanted to. Darwin was merely denounced as a tool of Satan. However, anyone who thinks this issue is over and done with can go today and have a good argument about evolution and natural selection with the numerous idiots who proclaim themselves to be scientific creationists.

Albert Einstein fared better, mainly because most people had no idea what he was talking about. However, from 1905 to his death in 1955 he became the target of every crank and scientific nitwit outside (and often inside) the lunatic asylums.

Today we will be discussing an idea, contrary to common sense, that has been developing in the past twenty years. So far its proposers have escaped extreme censure, though in the early days their careers may have suffered because no one believed them — or understood what they were talking about.

3.   BUILDING MODELS

The idea at the heart of chaos theory can be simply stated, but we will have to wind our way into it.

Five hundred years ago, mathematics was considered essential for bookkeeping, surveying, and trading, but it was not considered to have much to do with the physical processes of Nature. Why should it? What do abstract symbols on a piece of paper have to do with the movement of the planets, the flow of rivers, the blowing of soap bubbles, the flight of kites, or the design of buildings?

Little by little, that view changed. Scientists found that physical processes could be described by equations, and solving those equations allowed predictions to be made about the real world. More to the point, they were *correct* predictions. By the nineteenth century, the fact that manipulation of the

purely abstract entities of mathematics could somehow tell us
how the real world would behave was no longer a surprise. Sir
James Jeans could happily state, in 1930, "*all* the pictures
which science now draws of nature, and which alone seem
capable of according with observational fact, are *mathematical*
pictures," and ". . . the universe appears to have been designed
by a pure mathematician."

The mystery had vanished, or been subsumed into divinity.
But it should not have. It is a mystery still.

I would like to illustrate this point with the simplest problem of Newtonian mechanics. Suppose that we have an object
moving along a line with a constant acceleration. It is easy to
set up a situation in the real world in which an object so
moves, at least approximately.

To describe the problem mathematically, the scientist
writes down one simple equation:

$$dv/dt = a$$

This simply says that the rate of change of the speed, v, is a
constant, a.

We integrate this equation, *a purely abstract operation*,
nothing to do with the real world, and obtain the formal result:

$$v = v_0 + at$$

This gives us the speed, v, of the object at any time, given a
starting speed v_0 at $t = 0$. And since the speed is the rate of
change of distance, which is written, $v = dx/dt$, we can integrate
again — another purely *abstract* operation — to yield:

$$x = x_0 + v_0 t + at^2/2$$

which tells us the position of the object, x, at any time, in terms
of its initial position, x_0, and its initial speed, v_0.

If you have not met this sort of thing before, it may seem
baffling. What does this mathematical construct of the human
mind, *integration*, have to do with reality?

If you do have that feeling, it is totally appropriate. However, after a few years of solving equations like this, the sense
of wonder goes away. We take it for granted that the scribbling
we do on a piece of paper will describe the way that objects
really behave — and we are not surprised that the same equation will work for any object, accelerated by any force.

Well, we ought to be amazed. It is not just that we can *write
down* an equation for the relation between the acceleration

and the speed. It is that this integration process somehow corresponds exactly to something in the *real world*, so that when we have done our pencil-and-paper integrations, we are able to know where the object will be in reality.

No justification is usually offered for this in courses on mechanics and the calculus, other than the fact that it works. It becomes what Douglas Hofstadter in another context terms a "default assumption."

This is an especially simple example, but scientists are at ease with far more complex cases. Do you want to know how a fluid will move? Write down the three-dimensional time-dependent Navier-Stokes equation for compressible, viscous flow, and solve it. That's not a simple proposition, and you may have to resort to a computer. But when you have the results, you expect them to apply to real fluids. If they do not, it is because the equation you began with was not quite right — maybe we need to worry about electromagnetic forces, or plasma effects. Or maybe the integration method you used was numerically unstable, or the finite difference interval too crude. The idea that the mathematics cannot describe the physical world never even occurs to most scientists. They have in the back of their minds an idea first made explicit by Laplace: the whole universe is calculable, by defined mathematical laws. Laplace said that if you told him (or rather, if you told a demon, who was capable of taking in all the information) the position and speed of every particle in the Universe, at one moment, he would be able to define the Universe's entire future, and also its whole past.

The twentieth century, and the introduction by Heisenberg of the Uncertainty Principle, weakened that statement, because it showed that it was impossible to know precisely the position and speed of a body. Nonetheless, the principle that mathematics can *exactly model reality* is usually still unquestioned.

Now, hidden away in the assumption that the world can be described by mathematics there is another one; one so subtle that most people never gave it a thought. This is the assumption that chaos theory makes explicit, and then challenges. We state it as follows:

Simple equations must have simple solutions.

There is no reason why this should be so, except that it seems that common sense demands it. And, of course, we have not defined "simple."

Let us return to our accelerating object, where we had a simple-seeming equation, and an explicit solution. One requirement of a simple solution is that it should not "jump around" when we make a very small change in the system it describes. For example, if we consider two cases of an accelerated object, and the only difference between them is a tiny change in the original position of the object, we would expect a small change in the *final* position. And this is the case.

But now consider another simple physical system, a pendulum (this was one of the first cases where the ideas of chaos theory emerged). The equation that describes the motion of a simple pendulum, consisting of a bob on a string, can be written down easily enough. It is:

$$d^2q/dt^2 + k.\sin(q) = 0$$

Even if you are not familiar with calculus, this should seem hardly more complicated than the first equation we considered. And for small angles, q, its solution can easily be written down, and it exhibits the quality of simplicity, namely, the solution changes little when we make a small change in the starting position or starting speed of the pendulum bob.

However, when large angles, q, are permitted, a completely different type of solution becomes possible. If we start the bob moving fast enough, instead of swinging back and forward, like a clock, the pendulum keeps on going, right over the top and down the other side. If we write down the expression for the angle as a function of time, in one case the angle is a *periodic* function (back and forth) and in the other case it is constantly increasing (round and round). And the change from one to the other occurs when we make an *infinitesimal* change in the initial speed of the pendulum bob. This type of behavior is known as a *bifurcation* in the behavior of the solution, and it is a worrying thing. A simple equation begins to exhibit a complicated solution.

The mathematician Poincaré used a powerful graphical

method to display the behavior of the solutions of dynamical problems. It is called a *phase space diagram*, and it plots position on one axis, and speed on the other. For any assumed starting position and speed, we can then plot out where the solution goes on the phase diagram. (It works, because the equations of dynamics are what is known as second-order equations; for such equations, when the position and speed of an object are specified, that defines the nature of its whole future motion.)

If we make the phase space diagram for the case of the uniformly accelerating object, the result is not particularly interesting. It is shown in Figure 1, and consists of a set of parabolas.

Figure 1: Phase space diagram for uniform accelerated motion.

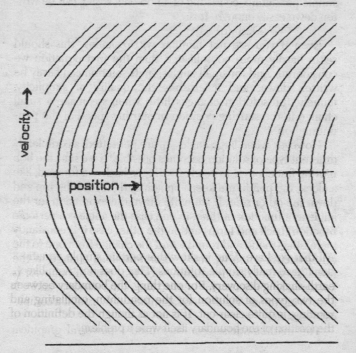

Things become more interesting when we do the same thing for the pendulum (Figure 2). Phase space now has two distinct regions, corresponding to the oscillating and the rotating forms of solution, and they are separated by an infinitely thin closed boundary. An infinitely small change of speed or position at that boundary can totally change the nature of the solution.

Figure 2: Phase space diagram for the simple pendulum

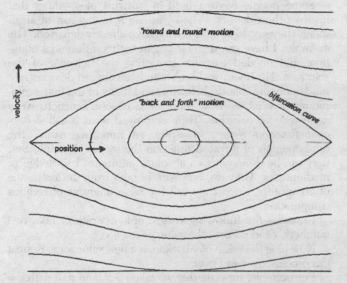

This kind of behavior can be thought of as a *sensitive dependence on the initial conditions*. In fact, at the dividing curve of the phase space diagram, it is an *infinitely* sensitive dependence on initial conditions.

At this point, the reasonable reaction might well be, so what? All that we have done is show that certain simple equations don't have really simple solutions. That does not seem like an earth-shaking discovery. For one thing, the boundary between the two types of solution for the pendulum, oscillating and rotating, is quite clear-cut. It is not as though the definition of the location of the boundary itself were a problem.

Can situations arise where this *is* a problem? Where the boundary is difficult to define in an intuitive way? The answer is, yes. In the next section we will consider simple systems that give rise to highly complicated boundaries between regions of fundamentally different behavior.

4. ITERATED FUNCTIONS

Some people have a built-in mistrust of anything that involves the calculus. When you use it in any sort of argument, they say, logic and clarity have already departed. The examples I have given so far began with a differential equation, and needed calculus to define the behavior of the solutions. However, we don't need calculus to demonstrate fundamentally chaotic behavior; and many of the first explorations of what we now think of as chaotic functions were done without calculus. They employed what is called *iterated function theory*. Despite an imposing name, the fundamentals of iterated function theory are so simple that they can be done with an absolute minimum knowledge of mathematics. They do, however, benefit from the assistance of computers, since they call for large amounts of tedious computation.

Consider the following very simple operation. Take two numbers, x and r. Form the value $y = rx(1-x)$.

Now plug the value of y back in as a new value for x. Repeat this process, over and over.

For example, suppose that we take $r = 2$, and start with $x = 0.1$. Then we find $y = 0.18$.

Plug that value in as a new value for x, still using $r = 2$, and we find a new value, $y = 0.2952$.

Keep going, to find a sequence of y's, 0.18, 0.2952, 0.4161, 0.4859, 0.4996, 0.5000, 0.5000 . . .

In the language of mathematics, the sequence of y's has *converged* to the value 0.5. Moreover, for any starting value of x, between 0 and 1, we will always converge to the same value, 0.5, for $r = 2$.

Here is the sequence when we begin with $x = 0.6$:
0.6000, 0.4800, 0.4992, 0.5000, 0.5000 . . .

Because the final value of y does not depend on the starting value, it is termed an *attractor* for this system, since it "draws in" any sequence to itself.

The value of the attractor depends on r. If we start with some other value of r, say r = 2.5, we still produce a convergent sequence. For example, if for r = 2.5 we begin with x = 0.1, we find successive values: 0.1, 0.225, 0.4359, 0.6147, 0.5921, 0.6038, 0.5981 . . . 0.6. Starting with a different x still gives the same final value, 0.6. (For anyone with a computer available to them and a knowledge of a programing language such as FORTRAN or BASIC, I recommend playing this game for yourself. The whole program is only a dozen lines long, and fooling with it is lots of fun. *Suggestion*: Run the program in double precision, if you have it available, so you don't get trouble with round-off errors. *Warning*: larking around with this sort of thing will consume hours and hours of your time.)

The situation does not change significantly with r = 3. We find the sequence of values: 0.2700, 0.5913, 0.7250, 0.5981, 0.7211 . . . 0.6667. This time it takes thousands of iterations to get to a final converged value, but it makes it there in the end. Even after only a dozen or two iterations we can begin to see it "settling-in" to its final value.

There have been no surprises so far. What happens if we increase r a bit more, to 3.1? We might expect that we will converge, but even more slowly, to a single final value.

We would be wrong. Something very odd happens. The sequence of numbers that we generate has a regular structure, but now the values alternate between two different numbers, 0.7645, and 0.5580. *Both* these are attractors for the sequence. It is as though the sequence cannot make up its mind. When r is increased past the value 3, the sequence "splits" to two permitted values, which we will call "states," and these occur alternately.

Let us increase the value of r again, to 3.4. We find the same behavior, a sequence that alternates between two values.

But by r = 3.5, things have changed again. The sequence has *four* states, four values that repeat one after the other. For r = 3.5, we find the final sequence values: 0.3828, 0.5009, 0.8269, and 0.8750. Again, it does not matter what value of x we started with, we will always converge on those same four attractors.

Let us pause for a moment and put on our mathematical hats. If a mathematician is asked the question, "Does the iteration y = rx(1-x) converge to a final value?", he will proceed as follows:

Suppose that there is a final converged value, V, towards which the iteration converges. Then when we reach that value, no matter how many iterations it takes, at the final step x will be equal to V, and so will y. Thus we must have V = rV(1 - V).

Solving for V, we find V = 0, which is a legitimate but uninteresting solution, or V = (r - 1)/r. This single value will apply, no matter how big r may be. For example, if r = 2.5, then V = $^{1.5}/_{2.5}$ = 0.6, which is what we found. Similarly, for r = 3.5, we calculate V = $^{2.5}/_{3.5}$ = 0.7142857.

But this is not what we found when we did the actual iteration. We did not converge to that value at all, but instead we obtained a set of four values that cycled among themselves. So let us ask the question, what would happen if we *began* with x = 0.7142857, as our starting guess? We certainly have the right to use any initial value that we choose. Surely, the value would simply stay there?

No, it would not.

What we would find is that on each iteration, the value of y changes. It remains close to 0.7142857 on the first few calculations, then it — quite quickly — diverges from that value and homes in on the four values that we just mentioned: 0.3828, 0.5009, etc. In mathematical terms, the value 0.7142857 is a solution of the iterative process for r = 3.5. But it is an *unstable* solution. If we start there, we will rapidly move away to other multiple values.

Let us return to the iterative process. By now we are not sure what will happen when we increase r. But we can begin to make some guesses. Bigger values of r seem to lead to more and more different values, among which the sequence will oscillate, and it seems as though the number of these values will always be a power of two. Furthermore, the "splitting points" seem to be coming faster and faster.

Take r = 3.52, or 3.53, or 3.54. We still have four values that alternate. But by r = 3.55, things have changed again. We now find *eight* different values that repeat, one after the other. By r = 3.565, we have 16 different values that occur in a fixed order, over and over, as we compute the next elements of the sequence.

It is pretty clear that we are approaching some sort of crisis, since the increments that we can make in r, without changing the nature of the sequence, are getting smaller and smaller. In fact, the critical value of r is known to many significant figures. It is r = 3.569945668 . . . As we approach that value there are 2^n states in the sequence, and n is growing fast.

What happens if we take r *bigger* than this, say r = 3.7? We still produce a sequence — there is no difficulty at all with the computations — but it is a sequence without any sign of regularity. There are no attractors, and all values seem equally likely. It is fair to say that it is *chaos*, and the region beyond the critical value of r is often called the *chaos regime*.

This may look like a very special case, because all the calculations were done based on one particular function, y = rx(1-x). However, it turns out that the choice of function is much less important than one would expect. If we substituted any up-and-down curve between zero and one (see Figure 3) we would get a similar result. As r increases, the curve "splits"

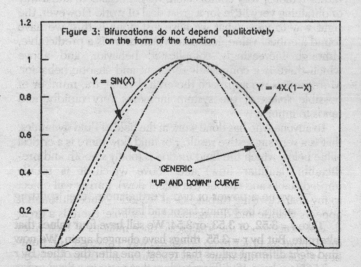

Figure 3: Bifurcations do not depend qualitatively on the form of the function

Y = SIN(X)

Y = 4X.(1-X)

GENERIC
"UP AND DOWN" CURVE

again and again. There is a value of r for which the behavior becomes chaotic.

For example, suppose that we use the form y = r sin(x)/4 (the factor of 4 is to make sure that the maximum value of y is the same as in the first case, namely, ¹/₄). By the time we reach r = 3.4 we have four different values repeating in the sequence. For r = 3.45 we have eight attractors. Strangest of all, the way in which we approach the critical value for this function has much in common with the way we approached it for the first function that we used. They both depend on a single convergence number that tells the rate at which new states will be introduced as r is increased. That convergence number is 4.669201609 . . . , and is known as the *Feigenbaum number*, after Mitchell Feigenbaum, who first explored in detail this property of iterated sequences. This property of common convergence behavior, independent of the particular function used for the iteration, is called *universality*. It seems a little presumptuous as a name, but maybe it won't, in twenty years time.

This discussion of iterated functions may strike you as rather tedious, very complicated, very specialized, and a way of obtaining very little for a great deal of work. However, the right way to view what we have just done is this: we have found a critical value, less than which there is a predictable, although increasingly complicated behavior, and above which there is a completely different and chaotic behavior. Moreover, as we approach the critical value, the number of possible states of the system increases very rapidly, and tends to infinity.

To anyone who has done work in the field of fluid dynamics, that is a very suggestive result. For fluid flow there is a critical value below which the fluid motion is totally smooth and predictable (laminar flow) and above which it is totally unpredictable and chaotic (turbulent flow). Purists will object to my characterizing turbulence as "chaotic," since although it appears chaotic and disorganized as a whole, there is a great deal of structure on the small scale since millions of molecules must move together in an organized way. However, the number of states in turbulent flow is infinite, and there has been much discussion of the way in which the single state of laminar flow changes to the many states of turbulent flow. Landau proposed that the new states must come into being one at a time. It was also assumed that turbulent behavior arose as a consequence of the very complicated equations of fluid dynamics.

Remember the "common sense rule": Simple equations must have simple solutions. And therefore, complicated behavior should only arise from complicated equations. For the first time, we see that this may be wrong. A very simple system is exhibiting very complicated behavior, reminiscent of what happens with fluid flow. Depending on some critical variable, it may appear totally predictable and well-behaved, or totally unpredictable and chaotic. Moreover, experiments show that in turbulence the new, disorganized states come into being not one by one, but *through a doubling process as the critical parameter is approached*. Maybe turbulence is a consequence of something in the fluid flow equations that is unrelated to their complexity — a hidden structure that is present even in such simple equations as we have been studying.

This iterated function game is interesting, even suggestive; but to a physicist it was for a long time little more than that. Physics does not deal with computer games, went the argument. It deals with mathematical models that describe a physical system, in a majority of cases through a series of differential equations. These equations are solved, to build an idea of how Nature will behave in any given circumstance.

The trouble is, although such an approach works wonderfully well in many cases, there are classes of problems that it doesn't seem to touch. Turbulence is one. "Simple" systems, like the dripping of water from a faucet, can be modeled in principle, but in practice the difficulties in formulation and solution are so tremendous that no one has ever offered a working analysis of a dripping tap.

The problems where the classical approach breaks down often have one thing in common: they involve a random, or apparently random, element. Water in a stream breaks around a stone this way, then that way. A snowflake forms from supersaturated vapor, and every one is different. A tap drips, then does not drip, in an apparently random way. All these problems are described by quite different systems of equations. What scientists wanted to see was *physical problems*, described by good old differential equations, that also displayed bifurcations, and universality, and chaotic behavior.

They had isolated examples already. For example, the chemical systems that rejoice in the names of the Belousov-Zhabotinsky reaction and the Brusselator exhibit a two-state cyclic behavior. So does the life cycle of the slime mold, *Dictyostelium discoideum*. However, such systems are very tricky to study for the occurrence of such things as bifurcations, and involve all the messiness of real-world experiments. Iterated function theory was something that could be explored in the precise and austere world of computer logic, unhindered by the intrusion of the external world.

We must get to that external and real world eventually, but before we do so, let's take a look at another element of iterated function theory. This one has become very famous in its own right (rather more so, in my opinion, than it deserves to be for its physical significance, but perhaps justifiably most famous for its artistic significance).

The subject is *fractals*, and the contribution to art is called the Mandelbrot Set.

5. SICK CURVES AND FRACTALS

Compare the system we have just been studying with the case of the pendulum. There we had a critical *curve*, rather than a critical value. On the other hand, the behavior on both sides of the critical curve was not chaotic. Also, the curve itself was well-behaved, meaning that it was "smooth" and predictable in its shape.

Is there a simple system that on the one hand exhibits a critical *curve*, and on the other hand shows chaotic behavior?

There is. It is one studied in detail by Benoit Mandelbrot, and it gives rise to a series of amazing objects (one hesitates to call them curves, or areas).

We just looked at a case of an iterated function where only one variable was involved. We used x to compute y, then replaced x with y, and calculated a new y, and so on. It is no more difficult to do this, at least in principle, if there are two starting values, used to compute two new values. For example, we could have:

$$y = (w^2 - x^2) + a$$
$$z = 2wx + b$$

and when we had computed a pair (y,z) we could use them to replace the pair (w,x). (Readers familiar with complex variable theory will see that I am simply writing the relation $z = z^2 + c$, where z and c are complex numbers, in a less elegant form).

What happens it we take a pair of constants, (a,b), plug in zero starting values for w and x, and let our computers run out lots of pairs, (y,z)? This is a kind of two-dimensional equivalent to what we did with the function $y = rx(1-x)$, and we might think that we will find similar behavior, with a critical *curve* replacing the critical value.

What happens is much more surprising. We can plot our (y,z) values in two dimensions, just as we plotted out speeds and positions for the case of the pendulum. And, just as was the case with the pendulum, we will find that the whole plane is divided up into separate regions, with boundaries between them. The boundaries are the boundary curves of the "Mandelbrot set," as it is called. If, when we start with an (a,b) pair and iterate for (y,z) values, one or both of y and z run off towards infinity, then the point (a,b) is *not* a member of the Mandelbrot set. If the (y,z) pairs settle down to some value, or if they cycle around a series of values without ever diverging off towards infinity, then the point (a,b) is a member of the Mandelbrot set. The tricky case is for points on the boundary, since convergence is slowest there for the (y,z) sequence. However, those boundaries can be mapped. And they are as far as can be imagined from the simple, well-behaved curve that divided the two types of behavior of the pendulum. Instead of being smooth, they are intensely spiky; instead of just one curve, there is an infinite number of them.

The results of plotting the Mandelbrot set can be found in many articles, because they have a strange beauty unlike anything else in mathematics. Rather than drawing them here, I will refer you to James Gleick's book, *Chaos: Making a New Science*, which shows some beautiful color examples of parts of the set. All this, remember, comes from the simple function we defined, iterated over and over to produce pairs of (y,z) values corresponding to a particular choice of a and b. The colors seen in so many art shows, by the way, while not exactly a cheat, are not fundamental to the Mandelbrot set itself. They are assigned depending on how many iterations it takes to bring the (y,z) values to convergence, or to a stable repeating pattern.

The Mandelbrot set also exhibits a feature known as *scaling*, which is very important in many areas of physics. It says, in its simplest terms, that you cannot tell the absolute scale of the phenomenon you are examining from the structure of the phenomenon itself.

That needs some explanation. Suppose that you want to know the size of a given object — say, a snowflake. One absolute measure, although a rather difficult one to put into practice, would be to count the number of atoms in that snowflake. Atoms are fundamental units, and they do not change in their size.

But suppose that instead of the number of atoms, you tried to use a different measure, say, the total *area* of the snowflake. That sounds much easier than looking at the individual atoms. But you would run into a problem, because as you look at the surface of the snowflake more and more closely, it becomes more and more detailed. A little piece of a snowflake has a surface that looks very much like a little piece of a little piece of a snowflake; a little piece of a little piece resembles a little piece of a little piece of a little piece, and so on. It stays that way until you are actually seeing the atoms. Then you at last have the basis for an absolute scale.

Mathematical entities, unlike snowflakes, are not made up of atoms. There are many mathematical objects that "scale forever," meaning that each level of more detailed structure resembles the one before it. The observer has no way of assigning any absolute scale to the structure. The sequence-doubling phenomenon that we looked at earlier is rather like that. There is a constant ratio between the distances at which the doublings take place, and that information alone is not enough to tell you how close you are to the critical value in absolute terms.

Similarly, by examining a single piece of the Mandelbrot set it is impossible to tell at what level of detail the set is being examined. The set can be examined more and more closely, forever, and simply continues to exhibit more and more detail.

There is never a place where we arrive at the individual "atoms" that make up the set. In this respect, the set differs from anything encountered in nature, where the fundamental particles provide a final absolute scaling. Even so, there are in nature things that exhibit scaling over many orders of magnitude. One of the most famous examples is a coastline. If you ask "How long is the coastline of the United States?" a first thought is that you can go to a map and measure it. Then it's obvious that the map has smoothed the real coastline. You need to go to larger scale maps, and larger scale maps. A coastline "scales," like the surface of a snowflake, all the way down to the individual rocks and grains of sand. You find larger and larger numbers for the length of the coast. Another natural phenomenon that exhibits scaling is — significantly — turbulent flow. Ripples ride on whirls that ride on vortices that sit on swirls that are made up of eddies, on and on.

There are classes of mathematical curves that, like coastlines, do not have a length that one can measure in the usual way. A very famous one, the "Koch curve," is sketched in Figure 4. The area enclosed by the Koch curve is clearly finite; but when we set out to compute the length of its boundary, we find that it is 3 x $^4/_3$ x $^4/_3$ x $^4/_3$ . . . Which diverges to infinity. Curves like this are known as *pathological curves*. The word "pathological" means diseased, or sick. It is a good name for them.

There is a special term reserved for the boundary dimension of such finite/infinite objects, and it is called the *Hausdorff-Besicovitch* measure. That's a bit of a mouthful. The boundaries of the Mandelbrot set have a fractional Hausdorff-Besicovitch measure, rather than the usual dimension (1) of the boundary of a plane curve, and most people now prefer to use the term coined by Mandelbrot, and speak of *fractal dimension* rather than Hausdorff-Besicovitch dimension. Objects that exhibit such properties, and other such features as scaling, were named as *fractals* by Mandelbrot.

Any discussion of chaos has to include the Mandelbrot set, scaling, and fractals, because it offers by far the most *visually* attractive part of the theory. I am less convinced that it is as important as Feigenbaum's universality. However, it is certainly beautiful to look at, highly suggestive of shapes found in Nature and — most important of all — it tends to show up in the study of systems that physicists *are* happy with and impressed by, since they represent the result of solving systems of differential equations.

Figure 4: A sick curve

6.   STRANGE ATTRACTORS

This is all very interesting, but in our discussion so far there is a big missing piece. We have talked of iterated functions, and seen that even very simple cases can exhibit "chaotic" behavior. And we have also remarked that physical systems also often exhibit chaotic behavior. However, such systems are usually described in science by *differential equations*, not by iterated functions. We need to show that the iterated functions and the differential equations are close relatives, at some fundamental level, before we can be persuaded that the results we have obtained so far in iterated functions can be used to describe events in the real world.

Let us return to one simple system described by a differential equation, namely, the pendulum, and examine it in a little more detail. First let's recognize that the phase space diagram that we looked at in Figure 2 applies only to an *idealized* pendulum, not a real one. In the real world, every pendulum is gradually slowed by friction, until it sits at the bottom of the swing, unmoving. This is a single point in phase space, corresponding to zero angle and zero speed. That point in phase space is an *attractor* for pendulum motion, and it is a *stable* attractor. All pendulums, unless given a periodic kick by a clockwork or electric motor, will settle down to the zero angle/zero speed point. No matter with what value of angle or speed a pendulum is started swinging, it will finish up at the stable attractor. In mathematical terms, all points of phase space, neighbors or not, will approach each other as time goes on.

A friction-free pendulum, or one that is given a small constant boost each swing, will behave like the idealized one, swinging and swinging, steadily and forever. Points in phase space neither tend to be drawn towards each other, nor repelled from each other.

But suppose that we had a physical system in which points that *began* close together tended to *diverge* from each other. That is the very opposite of the real-world pendulum, and we must first ask if such a system could exist.

It can, as we shall shortly see. It is a case of something that we have already encountered, a strong dependence on initial conditions, since later states of the system differ from each other a great deal, though they began infinitesimally separated. In such a case, the attractor is not a stable attractor, or even a periodic attractor. Instead it is called a *strange attractor*.

This is an inspired piece of naming, comparable with John Archibald Wheeler's introduction of the term "black hole." Even people who have never heard of chaos theory pick up on it. It is also an appropriate name. The paths traced out in phase space in the region of a strange attractor are infinitely complex, bounded in extent, never repeating; chaotic, yet chaotic in some deeply controlled way. If there can be such a thing as controlled chaos, it is seen around strange attractors.

We now address the basic question: Can strange attractors exist mathematically? The simple pendulum cannot possess a strange attractor; so far we have offered no proof that *any* system can exhibit one. However, it can be proved that strange attractors do exist in mathematically specified systems, although a certain minimal complexity is needed in order for a system to possess a strange attractor. We have this situation: simple equations can exhibit complicated solutions, but for the particular type of complexity represented by the existence of strange attractors, the system of equations can't be *too* simple. To be specific, a system of three or more nonlinear differential equations can possess a strange attractor; less than three equations, or more than three linear equations, cannot. (The mathematical statement of this fact is simpler but more abstruse: a system can exhibit a strange attractor if at least one Lyapunov exponent is positive.)

If we invert the logic, it is tempting to make another statement: *Any physical system that shows an ultra-sensitive dependence on initial conditions has a strange attractor buried somewhere in its structure.*

This is a plausible but not a proven result. I am tempted to call it the most important unsolved problem of chaos theory. If it turns out to be true, it will have a profound unifying influence on numerous branches of science. Systems whose controlling equations bear no resemblance to each other will share a *structural* resemblance, and there will be the possibility of developing universal techniques that apply to the solution of complicated problems in a host of different areas. One thing in common with every problem that we have been discussing is *nonlinearity*. Nonlinear systems are notoriously difficult to solve, and seem to defy intuition. Few general techniques exist today for tackling nonlinear problems, and some new insight is desperately needed.

If chaos theory can provide that insight, it will have moved from being a baffling grab-bag of half results, interesting conjectures, and faintly seen relationships, to become a real "new science." We are not there yet. But if we can go that far, then our old common sense gut instinct, that told us simple equations must have simple solutions, will have proved no more reliable than our ancestors' common sense instinctive knowledge that told them the Earth was flat. And the long-term implications of that new thought pattern may be just as revolutionary to science.

7. SOME READING

Gleick, J. *Chaos: Making A New Science*. Viking, 1987. You will read this book, love it, be swept up and carried along by it, and thoroughly enjoy the exciting ride. And when you are done, I defy you to tell me, on the basis of what you have read there, what chaos theory is, or how its underlying ideas serve as an integrating influence in science.

Prigogine, I., and I. Stengers. *Order Out of Chaos*. Bantam, 1984. This book is not primarily a discussion of chaos theory, but in three chapters (5, 6, and 9) it provides more meat on the subject than Gleick's whole book. From this work I drew the opening quotation of the article, "Classical Nightmares . . . and Quantum Paradoxes." Also, Prigogine's book, *From Being to Becoming* (Freeman, 1980) tackles the tough question of irreversible processes and quantum theory at a more advanced level than the Prigogine and Stengers text. Its third part should make your head ache. Both Prigogine books are harder reading than Gleick, and expect a lot more of the reader.

Hofstadter, D. *Scientific American*, November, 1981, reprinted as Chapter 16 of *Metamagical Themas*. Basic Books, 1985. Hofstadter, as always, looks for elegance. He finds it in the results of chaos theory, and describes what he finds as clearly as one could ask. I am a fan of Hofstadter. His *Gödel, Escher, Bach* (Vintage Books, 1980) examines the same question of the nature of the human brain as Roger Penrose's *The Emperor's New Mind* — and reaches exactly opposite conclusions.

ternative to the more academic "periodical cicadas." Perhaps their only function is to separate the old-timers in Washington from the new heads.

You don't know about the locusts? Why, weren't you born

THE SEVENTEEN-YEAR LOCUSTS

The Seventeen-Year Locusts occupy a special place in the Washington, D.C., scene. As a natural event, these tree-grasshoppers induce in even the least imaginative visitor a sense of wonder at the strangeness of Nature.

For sixteen years, the U.S. capital city has its usual swarms of cicadas. In July and August they fill the warm and muggy summer nights with their chirping and chittering. Then comes the seventeenth year. The locusts awaken in their hiding places underneath the tree roots and begin to crawl up out of the damp ground. For a few weeks they cover every tree and every shrub, so that you cannot walk in the garden without trampling them underfoot. At night they make a noise loud enough to drown the sound of low-flying aircraft on their runs along the Potomac to Washington's National Airport.

Why seventeen years? Is it some unfathomable confluence of natural events, a resonance of the planetary orbits? Or is it a precise biological chronometer, ticking away inside the pin-head brains, to bring them out in the exact week of that seventeenth summer? No one knows. But once in position on their twigs, the locusts seems quite happy to sit, green bodies motionless and bright red eyes unwinking.

The Seventeen-Year Locusts seem to serve no useful purpose. If they did not exist, it would be by no means necessary to invent them. They do not bite or sting, and although they suck the sap from tender young twigs, all evidence of that is gone in a couple of years. They do not scourge the earth, for the name "locust" is only a popular alternative to the more academic "periodical cicadas." Perhaps their only function is to separate the old-timers in Washington from the new hands.

"You don't know about the locusts? Why, weren't you here

in 1986? They'll be back again in 2003, just hang around awhile."

And then the arguments start, as other natives insist that they were last here in 1985, or 1987. For unlike the locusts, the Washingtonians seem to lack that precise memory and timing.

The insects themselves take no interest in the arguments, or indeed in much else. As one might expect, they seem confused about everything. They popped down for a nap when Ronald Reagan was running the show, when gasoline was under a dollar a gallon, and when "Dallas" was a top TV show. Now in 2003 some total unknown has appeared as President, gas is up to nine dollars a pint, and TV sets are used only as neural interfaces.

"What's going on here?" they say to each other. "Close your eyes for one minute in this darn town, and next thing you know you feel like a complete outsider."

Confusion is probably their dominant emotion. But I have my own concerns — ones that may explain another of Nature's great mysteries.

I see the day coming when the earth trembles and cracks into huge, mile-deep fissures. People in Washington — who value curiosity more than anything, even life itself — go to the edge and look down. Then they begin to scream and run about wildly.

It is quite useless, because they cannot escape. They are gripped in the monstrous jaws, lifted high into the air, and torn apart.

The Seventy-Million-Year Dinosaurs are back in town.

Afterword: *The Seventeen-Year Locusts*

Here is a universal law that I just invented: Stories under 2,000 words are excused Afterwords.

not accept any of these gifts.

Sebastian's second visit to the Takla Makan Shamo had to be very different. His three-week disappearance on the first trip had left the Chinese authorities uneasy; they did not want him back. For his part, he did not want anyone in China to

THE COURTS OF XANADU

The eagle's way is easy. Strike north-north-west from Calcutta, to meet the international border close to the little Indian town of Darbhanga. Fly on into Nepal, passing east of Kathmandu. After another hundred miles you encounter the foothills and then the peaks of the Himalayan range. Keep going — easy enough when you fly with the wings of imagination. You traverse silent, white-capped mountains, the tallest in the world, float on across the high plateau country of Tibet, and come at last to the Kunlun Mountains. Cross them. You are now in China proper, at the southern edge of the *Takla Makan Shamo*, one of the world's fiercest deserts, a thousand miles from east to west, five hundred from north to south.

If you are driving, or walking on real feet, you have to do things rather differently. The Himalayas are impassable. The Tibetan border is patrolled. Travel in the Tibetan interior is restricted.

Gerald Sebastian made the trip to the Takla Makan in two different ways. The first time he was alone, traveling light. He sailed from Calcutta to Hong Kong, flew to Beijing, and then took the train west all the way to Xinjiang Province. He was a celebrity, and his presence was permitted, even encouraged. However, his trip south from Urumqi, into the fiery heart of the Takla Makan desert, was not permitted. It was difficult to arrange, and it took a good deal of bribery.

Today's Chinese, you will be told by their government, do not accept tips or bribes. Just so.

Sebastian's second visit to the *Takla Makan Shamo* had to be very different. His three-week disappearance on the first trip had left the Chinese authorities uneasy; they did not want him back. For his part, he did not want anyone in China to know of his presence. This time he also had four people with him, and he needed a mass of equipment, including two large, balloon-wheel trucks.

The trucks were the obvious problem; the four people — five, if one includes Sebastian himself — would prove a worse one. The group consisted of the following: one world-famous explorer and antiquarian, Gerald Sebastian; one wealthy, decorative, and determined woman, Jackie Sands; one NASA scientist, Dr. Will Reynolds, as out of place on the expedition as a catfish on the moon; one China expert, Paddy Elphinstone, fluent in the *Turkic* language spoken in Xinjiang Province, and in everything else; and one professional cynic, con-man, and four-time loser, convinced in his heart that this expedition would be his fifth failure.

How is it possible to know what a man believes in his heart?

It is time for me to step out of the shadows and introduce myself. I am Sam Nevis. I was along on this expedition because I knew more about treasure-hunting, wilderness excavation, and survival in the rough than the rest of Sebastian's helpers put together — which was not saying much. And by the time that we were assembled in Sebastian's hotel room in Rawalpindi, ready to head north-east out of Pakistan, I already knew that the expedition was going to be a disaster.

It was not a question of funds, which is where three of my own efforts had failed. Gerald Sebastian had enough silver-tongued persuasiveness for a dozen people. How else could a man raise half a million dollars for an expedition, without telling his backers what they would get out of it?

I had seen him cast his spell in New York, three months earlier, and knew I had met my master. He was a bantam-weight, silver-haired and hawk-nosed, with a clear-eyed innocence of manner I could never match.

"*Atlantis,*" he had said, and the word glowed in the air in front of him. "Not in the middle of the Atlantic Ocean, as Colonel Churchward would have you believe. Not at Thera, or Crete, in the Mediterranean, as Skipios claims. Not among the Mayans, as Doctor Augustus Le Plongeon asserts. But *here*, where the world has never thought to look." He whipped out the map, placed it on the table, and set his right index finger in the middle of the great bowl of Xinjiang Province. "Right here!"

There were half a dozen well-dressed men and two women sitting at the long conference room table. They all craned forward to stare at the map. "Takla — Makan —Shamo," read one of them slowly. He was Henry Hoffman, a New York real estate multimillionaire who also happened to be Mr. Jackie Sands. He was seventy-five years old, and she was his third wife. He leaned closer to the map, peering through strong bifocals. "But it's marked as a *desert*."

"Exactly what it is." Gerald Sebastian had paused, waiting for the faces to turn back up to meet his eyes. "That's what the word *shamo* means, a sand desert — as distinguished from a pebble desert, which is a *gobi*. This is desert, extreme, wild, and uninhabited. But it wasn't always a desert, any more than there were always skyscrapers here on Manhattan. You have to look *under* the dunes, a hundred feet down. And then you will see the cities. Cities *drowned by sandstorms*, not water."

He reached into his case and pulled out another rabbit: the images taken by the Shuttle Imaging Radar experiments. He slapped them onto the table, and turned to Will Reynolds. "Doctor Reynolds, if you would be kind enough to explain how these images are interpreted . . ."

Reynolds coughed, genuinely uncomfortable at explaining his work to a group of laymen. "Well — uh — see, this is a strip taken by a synthetic aperture radar, the Shuttle Imaging Radar, on board the Shuttle Orbiter." He worked his hands together and cracked the knobby finger joints. Will Reynolds was a stork of a man, with a long neck, great ungainly limbs and a mop of black hair. "It's sort of like a photograph, but it uses much longer wavelengths, microwaves rather than visible light. Centimeters, rather than micrometers. So it doesn't just see what's *on* the surface. Where the ground is dry, it sees *under* the surface, too. And in a real desert, where there's been no rain for years or decades, it can see a long way down. Tens of meters. Here's some earlier SEASAT and SIR-A shots of the Sahara Desert, where it hasn't rained and you can clearly see the old river courses, far below the surface sand dunes. . . ."

His hesitancy disappeared as he slipped into his special subject, and he was off and running.

Gerald Sebastian did not interrupt. He would not dream of

interrupting. It was pure flummery, the oldest and best con-
man style, with the right amount of technical and authentic
detail to make it persuasive. Will Reynolds could not be
bought, that was obvious. But he could be *sold*, and Sebastian
had sold him on the project. Now he was showing the radar
images of the Takla Makan, pointing out what seemed to be
regular geometric figures under the sand dunes, where no
such figures could be expected.

Those shapes looked like the natural cracking patterns of
drying clay to me, but no one around the table suggested that.
What do investment bankers, art museum patrons, and the
rest of the New York *glitterati* know about clay cracks? And
what do they care, when it's only a half a million dollars at
stake, and you might be part of the team that finds Atlantis?
Nothing could beat that as cocktail party conversation.
Sebastian knew his pigeons.

Very well; but what was I doing, following Sebastian on his
wild chase to the world's most bleak and barren desert? I was a
professional, a fund-raiser and treasure-hunter myself.

To understand that, you have to remember an old gold-
miners' story. Two prospectors were out in the American West,
late in the nineteenth century; they had looked for gold unsuccessfully for forty years. They had dug and panned and
surveyed one particular valley from end to end, and found not
an ounce of gold anywhere in it. Finally, they decided that
there were better ways to get rich. They left the valley they had
explored so carefully and so unproductively, and headed for
the nearest big town. There they put every cent they had into
buying provisions, horses, and wagons, and they both set up
stores.

Then they started spreading the story: the worlds' biggest
gold find had just been made, back in the valley they had come
from. If you went for a stroll there, you would stumble over
fist-sized nuggets of twenty-four carat.

The run on horses, wagons, and supplies was incredible.
Everybody in town wanted to dash off to the wilderness and
stake a claim. The two old prospectors had cornered the market for transportation and supplies, and they could name their
price. They sold, and sold, and sold, until at last one of them
found he had only one horse and one wagon left. He jumped

into the wagon, whipped up the horse, and started to drive out of town. As he did so, he found he was running side by side with his old friend, also with horse and wagon.

"Where you heading?"

"Back to the valley — to get the gold!"

"Yeah!"

So I was along on Sebastian's ride. And I was sure that the same ghosts of golden discovery must fill and dominate the fine, phantasmagoric mind of Gerald Sebastian. He and I were cut from the same bolt of cloth. As the poet laureate of all confidence tricksters and treasure-seekers puts it, we were "given to strong delusion, wholly believing a lie."

In my own defense, let me point out that the full insanity of the enterprise was not obvious at once. It became apparent to me only when we assembled in Hong Kong, prior to flying to Pakistan.

There, in the regent Hotel in Kowloon, looking out over Hong Kong Harbor with its crowded water traffic, I tried to buy Jackie Sands a drink. A dry martini, perhaps, which is what I was having. Paddy Elphinstone, our China expert, had warned me that it would be my last chance at a decent alcoholic cocktail for quite a while.

Jackie smiled and ordered an orange juice. It was predictable. She was dark-haired, clear-skinned, and somewhere between thirty-eight and forty-four. Her hair stood out in a black cloud around her head, her eyes were bright, and she was so healthy looking it was disgusting. She seemed to glow. If she had ever tried alcohol, it must have been a long-ago experiment.

"Gerald is entitled to his opinion," she was saying. "But I have my own. I didn't come here expecting to find Atlantis. And I'm sure we won't find Atlantis."

"Then what will we find?" I asked the question, but young Paddy Elphinstone seemed even more interested in the answer. He had been drinking before we arrived, then accepted the drink that Jackie refused and quadrupled it. As the waiters went by, he gabbled at them in their own tongues, Tamil and Malay and Thai and Mandarin and Cantonese. Now he was leaning forward, his chin low down toward the table-top, staring at Jackie.

"Visitors," she said. "Old visitors."

Paddy laughed. "Plenty of those, to the Takla Makan. Marco Polo wandered through there, and the Great Silk Road ran north and south of it. The technology for horizontal well drilling in Turpan was imported all the way from Persia."

"I mean older than that. And farther away than that." Jackie reached out and put a carefully manicured, red-nailed hand on Paddy's. Wasn't she the woman I had imagined for twenty years, wandering the world at my side, the competent, level-headed companion that I had never managed to attract?

Her next words destroyed the fancy. "Visitors," she said. "Long, long ago. Aliens, from other stars. Beings who found the desert like home to them. They came, and then they left."

"Pretty neat trick," said Paddy. He was leaning back now, too drunk to pretend to sobriety. "Sure that they left, are you? Damn neat trick, if they did. D'yer know what Takla Makan means, in the local Turkic?"

I was sure that Jackie didn't. I didn't, either. I knew that Paddy had that incredible gift for languages, learning them as easily and idiomatically as a baby learns to talk. But I didn't know until that moment that Paddy Elphinstone was also an alcoholic.

"Takla Makan," he said again, and closed his eyes. His thin, straw-colored hair sagged in a cowlick over a pale forehead. "*Takla Makan* means this, Jackie Sands: 'Go in, and you don't come out . . .'"

At its western edge China meets three other countries: Russia to the north, Pakistan to the south, and a thin strip of Afghanistan between. The east-stretching tongue of Afghanistan would provide the easiest travel route, but it and Russia are both politically impossible. With no real choice, and a need for secrecy above all, Gerald Sebastian had arranged that we would move into China through Pakistan.

We drove from Rawalpindi to Gilgit, skirting the heights of the Karakoram Range. At Gilgit we made our final refueling stop, six hundred gallons for the trucks' enlarged tanks. Then we took the old path into Xinjiang, just as though we were heading for Kashi, on the western edge of the Takla Makan desert. Five miles short of the Chinese border we left the road and veered right.

I probably took more notice of our path than the others, because I was driving the first truck with Will Reynolds as companion and navigator. He was following our progress carefully, tousled dark head bent over maps and a terminal that hooked him into the Global Positioning System satellites. He called the turns for me for more than seven hours. Then, as the sun of early May began to set and the first sand dunes came into sight to the northeast, he nodded and folded the map.

"We're two hundred miles from the border, and we ought to be out of the danger area for patrols. Sebastian said he wants to stop early tonight. Keep your eyes open for a little lake ahead, we're going to stay by it."

I nodded, while Will put the map away and pulled out one of his precious radar images. Every spare moment went into them. Now he was trying to pinpoint our position on the picture and muttering to himself about "layover" location problems.

The lake, thirty yards across and fed by a thin trickle in a bed of white gravel, appeared in less than a mile. While the other truck caught up with us, I hopped out and bent down by the soda-crusted lakeside. The water was shallow, briny, and heavy with bitter alkalines.

I spat it out. "Undrinkable," I said to Sebastian, as he moved to join me.

He didn't argue, didn't want to taste if for himself to make sure. He knew why he had hired me, and he trusted his own judgment. "I'll get the desalinization unit," he said. "Tell the others. A gallon per person, to do what you like with."

"Washing?"

He gave me a remote smile and gestured at the pool's still surface.

Dinner — my job and Paddy's, we were the hired help — took another hour, cooking with the same diesel fuel that ran the motors and would power the hoist derrick. By the time we were finished eating, the first stars were showing. Fifteen minutes later the tents were inflated and moored. The trucks, packed with supplies and equipment, were emergency accommodation only.

We sat on tiny camp stools arranged in a circle on the

rocky ground. Not around the romantic fire of Sebastian's movies — the nearest tree was probably three hundred miles away — but around a shielded oil lamp, hanging on a light tripod. Gerald Sebastian was in an ebullient mood. He had wandered around the camp, putting everything that appealed to his eye on videotape, and now he was ready to relax. He was a rarity among explorers, one who did all his own camerawork and final program composition. He would add his commentaries back in America.

"The hard part?" he said, in answer to a question from Jackie. "Love, we're done with the hard part. We know where we're going, we know what we'll find there, we're all equipped to get it."

"What is it, d'you think?" said Paddy in a blurry voice. His words to me in Hong Kong concerning access to alcoholic drinks in China applied, I now realized, only to others. Paddy had brought along his own bottled supply, and from the way he was acting it had to be a generous one.

Instead of replying, Sebastian stood up and walked off to the trucks. He was back in a couple of minutes carrying a big yellow envelope. Without a word he slipped out half a dozen photo prints and passed them around the group. I felt the excitement goosepimpling the hair on my forearms. Sebastian had shown me pictures when we first talked, and I gathered he had shown others to Jackie Sands and Will Reynolds. But like a showman shining the spotlight on a different part of the stage for each different audience, he showed each set of listeners what it wanted to hear — and only that. I had asked a dozen times for more details, and always he had said, "Soon enough you'll see — when we get to Xinjiang." I had no doubt that even now there was another folder somewhere, one that none of us would see.

Back in the United States, Sebastian had produced for me only two photographs, of a ruby ring set in thick gold, and of a flat golden tablet the length of a man's hand, inscribed with unfamiliar ideographs. I couldn't relate either of those to Atlantis, but of course I didn't care. Atlantis was somebody else's part of the elephant.

The picture in my left hand was not one I had seen before. It was clear, with excellent detail and color balance, good enough to be used on one of Gerald Sebastian's TV documentaries. Some day it might be. For I was staring at a green statue, with a meter ruler propped alongside to show the scale, and although in fourteen years of wasted wandering I had seen the artifacts of every civilization on Earth, this, whatever it might be, was unlike any of them.

It was man-sized, and must weigh a quarter of a ton. The plumed helmet and tunic might be Greek or Cretan, the sandals Roman. The face had the Egyptian styling, while the sword on the heavy buckled belt was vaguely central Asian. And if I stretched my imagination, I could see in the composed attitude of the limbs the influence of Indonesia and Buddhism. Put the pieces together, and the sum was totally strange.

Strange, but not enough to excite me. The picture in my right hand did that. It was an enlargement of the statue's ornate belt. The buckle looked like the front of a modern hand calculator, with miniature numerals, function keys, and display screen. Next to it, attached to the belt but ready to be detached from it, was a bulbous weapon with sights, trigger, and a flared barrel. It was not a revolver, but it looked a lot like a power laser.

First things first. "Do you have the statue?" I asked, before anyone else could speak.

He had assumed his old seat in the circle. "If I did, I would not be here." He was sitting as immobile as a statue himself. "And if I thought I could obtain it alone, none of you would be here. Let me tell you a story. It concerns my earlier trip into the Takla Makan, and how I came to make it."

The lamp caught the keen profile and the dreamer's brow. The moon was rising. Far away to the northeast, the first desert dunes were a smoky blur on the horizon.

"I thought I knew it all," he said. "And then, three years ago, I was called in to help the executor of an estate in Dresden. Dull stuff, I thought, but an old friend called in a favor. You may ask, as I did, why me? It turned out that the old lady who died was a relative of Sir Aurel Stein, and she mentioned my name in her will." Paddy Elphinstone started, and Sebastian caught the movement. "That's right, Paddy, there's only one of him." He turned to the rest of us. "Aurel Stein was the greatest Oriental explorer of his time. And this was his stamping-ground" — he gestured around us — "for forty years, in the early part of this century. He covered China, Mongolia, and Xinjiang — Sinkiang, the maps called it in his day — like nobody else in the world. He lived in India and he died in Kabul, but he left relatives in Germany. It was more than a pleasure to look at that house in Dresden. It was an *honor*.

"Before I'd been in that place for an hour, I knew something unusual had been thrown my way. But it was a couple more days before I realized how exciting it was." He tapped the photographs on his knee. "Stein drew the statue, and described its dimensions. The pen-and-ink drawing was in the old lady's collection. Sir Aurel told in his journal exactly where he had found it, in a dry valley surrounded by dunes. He gave the location — or to be more accurate, he described how to reach the spot from Urumqi and the Turpan Depression. He knew it was an oddity and he couldn't identify its maker, but it was far too heavy to carry. Sixty years ago, that statue's belt didn't send its own message. Electronic calculators and power lasers didn't exist. So he left it there. He was content with the drawing, and he didn't set any great value on that. It could take an inconspicuous place in his works, and end up in the possession of an old German lady, dying in her late eighties in a Dresden rowhouse."

It was hard to be specific, but there was something different about Gerald Sebastian. I felt an openness, an eagerness in him since we had entered China, something that was quite different from his usual public persona. Evaluating his performance now, I decided that he was a little too obsessive to appeal to his own backers. He and Will Reynolds were brothers under the skin.

"I went there," he said. "Three hundred miles south of Urumqi, just as Sir Aurel Stein said, to the middle of the worst part of the desert. Of course, I didn't *expect* to find the statue. Chances were, if it were ever there, it was long gone. I knew that, so I went inadequately prepared and I didn't think through what I would do if I found it. But I had a look. Sam will understand that, even if the rest of you don't." He nodded his head at me, eyes unreadable in the lamplight. "Well, the valley was there, half filled with drifting sand. And I didn't have equipment with me. I spent one week digging — scrabbling, that's a better word — then I was running short of water." He slipped the photographs back into their envelope and stood up abruptly. "The statue was there. I found it on my last day. There was a gold tablet and a ruby ring, attached to the belt, and I took those. Then I photographed it, and I covered it with sand. It will be there still. We're going to lift it out this time and put it on the truck. And when we get it, we'll take it back for radioactive dating. My guess is that it is more than seven thousand years old."

He walked away, outside the circle of lamplight, over behind the two balloon-wheeled trucks. After a few seconds Jackie Sands followed him. Paddy was off in an alcoholic world of his own, eyes closed and mouth open. I looked at Will Reynolds, sitting hunched forward and tugging at his finger joints.

"Give me a hand to get Paddy to his tent, would you? It's getting cold, and I don't think he'll manage it on his own."

Will nodded and moved to the other side of Paddy. "I've seen it, you know," he said, as we lifted one to each arm.

I paused. "The statue?"

"Naw." He gave a snuffling laugh. "How the hell would I see the statue? The *valley*. It shows on the radar images, clear as day. And there's structure underneath it — buildings, a whole town, buried deep in the sand. I saw 'em, before I'd ever met Gerald Sebastian."

"He contacted you?"

"No. I wrote to him. You see, after I interpreted the images and realized what I might be seeing, I asked the applications office at Headquarters for field trip funding, to collect some ground truth. And they *bounced* it — as though it was some dumb boondoggle to get me a trip to China!" Between us, we stuffed Paddy Elphinstone into his tent and zipped the flap. If he wanted to undress that was his own affair. "That made me so mad," said Will, "I thought, damn you bureaucrats. If you don't want this, there's others might. I'd seen one of Sebastian's travel programs about China, and I wrote to him. The hell with NASA! We'll find that city without 'em."

Will turned and lurched off towards his own tent. He had

the height of a basketball player and none of the coordination.

Well, I thought, that's another piece of the elephant accounted for. So far as Will Reynolds was concerned, this illegal journey to China's western desert was just a field trip, a way to gather the data that justified his own interpretation of satellite images. I wondered, had Gerald Sebastian talked of Sir Aurel Stein's legacy in Dresden, and the follow-up trip to the Takla Makan desert *before* Will Reynolds had shown him those radar images? My skeptical soul assured me that he had not.

And yet I couldn't quite accept my own logic. While Sebastian had been speaking about Aurel Stein, a disquieting thought had been creeping up on me. From the day I was recruited by him, I had been sure that he and I had the same motives. Sure, he was smoother than I was, but inside we were the same. Now I wasn't sure. He was so terribly convincing, so filled with burning curiosity. Either his interest in exploration was powerful and genuine — or he was better at the bait-and-catch funding game than anyone in history. Was it somehow possible that *both* were true?

I lit a black Poona cheroot and stood there in the lamplit circle, noticing the temperature dropping fast around me. In this area, it would be well below freezing before dawn, and then back up to a hundred degrees by the next afternoon. I zipped up my jacket and started to put away the cooking equipment. With Paddy gone for the night, the number of hired help on the party was down to one.

The evening was not yet over. Before I had time to finish tidying up, Jackie Sands reappeared from the direction of the trucks. She was wearing a fluffy wool sweater, as dark, tangled and luxuriant as her hair. She made no attempt to help — I wondered if she had ever in her whole life cleared up after dinner — but sat down on one of the camp stools.

"Destroying your lungs," she said.

"Do you tell that to your hubby, too?"

There was a flash of teeth, but I couldn't see her facial expression. "It's not worth telling things to Henry. He stopped accepting inputs years ago on everything except stocks and bonds."

"Does he smoke?"

"Not any more. Doctor's orders."

"So he *does* accept other inputs."

This time a chuckle accompanied the gleam of teeth. "I suppose he does. But not from me."

I flicked the cigar stub away and watched its orange-red spark cartwheel across the dusty surface. "That's one nice thing about deserts. No fire hazard." I sat down on a camp stool opposite her. "What can I do for you, Mrs. Hoffman?"

"Miss Sands. I don't use my husband's name. Do you have to be so direct?"

"It's nearly ten-thirty."

"That's not late."

"Not for Manhattan. But social functions end early in the Takla Makan. I have to be up at five. And it's getting cold."

"It is." She snuggled deeper into her sweater. "I thought this was supposed to be a hot desert. All right, straight to business. I know why Gerald Sebastian organized this expedition. He did it for fame and fortune, equal parts. I know why Will Reynolds came along; he wants to protect his scientific reputation. And I understand Paddy. He's a born explorer, along for the sheer love of it, and if he doesn't drink himself to death he'll be world famous before he's forty. But what about you, Sam? You sit and listen to everybody else, and you hardly say a word. What's your motive for being here?"

"Why do you want to know? And if it comes to that, what's your motive?"

"Mm. You show me yours and I'll show you mine, eh?" She stared straight into the lamp and pursed her lips. "You know, being on an expedition like this is a bit like being on a small cruise ship. After a few days, you start to tell near-strangers things you wouldn't admit to your family."

"I don't have a family."

"No?" Her eyebrows arched. "All right, then, I'll do it. I'll play your game. A swap. Who first?"

"You."

"You're a hard man, Sam-I-am. Lordie. Where should I begin? Do you know what SETI is?"

"Settee? Like a couch?"

"No. SETI, like S-E-T-I — the Search for Extra-Terrestrial Intelligence. Heard of it?"

"No. I'm still looking for signs of intelligence on Earth. What is it, some sort of game?"

"Not to me. Just think what it will mean if we ever find evidence that there are other intelligent beings in the universe. It will change everything we do. Change the basic way we think, maybe stop us all blowing ourselves up. I believe the work is enormously important, and for nearly five years I've been giving money to promote SETI research."

"Henry's money?"

She sat up a little straighter. "My allowance. But most of the research work is highly technical, with radio receivers and electronics and signal analysis. I can't even understand how my money is spent."

"Which makes it sound like a classic rip-off."

"It does sound like that, I admit. But it's not."

Her voice was totally earnest. Unfortunately, that's one prime qualification to be a total sucker. "You *think* it's not," I said.

"Put it that way if you want to. I've never regretted giving the money. But then I heard about this expedition, and it really made me think. Sebastian says he has found Atlantis, with a technological civilization as advanced as ours. But I say, it's just as likely he found evidence of *visitors* to the earth, ones who came long ago."

"And just happened to look exactly like humans? That's too implausible."

"Not if they were truly advanced. Beings like that would be able to look just as they wanted to look. Anyway, Sam, you're on the wrong side of the argument. Suppose there's only a one in a thousand chance that what we are looking for is evidence of aliens. I'm still better off spending my money coming here, to do something myself, rather than being a little bit of something I don't even understand. Don't you agree?"

"Oddly enough, I do. It's one of the golden rules; stay close to the place your money is spent."

"But you don't accept the idea of visitors to this planet?"

"I don't reject it. I just say it's improbable."

"Right. But it's possible." She sounded short of breath. "And that's what I think, too. So that's me, and that's why I'm here, and the only reason I'm here. Now how about you?"

I didn't want to talk, but now I seemed committed to it. I lit another cigar and blew smoke toward the half-moon. "I'm going to be a big disappointment to you," I said, with my face averted. "You're on an expedition with a world-famous traveler and television celebrity, a NASA scientist, and a born explorer. I'm the bad apple in the barrel. You see, I'm a treasure hunter. I came with Gerald Sebastian for one simple reason: there's a chance — an outside chance, but a hell of a lot better than the odds that you'll find your extraterrestrials — that I'm going to walk away from this holding a whole basket of money. That's why I'm here."

"I don't believe you!"

I shrugged. "I knew you wouldn't. I didn't think you'd like it, and you don't. But it's true."

"You may have convinced yourself that it's true, but it isn't." She sounded outraged. "My God, if all you wanted was money, there are a hundred easier ways to get it. Play the Stock Market, work in a casino, go into the insurance business. You don't have to come to the ends of the earth to make money. I don't think you know your own motivation, or you want to hide it from me."

I threw away my second cigar — this one much less than half-smoked. "Miss Sands, how long have you been married?"

"Why, four years, I suppose. Five years in August. Not that I see why—"

"Do you love Henry Hoffman?"

"What! I — of course I do. I *do*. And it's no damned business of yours."

"But you left him for months to come on this expedition."

"I told you why!"

"Right. Do you enjoy sleeping with him? Never mind, ignore that, and let's assume you do. You're quite right, it *is* no business of mine. All I'm trying to say is that people do a lot of different things to make money, and it's no one else's concern *why* they do it. And sometimes the obvious assumptions about why people do things are right, and sometimes they are quite wrong. So why won't you believe me, when I tell you that I'm here for the simplest possible reason, to make my fortune?"

But she was on her feet, swiveling around and heading fast

for the dark bulk of the trucks. "Damn you," she said as she walked away. "My marriage is fine, and anyway it's none of your bloody business. Keep your big nose out of it."

She was gone, leaving me still with the clearing-up to take care of. Before I did that I picked up the lamp and went off to look for the cigar I had thrown away. The way things were going, before the end of this expedition I might be craving a half-smoked cigar.

I slept poorly and woke at dawn. When I emerged from my tent Paddy already had the stove going and water heated for coffee. Apparently he was one of those unfortunates who never suffer a hangover, which made his long-term prospects for full alcoholism all too good. One good hangover will keep me sober for months. He nodded at me cheerfully while he shaved. "Sleep well?"

"Lousy. I thought I could hear noises outside the tent — like people talking. I guess I was dreaming."

"No. You were listening to *them*." Paddy pointed his razor at the sand dunes to the north. "It's called *mingsha* — singing sand. It will get worse when we move deeper into the Takla Makan."

"I'm not talking about sand dunes, Paddy. I'm talking about *people*. Conversations, whistling, calling to animals. I even heard somebody playing the flute."

"That's right." He was intolerably perky for the early morning. "Hold on a minute." He put his razor down on the little folding table that held his coffee, towel, soap, and a cheese sandwich, and ran off to dive into his tent. A second later he reappeared with a paperback book in his hand.

"We're not the first people to visit this place, not by a long shot. It was a big obstacle for two thousand years on the Great Silk Road, and all the travelers skirted it either north or south. Marco Polo came by the Takla Makan seven hundred years ago, when he was traveling around on Kubla Khan's business. He called it the Desert of Lop. Here's what he says about the desert."

While I poured sweetened black coffee for myself, Paddy found his place in the book and began to read aloud. " 'In this tract neither beasts nor birds are met with, because there is no kind of food for them. It is asserted as a well-known fact that this desert is the abode of many evil spirits, which lure travelers to their destruction with extraordinary illusions . . . they unexpectedly hear themselves called by their own names, and in a tone of voice to which they are accustomed. Supposing the call to proceed from their companions, they are led away from the direct road and left to perish. At night, they seem to hear the march of a large cavalcade.' And here's another choice bit. 'The spirits of the desert are said at times to fill the air with the sounds of all kinds of musical instruments' — there's your flute, Sam — 'and also of drums and the clash of arms.' And it wasn't only Marco Polo. A Chinese monk, Fa Xian, passed this way in the fifth century, and he wrote that there were 'evil spirits and hot winds that kill every man who encounters them, and as far as the eye can see no road is visible, only the skeletons of those who have perished serve to mark the way.'"

Paddy closed his book and grinned happily. "Good stuff, eh? And nothing has changed. At least we know what we're in for over the next few weeks." He went to put the book back in his tent.

The dust-red sun was well above the horizon now, and the other three team members emerged from their tents within a couple of minutes of each other. Between cooking breakfast and striking camp, Paddy and I had no more chance for talk.

Gerald filmed our activities and the scenery around us, then disappeared into the second truck. But Jackie Sands gave me an extra nice smile and even helped collect the breakfast plates. Whatever had annoyed her so last night was apparently all forgotten or forgiven.

She had discarded yesterday's shirt and jeans in favor of a long, loose-fitting dress of white cotton and thick-soled leather sandals. The clothes made good hot-weather sense. So did the different hair styling, smoothing the viper's nest of tangles to long dark curls. But she had also applied heavy makeup and bright lipstick, and that was not so smart. I wondered if she would keep it up when we melted in the heart of the desert and the trucks' inside temperature soared over a hundred and ten.

And then I noticed the dark rings under her eyes, which makeup could not quite hide. Like me, Jackie had apparently suffered a disturbed night.

We were on our way by six. We planned to drive only in the early morning and late afternoon, resting through the worst heat of midday. Today we would be penetrating the true dune country of the desert. I thought that in spite of Gerald Sebastian's optimism, the tough part of the expedition was just beginning.

We drove almost due north, while the land ahead turned to rolling sand hills, enormous, lifeless, seemingly endless. Dun-colored, distinct, and sun-shadowed, each dune rose five or six hundred feet above the dead plain. By nine o'clock their profiles smoked and shimmered in dust and heat haze. It was easy to see why travelers regarded this desert as featureless and impassable. The dunes moved constantly, shaped by wind, creeping across the arid landscape. Nothing could grow here, nothing provided permanence.

And Will Reynolds, seated at my side, was in his element. His space images revealed the contour of every dune. He had known, before he left Washington, their extent, their shape, and their steepness. Months ago he had sat at his desk and plotted an optimum route, weaving us north to Gerald Sebastian's destination on an efficient and sinuous path that took advantage of every break in the dune pattern.

Now he was finally able to apply his knowledge. As I drove, and the thermometer above the truck's dashboard climbed implacably through the nineties, Will chuckled to himself and called out compass headings. At a steady twenty-five miles an hour, we snaked our way forward without a hitch.

Other than an occasional tamarisk bush, we saw nothing and no one. A billion Chinese people lived far to the east, on the alluvial plains and along the fertile river valleys, but no one lived here. This land made Tibet's high plateau appear lush and fertile, even to China's central development committee. According to Gerald Sebastian, the danger of our discovery was too small to worry about.

By ten-thirty, there was no scrap of shade from even the steepest of the dunes. We halted, raised the parasol over both trucks, and settled down to wait. That gave me my first chance to talk to Sebastian alone since we had stopped for dinner last night.

I followed him as he prowled outside the shady zone with his video camera. He spoke with his eye still to the viewfinder. "All right, Sam. Say it."

"You're the one who has to say it."

He turned to face me, squinting up at me in the strong sun. "I don't understand. What do you want?"

"An explanation." We automatically walked on up the dune, farther out of earshot of the others. The heat of the sand burned through our shoes. "Last night, you told us all that you took the ruby ring and the gold tablet from the statue on your last trip."

"Quite right, I said that. And it's quite true."

"So why didn't Sir Aurel Stein do the same thing, when *he* found and drew a picture of the statue?"

He looked me in the eye, the honest stare that was part of his stock-in-trade. "I don't know, Sam. All I can tell you is that he didn't take them. Naturally, I asked myself the same question."

"And how did you answer it?"

"First, I thought that maybe he planned to return for the statue itself, and so he left everything else behind, too. Then when Xinjiang was closed to foreigners, in 1930, he couldn't go back. It's a weak argument, I know, because we all carry what we can, and only leave behind what we can't haul with us. My second explanation is not much better. Aurel Stein didn't show the tablet and ring in his drawing; therefore, they were not there when he explored the valley. Someone else was there between his visit and mine. I'm sure you see what's wrong with that idea."

"People take things from archaeological sites. They don't leave them there."

"Exactly!" There was a furious, frenzied energy to Gerald Sebastian now, an effervescence that had not been there before we reached the Takla Makan. But he was not worried, only excited. "So what is the explanation? Sam, that's what we're going to find out. And this time we didn't come lacking equipment."

He was not referring to the pulleys, hoist, and derrick on

the truck. So what was it? I knew the complete inventory of the truck I was driving. Maybe Paddy Elphinstone could tell me about the other one.

"Don't worry, Sam," Sebastian was saying. "If I knew what had happened, I would have told you." He was interrupted by a cry from the camp. Jackie Sands was standing out from under the parasol, calling and waving her arms at us. We ran back to her.

"It's Will Reynolds," she said as soon as we were close enough. "He was sitting next to me, and suddenly he started to speak. He sounded all slurred, as though he was drunk. Then he tried to stand up and fell off his chair. I think he had a stroke. He's unconscious."

He wasn't, not quite. When we got to him his eyes were rolling from side to side under half-open lids and he was muttering to himself. I sniffed his breath, felt his pulse, then touched my fingers to his forehead.

"Not a stroke. And not drunk. He's overheated — get his shirt open and bring water. Where the devil is Paddy?"

Before I had an answer to that question, Will Reynolds was sitting up and looking about him. We had damp cloths on his wrists, temples, and throat.

"What happened?" he said.

"What do you remember?" I wanted to be sure that he was functioning normally.

"Over there." He pointed up at the brow of a dune, into the eye of the sun. "I saw them marching over the top of it and I stood up to shout to you and Gerald. Then I woke up here."

"Saw who?" said Jackie. She looked at me. "I was sitting there, and I didn't see a thing."

"The patrol, or whatever it was. A line of men and pack-horses and camels, one after another, parading across the top of the dune. There must have been fifty of them." He turned to Gerald. "That's one idea of yours out of the window. You said there was a negligible chance that we'd have trouble with Chinese patrols, and we run into one the first day. I guess they didn't see us down here." He tried to stand, then swayed and leaned back against me. "What's happened to me?"

"Just rest there," I said. "You're all right, Will. You've got a slight case of heatstroke. Take it easy today, and tomorrow you'll be back to normal."

The nature of his overheated fancy worried me. Had he, half-asleep, somehow overheard Paddy reading to me this morning, and built the idea of desert caravans into his subconscious? Now Paddy himself was returning from almost the direction that Will had pointed, shuffling along between two dunes and wearing a coolie hat that covered his head and shielded his shoulders. His walk told me that he was not sober.

"Where have you been?" Sebastian's voice was more than excited. It was demented.

Paddy's face had a blurry, unfocused look. "I thought I saw something." He made a vague gesture behind him. "Out there, between the dunes. Some *body*," he corrected, with the precision of the drunkard.

Add that to Will Reynolds' statement, and you had something to catch Sebastian's full attention.

"Who was it?"

Paddy shook his head, but before the gesture was complete Sebastian was running off between the dunes, following the weaving line of Paddy's footsteps. Then he went scrambling up the steepest slope of the nearest mountain of sand. Three minutes later he was back, slithering down amid a great cloud of dust.

"Of all the bloody bad luck!" When he got too agitated his upper-class accent began to fall apart. "One patrol per thousand square miles, and we run smack into it."

"You saw it?" I asked.

"I saw their dust, and that was enough." He ran to camp and began to throw things anyhow into the trucks. "Come on, we're getting out of here. If we head north we can run clear of them."

I folded down the parasol. "What about Reynolds? He's not fit to navigate."

"He can travel in the second truck." Sebastian hesitated for a moment, staring first at Paddy and then at Jackie. I could read his thoughts. Who was going to drive that one, if he navigated for me?

"Will Reynolds has the track through the dunes clearly

marked on his radar images," I said. "I'm pretty sure Miss Sands could call the turns for me."

"Do it." The trucks were loaded, and already he was hustling dazed Will and drunk Paddy into the second one. "And don't stop unless you need to consult with us. We'll be right behind you."

I swung up into the driver's seat and put my hand on the dashboard. We were in the hottest part of the afternoon. The gray exposed metal would blister skin. As Jackie moved to the seat beside me, and muttered her protest at the heat of the leather, I leaned out again. "What time do you want to make camp?" I called to Sebastian. "Sunset?"

"No. There should be a decent moon tonight. Keep going as long as you can see and stay awake." The engine behind me started, growling into low gear. His voice rang out above it. "There may be other patrols. We have to reach that valley — *soon*."

For the first hour it was the silence of people with too much to say. Jackie kept her head down, pored over the images, and called off the turns clearly and correctly. I stared at the land ahead, drove, sweated, and wondered why I had such a terrible headache.

"Will you do me a disgusting favor?" I asked at last.

"What? While you're driving?"

"Dig down into the knapsack behind you, and give me a cigar."

"Yuck."

When she reached out to put the lit cheroot in my mouth I turned to nod my thanks. She had wiped the makeup off her face with paper towels, and patches of sweat discolored the armpits and back of her white cotton dress. The dress itself had become dust-gray. Trickles of perspiration were running down her brow and cheeks.

"It will start to cool off in about two hours," I said.

"Two more hours of this. God." While I was still looking at her, she reached up with both hands and pushed the mass of dark hair deliberately off her head.

"You wear a wig," I said brainlessly.

"No. I wear six of them. A look for all occasions. Or almost all." She sighed and ran her hands through her hair. "My God, that feels good."

Her hair was short, almost boyish, a light blond showing the first lines of gray. Without the wig her face had a different shape, and oddly enough she looked younger.

She stared back at me with only a trace of embarrassment. "Well, Sam-I-Am, there's the dreadful truth. Next comes the glass eye and the wooden leg."

"Slipping down the ladder rung by rung. Have a cigar."

"I've not come to that yet. But I'd sell my best friend for a glass of chilled orange juice." She laughed. "You know, it's hard on Will, but I'm glad that I'm not riding in that other truck. Paddy's sloshed all the time, and I think Gerald is going crazy."

Her cheerful manner didn't quite convince.

"You had a fight with Gerald," I said.

"Why do you say that?"

"Guessing. You were both too keen for you to ride with me. And you looked exhausted this morning. You had a fight with him last night, after you left me."

"No. After dinner, and before I sat with you by the lamp. I suppose that's why I came to you — I wanted to avoid more contact with him."

"Thanks."

"It worked. He didn't try to come to my tent. But I had a terrible night anyway. I'm normally a great sleeper. Head on pillow, and I'm gone. Only last night . . ."

With most people I'd have suggested a sleeping pill. Jackie would no doubt have given me a lecture on drug abuse.

"Horrible dreams!" she went on. "I got up feeling like a wet Kleenex."

"Me too. Did you hear things outside?"

"Yes!"

"People talking, and animals, and music?" I slowed the truck and stared at her.

She frowned back at me. "No. Nothing like that. I heard storm noises, and rushing water, and horrible sounds like buildings falling over. In fact, in the middle of the night I was so scared I opened my tent and looked out to see what was happening. I thought there must be flash floods or something. But everything outside was quiet. I decided I must have been asleep without knowing it. And yet I still couldn't sleep. What's happening, Sam? Is it all nerves?"

Before I would accept that, I'd believe something more mundane, like bad food or water. Or even — I couldn't stop the thought — deliberate drugging or poisoning. Gerald Sebastian controlled all the water supply from the distillation unit. *Was* it no more than alcohol with Paddy, and heat stroke with Will Reynolds?

"You said Gerald was going crazy. What did you mean by that, Jackie?"

And now she did seem embarrassed. Her eyes moved to stare at the truck's radiator emblem. "I wish I hadn't said that, even though it's true enough. I don't think you have a very good opinion of me. So it probably won't surprise you to find out that Gerald and I are lovers."

"Surprise, no. Upset, maybe."

A quick sideways flash of her eyes in my direction. "Thanks, Sam. That's kind when I'm not looking my best. You know, that's the first nice thing you've said to me. You pretend to be a human icicle, but you're not. I'm glad. But I want you to know the Gerald wasn't the reason I'm on this expedition. I'm serious about the SETI work, and I wanted to come here long before he and I started anything."

"I believe you. Henry doesn't know?"

"Know, or care. He's fascinated by Gerald, thinks he's brilliant."

"So do I. He is."

"The Gerald Sebastian that I met in New York certainly was. He knew where he was going, how to get there, just what he wanted."

"Present company included?"

"I guess so. But once we reached Pakistan he changed completely. He's a monomaniac now. All day yesterday in the truck, while he drove, he talked and talked and talked."

"Of course he did. Jackie, this is his baby."

"You don't understand. He didn't talk about the expedition, the way he had in Hong Kong. Or rather he did, but not in a sensible way. He went on and on about *Atlantis* — about the rivers and lakes there, and the flower gardens, and fruit trees, and white sailboats moving along streets like Venetian canals.

Sam, he was totally dippy. As though he thought he had been there himself, and knew just what it was like. I tried to tell him, he had to get hold of himself, but it was useless. He couldn't stop. And Paddy was no help at all. He just sat there in the truck with a dreamy look on his face."

I remembered my discussion with Gerald Sebastian regarding Aurel Stein's failure to take the ring and gold tablet from the statue. He had seemed wildly excited, but as rational as you could ask. "I'm sorry, Jackie. I can't see Sebastian that way."

"Nor could I, three days back. Sam, he's your colleague and your boss. But Gerald and I were *lovers*, for Heaven's sake. Less than a week ago we couldn't get enough of each other. But last night after dinner, when we went to his tent . . ."

I could complete that thought, and also the whole proposition. Gerald hadn't wanted to make love to Jackie; Jackie needed her self-esteem; therefore, something must be seriously wrong with Gerald.

"Oh, don't be an idiot, Sam." And I hadn't said a word. "It's not that he's tired of me, or got other things on his mind. Anyway, I wouldn't get bent out of shape about Gerald and sex. I'm telling you, he's gone *crazy*."

It was her inconsistency that convinced me. She had wanted Sebastian in her tent right after dinner, but later she wanted to avoid him altogether.

Perfect, I thought. I'm on an expedition with a crazy leader, a drunk interpreter, a brain-fried navigator and a wild lady who thinks we will find little green men in the middle of the Takla Makan. Disaster on wheels.

And with all that to worry about, what thought poked its way again and again into my forebrain? Of course. It was Jackie's comment that I was a human icicle.

We had stopped talking. Maybe she thought I didn't believe a word she'd said, and was waiting for a chance to talk about her with Sebastian. Maybe she felt as exhausted as I did. My head was still aching, and I drove by instinct, following the route that Jackie gave me without thinking or caring where it led. The sun set, the moon came up, and we were able to cruise on without stopping. The temperature went from hot to cool to cold. About eight-thirty, Jackie stirred in her seat.

"I can go without dinner, Sam, but I have to have warm clothes. My legs are beginning to freeze. You have to stop."

I emerged from my reverie. The dunes were all around us. At night they became frozen ocean breakers, looming high and dark above the moving truck. Sometimes my tired eyes could see long shapes scudding across their flanks. Was this the illusion that had fueled Gerald Sebastian's sea-fantasies?

"How much farther to go?"

Jackie had put her wig on again and sat hugging herself. "No more than forty miles. Two hours, at the rate we've been going. But I don't care. I want to stop and rest."

I let us coast to a halt. "Gerald will never agree to it. When he's this close he'll want to get there tonight. In less than two hours the moon will set and it will be too dark to drive."

"We'll be there in the morning."

Jackie didn't understand treasure hunters. The idea of camping here, when we were so close to the valley . . .

Gerald popped out of the cabin of the other truck almost before it had stopped moving. "What's the problem?" His voice echoed off the dunes and he ran to peer in at us. "Why are you stopping?"

"My eyes," I said. "They're so tired I'm seeing double. And I'm cold and hungry. We have to take a break."

Jackie said nothing, but her hand touched my arm in appreciation.

"But we're almost there!" said Sebastian. "It's a straight run from here, a child could drive it."

"I know, but I need rest — and so do you."

He turned to stare at the moon. I could see his face, and although it was tired and lined his expression was perfectly sane. "Twenty minutes," he said after a moment. "That will give us time to eat. Then—"

"No." Jackie did not raise her voice. "You can do what you like, Gerald, but I'm not going any farther tonight. And Will Reynolds should be asleep in his tent, not jolting around in a truck. If you want to go on, you'll do it without Will and me."

There was a moment when I thought Sebastian would explode at her. Then he nodded, lowered his head, and marched without a word to the other truck.

❖   ❖   ❖

I could never earn a living as a fortune-teller. My premonition had told me that we were in for a grim evening. Instead it proved to be the most peaceful few hours since we had left Hong Kong.

Will Reynolds was fully recovered. Paddy was semi-sober. And Gerald Sebastian hid any angry feelings he had toward Jackie under icy politeness. Only his eyes betrayed him. They turned, at every gap in the conversation, to the north. On the other side of those moonlit dunes, less than forty miles away, lay his obsession. I could share his feelings.

We had halted at about eight forty-five. At nine-fifteen, when we had finished a meal of hot tinned beef and biscuits, Sebastian wandered away from the lamplight and stood looking wistfully up at the haloed moon. It was setting, and a northern breeze veiled its face with fine sand.

Abruptly he swung around and walked back to us. "I'm going on, Sam," he said to me. "I have to go on. You follow me tomorrow morning."

His voice carried the command of the expedition's leader. Jackie looked at me to raise an objection. I could not. I knew the desire too well. All I could do was wish that I could go with him.

"You have only one more hour of moonlight," I said.

"I know." He picked up a gallon container of water and climbed into the truck that I had been driving. "You're in charge here. See you tomorrow."

The truck rumbled away between the mountains of sand. We watched it leave in silence, following it with our ears for what felt like minutes. When the last faint mutter of the engine was lost, I was able to pick up in the new silence the sounds of the cooling landscape around us. It was the *mingsha* again, the song of the dunes as they lost their heat to the stars. There were faint, crystalline chimes of surface slidings, broken by lower moans of movement deep within the sandhills. It was easy to imagine voices there, the whistle and call of far-off sentinels.

"The dragon-green, the luminous, the dark, the serpent-haunted sea," said Paddy suddenly. He was gazing out beyond the circle of lamplight, and his eyes were wide. Without another word he stood up, turned, and went off to his own tent.

We stared after him. Within a couple of minutes Will Reynolds rose to his feet. He shivered, snorted, and glared at the fading moon. "Seen that in New Mexico," he said. "Dust halo. Sandstorm on the way. It'll be a bugger. Gotta get some sleep." He lurched away.

And then there were two. Jackie and I sat without speaking while the night grew colder and the sands murmured into sleep. "Did you understand what Paddy said?" she said at last.

I shook my head. Our thoughts had been running in parallel. "He seemed to be talking about the sea, too, but we're in one of the driest places in the world. Will Reynolds made a lot more sense. I've seen that haloed moon myself in desert country. It's caused by a high dust layer. If there's a sandstorm on the way we have to start early tomorrow, or Sebastian may be in trouble. We have all the food and the water distillation unit on this truck."

We left the camp just as it stood, the lamp still burning, and walked across to Jackie's tent. There we hesitated. "Goodnight, Sam," she said at last. "I don't know if I'll be able to sleep, but sweet dreams."

"And you, Jackie." Then, as she was putting her dark head into the tent, "I have some Halcion here. Sleeping tablets. If you'd like one."

She paused and pulled her head out of the tent. Then she held out her hand. "Just this once. Don't get me into bad habits."

"Tomorrow, your first cigar." I watched as she closed the tent, then walked back to turn out the lamp. The moon was on the horizon, a smoky, gray blur. Overhead no stars were visible. By the time that I stepped into my tent and climbed into my sleeping bag the night was totally dark.

Sleep is a mystery, a force beyond control. The previous night, with nothing to worry about, I had been restless. Tonight, hours away from what could be the greatest event of my life, I put my head down and enjoyed the dreamless, uninvaded slumber that we mistakenly assign to small children. I did not stir until Paddy unzipped my tent and announced that I would miss coffee and eggs if I didn't get a move on. Then I woke from a sleep so deep that for a moment I had no idea where I was.

Neither Paddy nor Will seemed to remember anything strange about their last night's behavior. We were in the truck before six-thirty, facing north into a cold, grit-filled wind. Visibility was down to less than two hundred yards and we would be reduced to map and compass. It promised to be slow work, and I intended to drive carefully. This truck contained a hundred pounds of plastic explosive, and no one knew why Gerald Sebastian had brought it. Plastic is safe enough without a detonator, everyone tells you so, but it makes an uncomfortable travel companion.

I asked Will, bent over his image, for a first direction. And it was then, as I slipped into first gear and looked beyond the closest dunes to a red-brown sky, that I learned my mistake.

Sleep had not been without dreams, and Gerald Sebastian's vision was a strong one — strong enough to infect others. Night memories came flooding back to me.

It was evening, with sunset clouds of red and gold. I stood next to the green statue, but it was no longer a lonely monolith half-buried in gray sand. Now it formed part of a great line of identical statues, flanking an avenue beside a broad canal. Laden pack animals walked the embankment, camels and donkeys and heavy-set horses, and I heard the jingle of metal on carved leather harnesses. A flat-bottomed boat eased along past me. The crew were tall, fair-skinned women with braided amber hair, singing to the music of a dreamy flute player cross-legged in the dragon's-head bow. Beyond the embankment, as far as I could see, buildings of white limestone rose eighty to a hundred feet above the water. They were spired and windowless, mellow in the late sunlight. The wind was at my back. I could smell apple blossom and pear blossom from the dwarf trees that grew between the statues.

I moved forward along the pebbled embankment. In half a mile the canal broadened to a lake bordered by lotus plants and water-lilies. Although the waters stretched to the purple haze of the horizon, I knew that they were fresh, not salt.

On the quiet lake, their sails dipping rose-red in the evening sun, moved dozens of small boats. It was obvious that they were pleasure craft, sailing the calm lacustrine waters for pure enjoyment.

As I watched, there was a sudden shivering of the landscape. The sky darkened, there was the sound of thunder. The buildings trembled, the road cracked, lake waters gathered and divided. The dream shattered.

"Sam!" The shout came from Jackie and Paddy in the back seat. I found we were heading at a thirty degree angle up the side of a dune, four-wheel drive scrabbling to give purchase on the shifting sands. A second before we tipped over I brought us around to head down again.

"Sorry!" I raised a hand in apology and fought back to level ground, horribly aware of our explosive cargo. "Lost concentration. It won't happen again."

Will had just got round to looking up. "North-west, not north," he said calmly. "Look, there's his tracks. Follow them where you can."

To our left, almost hidden by blown sand, I saw the ghostly imprints of balloon tires. New sand was already drifting in to fill them. I followed their line and increased our speed. In full day, the temperature in the truck began to inch higher.

After another ten miles the tire tracks faded to invisibility. But by that time we were on the final stretch, a long, north-running ridge that led straight to the valley. Less than an hour later we were coasting down a shallow grade of powdery white sand that blew up like smoke behind us.

"Half a mile," said Will Reynolds. "Look, all the contours are right. There's a whole city underneath us, deep in the sand." He thrust an image under my nose. It showed a broad pattern of streets, picked out as dark lines on a light background. I thought I recognized the curving avenues and sweep of a broad embankment, and saw again in my mind the white sails and the laden animals. But I had no time for more than a moment's glance. Then my attention moved to the valley ahead of us.

He was there. So was the truck. And so was the statue. When we turned the final lip of the valley I could see the green warrior standing waist-deep in a great pit. Sebastian must have been working all night to dig it clear. Now he was leaning over the back of the truck, so uniformly covered in white dust that he was himself like a stone statue. The derrick had already been swung out over the rear of the truck. Chains were clinched around the statue's broad belly and hooked to iron cables over the pulley. Red sticks of explosive stood near it on the sand, with detonators already in place.

Our diesel made plenty of noise but Sebastian did not seem to hear us. He was working the engine on the back of his truck. As Will Reynolds and I jumped down from the front seat there was a chattering of gears and the scrape and clatter of chains. The statue moved a little, altering its angle. The sound of the engine growled to a deeper tone. The chains groaned, the statue tilted and began to lift.

I understood the plastic explosive now, but it would be unnecessary. The statue was not anchored at its base. It moved infinitely slowly, but it moved, inching up from the depths. Sand fell way from it, and after a few more seconds the ponderous torso was totally visible.

Will and I slowed our pace down the slope. There was every sign that Sebastian had matters under full control. At the same time, I marveled that he could have done so much, alone, in such a short time. The valley was perhaps a quarter of a mile long and a hundred yards across. And the white sand was everywhere, a uniform layer of unguessable depth. Judging from its general level, no more than the top of the statue's head would have peered above it when the truck first arrived. To reach the point where the chains and tackle could be attached, Gerald Sebastian must have moved many tons of dry sand.

When we were still twenty yards away, and while Paddy behind me was calling out to the unheeding Sebastian, I looked along the line of the valley. In my mind I saw a hundred companion statues stretched beneath the lonely desert. As I stared, some final load of sand was shed at the figure's base. There was a faster whirring of gears, the cable moved quickly, and the whole statue was suddenly hanging in midair. Suspended on the flexible cable, the body turned. The blind, angry gaze swung to meet me, then on to survey the whole valley.

I did not think it then, but I thought of it later. And I

understood it for the first time, that simple epitaph of Tamburlaine the Great: "If I were alive, you would tremble."

As the swinging statue completed its turn, to look full on Gerald Sebastian, many things happened at once.

The sky darkened and the air filled with a perfume of apple and pear blossom, one moment before the plastic explosive by the pit blew up. A flash of white fire came from it, brighter than the sun. It blinded me. When I could see again, the statue was no longer hanging from the chains. It stood on the ground, eight and a half feet high, and towered into a leaden sky. As I watched, it moved. It turned, and took one ponderous, creaking step toward Gerald Sebastian.

He screamed and backed away, lifting his hands in front of his face. But he no longer stood on powdery desert sand. He stood on a broad avenue, at the brink of a great lake bordered by apple groves. The statue took another lumbering step forward. Gerald Sebastian seemed unable to turn and run. He backed into the lake, among the lotus flowers and lilies, until the water was to his knees. Then he himself became a statue, frozen, mouth agape.

The face of his pursuer was hidden from me, but as it bent forward to stare into Sebastian's eyes I heard a cruel, rumbling laugh. I ran forward across the avenue to the edge of the lake, as a great green hand reached out and down. Sebastian was lifted, slowly and effortlessly. He hung writhing in midair, the grip around his throat cutting off his new screams.

The other hand reached forward. Sebastian's jacket was ripped from his body. Carved jade fingers stripped from beneath his shirt a ruby ring and an engraved gold tablet, and tucked them into the statue's buckled belt. "Xe ho chi!" growled a deep voice. The meaning was unmistakable: "Mine!"

There was a roar of triumph. "Ang ke-hi!" Then the statue was wading into the water, still holding Gerald Sebastian in its remorseless grip. I ran after them, splashing through the blooming water-lilies. Soon I was waist-deep in the cool lake. I halted. The green colossus strode on into deepening waters, still carrying Sebastian. As his head dipped toward the surface he gave one last cry of terror and despair. The statue raised him high in the air, then plunged him under with terrible violence. He did not reappear.

The head swung to face the shore. The blind gaze focused, found me. The wide mouth grinned in challenge.

I turned and fled from the lake, blundering up onto the embankment with its line of fruit trees. The statue was out of the water now, striding back towards me. I ran on, to cower against the shelter of a squat gray obelisk. As my soaked clothing touched its stone base there was a second burst of white light. I became blind again, blind and terror-stricken. The statue was stalking the embankment. I could hear the clanking tread of its progress.

Where could I hide, where could I run to? Again I tried to flee. Something was clutching me, holding me at thigh level.

Sight returned, and with it the beginnings of sanity. I saw a stone statue before me, but it stood silent and motionless. On its belt sat a ring of ruby fire and an engraved gold tablet.

Beyond the silent effigy I saw for one moment the faint outlines of white buildings, cool green water, and a hundred tiny sails. A freshwater wind blew on my face, filled with lotus blossoms. But in moments, that vision also faded. Superimposed on its dying image appeared once more the dry, dusty valley, deep in the sterile desert. Another few seconds, and the ghostly outline of a truck flickered back into existence, then steadied and solidified. Its chains and tackle hung free, unconnected to the ancient statue beneath the derrick.

I stared all around me. Will Reynolds had fallen supine on the sand, face staring up at the overcast sky. Paddy was on his knees in front of me (but when had he run past me?), hands clapped over his ears. And it was Jackie, also on her knees, who was clutching me around the legs. She crouched with her face hidden against my thigh.

I began to stagger forward, pulling free of Jackie's grip. For Gerald Sebastian had reappeared. He was thirty yards away, facedown on the loose sand. But unlike Will he was not lying motionless. He was *swimming*, propelling himself toward me across the level surface with laborious strokes of arms and legs, striking out for an unseen shore. His breath came in great, shuddering spasms, as though he had long been deprived of air. Perhaps he had. His mouth was below the surface and he was choking on sand.

A few yards from him — unexploded and untouched — lay the sticks of red plastic.

I knelt by his side, turning his head so that he could breathe, and found that the eyes looking into mine were empty, devoid of all thought or awareness. And as I knelt there, clearing sand from his gaping mouth, sudden bright marks touched his upturned face. I heard a pattering on the dusty desert floor.

I stared up into the sky. In that valley, in the fiercest depths of the *Takla Makan Shamo*, a hundred-year event was taking place. It was raining.

Paddy Elphinstone had seen an army of warriors, swords unsheathed, sweeping down on us from across the valley. He had known that he was about to die. Jackie saw a city, perhaps the same one I had seen, but it was writhing and collapsing in the grip of a huge earthquake, while she was sliding forward into a great abyss that opened in the surface.

Will Reynolds, God help him, could not tell what vision had gripped him. Like Gerald Sebastian, he was *elsewhere*, in a mental state that permitted no communication with other humans.

When the rain shower was over I searched that valley from end to end, looking for anything out of place. There was the quiet, dusty slope, merging into the dunes in all directions. There was the truck, just where Gerald Sebastian had left it. There was the pit with the statue at its center, rapidly filling with new sand. A ruby ring and an engraved gold tablet were attached to the buckled belt. I took two steps that way, then halted. As I watched the sand steadily covered them. In the whole valley, nothing moved but the trickling sands.

With two terribly sick men in my charge, I had no time for more exploration. We had to leave, and I had to make a decision: would we drive north or south? In other words, would Will and Gerald receive treatment in China, or would we try to get them home through Pakistan to the United States?

Maybe I made the wrong choice, maybe it was the cowardly choice. I elected to run for home. With me driving one truck and Paddy, shocked to sobriety, the other, we set off southwest as fast as we could go. We drove night and day, cutting our sleep down as far as we dared and keeping ourselves going on strong coffee that Jackie and I brewed by the gallon.

Sixty hours later we were in Rawalpindi, and I was buying airline tickets for the long flight home.

New York again. I told the backers of the expedition the unpleasant truth: that we had taken nothing from the valley, and they had nothing to show for all their investment. They were perhaps a little upset by that, but they were far more upset when they heard what had happened to Will and Gerald, and read the medical prognoses. Either might recover, but no one could predict how or when. Henry Hoffman showed what a gentleman he was by arranging perpetual medical care at his expense for as long as the two might need it.

I went home. And it was then that I discovered I had lied — accidentally — to our financial backers. While we were still traveling I had looked at the videocamera tapes made by Sebastian on the trip, including one taken in the valley itself. It showed the same bleak desert that I remembered so well, dry sand and barren rock.

In addition to the videotapes, Gerald Sebastian had also shot four or five rolls of film, but I had no way of developing those until we returned home and I could get to a photolab. The films, with whatever latent images might be on their exposed surfaces, did not seem to me a high-priority item. I left them in the bottom of my luggage. At last, four days after I returned to my apartment in Albuquerque, I went to my modest photolab and developed them.

Five rolls showed Hong Kong and Pakistan, and our entry to western China. The sixth was different. I stared at the pictures for half an hour. And then I went to the telephone and placed a call to Jackie Sands in Manhattan. We talked for four hours, and all the time I realized how much I had been missing her.

"I know," she said at last. "We could talk forever, but I'm going to hang up now. Don't do anything silly, Sam. I have to see you, and I have to see it. I'll be on the next plane out."

She had to see what I had hardly been able to describe: the sixth film. There were just three exposures on it. The first was of the green statue, with only its head showing above the sand. In the other two, the statue was uncovered to waist level. It filled most of the frame, with an expression on its face that I could only now read (*If I were alive, you would tremble*). But there was enough space at the edges for something else to show: not the dry gray of desert sands, but the cool green of water; and on the surface of that water, dwarfed by distance and slightly out of focus, a score of tiny white sails, delicate as butterfly wings. At the very edge of the frame was a hint of a broad embankment, curving out of sight.

Jackie's plane would not arrive for another five hours, but I drove at once to the airport. I thought about her while I waited, and about one other thing. Gerald Sebastian had expected to find Atlantis. Jackie had sought aliens. Had they in one sense both been right?

There is nothing more alien to a modern American than yesterday's empires, with their arbitrary imperial powers, their cruelty, and their casual control over life and death. Humans make progress culturally, as well as technologically. Progress in one field may be quite separate from advances in the other. Suppose, then, the advanced civilization of an Atlantis; it might have technology far beyond our own, but it would have the bloody ways of a younger race. What would you expect from its emperors?

In ancient Egypt, Cheops had his Great Pyramid; Emperor Qin had his terra cotta army of ten thousand at Xian. But their technology was simple, and their monuments limited to stone and clay. Imagine a great khan, king of Atlantis, with powerful technology wedded to absolute rule. How would he assure his own memory, down through the ages?

I can suggest one answer. Imagine a technology that can imprint a series of images; not just on film, or a length of tape, but on an entire land, with every molecule carrying part of the message. The countryside is saturated with signal. But like the picture on an undeveloped film, the imprint can lie latent for years or thousands of years, surviving the change from fertile land to bleak desert, until the right external stimulus comes along; and then it bursts forth. Atlantis, or Xanadu, or whatever world is summoned, appears in its old glory. To some, that vision may be beautiful; to others, it is intolerable. The great khan, indifferent to suffering, laughs across the centuries and inflicts his legacy.

An idea, no more; but it fills my mind. And how can I ever test it? Only by going back to that lonely valley in the Takla Makan, providing again the stimulus of disturbance, and waiting for the result.

I would love to do it, whatever the risk. The opportunity exists. Jackie told me on the phone that Henry Hoffman, indulgent as ever, was not disappointed by the last expedition. He would be willing to finance another trip to the Takla Makan; and he will let me lead it.

An attractive offer, since to raise that much money myself would take years. To search for Xanadu. How can I say no? And yet it is not simple; for Jackie and I know the rules, even though we have never discussed them. We must begin right, or not at all. I am not Gerald Sebastian. If I let myself take Henry's money, I cannot also take his wife.

I make the decision sound difficult, but it is actually very easy. I learned the answer in the Takla Makan, and it is the only answer: for access to its rarest treasures, life offers but a single opportunity.

Xanadu has waited for thousands of years; it must wait a few years longer.

Afterword: *The Courts of Xanadu*

Most people whom I meet assume that I like to travel, just because I have seen a lot of the world. In fact, I hate it. Jet lag affects me more than most people, and my stomach, which I never treat kindly, objects strongly to changes of food and water. As for air travel — if Samuel Johnson had known about airports, flight overbooking, economy class legroom, airplane "cuisine," and weather delays, he would have found something to top his remark on a sailor's life, "a man in a jail has more room, better food, and commonly better company."

If I have seen much of the world, it is only because for twenty years I have had the rare privilege of viewing most of it from a few hundred miles above it, in the form of satellite images. I can be given a Landsat or a SPOT scene, and tell you from its appearance the approximate location, latitude, season, and climate. Put me on the ground in that same location, and I would have no idea where I was or what to do. I would sweat, freeze, starve, or panic.

Now, having said all that I also have to confess to being a travel book junkie. I like nothing better than to sit in a comfortable armchair, struggling vicariously across the barren Empty Quarter of Saudi Arabia, gasping in the rarefied air of the high Karakoram, or losing assorted fingers and toes on a winter journey to a colony of Emperor penguins. I yearn to visit Antarctica, Patagonia, and Serengeti, but only by spacecraft or the printed word. I like to travel, so to speak, clairvoyantly.

So when I came across a rare edition of the Travels of Marco Polo in a bookstore, I coveted it. A friend of mine was with me in the shop. He rolled his eyes at the price, and said, "You'll have to write a new story to pay for that."

He was right. I did, and you just read it.

C-CHANGE

It was early in 2043 that Hippolyte Martin discovered the trick that increased the speed of light by a factor of sixty million.

Since his work began as pure theory, he checked for the usual pitfalls. Had he divided an equation by zero, or subtracted infinite quantities from each side, or taken the wrong branch of a multiple-valued function?

He had not. His work was without flaw — and translatable from theory to practice. Most staggering of all, the change in light-speed could be *universal*. Everywhere would be affected once his device was in operation.

Hippolyte was a responsible scientist, so he sought the validity check of peer review. He published his work — or tried to. But he made the mistake of stating the consequences of his discovery, rather than offering pure theory.

He noted that the center of the galaxy was about thirty thousand light-years away. After the c-change that would become five light-hours. Even with ships hobbling along at one-hundredth of light speed, the whole galaxy was just a few weeks across. As for visits to the nearer stars, it was hardly worth taking along a change of clothing. Sirius and back, even allowing for the tedious business of acceleration and deceleration, was an afternoon jaunt.

Hippolyte made these points in his paper's introduction. The rejection letters ranged from studiously polite to suggestions that he needed psychological help.

Lesser men might have despaired, become enraged, or turned misanthropic. Hippolyte, fortified by the knowledge that he was right, did none of these. He assembled his c-change generator on board his spaceship, a little one designed to putter along at only a thousandth of the speed of light. For Hippolyte had a way to silence the skeptics: he would turn on the generator, head for the stars, and return with proof.

His work might be accepted before his return. Newly generated light would be affected, while light already on its way somewhere would not; so there would be immediate visible results. The Sun was eight minutes light-travel time from Earth. When the c-change was made, for eight minutes there would be two suns in the sky. One of those suns would be "old" light, sent out eight minutes earlier; the other would be newly generated light, zipping from Sun to Earth in a few microseconds.

There would be similar effects all through astronomy. For forty minutes there would be two Jupiters; twin Saturns would last twice as long. Alpha Centauri would shine in duplicate for four years, Sirius nearly nine. The new sky would be cluttered, twice as bright and populous as before, but would return to normal over years and centuries as doppelganger planets and stars vanished, one by one.

Hippolyte turned on his generator. As expected, the sky showed twice as many stars. He headed for the brightest one.

He was back ten days later, a shaken man. Earth was waiting, just as shaken. Computers, control systems, and other advanced electronics had all become pieces of instant junk. For light is just one form of electromagnetic radiation, and when its speed changed the other forms changed with it.

On the fourth day, people had remembered Hippolyte's "impossible" theory. They noted the disappearance of his ship from the solar vicinity. When he returned he was promptly charged with forty-nine civil offenses and eighty-six military ones.

He didn't seem to care.

"I wanted to give us the stars," he said. "So I built the generator. I'm sorry about the electronics. But it's not important."

His panel of judges boggled.

"Not important!" said the senior inquisitor. "Not important, to ruin the world's economy, to destroy the banking system, to reduce to a shambles the computer and communications system —"

"Not important," repeated Hippolyte. "You see, *they* are *there*. Just the way we imagined they might be. Advanced civilizations, millennia old, *millions* of years old, across the stars and galaxies.

"On my fourth planet I met their delegates. Three beings, all oxygen breathers. They treated me very nicely. They explained about the Intergalactic Trading Federation."

"He is mad!" exclaimed the panel's expert on the non-existence of extraterrestrial intelligence. "It can be *proved*, by rigorous arguments, that interstellar commerce is impossible. In fact, regular interstellar travel of *any kind* cannot be accomplished. The distances are too large, the travel times too extreme."

Hippolyte nodded. "I wondered myself how intergalactic commerce operated over such times and distances before the c-change. Yet they were *there*." He stared bleakly at the panel. "Is there by any chance an astronomer among you?"

The others turned to a pale woman with red hair, who jerked upright at becoming the center of attention.

"You, madam?" asked Hippolyte. "You must have noticed astronomical effects. What was your explanation for them?"

"We noticed that every light source *less* than a hundred light-years away appeared in duplicate. Anything *more* than a hundred light-years away did not; but we had no explanation."

"Then I, reluctantly, must give one." Hippolyte sighed, and turned to face the cameras. "I increased the speed of light, and thought I had made the change to the whole universe. What I did not realize, until the beings who greeted me explained, was that the speed of light is *already* sixty million times as big as the old Earth-measured value. It has the higher value everywhere, except within a hundred light-years of Sol.

"And even *within* that hundred light-year sphere, the speed of light had its high value until ten thousand years ago. Until, in fact, the intergalactic federation had a first good look at *humans*. That was when they put in the slow-speed barrier."

The panel was stunned to silence. Finally, the senior member spoke. "But you changed all that, didn't you? With your generator, we can go as fast—"

"No." Hippolyte shook his head sadly. "They are sorry, but they can't risk it. The Sol region goes permanently back to slow-speed — tomorrow."

Afterword: *C-change*

See the Afterword to "The Seventeen-Year Locusts."

UNCLEAR WINTER

A Miscellany of Disasters

1. INTRODUCTION

The scenario is almost too familiar.

War breaks out between the United States and Russia. The cause of the final conflict is not relevant, but both sides unleash the full force of their nuclear arsenals. Within hours, the energy of 25,000 one-megaton hydrogen bombs has been released. Most of the United States and Russia, including all the major cities, is reduced to a flaming wilderness of destruction and radioactive contamination.

And then the real trouble starts.

The initial explosions, together with the fires that they have created, carry gigantic amounts of dust and smoke high into the upper atmosphere. It lingers there, blocking out sunlight, for months or years. On the surface below, temperatures drop dramatically. The earth is darkened, crops are frozen or fail to mature, and starvation becomes a universal problem. The civilization of the world collapses, and the development of humanity is set back for hundreds or thousands of years.

This is "nuclear winter," a projected future that suggests that the Doomsday Machine of Dr. Strangelove is already in our possession. For it is not necessary that both sides release their bombs. If either one does, the subsequent winter will destroy the aggressor country along with the intended victim. A preemptive "first strike" does nothing to guarantee a nation's security.

The general concept of nuclear winter is not new. It goes

back at least to 1974, when a paper by J. Hampson was published in *Nature*. A year later, the National Academy of Sciences issued a report covering the same theme: "Long-Term Worldwide Effects of Multiple Nuclear-Weapon Detonations." It assumed that 10,000 one-megaton hydrogen bombs would be used in an all-out nuclear war, and drew the conclusion that the effects on the whole ecosystem would be small. The report was somewhat criticized as encouraging military solutions to general political problems, but mostly it was ignored. The whole subject was apparently of minor interest until 1983, when a paper, "Nuclear Winter: Global Consequences of Multiple Nuclear Explosions" was published by Turco, Toon, Ackerman, Pollack and Sagan. This "TTAPS" paper and subsequent press conferences introduced the phrase "nuclear winter." The idea then received wide circulation.

However, the validity of the TTAPS conclusions was not accepted everywhere. The subject quickly became a hot issue for debate. On the one hand, the proponents of nuclear winter felt that they had a new and irrefutable case against anyone who thought it might be possible to "win" a nuclear war. On the other hand, critics said the analysis was inadequate and misleading. The models were accused of being (literally) one-dimensional, of ignoring the heat reservoir capacity of the oceans, and of assuming that there would be too rapid atmospheric mixing, so that the southern hemisphere would suffer as badly as the northern one.

The Pentagon in particular didn't want to hear anything about nuclear winter. If the idea were valid, it made the point that our arsenals are just as dangerous to us as to any possible enemy.

The criticisms of the original models seem to be valid. However, none of them proves that there will be no nuclear winter effects. They merely reduce the estimated size of the effect.

Reduce it, by how much?

No one is sure. There has never been an atmospheric nuclear explosion providing more than a thousandth of the energy release of a full-scale nuclear war. Also, even the biggest atmospheric tests were not conducted in areas where forest or urban fires could result. Thus all the arguments rely a great deal on theoretical (and simplified) results, on analogy, and on preconceived ideas. And the key question, what would all-out nuclear war do on a long-term global scale, remains unanswered. So does a rather different, but equally important question: how do the risks of nuclear winter compare with other forms of disaster?

2. THIS IS THE WAY THE WORLD ENDS

All-out war is not the only way to produce the possible collapse of civilization predicted by nuclear winter. In this article we will examine some violent alternatives, and see how likely they are to serve as instruments as doom.

The production of nuclear winter effects, by any mechanism, calls for the release of a great deal of energy. The way that this energy is delivered to Earth's biosphere is important, but the easiest way to begin is by looking at the raw energy provided by different events.

Here are some prime candidates:
1) Nuclear war
2) Earthquakes
3) Volcanic eruptions
4) Meteorite impacts
5) Solar flares
6) Nearby supernovas

To provide a standard of comparison, we will first consider a natural energy source which is definitely not destructive to the biosphere: the tides.

3. TIDAL ENERGY

Humans harness a negligible fraction of tidal energy, although the available energy is huge. Other species do rather better, and the intertidal zones are the most biologically productive regions of the world, more so than even the tropical rain forests. On the average, waves powered by the tides deliver to the shoreline 0.335 watts per square centimeter, fifteen times as much energy as comes from the Sun. Even so, the coastal area is small compared with the open oceans, and almost all tidal energy remains untapped.

A ballpark figure for the total energy is easy to calculate (though not easy to find in the literature). Let's assume that the tides raise and lower the mean sea-level of Earth's oceans by two meters, twice a day. Since the oceans cover 70% of the globe, and the total surface area of Earth is about 500 million square kilometers, the total tidal energy proves to be about 2.8×10^{26} ergs.

This is a very large amount, but it looks even bigger than it is because the erg is a standard but very small energy unit. The daily output of a sizable (1,000 megawatt) power station is 8.64×10^{20} ergs. A one-megaton hydrogen bomb produces 4.2×10^{22} ergs, or a month and a half's production from a large power station.

This value of available tidal energy is probably good to within a factor of two, and we will not be trying to obtain results better than that.

4. NUCLEAR WAR

To compare tidal energy with the energy release of a full-scale nuclear war, we have to make some assumption about the number and size of the bombs that are available. We will employ the same figure as in the 1983 TTAPS paper, namely, 25,000 megatons of TNT equivalent. Since one million tons of TNT release 4.2×10^{22} ergs of energy, our nuclear war can produce a total of 10^{27} ergs (assuming all the missiles are fired, and they all work — an assumption that anyone who has had dealings with the Defense Department will have a lot of trouble swallowing).

The available daily energy of tides is thus about one-quarter of that produced by a full-scale nuclear war. However, that tidal energy is released twice *every day*; nuclear war can never be a regular event.

5. EARTHQUAKES

Earthquakes are interesting in their own right. However, I am going to give them short shrift. Although they do tremendous damage, they do it mainly at ground (and sea) level, and they do not send finely divided material high into the atmosphere. Earthquakes are thus not going to be a major source of nuclear winter effects.

There are two different scales used to measure the intensity of earthquakes. The better-known one, called the *Richter Scale*, was developed by C.F. Richter in 1935, and is now routinely reported for most earthquakes around the world. It is actually an energy scale, and a *logarithmic* scale, at that, so a Richter rating of, say, 7.5, releases ten times as much energy as one with a rating of 6.5, and a hundred times as much energy as one of 5.5.

As a rule-of-thumb, property damage begins with about magnitude 5. The largest recorded earthquakes rated 8.6 on the Richter Scale. There have been four of them: Alaska, on September 10, 1899; Colombia, on January 31, 1906; India, August 15, 1950; and Alaska, March 27, 1964. Judging from the reported effects, the Lisbon earthquake on November 1, 1755, probably had a magnitude between 8.7 and 9.0. The great Chinese earthquake of July 28, 1976, killed half a million people in Tangshan, and was 8.2 on the Richter Scale. The 1906 earthquake in San Francisco was rated at 8.3.

The other scale is called the *Mercalli Scale*, and it is less precise. It defines "degrees of intensity" between I and XII. An intensity II earthquake is barely perceptible to humans; intensity IX damages buildings and cracks the ground, and intensity XI shatters masonry buildings, bends railroad tracks, and destroys most free-standing structures.

I should point out that the Mercalli scale concerns itself only with effects on manmade structures. If there are none of those around, there is no rating on the Mercalli scale. This is rather like the old question, "If a tree falls in the forest and no one hears it, does it make a sound?" Is it an earthquake, if there are no manmade objects to be affected by it? The Mercalli scale would suggest that it is not.

The location of a volcanic eruption is not usually in any doubt. Locating an earthquake is trickier, and its point of maximum intensity, or *epicenter*, is determined by inference. However, it is useful to note that the total amount of energy release in a large volcanic eruption and a large earthquake seem to be very comparable. This emphasizes that energy release is only one of the significant variables, and probably not the most important one, when we look at the climatic effects of natural or man-made disasters.

6.   VOLCANIC ERUPTIONS

Volcanic eruption has been fairly well studied, but there is no equivalent of the Richter Scale for volcanoes.

Volcanic eruptions are often divided into two groups, termed Type A and Type B. Type B eruptions are in many ways more interesting and spectacular, since they are accompanied by gigantic explosions and produce large volumes of *ejecta* — lava, dust and ash thrown high into the air. Krakatoa, in 1883, and Mount St. Helens, in 1980, were both Type B events. Type B eruptions, foreshadowing thoughts of nuclear winter, send their dust high into the stratosphere, to produce colorful sunsets all around the world for several months.

Krakatoa is one of the most famous eruptions of historical times, perhaps because of the movie, "Krakatoa, East of Java" (a nice example of Hollywood's disregard of facts; Krakatoa is an island just *west* of Java). The Krakatoa eruption released an estimated 10^{25} ergs of energy — equal to a couple of hundred one-megaton hydrogen bombs. The sound of the explosion was heard 3,000 miles away, and the atmospheric shock wave circled the globe several times. At Batavia (now Jakarta), a hundred miles from the volcano, the air was so dark with dust that lamps had to be used at midday. Fifty-foot tidal waves hit the coast of Java and killed 36,000 people.

Yet there have been much bigger explosions. Tambora, in 1815, on the Indonesian island of Sumbawa, is estimated to have been 80 times as energetic an eruption as Krakatoa. The following year, 1816, was known as "the year without a summer," when crops failed to ripen throughout Europe. The most likely cause was a stratospheric layer of reflective dust from Tambora.

Biggest of all blow-ups during historical times, but one for which no eyewitness or contemporary records exist, was the destruction of the island of Thira (formerly Santorini) in the Aegean Sea north of Crete. From archaeological evidence and the examination of the shattered remnant of Thira, this eruption is estimated to have released 10^{27} ergs of energy. That is equal to the energy release of the world's whole stockpile of nuclear weapons. The eruption, occurring about 1470 B.C., also produced a monstrous tidal wave, hundreds of feet high, which may have been the agent that destroyed the Cretan Minoan civilization.

The most famous volcanic eruption of all time was probably that of Vesuvius, in A.D. 79. It covered the towns of Pompeii, Herculaneum, and Stabiae in twenty-foot layers of ash (65 feet in some places) and preserved everything nicely until systematic excavation began in 1763.

It also, as an incidental, killed the Roman naturalist and historian, Pliny the Elder, who had sailed across the bay of Naples to take a look at the eruption and perhaps to help people. He didn't try to leave until too late, and suffocated on the beach.

I know how he felt. Volcanoes are seductive viewing, and they induce strange psychological effects. In 1980, driving from Portland to Seattle, a friend and I made a detour to take a good look at the recently erupted Mount St. Helens. About five miles from the crater, the road had been closed off by the police. We were very annoyed at the time, but in retrospect they were doing the right thing. We would have kept going until we were far too close for safety.

The next morning, talking at breakfast, we found that we had both dreamed about that deformed, ash-covered peak, with the ominous gray smoke cloud sitting on top of it.

On the largest scale of things, the famous eruption of Vesuvius was no big deal. It released only an estimated 10^{24} ergs, less than one-tenth of a Krakatoa. By contrast, the 1912 eruption of Katmai in Alaska was twenty times as energetic as Krakatoa, but since it was in a sparsely populated area at the northern end of the Alaskan Peninsula, it attracted little global attention.

Type A eruptions are often just as energetic, but they are less noisy and colorful and don't get the same publicity. They produce great quantities of thermal energy, often heating the environment but not causing major explosions. They may involve huge lava flows, and even the creation of whole new volcanic islands. The most famous modern example is the island of Surtsey, created by a volcanic eruption off south-west

Iceland, in 1963. That event was estimated to have released 2×10^{24} ergs — one-tenth the energy of the Krakatoan eruption.

Table 1 shows values for some of the biggest and best-known (and some surprisingly little known) volcanic eruptions of both types.

Table 1: Volcanic Eruptions and Associated Energy Released

Volcano	Date	Type	Energy (ergs)	Megatons
Thira, Aegean	1470 BC	B	10^{27}	24,000
Laki, Iceland	1783	A,B	8.6×10^{26}	20,500
Tambora, Indonesia	1815	B	8.4×10^{26}	20,000
Katmai, Alaska	1912	B	2×10^{26}	4,800
Mauna Loa, Hawaii	1950	A	1.4×10^{25}	333
Krakatoa, Indonesia	1883	B	10^{25}	240
Surtsey, Iceland	1963	A	1.9×10^{24}	45
Vesuvius, Italy	1979	B	10^{24}	24
Mount St. Helens	1980	B	4.2×10^{23}	10

For comparison purposes:

Global nuclear war	?	B	1.1×10^{27}	25,000

Eruptions of Type A are mainly lava flows, whereas Type B eject large quantities of material with explosive force. The thermal energy of Type A eruptions is usually transferred slowly to the environment, through conduction and radiation.

7. METEORITE AND COMET IMPACTS

First, let us see how much energy a meteorite or a comet fragment will generate when it hits the Earth. This sounds like something that needs to be looked up in a reference work, rather than calculated directly. However, I will do it from first principles, because it is a nice example of being able to derive a result with almost no knowledge of physical constants.

The kinetic energy of a body hitting the Earth is $mv^2/2$, where m is the mass of the body, and v is the relative speed of the Earth and the object. We can put in any value we like for m —

and we will look at various sizes of impacting object. But what about v?

Suppose that the body is falling in towards the Sun from far away — perhaps from the Oort Cloud, which is the original home of the comets. Then its initial speed out there would be close to zero, and it would be accelerated all the way in towards the Sun by the solar gravitational field. Suppose that its speed relative to the Sun, by the time it hits the Earth, is v_c. The object has picked up as kinetic energy what it lost as potential energy, so

$$mv_c^2/2 = GmM/r$$

where G is the universal gravitational constant, M is the mass of the Sun, and r the distance of the Earth from the Sun at the time of the impact. Canceling the mass of the comet from the equation, we have

$$v_c^2/2 = GM/r \quad (1)$$

It looks from equation (1) as though we need to know G, M, and r in order to determine v_c. But we don't. For the Earth to be remain in orbit around the Sun, the gravitational force of the Sun on the Earth must balance the centrifugal force generated by the Earth's movement. This implies that if v_e is the speed of the Earth in its orbit,

$$v_e^2/r = GM/r^2,$$

or $v_e^2 = GM/r \quad (2)$

Comparing (1) and (2), we have:

$$v_c^2 = 2v_e^2 \quad (3)$$

This, a very well-known result, shows that all we need to know to determine the speed of the infalling comet is the speed of the Earth in its orbit around the Sun.

But that is easy to calculate. In one year, the Earth travels once around the Sun. The mean distance of the earth from the Sun is about 150 million kilometers (93 million miles) and the Earth moves roughly in a circle. Since there are 86,400 seconds in a day, the Earth moves 2π x 150,000,000 kilometers in 365 x 86,400 seconds, i.e., v_e = 29.89 kms/ second — say, 30 kms a second, accurate enough for our purposes.

Thus from equation (3), we at once have $v_c = \sqrt{2}v_e = 42.4$ kms/second.

The speed of the comet relative to the Earth is found by

compounding these two velocities. The motion of the Earth and the comet are roughly at right angles to each other, so the final relative velocity is $(v_c^2 + v_e^2)^{1/2}$ = 52 kms/second.

This result is something of an upper limit to the impact speed of an object hitting the Earth. It is appropriate for comet impact, but since asteroids orbit the Sun in the same direction as the Earth, and are coming from much closer than the Oort Cloud, they will hit with less speed, usually between 15 and 30 kilometers a second. On the other hand, a metallic asteroid is of higher density, has a more compact mass, and therefore delivers about as much energy as a faster-moving comet of the same size.

Meteorites are small asteroids and have quite different orbit characteristics from comets. They move in elliptical paths, almost always staying closer to the Sun than the orbit of Jupiter, and more hit in the afternoon than in the morning, by about a 3:2 ratio. Perhaps the computers of the missile defense systems should have a special test built into their code: If you detect a major impact, did it occur in the afternoon? If so, look a little closer before you start World War III.

The comet fragment will be traveling at 52 kms a second. A fragment one kilometer in radius and with the density of water masses about 4 billion tons. Impact with Earth generates 5×10^{28} ergs of energy — 5,000 Krakatoas, or 50 full-scale nuclear wars.

We need to know what size of fragment is reasonable, and how often such bodies are likely to hit the Earth. These are difficult questions, but we have at least a couple of available data points. First, a comet fragment* almost certainly did hit Earth, relatively recently. It happened early in the morning, on June 30, 1908, at a remote area of Central Siberia called Tunguska. Although the fragment was estimated to be no more than a couple of hundred meters across, it flattened a thousand square miles of forest and left so much dust in the high atmosphere that colorful sunsets were produced in western Europe seven thousand miles away.

---

* Why a comet, and not an asteroidal meteorite? Because no metallic or stony fragments were found at the scene of the impact.

According to our formulas, the energy produced by the Tunguska meteorite was about 5.4×10^{25} ergs — five Krakatoas, or a thousand one-megaton hydrogen bombs.

However, a full-sized comet should be much bigger than the Tunguska meteorite. For example, Halley's comet has a nucleus about 10 kms across. Its impact with the Earth would release 7.1×10^{30} ergs of energy — equal to 170 million one-megaton hydrogen bombs, or 7,000 nuclear wars.

One other point needs to be made here. The world's most famous comets are *periodic* comets, like Halley's comet or Encke's comet. These objects do not "fall from infinity," but are in orbits that bring them close to the Sun at regular intervals of a century or less. However, they are the exceptions of the cometary world. They were once part of the Oort Cloud, and fell in from there a long time ago; then Jupiter or one of the other planets perturbed their motion by a gravitational interaction, and gave them a less elongated orbit. Now they travel in paths that are relatively close to the Sun, and their days in the Oort Cloud are over forever.

There is evidence that major comet impacts have happened in the past, though fortunately not in historical times. Meteorite impact is the most popular theory to explain the disappearance of the dinosaurs in the late Cretaceous period, 65 million years ago, and also for an even more massive species extinction that occurred earlier, at the Permian/Triassic boundary 250 million years ago. The idea was proposed in 1980 by Alvarez and co-workers, originally to explain anomalous levels of iridium found in sedimentary deposits all around the world. It is holding up rather well, and is now supported by the discovery of so-called "shocked quartz" grains at widely dispersed locations around the world.

Evidence of other large meteorite impacts can be found in many places: Manicouagan Lake in Quebec, a water-filled ring crater 40 miles across, is believed to be an impact crater; so is the mile-wide Meteor Crater, Arizona, which was created about 20,000 years ago. The Sudbury nickel deposit in Ontario is also probably an "astrobleme," or asteroid-impact structure, that created the world's largest nickel ore body. The asteroid that hit Sudbury is estimated to have been moving at 15 kilometers a second, and have been 4 kilometers in diameter. If so, its impact delivered 3×10^{29} ergs, 300 times as much as a full nuclear war. (Note that a comet, the same size but with the density of water, would produce very much the same energy, at 4.5×10^{29} ergs.)

These are North American evidence of what I like to call "close encounters of the fourth kind." The Earth must have seen many events like them in its long history. Only the weathering effects of the atmosphere, plate tectonics, and biological organisms save Earth from being as heavily cratered as the Moon.

Small meteors hit the Earth every day, and are burned up in their passage through the atmosphere. How often do meteorite impacts of a substantial size occur? This is an area where there are very few solid data to guide us, but we can make plausible estimates by putting together several apparently unrelated facts. First, the Earth and Moon are close neighbors in celestial terms, and they should encounter about the same number of meteorites, once we make allowance for the Moon's smaller size. We can count the Moon's craters, and their number suggests that an object big enough to make a crater a mile across will hit every hundred thousand years or so. A comet fragment twenty meters in radius would do it. Allowing for Earth's larger size, something that big should hit us about every ten thousand years.

Statistical analysis of bodies in the asteroid belt also provides a rule-of-thumb, saying that for any asteroid of a particular radius, there will be ten times as many with one-third that radius. We are going to assume that the same distribution law applies to comets, too. (We have to — data on comet nucleus sizes are too sparse to establish any frequency/nucleus-size relationship.) The rule-of-thumb can readily be converted to a general formula that tells the number, n, of bodies of any radius, r, thus:

$$n = N10^{-\log(r/R)/\log 3} \quad (4)$$

where N and R are any pair of *known* values.

Assuming the impact of an object twenty meters in radius every ten thousand years, the size/number relationship of equation (4) allows us to calculate the frequency of an impact of any size of body, and we already know how to compute the associated energy release. Table 2 shows the average time between impacts for different sizes of cometary bodies.

The table tells us that there should have been only four impacts of something the size of Halley's Comet since the Earth was formed. Given the huge energy release this implies, that's just as well. Conceivably, four such events correspond to major species extinctions in Earth's history. (A detached attitude to such calamities is hard to achieve, but possible. I was driving James Lovelock, originator of the "Gaia" concept [more about Gaia later], down to the Museum of Natural History in Washington. On the way we somehow got onto the subject of all-out nuclear war. Lovelock surprised me very much by remarking that it would have very little effect. I said, "But it could kill off every human!" He replied, "Well, yes, it might do *that*; but I was thinking of effects on the general biosphere.")

Even if we keep our missiles in their silos and submarines, the planet will have seen a "nuclear war" energy release from a comet or meteorite impact an average of every two million years; a one-megaton hydrogen bomb equivalent every two thousand years; and a Hiroshima-sized event every 130 years. Historical evidence suggests that these rates are on the high side — not surprising, considering the tenuous nature of some of our assumptions. On the other hand, the reluctance of our ancestors to accept the idea of meteorites suggests that any fireball occurring, say, four hundred years ago, might have been misinterpreted* — or, in much of the world, not recorded.

It would be nice to think that explosions mimicking an atomic bomb in violence are rather rare. The response of a nervous nation to a Hiroshima-style fireball over one of its major cities is hard to predict.

---

* "I could more easily believe that two Yankee professors would lie than that stones would fall from heaven." — Thomas Jefferson

Table 2: Size, Frequency, and Effects of Comet Impacts

Size of body (radius in meters)	Frequency of occurrence (yrs)	Energy release (ergs)	Energy release (Megaton H-bombs)	Nuclear wars (1 nuclear war = 25,000 megatons)
2.5	128	8.8×10^{20}	0.02	
5	550	7.1×10^{21}	0.17	
10	2,340	5.7×10^{22}	1.4	
20	10,000	4.5×10^{23}	11	
40	43,000	3.6×10^{24}	86	
60	100,000	1.2×10^{25}	286	
100	292,000	5.7×10^{25}	1,350	
150	680,000	1.9×10^{26}	4,520	
250	2,000,000	8.8×10^{26}	21,000	0.84
500	8,500,000	7.1×10^{27}	169,000	6.8
1,000	36,000,000	5.7×10^{28}	1,360,000	54.3
2,500	250,000,000	8.8×10^{29}	21,000,000	838
5,000	1,060,000,000	7.1×10^{30}	169,000,000	6,760
10,000	4,500,000,000	5.6×10^{31}	1,347,000,000	54,000

The Hiroshima atomic bomb was about 20 kilotons TNT equivalent. The 2.5 meter comet fragment releases as much energy as one Hiroshima bomb, and the 5-meter fragment as much as nine such bombs. A 2.5-meter fragment impact can be expected every 128 years. Objects of this size and smaller will produce a fireball as they burn up in the atmosphere, but normally will not reach the surface of the Earth.

8.   STELLAR EVENTS

The energies of a nuclear war or a cometary impact are huge on the everyday scale of Earthly events, but they are minute compared with the power production of even the smallest and dimmest stars.

The Sun, a rather average G2-type dwarf star, emits 3.9×10^{33} ergs of radiative energy per second — that's four million nuclear wars a second. Fortunately the Earth intercepts only a tiny fraction of the solar bounty, roughly one two-billionth.

The question now is, can this energy change enough to threaten the survival of life on Earth?

The obvious danger in this case might seem to be an excess of radiation — of frying, rather than freezing — since there are no signs that the Sun is likely to go out for many billions of years. But could the Sun become much brighter? The sunlight delivered to the Earth is known as the "solar constant," and it is about 0.14 watts per square centimeter. Can the solar constant change, because of, say, a very large solar flare?

Well, over very long periods the solar constant has certainly changed. Life has existed on Earth for about three and a half billion years; and in that time, the solar constant has increased by at least thirty percent. If Earth's temperature simply responded directly to the Sun's output, two billion years ago the whole Earth would have been frozen over.

But in fact, the response of Earth's biosphere to temperature changes is complex, apparently adapting to minimize the effects of change. This is part of the whole Gaia concept, of life on Earth as a giant mechanism that regulates its own environment in an optimum manner. For example, as temperatures go up, the rate of transpiration of plants increases, so the amount of atmospheric water vapor goes up. That means more clouds — and clouds reflect sunlight, and shield the surface. In addition, increased amounts of vegetation reduce the amount of carbon dioxide in the air, and that in turn reduces the greenhouse effect by which solar radiation is trapped within the atmosphere. There are many other processes, involving other atmospheric gases, and the net effect is to hold the status quo for the benefit of living organisms.

However, there is a big difference between a 30% change that takes place over three and a half billion years, and one that takes place overnight. We need to know if a rapid change is possible.

The picture is a little bit confusing. The Sun emits almost all of its light energy at ultraviolet, visible, and infrared wavelengths (99% of the total between 0.276 and 4.96 micrometers). Measurement of the solar constant over this range shows very little change. On the other hand, there is a definite cyclic variation in solar output at X-ray and radio wavelengths, corresponding to the eleven-year cycle of sunspot activity and to other, longer periods. The fraction of energy emitted at these wavelengths is small, but the effects are certainly not negligible.

For example, although the Ice Ages took place before recorded history, there were two well-documented "Little Ice Ages," one from 1460 to 1550, the other from 1645 to 1715. These periods, known as the Spörer Minimum and the Maunder Minimum respectively, occurred at times when there were almost no sunspots on the Sun. Flamsteed, the first British Astronomer Royal, hardly saw a sunspot in forty years of observations. Isaac Newton, whose lifetime (1642–1727) neatly overlaps the Maunder Minimum, was in a similar position.

Conversely, the so-called "Grand Maximum" from 1100 to 1250, when Greenland was settled, has been studied by J.R. Eddy using carbon-14 dating of tree rings. It proves to be a period of prolonged sunspot activity and a warm Earth.

There is thus no doubt that quite small changes in solar output can have significant effects on the Earth's climate. The natural (but wrong) conclusion is that the major Ice Ages were caused by correspondingly larger changes to the solar constant. Actually, Milankovitch has produced convincing evidence that the Ice Ages correspond to changes in the Earth's orbit, rather than changes in solar output.

Theories of stellar evolution tell us that there have been slow, steady increases in solar heat production, over billions of years. But history offers no evidence of large, sudden excursions of the solar constant from its usual value. Sol is a remarkably stable furnace, having less effect on Earth's climate than the eccentricity of the Earth's orbit around the Sun.

As a competitor with meteors and nuclear wars to effect an abrupt end to human affairs, solar energy variation seems to be a non-starter.

9. SUPERNOVAS

With supernovas, we move into the big league. If Sol were to turn into a supernova, its light production could increase by a factor of a hundred billion, to 4×10^{44} ergs a second.

This sounds like a lot — it *is* a lot — but it is only a tiny part of the supernova's total energy production. Between ninety and ninety-nine percent of the energy in the explosion is carried off by neutrinos. Of the remainder, ninety to ninety-nine percent is in an exploding shell of matter, blasted outward at a twentieth of the speed of light. Only between one percent and one one-hundredth of a percent of the energy is emitted in the form of radiation.

The neutrinos appear at the moment of the explosion, whereas the emitted light and high-energy particles increase and then decrease in intensity over a period of weeks or months. The 1987A supernova in the Large Magellanic Cloud produced and emitted an estimated 10^{58} neutrinos in just a few seconds, and they carried off with them 3×10^{53} ergs — equivalent to one-tenth of the mass of the Sun.

Neutrinos interact with normal matter hardly at all, which is why they readily escape from the center of the supernova. A neutrino can pass through several light-years of lead before being captured. However, the number emitted in a supernova explosion is so large that the neutrinos alone would kill a human a billion kilometers away. If Sol were to became a supernova, we would be wiped out by the neutrinos shortly before we were vaporized by the flux of radiation.

Before we worry too much about that event, we ought to note that according to today's theories Sol cannot become a supernova. There are two types of supernova. Type I occurs only in multiple star systems, when a massive white dwarf receives enough matter from a stellar companion to render it unstable. Type II occurs when the core of a giant star, ten or more times the mass of the sun, collapses. (More details of what happens in both Type I and Type II supernovas are given in the article, "Something for Nothing.") Since our sun is neither a binary star nor a giant star, we seem to be safe. On the other hand, how much do you trust today's theories?

In our local stellar neighborhood there are candidate multiple star systems and giant stars. It is possible that one of those could produce a supernova. Is it then conceivable that the event would be energetic enough to destroy life on Earth, or at least produce a huge perturbation comparable with a nuclear war or a large meteor impact?

Let us look at the numbers.

The closest multiple star system to Earth is also the nearest star system, Alpha Centauri. It is a very unlikely candidate to become a supernova, but if it were to do so, would it harm the Earth? Alpha Centauri is 4.3 light-years away, more than 270,000 times as far as the Sun, and distance is the best protection.

The best protection in this case is not quite enough. If one of the three stars in the Alpha Centauri system became a supernova and produced 4×10^{44} ergs per second in the form of light, it would shine a third brighter than the Sun for a few weeks. The increased heat alone might not kill us, but the sleet of high-energy particles, carrying ten times as much energy as the light, would be even more destructive. However, we would have plenty of warning of the coming particle storm, since the radiation from Alpha Centauri would precede the particles by three-quarters of a century. Digging would become the new international pastime.

I can't help wondering how the world would react to the idea that, following a terrible time of heat and chaos, the worst was still to come. Would people believe the scientists' statements? Would they be willing to begin preparation *now*, for an event so far in the future that most people would not be there to experience it? Or would they shrug and say, "Let them handle it when it happens — it's their problem"? We have seen a lot of that attitude towards environmental pollution.

Supernovas vary in the violence of their explosions, but anything closer than 50 light-years might produce severe effects on the Earth, as much as if we had a sudden increase of ten percent in the solar constant.

Again, the *probability* of such an event is more important than the *possibility*. To determine this, we have to know the rate of occurrence of supernovas. The easiest place to look for supernovas is not in our own Galaxy, since much of that is obscured from us by interstellar dust clouds. It is better to look at neighboring galaxies, such as Andromeda, and count supernovas there. That exercise suggests that a supernova occurs maybe every century in a galaxy the size of ours, with an uncertainty on that number of at least a factor of two. Since the Galaxy contains about a hundred billion stars, and since there are about 1,000 star systems within 50 light-years of us, we can expect a supernova within this distance only once every 10 billion years. This is a simplistic argument, neglecting the different types of stellar populations, and where they lie within the Galaxy, but again we are looking for ballpark figures.

The closest and brightest supernova in recorded history occurred in A.D. 1054, and the remnant of that explosion now forms the Crab Nebula. The Crab supernova was bright enough to be visible during the day, but it had no harmful effects on Earth. It lies about 6,000 light-years away from us. We can expect a supernova this close or closer every 6,000 years. It is a little disturbing that the event actually occurred less than a thousand years ago, and it suggests that either supernovas are more frequent than we think, or more likely we are in a galactic region that favors supernovas. If a supernova as close as the Crab nebula occurs every thousand years in our galactic neighborhood, then we can expect a supernova within 50 light-years every couple of billion years.

One final question is of interest: how often will a supernova deliver the energy equivalent of a nuclear war to the Earth, in radiation and particles? Taking the total radiation and particle energy of a supernova as 10^{50} ergs, it is easy to calculate how far away the exploding star can be if the Earth is to intercept the necessary 10^{27} ergs. The answer is a little over a hundred light-years. Making the same assumption as before about the frequency of supernovas in our galactic neighborhood, this will happen every two and a half billion years. Apparently supernovas are not a major danger to the human race. (But of course, statistics being statistics, a nearby supernova could explode tomorrow.)

10. DANGER SIGNAL

It is time to pull all this together. We have looked at a number of ways that the world can end, or at least become a very unpleasant place for human habitation.

Those disasters do not form a complete list. There are many other ways for the human species to become extinct, some of which would leave the rest of the world intact (some would say, improved). Disease is one excellent candidate. We can imagine, for example, a mutation of AIDS. Suppose that a form of the AIDS virus were to appear that could be transmitted, like the common cold, through a sneeze. . . .

But that is a very different article. The key question for each event considered in the earlier sections is not, can it happen, but rather, what is the *chance* that it will happen?

Some events serve as triggers, to produce final effects beyond the obvious ones. Nuclear war, meteor and comet impact, and volcanic eruptions all serve to charge the upper atmosphere with dust, that cuts down sunlight and may produce results far more unpleasant than the original explosion. Similarly, a torrent of hard radiation and high- energy particles from a supernova may kill far more people in the long-term, from cancer, than die at once from burns.

Recognizing this, it is still instructive to compare the *direct* effects of each type of disaster. Table 3 shows the probable frequency of events equal in energy production to a full-scale nuclear war, derived from the discussion given earlier in this article.

It is very clear that nothing in Nature presents such a danger to the human race as our own actions. We know we can survive a volcanic eruption of the size of Thira; for one thing, it is *localized* in effect; for another, we have already survived such eruptions, essentially unscathed. We are not at all sure how much of our civilization would survive a nuclear war.

The message: our future lies in our own hands.

Anyone who is at all reassured by this conclusion is my

candidate for the Pollyanna award. To quote Pogo once again, "We has met the enemy, and it is us."

Table 3: Frequency of Disaster of "Nuclear War" Dimensions

Disaster	*Estimated Mean Time Between Occurrences*
Nuclear war	One hundred years*
Volcanic eruption	One thousand years
Meteorite/comet impact	Two million years
Supernova	Two and a half billion years
Solar instability	At least three billion years

*Based on the assumption that there is a one percent chance of full-scale nuclear war in any particular year. Am I unduly optimistic in thinking that this probability has actually gone down a great deal in the past five years? And not before time.

according to the aliens J and Marcus Aurelius Jackson are the reason that they came to the solar system — came, just in time to kill the dream.

In my case - it was a dream. In Marcus's case it was an

GODSPEED

The Genizee came.

Two weeks later, the Genizee went.

The aliens are the most self-sacrificing and noble saviors of humanity that anyone could imagine; or else they are the sneakiest and most evil species in the galaxy, following a diabolical agenda that no human is able to fathom.

Which?

Marcus Aurelius Jackson, a millionaire, a madman, a genius, and my long-time partner in science and short-time partner in crime, says the Genizee are villains. Everyone else on Earth says that they are heroes. Me, I just don't know.

Not yet. But thanks to Marcus, I *will* know. Soon. In the worst case, it may be for just a fraction of a second, before the end.

It sounds crazy to say it, but although I think of myself as sane and rational while Marcus is a lunatic who may cause my death and the death of everyone on Earth, I'm as bad in some ways as he is — because I can hardly wait to learn the answer. That question — *Which?* — has been sitting in my mind for four months going on forever, like an internal and eternal itch that can't be scratched.

I sit here, waiting for the reappearance of the television cameras or the end of the world, and I want to *know*.

In my case it is more than a theoretical issue. I was in the middle of the problem long before the arrival of the Genizee — before their existence was even suspected. More than that, according to the aliens, I and Marcus Aurelius Jackson are the reason that they came to the solar system — came, just in time to kill the dream.

In my case, it *was* a dream. In Marcus's case, it was an

obsession. I argue that there is an important difference between the two, though perhaps no else would agree.

Let me go back to the period BG — Before Genizee.

Before the aliens popped out of nowhere, most people thought that the world's space programs were going well. The United States had the Farside lunar base close to self-supporting, with a ninety-nine percent closed recycling of food, water, and supplies. Only the most complicated equipment was fabricated and shipped up from Earth. The Russians had their permanent Mars colony, at last, after three abortive tries and the loss of one hundred and forty-seven people. The C-J consortium had a mixed Chinese and Japanese expedition wandering the asteroid belt, and another approaching the Jovian moons. ESA had their own explorer — unmanned, this one — heading out for a second Grand Tour with smart probes of the outer planet atmospheres.

This is truly the Golden Age of space exploration, said the media.

Big deal.

Don't be surprised when I tell you that although space funding paid my salary, not one of the developments that I mentioned occupied my working attention for more than one minute a week. Marcus and I fumed at the self-congratulatory speeches from the politicians of all countries, and wept when the "great accomplishments" in space were touted by the world's media.

Couldn't they see — couldn't *everyone* see, as we saw so clearly — that even when the Moon and all the planets were explored and colonized, we would still be playing in our own backyard?

If humans were *serious* about exploring space, the solar system wouldn't do. We had to go to the stars, and we had to find a way to get there in a reasonable time. The fastest ship in existence, the Caltech/NASA Rocket Propulsion Lab's Continuous Electric Propulsion Planetary Probe (*Starseed* for short) was now heading for the inner edge of the Oort Cloud, but it would not arrive there for another ten years. That, measured in terms of my own life span, was surely not a *reasonable* time. And when it got there, three thousand astronomical units from the Sun, it would still be traveling at only one percent of lightspeed, and be only one hundredth of the way to the nearest star. Tau Ceti, our best bet for a close star with useful planets, would be a millennial journey for the RPL probe. Despite its name, the *Starseed* and its relatives were not and would never be the answer. They could not bring the stars within reach of humanity.

A faster-than-light drive: that was the way to go. The *only* way. Unfortunately, you couldn't even mention FTL to the Science Foundations who funded us. Marcus had tried it, and been ridiculed for his pains. Their committee of advisers was quite adamant. Nothing could go faster than light, the theory of relativity "proved" that, so not one cent should be wasted in trying. Instead we should spend the Foundation's money on something *useful*, like plodding ion drives or bone-jarring pulsed fission.

"Dummies!" said Marcus, when he got back to the lab. "Stupid jerks." He had said much the same thing to the committee, and it hadn't helped his case.

"I know," I commiserated. "They're a bunch of idiots. Curse 'em all."

I did a lot of cursing in those days, and without Marcus, that would have been all that I could do. With him, though, I had as my partner a top-drawer physicist who had studied the absolute basics of quantum theory and relativity, instead of taking them as gospel. He had done so with one goal in mind: looking for the loopholes.

They were there, of course. Everyone from Einstein onwards had pointed out that the two fields were inconsistent with each other. And even within the framework of those inconsistencies, the structure of spacetime at a subnuclear level had to be a sea of singularities, continuously forming and dissolving. The very notion of "travel" through such a discontinuous medium in its constant flux was meaningless, said Marcus. It was the learned advisers to our funding sources, sitting in their smug certainty, who needed to go back and do "something useful."

I knew he was smarter than me, and anyone else I'd ever met. When he said that he saw a ray of hope, I believed him. His failure with the committee, and their ridicule, didn't shake my faith in him one bit.

"We have to keep trying," I said. "Show them they're wrong."

He shook his head gloomily, but soon he was working harder than ever. Rejection merely drove him to greater efforts. In the next few months he developed the theory further, and it looked good (to him, I mean — I admit that I couldn't follow it).

The next steps had to be mine, though. I was the fix-it member of the team, because Marcus was terrible at practical details, and the diverse techniques for lubrication of egos that these days are lumped together as "human relationships" were quite beyond him.

So I "fixed it." With, if I say it myself, my usual efficiency. (I sometimes think that the only thing in life that I find truly irresistible is the challenge to finagle something that everyone else says can't be done.)

Money wasn't the issue. Marcus had inherited bundles of that, and had found little use for it, but the equipment that we needed couldn't be bought. It was available only through government programs. So the prototype construction, and the first small-scale tests, had to be worked secretly using materials bootlegged from approved conventional projects. If that sounds easy, remember that all the construction had to be done *in space*. Without assistance from Inventory Control, who owed me quite a few favors, it could not have been done at all. Even then, it was not totally invisible. Someday an enthusiastic auditor would discover that the equipment orders and use did not match, and the game would be over. Long before that I expected to have gone to Hell or Alpha Centauri.

It took five and a half years from the day of Marcus's key theoretical insight to the first space test. On that day the two of us, crowded into a small cargo capsule never intended for anything but free-fall storage, paused and looked at the little payload, then at each other.

"Well?" he said.

I nodded. He drew a long breath, shrugged, and toggled the switch.

The payload vanished without a sound.

The test transition — Marcus insisted that it shouldn't be called a test *flight*, since the payload would not be "traveling" through normal space — had been designed to carry an array of sensors eighty million kilometers to the vicinity of Mars, take a handful of pictures there, and return to the cargo capsule. It was supposed to be gone for just twenty minutes, almost all of it spent out near Mars.

Twenty minutes? I have known shorter months.

When the tiny payload popped back into existence, we both gasped. And when we examined the data it had collected, I at least got a lot more than I had bargained for.

The payload had not made the journey to Mars in a single hop. Instead, Marcus had programmed it to drop back periodically into normal space, make an instant navigation fix, and use that to direct the next transition. The resulting set of images was mind-blowing. The fixes had been taken every hundredth of a second, two hundred thousand kilometers apart. Seen in real time, they provided the series of frames that would have been obtained by a ship traveling at twenty million kilometers a second — nearly seventy times the speed of light. Godspeed.

I watched those movies about a hundred times in the next twenty-four hours, drunk with euphoria and the conviction that Marcus and I would ourselves be remembered as gods. We were the New Prometheans, the men who gave humanity the universe. (Like most people who play with fire, I had forgotten what happened to Prometheus.) I wanted to go public with our results, right away. As I told Marcus, we had more than enough evidence to justify funding for a complete series of operational tests.

At that point, he dug in and couldn't be budged. The establishment hadn't just said a polite "No thanks" to his theory, or pleaded poverty to explore it. They had *mocked* his ideas, suggesting that he was a crank or worse. Now he wanted to make a *manned* flight, go out in person farther than anything had ever been, and take hand-held pictures. Then he would come home, go to the skeptics who had told him he was a charlatan, show them our results, and invite them to stick it in their ear. Before that, he wanted complete secrecy.

Fame and fortune weren't enough, you see. He wanted *revenge*.

I should have refused to go along with him, but he always

burned a lot brighter than me. We argued for hours, until at last I gave in. He told me what he wanted for the Big Test: out a thousand astronomical units, so Marcus could get a shot of the *Starseed*, against a backdrop of the shrunken Sun and scarcely visible planets.

If finding the resources for the small test had been difficult, the new one — manned ship, life-support, full navigation and control systems — had me tearing out what was left of my hair. To be honest I also had a wonderful time, juggling three dozen people and organizations at once, but it was still another six months before I could go into his office and say, "Well, you asked for it, Marcus, and you got it. We're in business. All-up manned test for Project *Godspeed* is set for one week today."

"You actually got the flight permits, Wilmer?" — that's me — "How'd you fix it? I'd have bet it was impossible."

This had been one of our main worries. Stealing equipment had become fairly routine, and we had even managed to divert attention from our true activities by describing the *Godspeed* itself during the ship's construction as a "pulsed fission-fusion pre-experimental post-design model," which was enough to put off anyone. The earlier test had been on a scale small enough to hide. But the new one could not be concealed, since although the FTL transition should produce no detectable signal, according to Marcus the macroscopic quantum events leading up to it would make the *Godspeed*'s whole exterior sparkle and glitter like a cut gemstone catching the noonday sun.

"It *was* impossible," I said. "I had to use all my chips on this one. I wouldn't be surprised if we get caught."

"Who cares?" he said. "When we get back from this trip—"

And at that precise moment, when the day of glory was within reach, Sally Brown from Ground Operations came running into my office without knocking, switched on the little TV set that perched on the corner of my desk, and said breathlessly: "Messages and pictures. Coming in from space. All over the world, hundreds of different wavelengths. Not from Earth. From the stars."

I don't know what Sally Brown's words did to Marcus, but

they created in me such a conflict of emotions that I wanted to throw up. On the one hand, the arrival of aliens and their superior technology would make all our work for the past few years as obsolete as the horse and carriage; on the other hand, I would have what I had wanted for so long: access to the stars.

We froze in front of the TV screen, waiting for our first look at the Genizee.

What we got instead was a look at their ships, inside and out, and at their technical equipment. No pictures of aliens, not then. We learned later that they weren't sure Earth people were ready for three-foot-long cylinders of quaking black jelly, topped by a writhing mass of yellow spaghetti. Instead, we got pictures of technology.

Oddly enough, it was the sight of the ships that Marcus and I, alone of all the people on Earth, found hardest to take. The video signals had been beamed to Earth a few hours earlier, from just beyond the orbit of Saturn, along with a series of radio messages — in seven major Earth languages — proclaiming peaceful intentions and giving a projected arrival time at Earth equatorial orbit in less than a week. The radio messages we could take. But the ships . . .

Marcus caught on first. "Where is it?" he said, almost under his breath. "Wilmer, *where's the drive?*"

No one else would have been able to understand his question. But I did.

The form of certain technologies are dictated completely by the laws of chemistry and physics. That includes all propulsion technology. For instance, a rocket is a rocket, no matter whether the propellant is hot neutral gas, ionized particles, or radiation; and it makes little difference if the energy comes from chemical or nuclear processes. Similarly, a laser is a laser, regardless of wavelength or energy level. And the FTL drive that Marcus had conceived, and that we had both been working on so hard, had its own characteristic physics and signature.

The Genizee ships showed no sign of that signature. Either they had traveled across the interstellar void using a method which was so advanced that we could not recognize it; or — far more likely, in Marcus's paranoid view — they were deliberately withholding all information on their FTL drive.

Neither Marcus nor I could imagine a third possibility.

When the third option was proposed, Marcus did not believe it. He has never believed it, to this day.

In retrospect, the aliens broke it to us slowly and carefully.

First, they brought their three ships into orbit around the Earth, five hundred miles up, and sat there quietly for a week and a half, doing nothing except chatting over the radio and making sure that their mastery of Earth languages was complete. They told us a lot about themselves during that period, and asked for nothing in return but our idiomatic phrases. On the first day we learned that they came from the Tau Ceti system. (Marcus and I had been right on target, though we received little satisfaction from the thought.) Day Two they gave us a description of their civilization, with its five populated planets and moons and its links to other, more distant intelligences; all, according to the Genizee, were as peaceful, well-meaning and sympathetic as they were.

The fifth day brought a first look at the Genizee themselves. By that time they had soothed us so well that most people's reaction when they saw a picture of a Genizee was *sympathy* that any rational being had to live with being so ugly.

The sympathy faded a little when the Genizee told us that they lived, on average, for twenty-seven thousand Earth years. When asked if they would make the longevity formula available to humans, they replied, with an apologetic quiver, that there was no formula. The Genizee had always been so long-lived. Almost everyone except Marcus believed them. He was already full of dark surmise.

The bombshell dropped by the Genizee near the end of the second and final week confirmed his suspicions. Asked during a TV broadcast (the world had lived glued to TV sets since the arrival) about their journey to the solar system, they offered an implausible reply. They had not used an FTL drive at all, they said, but an efficient sub-lightspeed drive that allowed them to reach over half the speed of light. They had been on the way from Tau Ceti for twenty-five years. All their journeys between the stars were made at a fraction of lightspeed.

The blue ribbon panel of elderly scientists who had been assembled to interact with the aliens were, if you can believe it, *pleased* by that reply. It confirmed, they said, their own conviction, that faster-than-light travel was a physical impossibility. Nothing could ever move from one point to another, faster than light would cover the distance.

Well, said the Genizee, quaking apologetically, that's not exactly the case. In fact, the reason why we embarked on this long journey to Earth in person, rather than sending messages that you might not believe, or might think to ignore, was just this: Certain of your scientists have been conducting FTL experiments. . . .

No one had looked to Marcus Aurelius Jackson or me for help and advice when the Genizee arrived. Why should they? We were young and junior, without reputation or known accomplishments, and Marcus had already been branded as a crank. Even if we had offered our services, no one would have taken them, or listened to what we might have to say.

That changed in ten minutes — the ten minutes when the Genizee explained that faster-than-light travel was not impossible; that it offered enormous danger and possible total destruction to any species that attempted it, for reasons that they would be happy to explain to us; that such attempts were being conducted on Earth at this very moment; and that the Genizee had come here with two main goals: to pinpoint the location of those experiments, and to warn the inhabitants of Earth, telling them to cease and desist.

My own immediate reaction was total disbelief, with good reason. If the Genizee had been on the way for twenty-five years, they must have left twenty years *before* we had even the theory for an FTL drive. So they couldn't have started out for Sol just because they'd picked up evidence of what Marcus and I were doing.

It was Marcus himself, no fan of the Genizee, who quickly put me straight on that one. He had long known that any FTL drive would give rise to both *advanced* and *retarded* potentials, similar to those of conventional electromagnetic theory. Both potentials propagated through spacetime, and died out in magnitude — but the advanced potential moved *backwards* in time. The experiments that we had thought to be so secret might be detectable by the Genizee, before we had performed them.

They confirmed his comment later in the same broadcast. They could detect the signal from afar, they said, even as far away as Tau Ceti. But only when they came very close to Earth could their equipment pinpoint an exact *location*. They had done that now. They would be happy to provide that location to Earth authorities.

They did so, and added a few more minutes of stern warning on FTL drives. Half a dozen uses, they said, were often enough to cause "major repercussions" in the region of space.

Having said that, to everyone's amazement they started their ship drives and headed away from Earth.

It was bad for an emerging civilization, explained their departing message as the three ships lumbered off towards Saturn, to suffer major exposure to an older and more advanced one. Now that their warning had been delivered, the only responsible thing for them to do was to leave, and let us humans make our own way. Goodbye and good luck, people of Earth.

I gather that our scientists and politicians went into shock — they had been hoping for free technology from the Genizee, and had received nothing but talk. Marcus and I didn't take much notice at the time, because we had our own worries. Within hours of the last Genizee broadcast, our lab had been closed and was guarded by enough military men to fight a major war. Marcus and I were arrested. We were charged with theft of government equipment, misuse of grant funds, and travel without suitable permits.

Those crimes should not have been enough to hold us in confinement. They were. After what the Genizee had said, no one was willing to let us go free, not because of what they thought we *would* do, but because of what the aliens told them we *could* do.

Relax, said Marcus and I to each other. We can't really be kept in jail like this for more than a day. Can we?

What innocents! We sure could. For the first time in my life, I learned what was meant by a witch hunt. I doubt if one person in a million understood the explanation that the Genizee had offered of the dangers of a faster-than-light drive, but they didn't care. The Genizee themselves had fingered us, so we were guilty. We'd be kept under close guard, without a trial, unless the Genizee returned and said we were to be released.

I myself didn't understand what the Genizee warning was all about when I heard it, but my cell-mate was Marcus Aurelius Jackson. *He* knew what they were telling the whole world — and he didn't believe a word of it.

Marcus didn't just explain his views to me. He told the guards, our family members, and finally, after two months of work from me, the three members of the press who could be persuaded to come out to our maximum-security prison in the Nevada desert to interview us.

"A faster-than-light drive needs a tremendous amount of energy," he said to the three reporters. We were all sitting in one room, without bars between us, because I had been working hard on our guards, and finally had them to the point where they thought we might be crazy, but we were surely harmless. The room even had a tiny barred window, with only four guards posted inside, and another two just beyond the door.

"A huge amount of energy," went on Marcus. "The only practical — or even theoretical — way to get that much energy is from the vacuum itself. You have to tap into it."

"You mean, you get energy from nothing?" said the most junior of the press. He had an open, gullible face. The other two, one man and one woman, didn't look even vaguely interested, and I guessed that they thought of the whole trip as a chore they hadn't been able to wriggle out of.

"Not from *nothing*. From the vacuum!" That was one of Marcus's problems, because although it was clear from their facial expressions that this subtle distinction was far beyond all the reporters, he swept right on: "Now, the energy available from the vacuum is so big, you tend to think of it as unlimited. But the Genizee insist that tapping the zero point energy sets up a local stress in space, which ultimately must be relieved. If you remove local energy past a certain critical point, they say, there will be a jump to a lower-energy ground state. The only more stable state is a black hole. The whole region pinches off from the rest of the universe."

"In other words," I said. "The rest of universe will get rid of the stressed region by making it *vanish*." I saw the open mouths, and wondered if I was being as obscure as Marcus. But he had been over this with me again and again, until I had something that made sense to me inside my head. My picture might be over-simple, but the reporters ought to find it easier going.

"Imagine that there are a whole lot of elastic bands," I went on, "all over the universe. Somebody starts to stretch one, in one place. That's what we were doing, when we tested the drive. You can stretch it a fair bit, and nothing happens. All the other bands give a tiny bit, and everything settles down again. But if you go on stretching, there finally comes a point where something has to give. The band breaks. When it does, everything *can't* go back the way it was. You've got snapped elastic, and you're catapulted right out of this universe."

"And that's what the Genizee are warning us about?" said the young reporter.

"They were. But it's *not true*," said Marcus hotly. "When I heard what they were saying, I went back and did all the calculations over from scratch. There's no backlash effect. Spacetime makes a small and quiet adjustment — maybe the local curvature decreases by one part in ten to the twentieth. An FTL drive is quite safe."

"But that means the Genizee were *lying* to us," said the woman reporter, in an annoyed tone. "Are you suggesting that they *didn't* come all this way on those ships? Or that they *didn't* take a quarter of a century to get here?"

"Both!" said Marcus loudly. The guards stirred, and made sure their weapons were at hand. "They were lying about *both*. They didn't come all the way in those ships, and they didn't take a quarter of a century to get here. They came from Tau Ceti — if that's really their home, and they're not lying about that, too — in a big, fast ship, with a faster-than-light drive. They parked the mother ship out beyond Saturn, where we couldn't see it. Then they switched to their slow little ships, and came crawling in the rest of the way to Earth."

Marcus was losing any shred of credibility he might have

had, because the youngest of the reporters at once asked the obvious question: "But *why* would they lie to us? What good would it do them?"

"They don't want us to use the FTL drive. They want to bottle us up, here in the solar system. They don't *want* humans out among the stars. I think they're *scared* of us, because we're smarter than they are."

It sounded paranoid, even to me. He was wasting his breath anyway. Even if the reporters believed him, and it was clear to me that they didn't, they would never find an editor willing to run the story. The Genizee, initially repulsive in appearance, had not stayed long enough for humans to learn their possible defects. Their slow and bumbling speech patterns and apparent confusion, which Marcus considered evidence of human superiority of thought, were to most people part of their appeal. The Genizee had become everyone's favorite alien, and you couldn't get away with a bad word about them. The stores were packed with cute little mop-topped black jelly cylinders — although for aesthetic reasons the toys didn't have the disgusting layer of slime that allowed the amphibian Genizee to function out of water.

When it was Marcus Aurelius Jackson against the Genizee, MAJ didn't have a chance. After all, hadn't the altruistic Genizee taken many years of their own lives, just to come to Earth and deliver a warning? And weren't they, even now, creeping back across the light-years in their cramped, uncomfortable little ships, with twenty-five years still to go? How many Earth people would do something like that, even to save their own closest relatives? *Especially* to save their closest relatives.

So, although Marcus went on talking, I knew he was wasting his time. He wouldn't get one inch of column space or a second of air time for his unpopular views.

As it turned out, I was wrong. "MAD DOG SCIENTISTS UNREPENTANT!" shouted the only headline. And underneath: "Death Penalty Favored for Insane Inventors."

Marcus is an interesting case for the psychologists. When his idea of a faster-than-light drive was ridiculed, he redoubled his efforts. And when his just-as-heretical views of the Genizee

were pooh-poohed, he at once turned all his efforts from conjecture to possible methods of proof.

"There has to be a way to show that I'm right," he said.
"Wilmer, let me try something out on you."

I said nothing. When you are living together in one locked
room, it is hard to avoid a discussion.

"Point one," went on Marcus. "According to me, the
advanced potential from our test must damp out rapidly as it
goes backwards in time. The Genizee say they picked it up a
quarter of a century ago, but I say it fades to background level
and becomes undetectable in a year or less. If I'm right — and
I am — they can't have picked up evidence of our test more
than a year before they got here.

"Point two. They say they came from Tau Ceti, and their departure trajectory supports that idea. Even if they didn't,
though, they certainly came from outside the solar system. The
nearest star is over four light-years away. Four light-years or
more in one year or less means they *had* to have come using a
faster-than-light ship.

"Point three. They left two weeks ago. If they really intend
to fly all the way back to Tau Ceti, or any other interstellar destination, in those sub-light ships, they are still in the early
acceleration phase of the trip. Even with the most efficient
propulsion system I can imagine, it will take them nearly a year
to work their way up to half the speed of light."

He stared at me. "Do you see what that means?"

"It means they're still a hell of a long way from home.
They're as altruistic as everyone believes."

"*No.*" If the press could have seen Marcus now, they would
have felt that their MAD DOG SCIENTISTS UNREPENTANT
headline was thoroughly justified. "Wilmer, it means that if
they were telling the truth about how they came here, and how
they are going back, and where they are going back to, then
*anyone with an FTL ship could fly out and catch up with
them.* If they aren't where they should be, then they are lying,
either about coming from Tau Ceti or about the drive. One lie
is enough to discredit everything they said to us. If you ask me,
they're already back home, wherever they came from — and
I'll bet money it's not Tau Ceti — having a good laugh at the
credible people of Earth."

I looked at him, then let my eyes roam around the feature-less beige walls of the room. "Let *me* try something out on *you*, Marcus. Point one. There is just one FTL drive in the solar system, and it is impounded, up in orbit and protected by maximum security guards, because everyone on or off Earth is terrified of it. If they weren't afraid to touch the thing, they'd have destroyed it long ago.

"Point two. There are just two human beings who know how to fly that ship. No one else will go near the *Godspeed*.

"Point three. Those two humans are locked away in an underground room in a building in the middle of the Nevada desert. They have no tools, no friends, no money, and no way of getting to space, still less of reaching the *Godspeed*. Forget it, Marcus, you could never do it, not in a thousand years."

"I know I couldn't," he said. He was still staring at me. I felt a quivery feeling in my stomach, as though my recent breakfast had suddenly been converted to live worms.

"I know I couldn't," he said again. "That's not my line. But you, Wilmer, if you—"

"It's impossible."

"I'm sure it is."

"*Totally* impossible."

"Yeah." He stood up and went over to lie on his bed without another word.

After a few seconds I went across to my own bed, lay down on it, and closed my eyes. I decided that I hadn't been totally honest when I was speaking to Marcus. I still had friends out-side, and I still had some equity with them for past favors. I had cultivated our guards, too, drawing a little on Marcus's wealth, to the point where they normally left us to ourselves, but would do the odd paid favor for me provided it was obvi-ously no threat to them or to anyone else. So far as the security around the *Godspeed* was concerned, I had probably exagger-ated that. No one would be too worried, as long as it was known that Marcus and I were locked up here. . . .

I shivered, and stopped my thinking right there. What was Marcus trying to make me do? Help him to destroy the pair of us, and the whole of the human race as well? But he had touched that dark, hidden spot where the true ego dwells.

Now the live worms in my stomach had crawled up my throat into my brain, and set it on fire.

If we escaped from prison, the alarm would go off at once. The search for us would begin. The two of us would never make it far outside the prison walls, let alone into space, and the guards around the *Godspeed* itself would be tripled in numbers and placed on maximum alert.

But it took only one person to fly the *Godspeed*. And there would be real juggling to be done here, inside the prison, to hide the fact of that one person's escape.

Marcus, then, to pilot the ship and to design the programs that would allow the sort of freeze-frame sequence of hops that the unmanned payload had taken to Mars, searching at each transition for the Genizee ships. I, to stay here, and to arrange matters — how, for God's sake? I had no idea — so that no one knew that Marcus was missing, until he was on his way in the *Godspeed*.

I opened my eyes. Marcus was sitting up on his bed, gazing at me expectantly.

"Any good?" he asked.

"Go to hell." I closed my eyes again. What did he take me for? I had been lying there for maybe three minutes. Extraordinary things can sometimes be done in real time. Miracles take a little longer.

A "little longer" in this case turned out to be six weeks. Everything had to be choreographed tighter than a five-ship orbital rendezvous. I broke the problem down into discrete pieces, each one requiring a solution if the whole effort were to succeed. Marcus had to escape from here unnoticed. Then I had to conceal the evidence of his disappearance for at least five days. Marcus would need that much time to travel from Nevada, all the way out to the *Godspeed*. Then he had to have credentials that would allow him to board the ship, and he had to remain there undisturbed. After that he would be on his own.

I was prepared for a year-long effort, with a good chance of failure at the end of it. It is a curious fact that my six-week success was possible only because I had been placed in prison. Given enough money, and Marcus had plenty of that, a man can get anything in jail that he can get outside it — plus a whole lot more. Prisons, as I quickly learned, are the natural focal points for any imaginable legal or illegal activity.

You want Marcus Aurelius Jackson to take part in the sensory deprivation experiments now being conducted in this very jail? The external university team responsible for the experiments will be glad to have him. To them, one healthy prisoner is much like another, and the recommendation of the guards is all that they ask. Bringing someone *into* a prison, to enter the sensory deprivation tank in place of Marcus, costs a few thousand dollars. Getting Marcus out in that man's clothes is more expensive, but not much harder.

Not everything is so cheap. You would like a set of forged credentials, showing that you are a Nevada businessman making a trip up to space with a need for commercial secrecy? No problem, except money and lots of it. Many of the world's best forgers are already behind bars, ready to serve you.

The one piece of the puzzle that I couldn't see how to solve would be on board the *Godspeed* itself. Marcus didn't want company on his journey, so somehow he had to arrange to be left *alone* on the ship, long enough to make the first FTL transition.

While I was still pondering that, Marcus was worrying a different issue.

"I hope the ship's power plant has been left on," he said, as we were transferring some of his money to an anonymous bank account. "It would be a pain to have to bring all the systems back on-line."

I stared at him. "Thanks, Marcus. That's what I needed."

His new forged credentials showed that he was a specialist in industrial safety, flying out to the *Godspeed* to power-down the ship's dangerous nuclear equipment so that it would not explode. With that in hand, and a few casual words as he went aboard, it would be difficult to get anyone else to stay within a thousand kilometers.

On the final morning we shook hands, for the first time in our long acquaintance. The door was unlocked from the outside. Marcus left the room, and a man in his twenties wearing a bewildered look and a bad case of acne appeared in his place. Within the hour he had been collected. I wondered briefly if he even knew what sensory deprivation experiments were. From the look of him, it would be little change from his existing condition.

I settled down, to estimate Marcus's progress. Now he would be approaching the airport, dropping off the rented car that had been arranged for him outside the prison and collecting his ticket. Now he should be at the space facility, undergoing a routine physical check that included a DNA identification. He ought to pass that easily — I had rented the best illegal hacker that money could buy, to slot an ID for Marcus into the right computer data bank. Eight hours later he should be ascending to orbit, and four hours after that he would be in an orbital transfer vehicle, on his way to the *Godspeed*.

I kept the TV on, twenty-four hours a day. No news was good news, of course, until Marcus reached the *Godspeed* and could take the final step.

I had plenty of time to wonder if my faith in Marcus was too great. It was one man against the world, his authority against the word of the Genizee.

This morning, right on schedule, the television came alive. Every channel reported the inexplicable disappearance of the *Godspeed*. It was obvious that they had no idea what was happening, since the commentators were worried about the fate of the "safety inspector" who had been on board at the time. Within the hour, I was being questioned.

I saw myself on television, and learned to my relief that Marcus Aurelius Jackson was "in prison, but unavailable for comment." I said that I could tell them nothing useful. I thought that I looked worried.

I was worried. And now, late in the afternoon, waiting for another television interview, I look at my guards and at the afternoon sun streaming in through the bars of the little window, and I am still worried.

Although Marcus and the *Godspeed* left only ten hours ago, they ought to have been back long since. Following the path supposedly set by the Genizee would have taken our ship only a few seconds, even with the brief pauses between transitions needed to drop back into normal space and scan for the Genizee ships. Marcus could have traveled out half a light-year, well past the place they ought to have reached with their slow ships, and still been back hours ago.

Strange thoughts have been running through my head. Suppose that Marcus found the Genizee ships, and they destroyed him so that he could not return and tell? We had never asked if their ships carried weapons. Then I realize that my thought is totally illogical. Marcus could find the Genizee only if they had told us the truth, and were lumbering along in their slow ships. In that case, they would have nothing to hide from us.

But perhaps Marcus, having failed to find any trace of the Genizee on the way to Tau Ceti, had decided that they were concealing from us their true place of origin. It would be easy for him to take the *Godspeed* out for a second journey, toward some other probable stellar target. And if that produced no result, he might go out again. How many trips might he make, before he had enough evidence to prove to anyone back on Earth that the Genizee had been lying?

I know Marcus very well. It is part of his nature that he likes to be absolutely sure of things. He will not risk being mocked again. I would settle for one trip out, and rest my case. He might feel he had to make a dozen.

And that leads to another thought entirely. Half a dozen full-scale shots of the FTL drive, according to the Genizee, could lead to "major repercussions" in a region of space.

How big a region? The Genizee were talking of the collapse to a black hole of part of spacetime, with the separation of that region from the rest of the universe. Are we dealing with the collapse of something the size of a ship . . . or a planet . . . or a solar system? Would the collapse take place violently, or quietly and unobtrusively? And would the *Godspeed* itself be inside that region, or excluded from it? Might Marcus and his ship, left outside, become the only evidence in the whole universe that humans had ever existed?

Those are the sort of questions I am not equipped to answer. I wish that Marcus were here, to assure me that the Genizee were certainly lying, that I am talking nonsense, that I have nothing to worry about. I take some comfort from the setting sun, shining as usual through the little barred window.

But I wish that dusk would come quickly. I want to look for the stars.

Afterword: *Godspeed*

Putting together a collection like this reveals to a writer his or her own obsessions. I see appearing again and again here one of my own convictions: that the biggest problem in physics today is the nature of space-time. The "space-time continuum" cannot be a continuum, if quantum theory and general relativity are both to be correct. It must be a far more complex geometrical entity, smooth when viewed at the macroscopic level (the way we see it), infinitely complex and turbulent when viewed at the sub-microscopic level of the Planck length (10^{-35} meters).

That idea appears in "A Braver Thing," in the article "Classical Nightmares . . . and Quantum Paradoxes," in "Nightmares of the Classical Mind," and now again in "Godspeed." The problem preoccupies many other people, particularly workers in superstring theory. Most people believe that we will need a major conceptual breakthrough, including perhaps a totally new type of mathematics, before we have a good understanding of quantized space-time.

My own worries are a bit different, and far simpler. When Newton produced his System of the World, most of his contemporaries could grasp the concepts in general, but they found that the calculus needed to work with the theory was quite beyond them. They were too rooted in the geometrical approach. When Faraday and Maxwell introduced fields as a central notion in physics, their older contemporaries faced a similar problem. They were too solidly grounded in classical mechanics. In the twentieth century, relativity and then quantum theory offered the same shock of adaptation to the older generation.

Here is my worry: Suppose that ten or twenty years from now, a conceptual breakthrough is finally made. A new understanding of the nature of space-time is achieved, the problem that has interested me for so long. But I'm rooted in the "old" ideas of the late twentieth century. Suppose that I'm too set in my views to get my head around the explanation of my own obsession?

One other thing, about the story rather than my own

mental insecurities. I decided about two and a half years ago that Godspeed was a perfect name for a faster-than-light drive. I wanted to do a novel on the subject (I'm halfway through writing it at the moment), but I was busy with other things and worried that someone else would steal "my" title. So I wrote the short story, more or less to protect the word, and sold it to Analog. Everything worked better than I expected, and "Godspeed" became a 1991 Hugo finalist.

DANCING WITH MYSELF

A diary has its uses, even if it is the sort of random, fragmented, fill-it-out-two-days-late sort of diary like mine.

For instance, from my official work log I know that the second phase began seven months ago today. But only from my personal diary can I deduce that on that morning I woke up well before dawn. "Mylanta. Time runs, the stars move still, the clock will strike . . ." say my useful notes. And then, without any separating punctuation, "Nicotiana smells heavenly."

With this sort of assistance, I know that I got up suffering from indigestion, looked at the clock, and then went to the open window. And having got that far, I would guess that I heard a pre-dawn whisper of waking birds in the three oak trees at the end of the yard, stayed at the window to seek a glimpse of a raccoon padding thoughtfully across the lawn, and looked for but could not see the dark red blossoms of flowering tobacco below my bedroom window.

But that was all. No portents, nothing to tell me, in spite of that quote from Faustus, that something extraordinary had begun. I had done a hellish thing, but no Mephistopheles came to drag me off to Hades.

We were only two days short of summer solstice. I watched until the sun was on the horizon, then I went to shower and eat breakfast; toast and tea and jelly, and one scrambled egg. (No help from my diary; unless I am traveling, my stomach insists on a standard meal first thing in the morning.)

By eight o'clock I was walking down the hill towards the six-hundred acre campus. By eight-fifteen I was in the lab, staring at the new equipment, most of it uncrated, that lined the room's walls.

"Good morning, Alison," said Oscar Horowitz's voice from the lab's inner recesses. "I've had the same worry. We thought we wanted it all these years. Now we've got it we're not sure."

Oscar could see me, but I couldn't see him. I walked back to where he was tucked away in his own corner, behind a row of reagent racks and a gunmetal file cabinet.

"Good morning, Oscar."

We had shared three thousand good mornings, so when he stood up I assume that I looked at him with no particular interest.

I don't think anyone, under any circumstances, would call Oscar Horowitz a handsome or an attractive man. He was in his late thirties, badly overweight, and in deplorable physical condition. I had never seen him move faster than a walk. His dark hair had already thinned to a frizzy mat that could not conceal the scalp beneath despite ingenious combing, and he had a fondness for donuts that most mornings (but not today) left a faint dusting of powdered sugar on his cheek or chin.

He was no beauty. On the other hand, nor was I.

"If we don't uncrate that chromatography unit and plug it in this morning," I said, "the Receiving Department will be all over us. We promised last week we'd report on its condition."

"They send us too much, too much at once," replied Oscar.

"Mm. 'To be a prodigal's favorite, then, worse truth, a miser's pensioner.' Except in our case Wordsworth had it the wrong way round. If we were *accustomed* to new equipment we'd take all this in our stride and ask for more."

"I'll unpack it." Oscar put down his coffee cup. "In fact, I'll do that right now. It's my turn."

When two people share a small lab, and neither is senior to the other, peaceful co-existence is best guaranteed by strict alternation of duties. Oscar was right, it was his turn. I had taken delivery, just two days earlier, of a new microtomy and staining system that neither one of us knew how to use. I didn't feel like fighting more manufacturers' manuals, and in any case I had a nine o'clock class.

I nodded appreciation and walked on back to my own desk, hemmed in by three tall bookcases. The mail had already been delivered. My in-tray held the latest issues of two monthly journals, plus five preprints that I had requested.

I sat down, riffled through one of the journals for a few seconds, and reflected on the changing status of the Biology

Department. As recently as three months ago, the university had refused to subscribe to this journal, arguing that it was expensive and only one faculty member had the slightest interest in its contents. Now anything that Oscar or I ordered was on our desk within a few days.

The winds of change, or maybe of fear. For four years Oscar and I had submitted proposals to the National Science Foundation and the National Institutes of Health, and seen our requests refused outright or squeezed down to a hardly useful pittance. Small private universities, with tiny Biology Departments and no Nobel Laureates, were not the places that the ball of Government funding came to rest. Last year we had gone through the usual ritual, with the usual pessimism, only to find that somewhere, far upstream in the government funding process, a mighty dam had broken. Our research was on replacement processes in the replication of DNA, a long way from the RNA retrovirus that causes AIDS. But our principal keywords, Blood and Phages and Transcription, had somehow hurled our proposal into the *thallweg* of AIDS mainstream research. Suddenly we had a million dollar grant, fancy new hardware, and enough soft money for a dozen graduate students.

But in spite of all that, we had made no additions to the faculty. We still had our undergraduates, and we still had to teach courses. Cell Biology was still Cell Biology, and the arrival of grant funds had not conferred instant knowledge and wisdom on our students. In fact, judging from the results of my last class test, the opposite case could be made.

I checked my appearance in a mirror hanging from the bookcase in front of my desk. Undergraduates are all right, but there is no point in giving them ammunition. Then I picked up my notes (the eighth time that they had been used for the course — time to stop updating with hand scribbles, and generate a new typed set) and walked to the far end of the lab. If I initiated an experimental run now it should be completed by the time that my class was over.

As I did so I glanced at the computer summary. Apparently yesterday had been another wasted day. All the runs had produced negative results. If our "universal DNA converter" could exist, we seemed as far as ever from creating it.

❖   ❖   ❖

Our lab was halfway up the hill, and the Glenney Lecture Hall was at the bottom next to the big lake. I walked across the grass, avoiding groups of students sunbathing, walking dogs, and playing frisbee. Even at the best of times, I often felt that no more than ten percent of our student body was trying to learn anything. Now, with bright sunshine and term almost over, the end-of-year feeling was everywhere.

The sun was in my eyes and I had to descend a steep flight of stairs, so I did not recognize Susan Carter waiting for me at the bottom until I was only a step or two away from her.

"Doctor Benilaide?" She was a raven-haired girl with a clear complexion and a sumptuous figure, and when I saw her surrounded by would-be boyfriends I was sometimes inclined to excuse her indifferent grades. She had somehow made it to her senior year, but she obviously lived in the middle of a continuous sexual thunderstorm. Horny adolescent males homed in on her, showed off in her presence, propositioned her during lectures, tried to talk her into evening dates instead of homework, and interrupted her every thought. Two of them waited for her now, standing at the side of the stone steps.

"Doctor Benilaide," she said again. "I know it's late to ask, but do you think I could change to an Incomplete?"

I shook my head. She wasn't stupid, but this was still the student who through an entire class quiz in Cell Biology had managed to refer to the subject as cetology. "Sorry, Susan, I couldn't even if I wanted to. The final grades went into the computer two days ago."

She didn't argue, just nodded sadly and gave me a heart-melting look. I walked on towards the class, a class she was supposed to be attending but where I surely would not see her. When I was almost out of earshot I heard one of her attendant jocks laugh and say: "I told you. That's Professor Been-a-laid. Never even been asked, I'd say. She flunks everybody who looks halfway human."

Halfway human. That's right, pinhead, and that's you.

Two semesters ago I had flunked him.

And did his remark upset me, when I had heard it a hundred times before? Damn right it did.

❖   ❖   ❖

My class was down to twenty-two people, from its mid-term maximum of twenty-six. Not bad, given the fine weather and the end of term. I dumped the pile of exam books on the front desk, and while the students dashed in to hunt for their own sets I went to the board and picked up a red magic marker (blackboard and chalk is better, I know, but as the years go by I am increasingly allergic to chalk dust).

I drew a vertical line down the middle of the board, and wrote a heading in each half: MITOSIS on the left, MEIOSIS on the right. Then I waited. It was pointless to begin the class until each student had noted his own score and looked at my comments on the answers.

"We'll be taking this up again next semester," I began at last. "But given the confusion in some of your answers, I'm going to hit this one more time and let it sink in over the summer. Cell division can get complicated, but the principles fit on one blackboard. Basic rule: cells divide in two fundamentally different ways. *Mitosis* means that the DNA in the cell is duplicated exactly, to give double the amount. Each chromosome is exactly copied in the process, and then the cell goes on to divide, and become two cells. *Mitosis is non-sexual.*" I wrote those words in the first column and underlined them. "When plants or animals lacking separate male and female forms reproduce, their DNA duplication *has* to be done through mitosis. Look at that T in the middle of the word, miTosis, and remember." I wrote: *If you have TEA, you don't have sex.*

"Unfortunately, the textbooks often don't help. They refer to cells produced following mitosis, through simple cell division, as *daughter* cells. That is a bad name. They are better called neuter offspring."

While I was talking I looked around the class. Half a dozen students, including a Chinese girl and Italian twin boys in the front row, were hanging on my every word. Needless to say they had been having no trouble at all. The focal point of classroom ignorance was near the back, where three T-shirted youths drooped over their desks in attitudes of extreme exhaustion or boredom. They stirred and nudged each other when I mentioned the word sex, but no matter what I said they would go out of the room as uninformed as when they came in. It was no consolation to realize that their parents were paying fourteen thousand a year for the privilege of having their children learn nothing.

I sighed, and went on. "Meiosis, on the other hand, only takes place in *sexual* organisms. And it's easy to see why it's necessary. When anything, from a mosquito to a hippopotamus, develops by fusion of a sperm and an egg, the DNA from both is in the offspring. So if the sperm cell and the egg cell each had the same amount of DNA as other cells of the body, the offspring would have twice too much DNA. To prevent that, there is another form of cell division called *meiosis*. Each of you is a product of meiosis. You all had a father and a mother, and half your DNA came from each of them. In meiosis, cells are produced with half as many chromosomes and half as much DNA as a normal body cell. These are called *gametes* — that's either the sperm or the ovum — and when they merge to make a fertilized cell that's a *zygote*. . . ."

We had been through this six times in class. How was it possible for students to miss the point, over and over again? Was I that bad a teacher? I stared at seventeen faces, half a dozen following me, half a dozen yawning or doodling, the rest as perplexed as if I were addressing them in Mandarin.

Then I wondered if it was all relative. I was groping too, and just as out of my depth. Maybe I was missing some obvious point in my research, shunning the self-evident as badly as my dimmer class members. (Last year one of my students had gone half a semester in Cell Biology before I found that he didn't know what a helix was. Others told him it was a sort of spiral, and he'd visualized the flight of a football.)

While I went through the description of meiotic cell division and homologous chromosome pairs, my mind wandered back to our failing experiments.

Oscar and I were trying to create a universal DNA converter — a "general DNA eater," unlike anything in nature. If we were successful, the organism we were working on should also handle viral genetic material, so our NIH grant was not illogical. Our starting point had been the most basic observation in molecular biology, that a DNA molecule does one thing superbly well: it *copies* itself, with a tiny error rate. It also, through the intermediary of the RNA molecule, controls the workings of the cell that contains it. Every cell uses the information in its own DNA, both to run operations and control cell division.

Viruses are nothing more than parasitic chunks of DNA or RNA, wrapped in a coat of protein. Once a virus enters a cell it makes use of the DNA and protein "production line" there to form many copies of itself, until the cell bursts open and releases a slew of new viruses.

So why don't you die, when you get a viral infection like polio or the common cold? You don't, because your body has its own immune system, a set of "defensive" cells that mop up viruses — eat them — and dissolve their alien DNA or RNA. The terrible thing about AIDS is that HIV — the Human Immunodeficiency Virus — infects, and destroys, the cells of the body that are supposed to protect us.

Oscar had had the first idea. Then I thought of a way to build the experimental system. When it showed promise, we wrote our proposal. Our "DNA converter" changed DNA in the body to a "template DNA form" that we provided. When a DNA molecule begins to make a copy of itself, it unravels the ends of the double helix, to separate and leave exposed a purine or pyrimidine pair. New purine and pyrimidine molecules (adenine, guanine, cytosine, or thymine) attach themselves to make two new pairs and start production of a new double helix. Oscar had argued that the place to attack was at the point when the original double helix is in the process of unraveling. We also had a scheme to prevent our virus-gobbler happily eating *every* piece of DNA in the human body — an important detail, since your own DNA is in every cell of you.

But our experiments, after a fine start, refused to follow the theory. We weren't blaming anyone, but every evening we would look at each other and secretly wish that one of us were smart enough to decide what was going wrong.

We were missing — what?

When the class ended I went to the cafeteria in the basement, bought a carton of low-fat milk, and sat in the sun on a wooden bench just outside the side entrance of the building. I knew that once I was back in the lab I would be swept up in experimental detail; what I needed now was an *idea*.

Oscar liked to describe things in mechanical terms. To him, we were making the smart little engine that *could*, the "Mean Machine" that would one day eat up any bad virus on Earth.

I preferred a more biological analogy. Our new organism had "eyes," chemical detectors sensitive to the presence of "unwinding proteins" that were present when DNA replication began. It had "hands," enzymes that grabbed hold of the DNA as the double helix separated. There was "memory," the template that defined the final required DNA composition. There were "muscles" in the form of abundant ATP — adenosine triphosphate, that provided the energy for nucleotides to be stripped off the sugar and phosphate bases of the DNA, and for other purine and pyrimidine molecules to replace them.

And finally, there was reproduction. Our Mean Machine was self-replicating — and mortal. It would make copies to spread through every cell, but when it could no longer find DNA suitable for conversion it would die, quietly and with no effects on the host organism.

If I had to point to one place as the *soul* of our device, it would be the memory template. That was a DNA molecule, or a set of them, and the DNA to be converted had to be close in form to the template, otherwise the energy needed for conversion would be too great. For example, we could never convert plant DNA to animal DNA, or animal to viral form. They were too different, and Oscar's little engine that could, couldn't.

I squeezed the empty milk carton flat between my hands. How about this idea: we had used the most convenient source of animal DNA for our template, and made other DNA match it. Suppose the template itself had developed anomalies, and was foiling the match? We could find that out easily enough, with one of our new lab gadgets.

I was standing up from the bench when someone moved in front of me. It was Susan Carter.

"It's not about my grade, Doctor Benilaide," she said, before I could utter a word. "I know that's all fixed and done with."

"You weren't in my class this morning."

"I know. I'm sorry." She waved a piece of paper in her right hand. "I had to get this. That's why I want to talk to you. It's about next year."

"What about next year?" I started uphill, and she fell into step beside me.

"Professor Sawyer told me you were taking graduate students. I wondered how to apply." She thrust the piece of paper out in front of me. "That's why I missed your lecture today, they told me if I wanted my grade transcript I had to get it this morning."

In bright sunlight my eyes seemed almost as good as ever. Surely I could hold off on spectacles for another year or two. I stared at the smudgy computer listing as we approached the biology lab and had quite a surprise: an isolated D, but mostly C's, with three B's and one A.

"Susan, you did worse in my courses than anything else!"

"I know. But they were the most interesting."

"And you did best in chemistry."

"Yes, but I don't *like* chemistry. And Professor Sawyer told me that the more chemistry a biologist knows, the better. He says lots of biology teachers don't know a thing."

Thank you, Hank Sawyer. I owed him something, but I was not sure what.

"You think you can do better as a graduate student than as an undergraduate? It's tougher."

"I hope I can. I'd sure try."

"Come in for a moment." We had reached the door of the lab. "While you're here, you can give me some of your skin and blood."

I laughed at her astonished expression. "Just to add to our tissue bank. We grab anyone who comes by here." I walked inside. "Come on."

After a couple of timid trial stabs she pricked her thumb with a sterilized needle and squeezed half a dozen globules of dark-red blood onto the little plastic shield. While she did so I took a closer look at her grade transcript.

"When are you leaving campus for the summer?"

"The middle of next week. Liz Willis and I are driving west together, but she has five days of make-ups before she can go."

"Fine." I carefully labeled the blood sample and put it in the refrigerated rack, along with similar ones from me, Oscar, and half the faculty. "Write a survey of the role of reverse transcriptase in RNA virus reproduction, and give it to me before you leave. Fifteen pages, no more. If it's good I'll see what I can do about next year."

"I'll try to make sure it is." She couldn't keep the big grin off her face. "Thank you, Doctor Benilaide. I know I've given you some dumb answers in class, but I'll make this report the best I can do."

We were walking back to the door. When we arrived there my body language ought to have told her that the meeting was over, but at the threshold she halted and turned to face me.

"This is nothing to do with next year"— her eyes suddenly would not meet mine and her words came out in one embarrassed rush — "but I want to tell you how bad I feel about what Danny Fischer said this morning."

The young are marvelous. An older person would have at least given me the option of pretending that I hadn't *heard* Danny Fischer's words.

"It was nothing. Just someone being a jerk."

"I told him that if I never see him again that's too soon," she continued. "And he's dead wrong." Her cheeks were flaming pink. "Liz and I think you're very attractive. You could be married in a minute if you wanted to. People like you should be married."

"Thank you again." I took her gently by the arm and steered her outside. "Don't forget, I'll need that paper by the middle of next week."

I closed the door and leaned against it. I didn't know whether to laugh or cry. One thing was certain, if Susan Carter did research with me I was going to have my hands full. Your graduate students are like your children, you find you are involved in their health problems, love lives, hobbies, families, and diet, their job applications and their interviews, their hopes and their dreams. But I liked that. It was the closest to my own children that I was ever likely to get. Acute endometritis when I was twenty-six (thank the IUD) had left enough scar tissue that my gynecologist told me I was sterile "at the ninety-five percent probability level." As she told me, that was in some ways worse than assured sterility. There was the depression of knowing you almost certainly could not have children, coupled with the worry that you might become pregnant.

At the moment that was not a problem. The last love of my life had been almost two years ago. I went to look for Oscar, hidden away behind his racks. He and I never discussed such things as sex and children, but I judged him to be mildly heterosexual. Some day, almost without thinking about it, he would probably marry and become a kind, loving, and rather absentminded husband and father.

"Any great thoughts?" Oscar had heard me coming, and was peering at me through a gap in a reagent rack.

"The younger generation are clearly unfitted to run the world, but one day they're going to do it anyway. No good ideas. How about you?"

"Not an idea, exactly. But behold, I tell you a mystery." He stood up and stepped delicately out from behind his desk, holding a listing. "Have you looked at the total amount of chemical energy that our little critter uses during the experiments?"

"Not in detail. I know it's too little for us to have changed replication in the way we'd like, and the comparison of initial and final DNA composition confirms that. It's the same at the end as when it began."

"I know. But I just calculated how much energy we'd be using if every DNA base was being *examined* during the replication process, and there was no *substitution* going on. I get a result within a few percent of the energy the process is actually using."

"Telling us what?"

"I'm not sure. Telling us that the experimental DNA is being compared with the template, at every nucleotide site — and then no changes are being made?" He handed me the listing. "Here's the program, with my formulas for energy use built into it. Over to you, Alison. I have to go to another one of those godawful Interdepartmental Studies meetings. But I think there has to be something wrong with your experimental set-up."

Easy enough for Oscar to say, but I had checked the experiment over and over, to the point where if anything *were* wrong, I would probably be the last person on earth to see it.

I took his listing. However, instead of going back to the experiment I went to my computer terminal. Thanks to Oscar's passion for completeness, the entire data base for all our experiments was on-line, right back to the first run. He had arranged his new program to pull out the data for any single run and perform the energy calculation. But it was an easy change to add a program loop, so that Oscar's calculation would be performed for every experiment in the data bank.

While the computations were being executed I attached to my own directory in the Administration files and called up my grade assignments for the current semester. I had given Susan Carter a D. Now I changed it to a "To be assigned" category.

Unfair to the other students? Probably. I was not going to worry about that. Show me a totally impartial teacher, and I'll show you a robot.

The results of Oscar's program were buzzing out of the electrostatic printer, line by line. I went over to watch them. The computer was analyzing each experimental run in chronological order. The first page looked fine. The energy used was consistent with the desired DNA modification.

The change appeared gradually, in the middle of the second page. A run appeared in which the ATP energy used was far too low — and it was also a failed experiment, in which the DNA "fingerprinting" showed that there had been no modification in the DNA sequence of our test material. The fingerprinting method was very precise, the same equipment and technique that was used routinely in forensic DNA work. Every individual in the world was different, and every one distinguishable, and the method's reliability was the main reason that Oscar and I had decided to employ human DNA in our initial experiments. I found it hard to believe that we could be having trouble with the initial and final DNA matching.

A couple of runs later, the same anomaly appeared again. And then, as though the problem were itself infectious, the low energy use came more and more often. In the runs of the past thirty days, almost every energy use was too low, and no DNA modification seemed to be taking place in them.

It *had* to be a problem with my experimental set-up. And yet I was sure it couldn't be.

When you have eliminated the impossible . . .

After the results had been printed I set out to examine the sequence in more detail, particularly the place where the problem first seemed to appear.

For no better reason than easy availability, I had used DNA from my own cells as the "template" for all our experiments. The DNA that we were trying to convert using our biological engine had been taken from a variety of individuals, and carefully stored in our "DNA library" in the form of tissue samples. Some people, such as Oscar, had provided samples more than once, and appeared in the DNA library several times. And it was that fact that finally offered some hint of a pattern.

Two months ago, our experiments seemed to be working. And as long as we used DNA that had been in the library at least that long, the experiments worked still. But with samples that had been acquired more recently, the chance of a failed experiment increased. In the past three weeks only four runs had shown success, and two of them employed DNA that had been in the library for more than two months. The other two — I felt my skin begin to goose-pimple — were from visiting scientists, strangers who had stopped by the lab for a brief visit and been talked into giving us a little bit of blood and skin. The other samples in our library were from people that Oscar and I saw and worked with every day.

I took a clean piece of paper and went back to my desk. By the time that Oscar reappeared carrying a pastrami sub sandwich and a giant Pepsi, I had the relevant facts pared down to a minimum and laid out as cleanly as I could. He read them aloud as he ate, holding the edges of the page with his greasy fingers.

"One. All the experiments looked good until two months ago.

"Two. We have not changed the form of the organism in that period." He looked up. "Is that true, Alison? What about the DNA in the template?"

"Unchanged. We've used my DNA as the template in every experiment."

"OK. Three. In all failed experiments, the actual energy used is consistent with all the molecular *comparisons* being made, but with no *replacements* along the DNA molecule.

"Four. When we use samples that have been in our tissue bank for a couple of months, the experiments still work.

"Five. When we use samples that have entered the bank more recently, the experiments usually fail.

"Six. The exception to that statement occurs when the recent tissue came from *visitors* to the lab. Then the experiment works. Jesus. Are you sure of that?"

"Positive. I'll show you the output."

He shook his head, put down my sheet of paper, and picked up his Pepsi. Amazingly, he had left his sandwich half-uneaten. For the next two minutes he sucked in silence on his straw. I knew enough not to interrupt. One look from Oscar was enough to break most pieces of experimental equipment, but he was a top-notch theorist.

At last he put down his cup, rubbed his hands absentmindedly on his napkin and then on his trousers, and said: "You know, I've been assuming that the experiments didn't work because there was insufficient energy available to make the DNA conversion to the template form."

"That's right. We knew we had to begin with DNA close to the final structure. Maybe we just weren't close enough."

"But that's not what's happening here. Look at the energy used — it's not that the process *starts* replacement, and then quits because there's not enough energy available. It's that comparisons are made with the given form and the template, and then *no* replacements are performed. Not one."

"Because the initial and final forms are too dissimilar."

He shook his head. "The replacement process should at least *begin*. No, the only way to get the results we're seeing is for the given form and the template to be *identical*, so our little engine can't find a thing to replace. Our organism examines every nucleotide base, but if the match is already perfect it won't do more than look."

"But that makes no sense, either. I'm taking the samples right from our tissue bank. Every one comes from a different person."

"I know, it sounds crazy. But there's a simple way to test what I'm saying. You've been running the initial and final forms through the DNA fingerprint process. We can run a

comparison between template DNA and tissue sample DNA
—*before* you do the experiment."

It was a ridiculous suggestion. But it was the only suggestion
we had.

And so we did it.

The Jeffreys' DNA fingerprint technique was developed
over in England, at Leicester University. It produces thirty to
forty dark bands on X-ray film, corresponding to repeating
nucleotide sequences in the long DNA molecule. And while it
is not totally infallible, it is close to it. The probability that two
individuals will show the same banding on the developed film
is less than one in ten billion (there are five billion people on
the earth). When we compared the DNA in our tissue bank
with my own DNA, I was convinced that we would see evident
differences. And when we didn't, I was just as convinced there
had to be something wrong with the fingerprint matching
machine. All the recently acquired DNA samples — including
the one taken from Susan Carter, less than two hours earlier!
— matched mine perfectly, band for band. And the banding of
every sample that had been in the tissue bank for three
months or more was instantly recognizable as different from
my banding pattern.

Finally Oscar quietly took a sample from his own skin with a
scalpel, and fed that into the matching machine. Ten minutes
later we had the developed film. It correlated perfectly with
my DNA. But an old sample of his from three months ago,
kept in the tissue bank, had a totally different band pattern.

"Oscar, this is crazy." I felt we should be laughing hysteri-
cally. "According to this, you're me! *Everybody* is me!"

But he wasn't laughing at all. He was staring at his own arm
in disbelief, at the place where he had removed the skin sample. "The Mean Machine," he muttered. "The one thing we
didn't test it for — didn't think we needed to test it."

"Test for what?"

"We knew it reproduced — we designed it that way, so
there would be enough of it to work in every cell. But it does
more than reproduce. It's *contagious*. And by the look of it,
strongly contagious."

As contagious as the vision that Oscar was seeing. The
organism was in me — naturally; but in my case it did nothing,

since there was nothing for it to do. I already had my own
DNA, and no one else's. But if it could be communicated by
casual contact, it would have jumped quickly to Oscar — to
the rest of the faculty — to the students. There had been a
widespread complaint a few weeks ago of students running a
low-grade fever, not enough to keep anyone in bed but enough
for them to notice it. If the whole campus was by now infected,
only visitors would have different DNA to offer our tissue
bank. And when they left . . .

Now I had a clear mental picture of thousands of students
at the end of term, streaming away from the campus to every
part of the country. The organism would already be in California, in Texas, in Maine, in Wisconsin. With modern travel, how
long before it was in Europe, Australia, or China?

I brought my racing thoughts under better control. If Oscar
had been "infected," so that his DNA had been replaced with
the template for my DNA . . .

"Oscar, it can't be what you're thinking. We have to be
wrong about this. You're still you — you don't look like me, act
like me, think like me."

"Of course not. Alison, we know that the template matching
only takes place during cell replication. Nerve cells don't replicate — my brain is my own, and it always will be. Muscles, too,
those cells don't divide. But my skin, and my blood, and my
liver and spleen, they will have changed to your DNA patterns.
They are *you*. There's nothing terrible about that. People do
very well with blood from other people. So even if we can't
change everyone's DNA back to their own form it won't be the
end of the world. Of course . . ."

It was his turn to fade off into silence, while I shivered. We
had been struck by the same thought at the same time.

"Oscar," I said. "We made the organism to affect replication
— to work during mitosis. But it must work in meiosis, too.
Every sperm and every ovum will carry only my sex chromosomes . . . X chromosomes. And all human offspring with two
X chromosomes—"

"—are female."

No males. Which, in just one generation, *would* be the end
of the world.

❖   ❖   ❖

To tell, or not to tell. Ought we to go public at once? Oscar and I spent the rest of the day sequestered in our lab, doors locked, telephone calls ignored.

I felt we had no choice; we had to call Washington at once and talk to the Surgeon General's office.

Oscar disagreed, strongly. He made some good points. First, we had to do more tests to make sure we were right in our conclusions. Second, if we were right the whole campus was *already* infected, with no one feeling any the worse. Third, talk of a strongly contagious "plague" would cause widespread panic. And fourth, there was not a damned thing that anyone could do about the problem.

"Do you want people to hide away in their houses?" he said. "To stop shaking hands, refuse to meet strangers, lock us away and create new leper colonies? Look at me, Alison, do I seem sick?"

He did not. If anything he looked rather healthier than usual, a little thinner and a little less seedy. I agreed to wait, at least long enough for us to learn a bit more.

That was seven months ago. We are still waiting, but let me remove the suspense: in our first wild panic, Oscar and I had both committed a scientific blunder for which I would have flunked a freshman. Human males have a chromosome — the Y chromosome — that is completely absent in females. In its place, normal females have an X chromosome (occasionally, as in Turner's syndrome, a female will have nothing). The X and Y chromosomes are totally different, in structure and especially in size, so there was no way that my DNA's X-chromosome template could ever be close enough to a man's Y-chromosome to convert it. All the DNA comparisons in our experiments, naturally enough, had been for *autosomal* DNA — DNA in chromosomes that are not sex chromosomes.

So boys will continue to be born as well as girls, we have not deprived the human species of its future, and our globe is much the same as it was before my DNA spread across its face.

Much the same, but not quite. The body cells of skin and liver and blood and spleen — and ductless glands — that suffer

DNA replacement are not usually associated with the "higher" human functions of thought and emotion. Oscar and I had wondered if we would ever know how far and fast our new organism had spread. General human behavior should not change, but we could hardly go up to Canada or down to Mexico, and ask random strangers to contribute tissue samples to compare with mine.

But maybe we wrongly define the higher human functions. How we think and feel about everything except questions of pure logic is decided maybe five percent in our brains, ninety-five percent in our *glands*. And how many events in human history have been the result of logical thought? Just try to name one.

Anyway, neither I nor Oscar drew the immediate conclusion when cigarette manufacturers reported a catastrophic drop in U.S. sales, and raged against the new anti-smoking campaigns. And Oscar never reads the newspapers or watches television, so I was the one who picked up a different anomaly.

War makes it into the headlines much easier than peace. The people of Northern Ireland have been fighting over their border for too many generations to count. But four months ago, a snippet in the Overseas News section of our local paper pointed out that it was an unprecedented sixty days since the last violent incident. Maybe the Irish Protestants and Catholics disliked each other as much as ever, but for some reason they were not resorting to bloodshed.

I began to take a new interest in worldwide politics.

A month later, a strange quiet spread across the Middle East; no bombings in Beirut, no hostage-taking in Lebanon, a twenty-year trading agreement between Iraq and Iran. Farther east, the civil war in Sri Lanka ran out of steam, the Sino-Soviet border was peaceful, Indonesia held orderly elections, and the bloody Philippines riots ended. By that time, everyone could sense a new current in international relations. Five years ago, the Soviet Union and the United States had been busy in all-out arms escalation. But last week our leaders cut through the diplomatic red tape and agreed to a far-reaching treaty, reducing nuclear stockpiles and slowing conventional weapons development. The whole world began to breathe easier.

And so did I. Oscar (thirty pounds lighter and exercising every day, to his own astonishment and under the iron hand of Susan Carter) tells me that I ought to be ecstatic rather than simply relieved. "You make Alexander the Great and Genghis Khan look like amateurs," he said. "Alison Benilaide is conquering the whole globe. She's irresistible and she's ubiquitous, billions of her, marching through Georgia, invading Delhi and Moscow and Beijing, leaping international borders at a single bound. They're all you, Alison. You are the original Ur-Mother. You should be *proud* of your DNA, not ashamed."

And finally, I think I am. I feel pride, and I would not argue if it were described as maternal. Our little engine that could may not be able to change most of the brain, but it seems to manage very well elsewhere, in the places that define our emotions and our innermost feelings. My DNA knows what it's doing. And like the rest of me, it is apparently a pacifist.

So Oscar and I didn't destroy the world. I rather think we saved it. For that, you don't get medals. On the other hand, you don't need them.

Afterword: *Dancing with Myself*

This story, like "Tunicate, Tunicate, Wilt Thou Be Mine," began as a title. It also began at a time I can precisely define. I was at a Saturday night "prom" dance at Disclave, a local science fiction convention, on May 28, 1988. I suspect that I'm the world's worst dancer, but somehow I had managed to commit myself to dancing at least once. So I was moving around the floor in a bewildered sort of way, trying not to think too much about where my feet were going, and the disk jockey, who was later threatened with physical violence for playing advanced heavy metal when people wanted tunes they already knew, put on, presumably by accident, a great Billy Idol record, "Dancing with Myself."

And I, in the bemused mood where you know that at most one half of your brain is working, said to myself, "I can write a story with that title. And I know exactly what it will be about: DNA copying and the human genome."

I was halfway through writing another story, "Humanity Test," at the time, so I didn't get to "Dancing with Myself" for another month. But the story was finished by the end of June 1988.

Now let's talk about other timing. "Dancing with Myself" was purchased by Analog, and published in the August 1989 issue. Four months later that most visible symbol of the Cold War, the Berlin Wall, came down. Two years after that the whole Soviet Union fell apart. The threat of global nuclear war, for the first time in most people's lives, diminished. It no longer seems high on anyone's list of worries.

So things happened just about on the schedule suggested in "Dancing with Myself." Do I take credit, then, for "predicting" the vast changes in the world that took place in the four short years since I wrote the story?

You bet I do; but I don't expect anyone else on the planet to agree with me.

SOMETHING FOR NOTHING

A *Biography of the Universe*

1.   THE TRUE PROFESSIONAL

Biographies, of everyone from Charles Darwin to Nancy Reagan to Saddam Hussein, are a popular form of literature. Sometimes they are written because the author has had a long-term fascination or close relationship with the subject. Charles Darwin himself, for example, wrote a short biography of his polymath grandfather, Erasmus Darwin.

Just as often, however, biographies are written on commission, at the request of a publisher. One definition of a "truly professional" writer is a person who is willing to write about anything, at any length and to any deadline, provided only that the job is well-paid. If you would like to be such a professional, now or in the future, imagine the following situation: A publisher comes to you and asks you to write a biography. It is of a man you have heard of but never met.

You ask a few reasonable questions. How old is this person?

"I'm not sure. Somewhere between thirty and sixty."

"Do you have people that I can talk to who have known him all his life?"

"No."

"Well, I mean known him for *most* of his life."

"No."

"How about *some* of his life."

"I suppose so. I can give a fair amount of information about what he has been doing for the past half minute."

If you would take the assignment, you are a truly professional writer. You might also, with a little training, make a good cosmologist.

A cosmologist seeks to understand the nature and history of the whole universe. The age of the universe is not known with great precision, but we believe it to be between ten and twenty billion years. Let's say for the moment that it is fifteen billion.

We have been able to study the universe in detail for less than four hundred years, since the invention of the telescope in about 1608. That's about one thirty-seven millionth of its fifteen billion year lifetime. One thirty-seven millionth of the life of a forty-five year old is thirty-eight seconds.

The task of writing a biography of the universe with so little solid information sounds hopeless. There is a chance of success only because the basic physical laws of the universe that govern events on both the smallest scale (atoms and subatomic particles) and the largest scale (stars, galaxies, and clusters of galaxies) have not changed since its earliest days.

That constancy is of course an *assumption*, not a fact; but there are reasons to make it, and we will come to those in due course.

Let me make one more introductory point. New biographies of old celebrities often promise "amazing new revelations." These are normally, for obvious reasons, set at the end of the book, with the first three-quarters devoted to rehashing the same old material. I will be following this tried and tested philosophy. You will find little in the opening sections that was not in textbooks twenty or more years ago, and most of what I write is standard scientific dogma. I will provide due warning when the doubtful material appears.

2. STARS...

I said that we've been studying the external universe for only four hundred years. That's an understatement if we accept that stars and planets must have been the subject of speculation since mankind first looked up and wondered about those points of light in the sky. However, no one had any idea until four hundred years ago what planets and stars *were*, or of their sizes, distances, and composition.

The modern view, that all stars are giant globes of hot gas, developed after 1609, when Galileo turned his homemade telescope upwards. He found that the Sun was not the perfect, unmarked sphere that traditional teaching required, but a rotating object with lots of surface detail, like sunspots and solar flares.

Over the next couple of hundred years, the size and the temperature of the sun were pinned down fairly well. It is a great ball of gas, about a million miles across, with a surface at 6,000 degrees Celsius. What was not understood at all, even a hundred years ago, was the way that the sun *stays* hot.

Before 1800, that was not a worry. The universe was believed to be only a few thousand years old (Archbishop Ussher of Armagh, working backwards through the genealogy of the Bible, in 1654 announced that the time of creation was 4004 B.C., on October 26, at 9 o'clock in the morning. No messing about with uncertainty for *him*.)

In the eighteenth century, the scriptural time-scale provided by religion prevented anyone worrying much about the age of the Sun. It presumably started out very hot and burning in 4000 B.C., and so it hadn't had time to cool down yet. If it were made entirely of burning coal, it would have lasted long enough.

Around 1800, the geologists started to ruin things. In 1785, James Hutton read his *Theory of the Earth* to the Royal Society of Edinburgh, advancing the idea of *uniformitarianism* in geology. He published it in the *Proceedings* of the society three years later, and then an amplified form in two volumes in 1795. It did not make great waves, but after Hutton's death John Playfair published (in 1802) a shorter and more accessible version.

Uniformitarianism, in spite of its ugly name, is a beautiful and simple idea. According to Hutton and Playfair, *the processes that built the world in the past are exactly those at work today*: the uplift of mountains, the tides, the weathering effects of rain and air and water flow, these shape the surface of the Earth. This is in sharp distinction to the idea that the world was created just as it is now, except for occasional great catastrophic changes like the Biblical Flood.

The great virtue of Hutton's theory is that it removes the need for assumptions. The effectiveness of anything that shaped the past can be measured by looking at its effectiveness today.

The great *disadvantage* of the theory, from the point of view of anyone pondering what keeps the Sun hot, is the amount of time is takes for all this to happen. We can no longer accept a universe only a few thousand years old. Mountain ranges could not form, seabeds could not be raised, chalk deposits be laid down, and solid rocks could not erode to powder, in so short a time. Hutton and Playfair, and later Charles Lyell who further developed and promoted the same ideas, needed many millions of years in which to work. And it was clearly preposterous to imagine the Sun as orders of magnitude *younger* than the Earth.

A Sun made of burning coal would not do. Hermann von Helmholtz and Lord Kelvin independently proposed a solution that could give geology more time. They suggested that the source of the Sun's heat was not burning, but *gravitational contraction*. If the material of the Sun were slowly falling inward on itself, that would release energy.

If the source of such energy feels obscure, take a hammer and smack a flat stone hard with it, many times in succession. After thirty or forty blows, feel the hammer and the stone. They will both be warmer, heated by the energy of the hammer blows. Now instead of holding the hammer, raise it by a pulley and then drop it. Do this a number of times, and the hammer and stone still become warmer. The heat is now produced by gravity, pulling the hammer down. That was exactly, according to Lord Kelvin, what was heating the Sun.

The amount of energy produced by the Sun's contraction could be precisely calculated. Unfortunately it was not enough. While Lord Kelvin was proposing an age for the Sun of 20 million years the ungrateful geologists, and still more so the biologists, were asking considerably more. Charles Darwin's *Origin of Species* came out in 1859, and evolution seemed to need much longer than mere tens of millions of years to do its work. The biologists wanted hundreds of millions at a minimum, and they preferred a few billion.

No one could give it to them during the whole of the 19th century. Lord Kelvin, who no matter what he did could not come up with any age for the Sun greater than 100 million years and was in favor of a number far less, in particular became an arch-enemy of the evolutionists. An "odious spectre" is what Darwin called him. But no one could refute his physical arguments. A new scientific revolution was needed before an explanation was available for a multi-billion year age of the Sun.

That revolution began in the 1890's, when in quick succession Röntgen discovered X rays (1895), Becquerel discovered radioactivity (1896) and Thomson (J.J. Thomson, not William Thomson — no relation) discovered the electron (1897). Together, these discoveries implied that the atom, previously thought to be an indivisible particle, had an interior structure and could be broken into smaller pieces.

Skipping as lightly over the next quarter of a century of enormous intellectual effort as we did over the period 1600–1800, by the end of the 1920's we reach a time when it was realized that not only could atoms split, to form smaller atoms and subatomic particles, but light atoms could *combine*, to form heavier atoms. In particular, four atoms of hydrogen could fuse together to form one atom of helium; and if that happened, huge amounts of energy could be produced. (That's what a hydrogen bomb does.)

Perhaps the first person to realize that nuclear fusion was the key to what makes the sun go on shining was Arthur Eddington. Certainly he was one of the first persons to develop the idea systematically, and equally certainly he believed that he was the first to think of it. There is a story of Eddington sitting out one balmy evening with a girl friend. She said, "Aren't the stars pretty." And he said, "Yes, and I'm the only person in the world who knows what makes them shine."

It's a nice story, but it's none too likely. Eddington was a lifelong bachelor, a Quaker, and a workaholic, by all accounts too busy to have much time for idle philandering. (Just as damning for the anecdote, Rudolf Kippenhahn, in his book *100 Billion Suns*, tells exactly the same story with minor word changes — but about Fritz Houtermans, who also played an important part in explaining the hydrogen-to-helium energy conversion.)

Astronomy, mathematics, and physics formed Eddington's

life, and he was a superb theoretician. But even he could not say *how* the hydrogen fused to form helium. That insight came ten years later, with the work of Hans Bethe and Carl von Weizäcker, who in 1938 discovered the "carbon cycle" for nuclear fusion.

However, Eddington didn't have to know *how*. He had all the information that he needed, because he knew how much energy would be released when four hydrogen nuclei changed to one helium nucleus. All he required was the mass of hydrogen, the mass of helium, and Einstein's most famous formula, $E = mc^2$.

From that, Eddington worked out how much hydrogen would have to be converted to provide the Sun's known energy output. The answer is around 600 million tons a second.

Before we say, wow, what a huge amount, we ought to think of it as a fraction of the *total* mass of the Sun. That mass is around 2×10^{27} tons, a number big enough to be almost meaningless. But we can put both numbers into a useful perspective, by noting that 600 million tons a second for one billion years is about 2×10^{25} tons — or one percent of the Sun's mass. Now, the Sun is about 65 percent hydrogen. So to keep the Sun shining as brightly as it shines today for five billion years* would require only that during that period, less than eight percent of the Sun's hydrogen be converted to helium.

Why pick a period of five billion years? Because other evidence suggests an age for the Earth of about 4.5 billion years. Nuclear fusion is all we need in the Sun to provide the right time-scale for geology and biology on Earth. More than that, the Sun can go on shining just as brightly for another five billion years, without totally depleting its source of energy.

But how typical a star is the Sun? It certainly occupies a unique place in our lives. All the evidence, however, suggests that the Sun is a rather normal star. There are stars scores of times as massive, and stars tens of times as small. The upper limit is set by stability, because a contracting ball of gas of more

---

* The Sun has actually been getting brighter. Over the past three and a half billion years it is estimated to have increased in energy production by 30 percent.

than about 90 solar masses will oscillate more and more wildly, until parts of it are blown off into space and what's left will be 90 solar masses or less. At the lower end, below a certain size, maybe one-twelfth of the Sun's mass, a starlike object cannot generate enough internal pressure to initiate nuclear fusion, and so should perhaps not be called a "star" at all.

The Sun sits comfortably in the middle range, designated by astronomers as a G2-type dwarf star, in what is known as the *main sequence* because most of the stars we see can be fitted into that sequence.

The life history of a star depends more than anything else on its mass. That story also started with Eddington, who in 1924 discovered the *mass-luminosity law*. The more massive a star, the more brightly it shines.* This law does *not* merely restate the obvious, that more massive stars are bigger and so radiate more simply because they are of larger area. If that were true, because the mass of a star grows with the cube of its radius, and its surface area like the square of its radius, we might expect to find that brightness goes roughly like mass to the two-thirds power. (Multiply the mass by eight, and expect the brightness to increase by a factor of four.) In fact, the brightness goes up rather faster than the *cube* of the mass (multiply the mass by eight, and the brightness increases by a factor of more than a *thousand*).

The implications of this for the evolution of a star are profound. Dwarf stars can go on steadily burning for a hundred billion years. Massive stars squander their energy at a huge rate, running out of available materials for fusion in just millions of years.

The interesting question is, what happens to massive stars when their central regions no longer have hydrogen to convert to helium? Detailed (and difficult) models, beginning with Fred Hoyle and William Fowler's fundamental work on stellar nucleosynthesis in the 1940's, have allowed that question to be answered in the past forty years.

---

* I say *shines*, rather than appears to shine, because the brightness of the stars we see depends on how far away they are. The *absolute magnitude* of a star means its brightness as it would appear from a standard distance. The mass-luminosity law works in terms of the absolute magnitude.

Like a compulsive gambler running out of chips, stars coming to the end of their supply of hydrogen seek other energy sources. At first they find it through other nuclear fusion processes. Helium in the central core "burns" to form carbon, carbon burns to make oxygen and neon and magnesium. These processes call for higher and higher temperatures before they are significant. Carbon burning starts about 600 million degrees (as usual, we are talking degrees Celsius). Neon burning begins around a billion degrees. Such a temperature is available only in the cores of massive stars, so for a star less than nine solar masses that is the end of the road. Many such stars settle down to old age as cooling lumps of dense matter. Stars above nine solar masses can keep going, burning neon and then oxygen. Finally, above 3 billion degrees, silicon, which is produced in a process involving collisions of oxygen nuclei, begins to burn, and all the elements are produced up to and including iron. By the time that we reach iron, the different elements form spherical shells about the star's center, with the heaviest (iron) in the middle, surrounded by shells of successively lighter elements until we get to a hydrogen shell on the outside.

Now we come to a fact of great significance. *No elements heavier than iron can be produced through this nuclear synthesis process in stars*. Iron, element 26, is the place on the table of elements where nuclear binding energy is maximum. If you try to "burn" iron, fusing it to make heavier elements, you *use* energy, rather than producing it. Notice that this has nothing to do with the mass of the star. It is decided only by nuclear forces.

The massive star that began as mainly hydrogen has reached the end of the road. The final processes have proceeded faster and faster, and they are much less efficient at producing energy than the hydrogen to helium reaction. Hydrogen burning takes millions of years for a star of, say, a dozen solar masses. But carbon burning is all finished in a few thousand years, and the final stage of silicon burning lasts only a day or so.

There are obvious next questions: What happens now to the star? Does it sink into quiet old age, like most small stars? Or does it find some new role?

Actually, we have one more question to ask. We can explain through stellar nucleosynthesis the creation of every element lighter than iron. But more than 60 elements *heavier* than iron are found on Earth. If they are not formed by nuclear fusion within stars, where did they come from?

They were not, as you might argue, "there from the beginning"; but in order to prove that assertion we need some additional facts.

In the best cliff-hanger tradition, therefore, I am going to leave our massive star, running faster and faster through its sources of energy, down to the last one left (silicon to iron), and wondering where it can possibly go next.

We will come back to that mystery, and also to the problem of the source of heavy elements, in a little while. First, however, we must explore another important piece of the universe.

3.   . . . AND GALAXIES

The ancient astronomers, observing without benefit of telescopes, knew and named many of the stars. They also noted the presence of a hazy glow that extends across a large fraction of the sky, and they called it the *Milky Way*. Finally, those with the most acute vision had noted that the constellation of Andromeda contained within it a much smaller patch of haze.

The progress from observation of the stars to the explanation of hazy patches in the sky came in stages. Galileo started the ball rolling in 1610, when he examined the Milky Way with his telescope and found that he could see huge numbers of stars there, far more than were visible with the unaided eye. He asserted that the Milky Way was nothing more than stars, in vast numbers. William Herschel carried this a stage farther, counting how many stars he could see in different parts of the Milky Way, and beginning to build towards the modern picture, of a great disk made out of billions of separate stars, with the Sun in the plane of the disk but well away (30,000 light-years) from the center.

At the same time, the number of hazy patches in the sky visible with a telescope went up and up as telescope power increased. Lots of them looked like the patch in Andromeda, which had long been known as the *Andromeda Nebula* (nebula = mist, in Latin).

A dedicated comet hunter, Charles Messier, annoyed at constant confusion of hazy patches (uninteresting) with comets (highly desirable) had already plotted out their locations so as not to be bothered by them. This resulted in the *Messier Catalog*: the first and almost inadvertent catalog of *galaxies* (galaxy = milky).

But what *were* those fuzzy glows identified by Messier?

The *suspicion* that the Andromeda and other galaxies might be composed of stars, as the Milky Way of our own galaxy is made up of stars, was there from Galileo's time. Individual stars cannot be seen in most galaxies, but only because of their distance. The number of galaxies, though, probably exceeds anything that Galileo would have found credible. Today's estimate is that there are about a hundred billion galaxies in the visible universe — roughly the same as the number of individual stars in a typical galaxy, such as our own. Galaxies, fainter and fainter as their distance increases, are seen as far as our telescopes can probe.

In most respects, the distant ones look little different from the nearest ones. But there is one crucial difference, and it is the main reason for introducing the galaxies at this point.

Galaxies increase in numbers as they decrease in apparent brightness, and it is natural to assume that these two go together: if we double the distance of a galaxy, it appears one-quarter as bright, but we expect to see four times as many like it if space is uniformly filled with galaxies.

What we would *not* expect to find, until it was suggested by Carl Wirtz in 1924 and confirmed by Edwin Hubble in 1929, is that more distant galaxies appear *redder* than nearer ones.

To be more specific, particular wavelengths of light emitted by galaxies have been shifted towards longer wavelengths in the fainter (and therefore presumably more distant) galaxies. The question is, what could cause such a shift?

The most plausible mechanism, to a physicist, is called the *Doppler Effect*. According to the Doppler Effect, light from a receding object will be shifted to longer (redder) wavelengths; light from an approaching object will be shifted to shorter (bluer) wavelengths. Exactly the same thing works for sound, which is why a speeding police car's siren seems to drop in pitch as it passes by.

If we accept the Doppler effect as the cause of the reddened appearance of the galaxies, we are led (as was Hubble) to an immediate conclusion: the whole universe must be *expanding*, at a close to constant rate, because the red shift of the galaxies corresponds to their brightness, and therefore to their distance.

Note that this does *not* mean that the universe is expanding *into* some other space. There is no other space. It is the *whole* universe — everything there is — that has grown over time to its present dimension.

And from this we can draw another immediate conclusion. If that expansion had proceeded in the past as it did today, there must have been a time when everything in the whole universe was drawn together to a single point. It is logical to call the time that has elapsed since everything was in that infinitely dense singularity *the age of the universe*. The Hubble galactic redshift allows us to calculate how long ago that happened.

Our estimate is bounded on the one hand by the constancy of the laws of physics (how far back can we go, before the universe would be totally unrecognizable and far from the places where we believe today's physical laws are valid); and on the other hand by our knowledge of the distance of the galaxies, as determined by other methods.

Curiously, it is the second problem that forms the major constraint. When we say that the universe is between ten and twenty billion years old, that uncertainty of a factor of two betrays our ignorance of galactic distances. When (and if) the Hubble space telescope performs as it was originally supposed to do, we will obtain a better estimate of the distance of the nearer galaxies; from that we will be able to reduce the uncertainty in the size and age of the universe.

I want to pause here and point out how remarkable it is that observation of the faint agglomerations of stars known as galaxies leads us, very directly and cleanly, to the conclusion that we live in a universe of finite and determinable age. A century ago, no one could have offered even an approximate age for the universe. For an upper bound, most non-religious scientists would probably have said "forever." For a lower bound, all they had was the age of the Earth.

It's fascinating to note that at first, Hubble's work seemed to re-introduce the crisis of the early nineteenth century (Earth and Sun older than universe). Using the estimated galactic distances of the 1920's led to an age for the universe of only 2 billion years, compared with the required 4.5 billion year age of the Earth and Sun. However, over the next 30 years the estimated distances of the galaxies was gradually increased. Today's age for the universe, of ten to twenty billion years, is totally consistent with the age of the Earth, Sun and stars.

Answering one question, How old is the universe, inevitably leads us to another: What was the universe like, ten or twenty billion years ago, when it was compressed into a very small volume?

In particular, can we say if the 60 and more elements heavier than iron that we know today were created in the distant past?

Surprisingly, we can deduce a good deal about the early history of the universe, and the picture is a coherent one, consistent with today's ideas of the laws of physics. We can also, quite specifically, say something about the formation of elements during those earliest times. We will do that, before we go back to explore the fate of our fuel-depleted massive star, poised on the brink of nuclear burn-out.

4. EARLY (BUT NOT TOO EARLY) TIMES

After Albert Einstein had developed his general theory of relativity and gravitation, he and others used it in the second decade of this century to study various simplified theoretical models of the whole universe.

Einstein could construct a simple enough universe, with matter spread through the whole of space. What he could *not* do was make it sit still. The equations insisted that the model universe either had to expand, or it had to contract.

To make his model universe stand still, Einstein introduced in 1917 a new, and logically unnecessary, "cosmological constant" into his own general theory. With that, he could build a stable, static universe. He later described the introduction of the cosmological constant, and his refusal to accept the reality of an expanding or contracting universe, as the biggest blunder of his life.

When Hubble's work showed the universe to be expanding, Einstein at once recognized its implications. However, he himself did not undertake to move in the other direction, and ask about the time when the contracted universe was far more compact than it is today. That was done by a Belgian, Georges Lemaître. Early in the 1930's Lemaître went backwards in time, to a period when the whole universe was a "primeval atom." In this first and single atom, everything was squashed into a sphere only a few times as big as the Sun, with no space between atoms, or even between nuclei. As Lemaître saw it, this unit must then have exploded, fragmenting into the atoms and stars and galaxies and everything else in the universe that we know today. He might justifiably have called it the *Big Bang*, but he didn't. That name seems to have been coined by Hoyle (the same man who did the fundamental work on nucleosynthesis) in 1950. It is entirely appropriate that Hoyle, whose whole career has been marked by colorful and imaginative thinking, should have named the central event of modern cosmology.

Lemaître did not ask the next question, namely, where did the primeval atom come from? Since he was an ordained Catholic priest, he probably felt that the answer to that was a given. But there are other answers, which we will get to in due course.

Lemaître also did not worry too much about the composition of his primeval atom — what was it made of? It might be thought that the easiest assumption is that everything in the universe was already there, much as it is now. But that cannot be true, because as we go back in time, the universe had to be hotter as well as more dense. Before a certain point, atoms as we know it could not exist, because they would be torn apart by the intense radiation that permeated the whole universe.

The person who did worry about the composition of the primeval atom was George Gamow. In the 1940's, he conjectured that the original stuff of the universe was nothing more than densely packed neutrons. Certainly, it seemed reasonable to suppose that the universe at its outset had no net charge, since it seems to have no net charge today. Also, a neutron left to itself has a fifty percent chance that it will in about thirteen minutes decay radioactively, to form an electron and a proton.* One electron and one proton form an atom of hydrogen; and even today, the universe is predominantly atomic hydrogen. So neutrons could account for most, if not all, of today's universe.

An old name for the prime material out of which the universe was made is *ylem*. At the time of the 1952 American Presidential campaign, dedicated Republicans announced their preference for candidate General Dwight Eisenhower, nicknamed "Ike," by wearing lapel buttons that said, "I Like Ike." George Gamow, as colorful, interesting and opinionated a physicist as the twentieth century has produced, went around that year wearing a button that said "I Like Ylem."

(He also wrote popular treatments of science. My own favorite of those works is *Thirty Years That Shook Physics* [see Bibliography] in which Gamow comments on the rise of the quantum theory by describing the lives and personalities of the physicists who created it. He naturally, but regrettably, omits anecdotal descriptions of one of the major spirits of that scientific revolution, George Gamow.)

If the early universe was very hot and very dense and all hydrogen, some of it ought to have fused and become helium, carbon, and other elements. The question, *How much of each?* was one that Gamow and his student, Ralph Alpher, set out to answer. They calculated that about a quarter of the matter in the primeval universe should have turned to helium, a figure very consistent with the present composition of the oldest stars. They published their results on April 1, 1948. In one of physics' best-known jokes, Hans Bethe (pronounced *Bayter*, as Americans pronounce the Greek letter *Beta*) allowed his name to be added to the paper, although he had nothing to

---

* So after 26 minutes, three neutrons out of four will have decayed; after 39 minutes, seven out of eight, and so on. You might think that would mean that neutrons ought to have disappeared early in the history of the universe. However, that rapid decay only happens to *isolated* neutrons. Bound inside a nucleus a neutron is quite stable, and most elements have more neutrons inside the nucleus than they have protons.

do with its writing. The authors thus became Alpher, Bethe, and Gamow.

What Gamow and Alpher could not do, and what no one else could do after them, was make the elements heavier than helium after the Big Bang that began the universe.* In fact, Gamow and colleagues proved that heavier element synthesis did *not* take place. It could not happen very early, because in the earliest moment, elements would be torn apart by energetic radiation. At later times, the universe expanded and cooled too quickly to yield the needed temperatures.

Heavier element formation, as we have seen, had to be done by *stars*, during the process known as stellar nucleosynthesis. The failure of the Big Bang to produce heavier elements confirms something that we already know, namely, that the Sun (and with it the whole Solar System) is much younger than the universe. Sol, at maybe five billion years old, is a second, third, or even fourth generation star. Some of the materials that make up Sun and Earth derive from older stars that ran far enough through their evolution to produce elements up to iron, by nuclear fusion.

Apart from showing how to calculate the ratio of hydrogen to helium after the Big Bang, Gamow and his colleagues did one other thing whose full significance probably escaped them. In 1948 they produced an equation that allowed one to compute the *present* background temperature of the universe from its age, assuming a universe that expanded uniformly since its beginning in the Big Bang. Whether Gamow was skeptical of his own equation or not is difficult to say, but the fact remains that he never agitated for experiments to look for such background radiation — and when he had a bee in his bonnet, Gamow was as good as anyone at stirring up action. The background radiation, corresponding to a temperature of 2.7 degrees above absolute zero, was discovered by Arno Penzias and Robert Wilson in 1964 — discovered *by accident*, at the very time when a Princeton group a few miles away were planning to look deliberately. Penzias and Wilson head

---

* This is a little bit of an overstatement. Actually, a smidgeon of deuterium and lithium can be produced, too, but not enough to make a difference.

the list of "lucky" Nobel Prizewinners, since if they had not received their 1978 award for discovery of the leftover (or "relict") cosmic background radiation, it is hard to believe they would have received the award for anything else.

If our biography of the universe is to be complete, we need to explore the time of its birth in more detail, turning the clock back well beyond the time when hydrogen fused to helium. That happened, we now believe, when the universe was between three and four *minutes* old. Before exploring such early times, and trying to make the extraordinary statement of the previous sentence plausible, let us take off the hook our massive star, ten or more solar masses, that had run out of fusion fuel at the end of Section 2 and seemed to have nowhere to go next.

5. BIG BANGS (BUT NOT *THE* BIG BANG)

We have a star, of ten or more solar masses, running out of energy. The supply provided by the fusion at its center of silicon into iron is almost done, radiating away rapidly into space. In the middle of the star is a sphere of iron "gas" (technically, a *plasma*) about one and a half times the mass of the sun and at a temperature of a few billion degrees. It *acts* like a gas because all the iron nuclei and the electrons are buzzing around freely. However, the core density is millions of times that of the densest material found on Earth. Outside that central sphere, like layers of an onion, sit shells of silicon, oxygen and carbon, helium and neon and hydrogen, and smaller quantities of all the other elements lighter than iron.

When the source of fusion energy dries up, iron nuclei capture the free electrons in the iron gas. Protons and electrons combine. The energy that had kept the star inflated is sucked away, and the core collapses to become a ball of neutrons, only a few miles across.

That near-instantaneous gravitational collapse unleashes a huge amount of energy, enough to blow all the outer layers of the star clear away into space. What is left behind is a "neutron star"; a solid sphere of neutrons.

How much is a "huge" amount of energy? Well, when a star collapses and then blows up like this, in what is known as a *supernova*, it shines as brightly as a whole galaxy — which is to say, its brightness can temporarily increase by a factor of one hundred billion. If that number doesn't tell you much, try it this way: if a single candle in Chicago were to "go supernova" and increase in brightness one hundred billion times, you would easily be able to read a newspaper by its light in Washington, D.C.

The explosion of the supernova also creates pressures and temperatures big enough to generate all the elements heavier than iron that could *not* be formed by standard nucleosynthesis in stars. So finally, after a long, complex process of stellar evolution, we have found a place where substances as "ordinary" as tin and lead, or as "precious" as silver, gold, and platinum, can be created.

For completeness, I want to point out that there are actually *two* types of supernova, and that the other can also produce heavy elements. However, the second kind cannot happen to an isolated star. It occurs only in binaries, pairs of stars, close enough together that material from one of them can be stolen gravitationally by the other.

The star that does the stealing must be a small, dense star of the type known as a *white dwarf*, while its partner is usually a larger, diffuse, and swollen star known as a *red giant*. As more and more matter is stolen from the more massive partner, the white dwarf star *shrinks* in size, rather than growing. When its mass reaches 1.4 times the mass of the Sun (known as *Chandrasekhar's limit**) it collapses. The result is again a huge explosion, with a neutron star left behind as a possible remnant. The outgoing shock wave creates heavy elements, and ejects them along with the rest of the star's outer layers away from the binary system. If the nearest stellar system to us, the triple star complex of Alpha Centauri, were to turn into a supernova (it can't — at least according to current theory) the flux of radiation and high-energy particles would probably wipe out life on Earth.

---

* Subrahmanyan Chandrasekhar, one of the great men of modern astrophysics, did his first analysis of white dwarf structure in 1930, on the ship that took him from India to England. He shared the 1983 Nobel Prize for physics (with William Fowler) for his work on stellar structure.

I think of supernovas as rather like nuclear power stations. What they produce is immensely important to us, but we prefer not to have one in our own local neighborhood. If you want a physics question which must have a definite answer, but one which today we cannot even approach, consider this: *Where was the supernova explosion or explosions that produced the heavy elements on Earth?*

6. ALL THE WAY BACK

"Oh, call back yesterday," said Salisbury, in Shakespeare's *Richard the Second*. "Bid time return."

Let us do that. We are going to run the clock backwards, towards the *real* Big Bang, as opposed to the trifling explosions known as supernovas. For although most new-born babies look much alike and are subjects of limited interest except to parents, the universe by contrast appears more and more interesting, the closer we get to its origin.

How far back do we want to start the clock? Well, when the universe was smaller in size, it was also hotter. As we pointed out in Section 4, in a hot enough environment, atoms as we know them cannot hold together. High-energy radiation rips them apart as fast as they form. A good time to begin our backward running of the clock might then be the period when atoms could form, and persist as stable units. Although stars and galaxies would not yet exist, at least the universe would be made up of familiar components, hydrogen and helium atoms that we would recognize.

Atoms form, and hold together, somewhere between half a million and a million years after the Big Bang. Before that time, matter and radiation interacted continuously. After it, matter and radiation "decoupled," became near-independent, and went their separate ways. The temperature of the universe when this happened was about 3,000 degrees. Ever since then, the expansion of the universe has lengthened the wavelength of the background radiation, and thus lowered its temperature. The cosmic background radiation discovered by Penzias and Wilson, at 2.7 degrees above absolute zero, is nothing more than the radiation at the time when it decoupled from matter, now grown old.

Continuing backwards: even before atoms could form, helium and hydrogen nuclei and free electrons could be created; but they could not remain in combination, because radiation broke them apart. The form of the universe was, in effect, controlled by radiation energetic enough to prevent the formation of atoms. This situation held from about three minutes to one million years A.C. (After Creation).

If we go back to a period less than three minutes A.C., radiation was even more dominant. It prevented the build-up even of helium nuclei. As noted earlier, the fusion of hydrogen to helium requires hot temperatures, such as we find in the center of stars. But fusion cannot take place if it is *too* hot, as it was before three minutes after the Big Bang. Before helium could form, the universe had to "cool" to about a billion degrees. All that existed before then were electrons (and their positively charged forms, positrons), neutrons, protons, neutrinos (a mass-less, charge-less particle) and radiation.

Until three minutes A.C., it might seem as though radiation controlled events. But this is not the case. As we proceed farther backwards and the temperature of the primordial fireball continues to increase, we reach a point where the temperature is so high (above ten billion degrees) that large numbers of electron-positron pairs can be created from pure radiation. That happened from one second up to 14 seconds A.C. After that, the number of electron-positron pairs decreased rapidly. Less were being generated than were annihilating themselves and returning to pure radiation. After the universe cooled to ten billion degrees, neutrinos also decoupled from other forms of matter.

Still we have a long way to go, physically speaking, to the moment of creation. As we continue backwards, temperatures rise and rise. At a tenth of a second A.C., the temperature of the universe is 30 billion degrees. The universe is a soup of electrons, protons, neutrons, neutrinos, and radiation. As the kinetic energy of particle motion becomes greater and greater, effects caused by differences of particle mass are less important. At 30 billion degrees, an electron easily carries enough energy to convert a proton into the slightly heavier neutron. Thus in this period, free neutrons are constantly trying to decay to form protons and electrons; but energetic proton-electron collisions kept right on re-making neutrons.

We will keep the clock running. Now the important time intervals become shorter and shorter. At one ten-thousandth of a second A.C., the temperature is one thousand billion degrees. The universe is so small that the density of matter, everywhere, is as great as that in the nucleus of an atom today (about 100 million tons per cubic centimeter — a fair-sized asteroid, at this density, would squeeze down to fit in a matchbox). Modern theory says that the nucleus is best regarded not as protons and neutrons, but as *quarks*, elementary particles from which the neutrons and protons themselves are made. Thus at this early time, 0.0001 seconds A.C., the universe was a sea of quarks, electrons, neutrinos, and energetic radiation.

We can go farther, at least in theory, to the time, 10^{-35} seconds A.C., when the universe went through a super-rapid* "inflationary" phase, growing from the size of a proton to the size of a basketball in about 5×10^{-32} seconds. We can even go back to a time 10^{-43} seconds A.C. (called the *Planck time*), when according to a class of theories known as *supersymmetry* theories, the force of gravity decoupled from everything else, and remains decoupled to this day.

But at this point I want to pause, and ask, Does it make any *sense* to go back so far? We are already far beyond the realm in which the physical laws that we accept — and can test — today can be expected to apply. Are we, at this stage, any more plausible than Archbishop Ussher, who was presumably quite convinced that he had pinned down the time of creation?

More to the point, does that early history of the universe make any difference to *anything* today?

Oddly enough, it does. That early history of the universe was crucial in deciding the whole structure of today's universe.

The universe is expanding. Every cosmologist today agrees on that. Will it go on expanding forever, or will it one day slow to a halt, reverse direction, and fall back in on itself to end in a Big Crunch? Or is the universe poised on the infinitely narrow

---

* "Super-rapid" is an appropriate description, because during the inflation period the universe was expanding in size millions of times faster than the speed of light.

dividing line between expansion and ultimate contraction, so that it will increase more and more slowly, and finally (but after infinite time) stop its growth?

The thing that decides which of these three possibilities will occur is the total amount of mass in the universe, or rather, since we do not care what form the mass takes and mass and energy are totally equivalent, the future of the universe is decided by the total mass-energy content per unit volume.

If the mass-energy is too big, the universe will end in the Big Crunch. If it is too small, the universe will fly apart forever. And only in the Goldilocks situation, where the mass-energy is "just right," will the universe ultimately reach a "flat" condition. The amount of matter needed to stop the expansion is not large, by terrestrial standards. It calls for only three hydrogen atoms per cubic meter.

Is there that much available?

If we estimate the mass and energy from visible material in stars and galaxies, we find a value nowhere near the "critical density" needed to make the universe finally flat. If we arbitrarily say that the critical mass-energy density has to be equal to unity just to slow the expansion, we observe in visible matter only a value of about 0.01.

There is evidence, though, from the rotation of galaxies, that there is a lot more "dark matter" present there than we see as stars. It is not clear what this dark matter is — black holes, very dim stars, clouds of neutrinos — but when we are examining the future of the universe, we don't care. All we worry about is the amount. And that amount, from galactic dynamics, could be at least ten times as much as the visible matter. Enough to bring the density to 0.1, or possible even 0.2. But no more than that.

One might say, all right, that's it. There is not enough matter in the universe to stop the expansion, by a factor of about ten, so we have confirmed that we live in a forever-expanding universe.

Unfortunately, that is not the answer that most cosmologists would really like to hear. The problem comes because the most acceptable cosmological models tell us that if the density is as much as 0.1 today, then in the past it must have been much closer to unity. For example, at one second A.C., the density would have had to be within one part in a million billion of unity, in order for it to be 0.1 today. It would be an amazing coincidence if, by accident, the actual density were so close to the critical density.

Most cosmologists therefore say that, today's observations notwithstanding, the density of the universe is really *exactly* equal to the critical value. In this case, the universe will expand forever, but more and more slowly.

The problem, of course, is then to account for the matter that we don't observe. Where could the "missing matter" be, that makes up the other nine-tenths of the universe?

There are several candidates. At this point it might be good to honor the promise made in Section 1, that I would announce it in advance when we reached the highly speculative science. We are certainly there now, and perhaps I ought to point out that to some workers we got there some time ago. To them, the Big Bang itself is not the preferred cosmological theory.

One suggestion is that the universe is filled with energetic ("hot") neutrinos, each with a small but non-zero mass (as remarked earlier, the neutrino is for most purposes assumed to be mass-less). Those neutrinos would be left over from the very early days of the universe — so we are forced back to studying the period soon after the Big Bang. However, there are other problems with the Hot Neutrino theory, because if they are the source of the mass that stops the expansion of the universe, the galaxies, according to today's models, should not have developed as early as they did in the history of the universe.

A few years ago, observations from a short-duration rocket experiment sent up in February 1987 seemed to give evidence that the cosmic background radiation had features in its spectrum that argued against hot neutrinos. However, COBE (the Cosmic Background Explorer) satellite, launched last year, showed a very smooth spectrum for the background radiation, and hot neutrino theories gained a few points.

What about other candidates? Well, the class of theories already alluded to and known as supersymmetry theories require that as-yet undiscovered particles ought to exist.

There are *axions*, which are particles that help to preserve certain symmetries (charge, parity, and time-reversal) in elementary particle physics; and there are *photinos*, *gravitinos*, and others, based on theoretical supersymmetries between particles and radiation.* These candidates are slow-moving (and so considered "cold") but some of them have substantial masses. They too would have been around soon after the Big Bang. These slow-moving particles clump more easily together, so the formation of galaxies could take place earlier than with the hot neutrinos. We seem to have a better candidate for the missing matter — except that no one has yet observed the necessary particles. At least neutrinos are known to exist!

Supersymmetry, in a particular form known as *superstring theory*, offers at least one other possible source of hidden mass. This one is easily the most speculative. Back at a time, 10^{-43} seconds A.C., when gravity decoupled from everything else, a second class of matter may have been created that is able to interact with normal matter and radiation, today, only through the gravitational force. We can never observe such matter, in the usual sense, because our observational methods, from ordinary telescopes to radio telescopes to gamma ray detectors, all rely on *electromagnetic* interaction with matter. The "shadow matter" produced at the time of gravitational decoupling lacks any such interaction with the matter of the familiar universe. We can determine its existence only by the gravitational effects it produces; which, of course, is exactly what we need to "close the universe." Unfortunately, the invocation of shadow matter takes us back to such an early time that if we are sure of anything, it is that the universe was unrecognizably different then from the way that it is today.

7. ORIGINS

We have discussed the present state of the universe. We have discussed the early state of the universe. What we have not done, any more than Georges Lemaître or George Gamow

---

* Specifically, between the *fermions*, particles such as protons, neutrons, and electrons, and the *bosons*, particles such as photons.

did, is to ask the most basic question: *Where did the universe come from?*

The answer, until twenty years ago, was probably, *Nobody can say.* The most popular modern answer, perhaps not much more satisfying, is: *It came from nothing.*

That statement may call for a little explanation. Since this article is already becoming rather long and we are nowhere near the end, a little explanation is all I will give. However, I am not sure that a long explanation would be any more persuasive.

We need an idea from quantum theory. One of the best-established concepts of that subject, and one of the most famous, is the *Heisenberg Uncertainty Principle.* In its most familiar form, this states that one cannot know both the precise *position* and the *velocity* of a particle simultaneously. A more general formulation if that one cannot specify the values simultaneously of any pair of "conjugate variables," such as *position* and *momentum*; or, to pick the pair that we want, of *energy* and *time.*

This means that there can be a large uncertainty or fluctuation in energy, provided only that the *duration* of the uncertainty is short enough. Conversely, if the energy fluctuation has zero *net* energy, then it can be around for an indefinitely long time.

The first person to suggest in print that the whole universe might be nothing more than an energy fluctuation with zero net value was Edward Tryon, in a paper published in *Nature* in 1973. At the time, his suggestion was cheerfully ignored.

It certainly sounds ridiculous on first hearing. We sit in a universe that absolutely fizzles with energy, everything from gigantic stellar furnaces, like our own sun, pumping innumerable gigawatts into space every second, to supernovas, briefly shining a hundred billion times as bright. How can anyone propose that the universe has zero net energy?

To see that, we have to go back to Lord Kelvin, and his suggestion that the Sun shone because of its own contraction. If solar contraction releases energy, then moving the atoms that compose the Sun farther and farther apart must *require* energy.

How much energy would it take to move the atoms of the Sun from very close together, to indefinitely far apart? The answer to that, known for fifty years, is a curious one: the total energy needed is exactly the amount that would be produced were the Sun's mass totally converted to energy. In the language of the physicist, the rest mass energy of the Sun is equal and opposite to its gravitational potential energy.

Exactly the same argument can be applied to the whole universe, to show that the total material energy (matter plus radiation) is equal and opposite to the total gravitational potential energy. The net energy is thus exactly zero. And a fluctuation of zero energy, according to the Heisenberg Uncertainty Principle, can sustain itself for an indefinitely long time.

The universe was created out of nothing, by a zero energy fluctuation. And one day it may simply disappear, when the vacuum fluctuation that created it pops out of existence.

If this explanation appears unsatisfactory, let me point out that there are alternative theories, all at least as implausible on first hearing as Tryon's "vacuum fluctuation" universe. The "steady state universe" of Bondi, Gold, and Hoyle, popular in the early 1950's but banished from serious consideration later in that decade by observations from radio astronomy, has been revived recently by Hoyle and refurbished with the aid of a concept of cosmology known as *inflation*. In the steady state universe, the origin of the universe does not have to be described, because the universe has been around forever.

The "no boundary" universe of Stephen Hawking is a more recent idea. It does not posit an eternal universe in the sense of the steady state theory, but instead it suggests that the apparently unique moment of the Big Bang is an artifact, created by the way that we choose to measure things.

The idea proposed by Hawking sounds like a simple change of coordinates, but it is much more than that. Anyone who looks at the early history of the universe, in which significant events occur closer and closer together as we approach the moment of creation, will suspect that maybe we are using the wrong method of measuring time. Our system applies well today, but perhaps it was totally wrong near the Big Bang. To take one example, suppose that we define a transformation of the usual time coordinate, t, as measured from the moment of the Big Bang, and replace it with a new "time" variable, T, defined by: $T = \log(t_N/t)$

In this formula, the constant t_N is the present age of the universe, which we'll take to be 15 billion years (the actual present age is not important). As we go backwards in time to the different events of Section 6, Table 1 lists the values we find for t and T:

Table 1

Event	t	T
Today	15 billion years	0
Birth of solar system	4.6 billion years	0.51
Galaxy formation begins	1 billion years	1.18
Atoms form	1 million years	4.18
Helium forms	3.75 minutes	15.32
Electron/positron pairs vanish	30 seconds	16.20
Neutrinos decouple	1 second	17.67
Nuclear matter density	0.0001 seconds	21.67
Inflation of universe	10^{-35} seconds	51.67
Gravity decouples	10^{-43} seconds	60.67

The values of T are increasing as t tends to zero, as the Table shows; but they are not outlandish even when t is very close to zero. The crowding of events closer to the Big Bang is no longer evident. However, the singularity at t = 0 is still present in this picture — whereas in Hawking's model, there is no Big Bang at all. I'm not sure which I like better.

8. THE INCOMPLETE BIOGRAPHER

In order to know what the universe is like today we were forced back, much as we might like to have avoided it, to the earliest times.

However, we are now able to draw a quick sketch of the object whose biography we set out to write.

The moment of birth is shrouded in mystery. But we have been able to describe, in rather definite terms, everything from a fraction of a second after that birth, through the annihilation of electron-positron pairs, through the formation of neutrons, on past the formation of helium nuclei, and then to the production of stable hydrogen and helium atoms. The heavier elements came much later, by high-temperature cooking in the interior of stars and through stellar explosions as supernova, but the mechanics of that process are reasonably clear.

We also believe that we understand fairly well the way in which radiation "decoupled" from matter, so that the universe of matter became almost transparent to radiation when it was about a million years old. We observe today the leftover, or "relict" radiation from that time, as a cosmic background radiation at about 2.7 Kelvins, i.e., 2.7 degrees above absolute zero. It gives us our most direct information about the early days of the universe.

We also see, by direct observation, a universe in which stars are aggregated in the great hundred-billion star groupings we call galaxies; and the galaxies, receding faster and faster at greater distances, are themselves scattered through the whole of visible space.

We believe that there is just enough matter in the universe to slow its final expansion to zero. That belief is based on faith in our cosmological theories, since we cannot detect most of that matter. In fact, we observe directly only one percent, and infer another ten percent by gravitational effects on the rotation of galaxies.

What is missing in the biography? Oddly enough, the biggest historical gap is not at the *beginning* of the universe, though certainly things there become very speculative. But the big blank spot occurs during the adolescence of the universe, between the time it was a million and a billion years old.

We know surprisingly little about that period. It was then, in all likelihood, that the formation of galaxies began; perhaps also the formation of stars. The problem is, the only way to make direct observation is to peer deep, deep into space, seeking light which set out on its journey when the Big Bang was less than a billion years in the past and is only just reaching us.

That light, on its way for something over ten billion years, has been shifted in wavelength by the expansion of the universe to five or more times its original wavelengths. If we want to observe in visible light, we have to examine sources that originally generated signals in the far ultraviolet region of the spectrum. And signals, originally visible, reach us as shortwave infrared radiation — at wavelengths for which the Earth's atmosphere is likely to be opaque.

There is one other way in which this brief biography is clearly incomplete. For any biography, unless it is of a dead person, is always incomplete. The universe is anything but dead. It still exists, it is still changing, and we are still observing it.

How far along in its evolution is the universe, today? From a strictly qualitative point of view, one might say that it is by definition halfway. The whole of time can conveniently be divided into three parts: we have the past, and the future, and the moving knife-edge of the present that separates the two.

That seems to me like cheating. I like numbers, and I would like a numerical answer. If the universe is 10 to 20 billion years old *now*, for how many more years will it exist?

Some may find that a meaningless question. How can the universe possibly *not* exist? It sounds like a metaphysical issue, the same as asking what was there before the universe.

But there are ways in which the universe can go through a change whereby no *information* about anything in the universe that we know can possibly survive, including the physical laws.

Suppose that the Universe collapsed back into a Big Crunch. After that happened one could with justice say that at least *our* universe no longer existed. And yet in another sense we will find that we always have an infinite amount of time available to us.

9. ALTERNATIVE FUTURES

"When I dipped into the Future far as human eye could see," said Tennyson in *Locksley Hall*. Writing in 1842 he did pretty well, foreseeing air warfare and universal world government. We can go a long way beyond that.

Let's start with the "near-term" future. In another five billion years or so our own Sun will run out of fusion fuels and begin to swell up to become a red giant star. In doing so it will expand far enough to include Earth's orbit within it.

That should not be a problem for humanity. Long before

five billion years have passed we will have moved beyond the solar system. We can go, if we like, to sit around a smaller star. It will be less prodigal with its nuclear fuel, and we can enjoy its warmth for maybe a hundred billion years. By that time the needs of our descendants will be quite unknowable.

However, before that time something qualitatively different may have happened to the universe.

We have stated a preference for a "just-closed" Universe that expands forever, but slower and slower. That happens when the mass-energy density is just enough. Suppose, however, that the mass-energy density is *more* than enough to close the universe. Then the present expansion must be followed by a contraction. At last there will come a Big Crunch, rivaling the Big Bang in its temperatures and pressures. Everything familiar to us, certainly including life, will be destroyed in that final moment of infinite extremes.

The Big Crunch could happen as "soon" as 50 billion years from now, depending on how much the mass-energy exceeds the critical amount. We think we know from observation that the mass-energy density is not more than twice the critical density. That would mean we face about 20 billion more years of expansion, followed by at least 30 billion years of collapse.

Does this mean that life cannot in this case go on forever?

Yes and no. Life cannot survive the Big Crunch. Thus if we continue to measure time in the usual way, life therefore exists for a finite time only. However, it can be shown that there is enough time (and available energy) between now and the Big Crunch to think an infinite number of thoughts. From that point of view, if we work with *subjective* time then life can survive long enough to enjoy infinite numbers of thoughts — "forever" according to one reasonable definition. It is all a question of re-defining our time coordinates, as we did earlier.

Suppose, however, that the universe is forever expanding, or tends to final flatness. It can still be shown that an infinite number of thoughts can be thought. Curiously enough, in an ultimately flat universe an infinite number of thoughts can be thought with the use of only a finite amount of energy! That's just as well, because in such a universe, energy becomes less and less easy to come by as time goes on.

Freeman Dyson analyzed the expanding universe situation in detail in 1979, and found that although thoughts can go on into the far future they have to proceed more and more slowly. No more "lightning flashes of wit." Instead it will all be Andrew Marvell's: "My vegetable love should grow, vaster than empires and more slow." All thought must be "cool calculation."

Meanwhile, such thought goes on against the background of an expanding universe that is radically (but slowly) changing. First, all ordinary stellar activity, even of the latest-formed and smallest suns, will end. That will be somewhat less than a million billion (say, 10^{14}) years in the future.

After that it is quiet for a while, because everything is tied up in stellar leftovers, neutron stars and black holes and cold dwarf stars.

Then the protons in the universe begin to decay and vanish.

That requires a word of explanation. A generation ago, the proton was thought to be an eternally stable particle, quite unlike its cousin, the unstable free neutron. Then a class of theories came along that said that protons too may be unstable, but with a vastly long lifetime. If these theories are correct, the proton has a finite lifetime of at least 10^{32} years. In this case, as the protons decay all the stars will finally become black holes.

The effect of proton decay is slow. It takes somewhere between 10^{30} and 10^{36} years for the stellar remnants all to become black holes. Note that on this time scale, everything that has happened in the universe so far is totally negligible, a tick at the very beginning. The ratio of the present age of the universe to 10^{36} years is like a few nanoseconds (1 nanosecond = 10^{-9} seconds) compared with the present age of the universe.

Long after the protons are all gone, the black holes go, too. Black holes evaporate, according to a theory developed by Stephen Hawking, because they have an effective temperature, and quantum theory allows them to radiate to an environment of lower temperature. Today, the universe is far too hot for a black hole of stellar mass to be able to lose mass by radiation and particle production. In another 10^{64} years or so, that will not be true. The ambient temperature of the expanding universe will have dropped and dropped, and the black holes will evaporate. Those smaller than the Sun in mass will go first, ones larger than the Sun will go later; but eventually all will go.

In this scenario, the universe, some 10^{80} years from now, will be an expanding ocean of radiation.

Not everyone accepts the idea of proton decay, so we must consider the alternative. Suppose, then, that the proton is *not* an unstable particle. Then we have a rather different (and longer) future for the universe of material objects.

All the stars will continue, very slowly, to change their composition to the element with the most nuclear binding energy: iron. They will be doing this after some 10^{1600} years.

Finally (though it is not the end, because there is no end) after somewhere between 10 to the 10^{26} and 10 to the 10^{76} years,* a time so long that I can find no analogy to offer a feel for it, our solid iron neutron stars will become black holes.

Is this the end of the road? No. The black holes themselves will disappear, quickly (on these times scales) evaporating to radiation. The whole universe, as in the previous scenario, becomes at last pure radiation. This all-encompassing bath, feeble and far-diluted, is much too weak to permit the formation of particles. So in our distant future, radiation is all.

Or nearly all. Still, by careful use of the tiny amounts of energy available, it is possible that some few corporeal bodies may be preserved, and some form of memory, thought, and intelligence may endure.

There it is, the Universe, as far ahead as we can see or imagine.

How good is this long-term projection? Well, the events and the times are as good as today's science can offer. But why do I keep thinking of Archbishop Ussher, and 4004 B.C.?

---

* We have raised the stakes again. 10 to the 10^{26} is the number 1 followed by 10^{26} zeros. The possible future is not just longer than the past. It is *unimaginably* longer. To my knowledge, nothing in physics involves numbers as large as the possible future of the universe.

10. FAR-OUT THINKING

Some readers may still be feeling that I have not made good on my promise of Section 1, where I said I would offer "amazing new revelations." All right then. Try this:

The existence of God depends on the existence of a sufficient amount of missing matter in the universe.

That ought to be amazing enough for anyone. Yet it is proposed, as a quite serious physical theory, by Frank Tipler. I'm going to butcher his argument when I offer it in brief summary, but anyone who wants the full development can find it in Tipler's paper: "The Omega Point as *Eschaton*: Answers to Pannenberg's Questions for Scientists," published in *Zygon*, Volume 24 (June 1989). I don't think you will find the word "eschaton" in a standard dictionary, but it means the final state of all things, and therefore includes the final state of the universe.

Tipler argues that only certain types of possible universes allow a physicist to deduce (he says *prove*) the existence of a God with the powers of omnipresence, omniscience, and omnipotence. The key ideas are that:

(1) the universe must be such that life can continue for infinite (subjective) time,

(2) spacetime, continued into the future, must have as a boundary a particular type of termination, known as a c-boundary, and

(3) the necessary c-boundary must consist of a single point of space-time.

Then, and only then, according to Tipler, God with omnipresence, omniscience, and omnipotence can be shown to exist. I will not try to reproduce his logic, which is difficult but not implausible. I will only point out that his arguments require that the universe be *closed*. It cannot be expanding forever, or even asymptotically flat, otherwise his theories will not work.

But as we saw in Section 6, there is not enough visible matter to close the universe. Even if we throw in the invisible matter that seems to control the galaxies gravitationally, we are still short by a factor of five to ten.

In Section 6, the question of the missing matter and the

closed or open universe seemed like an interesting one, but not one that could say anything about religion. Now Tipler has raised the stakes. He argues that the existence of a God, including the concepts of resurrection, eternal grace, and eternal life, depends crucially on the *current* mass-energy density of the universe.

We saw, earlier in this article, the curious way in which observation of the remote patches of haze known as nebulas showed that the universe began a finite time ago. That was a striking conclusion: simple observations today decided the far past of the universe.

I leave you with a far stranger notion to contemplate: The search for and measurement of "hot" neutrinos and "cold" photinos and axions tell us about the far future of the universe; and those same measurements may have application not only to physics, but possibly to theology.

11. SOME READING

Gamow, G. *Thirty Years That Shook Physics*. Dover reprint of Doubleday text, 1966.

Gribbin, J. *In Search of the Big Bang*. Bantam Books, 1986. The most complete popular work around on this subject, and the most readable. What more can I say, except perhaps that I go to this book (and borrow from it) early and often?

Gribbin, J., and M. Rees. *Cosmic Coincidences*. Black Swan Press, 1991. This is an English edition, and I don't know if there is an American one. Just to complicate life further, the book was first published in 1990, by Heinemann, with a different title: *The Stuff of the Universe*. This book tackles the problems of the origin and large-scale structure of the universe with hair-raising panache.

Weinberg, S. *The First Three Minutes*. Basic Books, 1977. This was the first book to tackle the early history of the universe for a broad audience. Although fourteen years old, the material in it is still valuable and informative.

Kippenhahn, R. *100 Billion Suns*. Basic Books, 1983. Originally published in German in 1980. Kippenhahn spent his life in the middle of stellar evolution research, and his book shows the realism and recognition of difficulties of one "who was there."

Mitton, S. *Exploring the Galaxies*. Scribner, 1976. This book, because it describes the galaxies more than their origins, has dated very little although it is fifteen years old. The author refuses to talk down to the audience, uses "boring detail" and equations when they are necessary, and is to be commended for it.

Eiseley, L. *Darwin's Century*. Doubleday, 1958. A relatively old book, but since it is describing events that happened a century or more earlier, that doesn't really matter. Great coverage of the Darwin and Kelvin argument on the age of the Earth and Sun; beautifully written, too.

Barrow, J.D., and F.J. Tipler. *The Anthropic Cosmological Principle*. Oxford University Press, 1986. Tipler is the foremost advocate of the "We *are* alone" school, and he is thus at odds with all the SETI (Search for Extraterrestrial Intelligence) believers. Tipler says, and this book argues at length (you might say extreme length — it's over 700 pages) that humans are probably the only intelligent species in the universe; and in the long run we and our descendants (who will probably not be flesh and blood, but our descendants nonetheless) will take over the universe.

Tipler, F.J. "The Omega Point as *Eschaton*: Answers to Pannenberg's Questions for Scientists." *Zygon*, Volume 24 (June 1989). Seeks to prove the existence of God by arguments drawn from today's physical theories. I break my usual rule and include an article (and one that is not easy to find) simply because I know of no reference to it in a book. This is also the perfect choice for a final reference.

S.M. STIRLING
and
THE DOMINATION OF THE DRAKA

In 1782 the Loyalists fled the American Revolution to settle in a new land: South Africa, Drake's Land. They found a new home, and built a new nation: The Domination of the Draka, an empire of cruelty and beauty, a warrior people, possessed by a wolfish will to power. This is alternate history at its best.

"A tour de force."   **—David Drake**

"It's an exciting, evocative, thought-provoking—but of course horrifying—read."
    —Poul Anderson

MARCHING THROUGH GEORGIA
Six generations of his family had made war for the Domination of the Draka. Eric von Shrakenberg wanted to make peace—but to succeed he would have to be a better killer than any of them.

UNDER THE YOKE
In *Marching Through Georgia* we saw the Draka's "good" side, as they fought and beat that more obvious horror, the Nazis. Now, with a conquered Europe supine beneath them, we see them as they truly are; for conquest is only the *beginning* of their plans . . . All races are created equal—as slaves of the Draka.

THE STONE DOGS
The cold war between the Alliance of North America and the Domination is heating up. The Alliance, using its superiority in computer technologies, is preparing a master stroke of electronic warfare. But the Draka, supreme in the ruthless manipulation of life's genetic code, have a secret weapon of their own. . . .

A SIMPLE SEER

In a display he had never before witnessed, the Stone threw off rays of red and purple light, erupting like gobbets of liquid rock and sparks from the vent of a volcano. Amnet felt the heat against his face. At the focus of the rays was something bright and golden, like a ladle of molten metal held up to him. Without moving, he felt himself pitching forward, drawn down by a pull that was separate from gravity, separate from distance, space, and time. The heat grew more intense. The light more blinding. The angle of his upper body slid from the perpendicular. He was burning. He was falling. . . .

Amnet shook himself.

The Stone, still nestled in the sand, was an inch from his face. Its surface was dark and opaque. The fire among the twigs had burned out. The alembic was clear of smoke, with a puddle of blackened gum at its bottom.

Amnet shook himself again.

What did a vision of the end of the world portend?

And what could a simple aromancer do about it?

MERCEDES LACKEY

The Hottest Fantasy Writer Today!

URBAN FANTASY

Knight of Ghosts and Shadows with Ellen Guon

Elves in L.A.? It would explain a lot, wouldn't it? Eric Banyon is a musician with a lot of talent but very little ambition—and his lady just left him lovelorn in a deserted corner of the Renaissance Fairegrounds, singing the blues and playing his flute. He couldn't have known the desperate sadness of his music would free Korendil, a young elven noble, from the magical prison he has been languishing in for centuries. Eric really needed a good cause to get his life in gear—now he's got one. With Korendil he must raise an army to fight against the evil lord who seeks to conquer all of California. And Eric's music will show the way....

Summoned to Tourney with Ellen Guon

Elves in San Francisco? Where else would an elf go when L.A. got too hot? All is well there with our elf-lord, his human companion and the mage who brought them all together—until it turns out that San Francisco is doomed to fall off the face of the continent. Doomed that is, unless our mage can summon the Nightflyers, the soul-devouring shadow creatures from the dreaming world—creatures no one on Earth could possibly control....

Born to Run with Larry Dixon

There are elves out there. And more are coming. But even elves need money to survive in the "real" world. The good elves in South Carolina, intrigued by the thrills of stock car racing, are manufacturing new, light-weight engines (with, incidentally, very little "cold" iron); the bad elves run a kiddie-porn and snuff-film ring, with occasional forays into drugs. *Children in Peril—Elves to the Rescue*. (Part of the SERRAted Edge series.)

HIGH FANTASY

Bardic Voices: The Lark & The Wren

Rune could be one of the greatest bards of her world, but the daughter of a tavern wench can't get much in the way of formal training. So one night she goes up to play for the Ghost of Skull Hill. She'll either fiddle till dawn to prove her skill as a bard—or die trying....

Also by Mercedes Lackey:

Reap the Whirlwind with C.J. Cherryh
Part of the Sword of Knowledge series.

Castle of Deception with Josepha Sherman
Based on the bestselling computer game, *The Bard's Tale*.™

The Ship Who Searched with Anne McCaffrey
The Ship Who Sang is not alone!

Wheels of Fire with Mark Shepherd
Book II of the SERRAted Edge series.

When the Bough Breaks with Holly Lisle
Book III of the SERRAted Edge series.

Wing Commander: Freedom Flight with Ellen Guon
Based on the bestselling computer game, *Wing Commander*.™

PRAISE FOR
LOIS McMASTER BUJOLD

What the critics say:

The Warrior's Apprentice: "Now here's a fun romp through the spaceways—not so much a space opera as space ballet.... it has all the 'right stuff.' A lot of thought and thoughtfulness stand behind the all-too-human characters. Enjoy this one, and look forward to the next." —Dean Lambe, *SF Reviews*

"The pace is breathless, the characterization thoughtful and emotionally powerful, and the author's narrative technique and command of language compelling. Highly recommended." —*Booklist*

Brothers in Arms: "... she gives it a geniune depth of character, while reveling in the wild turnings of her tale.... Bujold is as audacious as her favorite hero, and as brilliantly (if sneakily) successful." —*Locus*

"Miles Vorkosigan is such a great character that I'll read anything Lois wants to write about him.... a book to re-read on cold rainy days." —Robert Coulson, *Comics Buyer's Guide*

Borders of Infinity: "Bujold's series hero Miles Vorkosigan may be a lord by birth and an admiral by rank, but a bone disease that has left him hobbled and in frequent pain has sensitized him to the suffering of outcasts in his very hierarchical era.... Playing off Miles's reserve and cleverness, Bujold draws outrageous and outlandish foils to color her high-minded adventures." —*Publishers Weekly*

Falling Free: "In *Falling Free* Lois McMaster Bujold has written her fourth straight superb novel.... How to break down a talent like Bujold's into analyzable components? Best not to try. Best to say 'Read, or you will be missing something extraordinary.'" —Roland Green, *Chicago Sun-Times*

The Vor Game: "The chronicles of Miles Vorkosigan are far too witty to be literary junk food, but they rouse the kind of craving that makes popcorn magically vanish during a double feature." —Faren Miller, *Locus*

MORE PRAISE FOR
LOIS MCMASTER BUJOLD

What the readers say:

"My copy of *Shards of Honor* is falling apart I've reread it so often.... I'll read whatever you write. You've certainly proved yourself a grand storyteller."
—Liesl Kolbe, Colorado Springs, CO

"I experience the stories of Miles Vorkosigan as almost viscerally uplifting.... But certainly, even the weightiest theme would have less impact than a cinder on snow were it not for a rousing good story, and good storytelling with it. This is the second thing I want to thank you for.... I suppose if you boiled down all I've said to its simplest expression, it would be that I immensely enjoy and admire your work. I submit that, as literature, your work raises the overall level of the science fiction genre, and spiritually, your work cannot avoid positively influencing all who read it."
—Glen Stonebraker, Gaithersburg, MD

" 'The Mountains of Mourning' [in *Borders of Infinity*] was one of the best-crafted, and simply best, works I'd ever read. When I finished it, I immediately turned back to the beginning and read it again, and I can't remember the last time I did that." —Betsy Bizot, Lisle, IL

"I can only hope that you will continue to write, so that I can continue to read (and of course buy) your books, for they make me laugh and cry and think ... rare indeed." —Steven Knott, Major, USAF

What do you say?

Send me these books!